THE
DYING DAYS

A Novel

by

SHANNON PATRICK SULLIVAN

©2006, Shannon Patrick Sullivan

Canada Council for the Arts   Conseil des Arts du Canada   GOVERNMENT OF NEWFOUNDLAND AND LABRADOR

We gratefully acknowledge the financial support of The Canada Council for the Arts, the Government of Canada through the Book Publishing Industry Development Program (BPIDP), and the Government of Newfoundland and Labrador through the Department of Tourism, Culture and Recreation for our publishing program.

All rights reserved. No part of this work covered by the copyrights hereon may be reproduced or used in any form or by any means—graphic, electronic or mechanical—without the prior written permission of the publisher. Any requests for photocopying, recording, taping or information storage and retrieval systems of any part of this book shall be directed in writing to the Canadian Reprography Collective, One Yonge Street, Suite 1900, Toronto, Ontario M5E 1E5.

Cover Design: Maurice Fitzgerald

Published by
Killick Press
an imprint of CREATIVE BOOK PUBLISHING
a Transcontinental Inc. associated company
P.O. Box 1815, Station C.
St. John's, Newfoundland A1C 5P9

Printed in Canada by:
Transcontinental Inc.

National Library of Canada Cataloguing in Publication

Library and Archives Canada Cataloguing in Publication

Sullivan, Shannon Patrick, 1976-
    The dying days : a novel / by Shannon Patrick Sullivan.

ISBN 1-897174-04-7

    I. Title.

PS8637.U558D93 2006   C813'.6   C2006-902652-1

For Nicole Stockley and
Shauna Gammon,
for being there.

"Fear no more the heat o' the sun,
Nor the furious winter's rages;
Thou thy worldly task hast done,
Home art gone, and ta'en thy wages:
Golden lads and girls all must,
As chimney-sweepers, come to dust."

William Shakespeare, *Cymbeline*

Prologue
In which Inevitable Things occur

Christopher Prescott hated Mondays. This was not an irrational hatred, but was well-founded upon the patterns which had traced their way through Christopher's twenty-seven years. Consider:

It had been a Monday when, at age fifteen, Christopher had finally struck up the nerve to ask Kelsey Pennywell out on a date. Christopher was shy and bookish as a teenager — and, in truth, continued to be so to this day, although now he was a little less shy and a little less bookish — and while his high school peers quickly found themselves pairing off, the prospect of pursuing any sort of romantic liaison filled the young Christopher with a palpable sense of panic. But Christopher found in himself an unusual confidence when it came to Kelsey, one kindled by two months of coy smiles in the classroom and brief but treasured conversations by the lockers. Plus she was smart and pretty and, like him, cheered for the Maple Leafs, so it seemed to be a match made in heaven. But on that Monday in April, when Christopher had nervously suggested they go ice skating together sometime, Kelsey had just coughed embarrassedly, and walked away mumbling something about not thinking of Christopher like that. And afterward, their conversations by the lockers became much briefer, and far rarer.

It had been a Monday, too, when Osric finally breathed his last. Fat and half-blind, the hungry grey cat had wandered into Christopher's home the day before his twenty-fifth birthday, while he was helping his mother ferry the groceries in from the car. Hefting two bags of potatoes, Christopher had nearly tripped over the feline as he sprawled on the kitchen floor, munching at a stick of celery which had spilled from one of the supermarket bags. Christopher tried his best to find the cat's owner — he couldn't believe that such a mammoth animal had been on the street for long — but none came forward, and by that time the behemoth had inveigled his way into the Prescott family. The cat's name had been Cecily's idea, and while Christopher suspected it was the peculiar byproduct of too many nights spent labouring over the works of the Bard, he was not prone to casually dismissing his one and only girlfriend's flights of inspiration, no matter how unusual. In no time, Osric had so firmly ensconced himself in the Prescotts' hearts that Christopher could no longer imagine the house without him. And this made things all the more gutwrenching on that dark and drizzly Monday eight months later, when the cat's heart finally gave up trying to support his massive frame, and Osric left Christopher's life as abruptly as he had entered it.

It was scarcely surprising, then, that the day Cecily chose to leave Christopher was, of course, a Monday.

They had met three years earlier at Memorial University's graduate student pub. It had been a crisp but clear winter's day when Christopher had arrived for lunch. By the time his meal was consumed and his pint of Guinness emptied, he was rather startled to discover that a raging blizzard had ambushed the city of St John's, and the wisest recourse seemed to be to stay put. He was the only customer in the place at this point — any others having apparently been aware of the weather forecast and fled before the snow got too thick — and soon found himself engaged in casual conversation with the waitress.

At some point, she had introduced herself as Cecily Bond, honours student in the final throes of her thesis for the English department. And Christopher had told her his name and confessed that he was a mere mathematician, barely started on his doctorate. By the time the snow finally abated, three hours had passed, the conversation had devolved into mindless, wonderful silliness... and somehow, almost by accident, Christopher found himself with a date to the movies.

The movie led to dinner which led to a walk in Bowring Park where, upon one of the snow-covered lawns, Christopher belatedly enjoyed the first tentative kiss of a life which no longer seemed quite so unlucky. Before long, Cecily had decided against moving to Toronto to begin her Masters and had instead opted to remain in St John's so she could be with him. And from that point, it was just a matter of time before Christopher moved out of the house he had sometimes feared he'd never leave, and came to live with Cecily in her basement apartment, Osric in tow.

But as their second year together neared its end, and their friends started to make allusions to marriage which became progressively less subtle, Christopher and Cecily's relationship began to crumble. The cause was never really obvious, not even in retrospect; instead, it was almost sinister in its insidiousness. Having learned that he could, in fact, be part of a successful and vibrant romantic partnership, did Christopher begin to wonder what it would be like to be with somebody else? Was it the way that, as time wore on, Cecily was letting herself become less defined as an individual in her own right, and more as simply one half of a couple?

Either way, the final straw was a bachelorette party (ironically, for one of Christopher's best friends). The night would take the girls on a pubcrawl through the fabled George Street area of the central core of old St John's. Cecily had initially been reluctant to go, having long professed a dislike for the downtown bar scene. In a fit of further irony, it was Christopher who had encouraged her to go out and enjoy herself, having become vaguely aware that Cecily no longer seemed quite as happy with herself as she had once been.

Christopher never learned exactly what transpired that Saturday night. From what he could gather, a few drinks too many, too quickly, had been the catalyst for all of Cecily's pent-up frustrations finally boiling to the surface, searing away her inhibitions and leading to things he tried hard not to imagine. He knew something was terribly wrong when she seemed all but oblivious to him on Sunday. And as much as he tried to attribute this to the effects of a bad hangover, it came as disturbingly little surprise when, on Monday morning, she sat him down on a chair in the kitchen and, with a tremble in her lower lip and an unmistakable quaver in her voice, asked him to move out, and move on.

Christopher's first inclination, of course, was to fight — to try to force Cecily to see that she was making a rash decision, ruining perhaps the best thing that ever had and ever would happen to either of them. But midway through his opening salvo, his voice broke and he slumped back onto the chair in defeat, because he knew that he would have eventually said to her much the same words now ringing in his own ears. And while the circumstances of their break-up tore at his insides, made him want to scream in rage or wail in anguish, he knew deep down that this had become inevitable. The magic of their life together was lost, never to be rediscovered.

Chapter One
In which Unusual Sights are beheld

Christopher sat at the bar and peered blearily at the dregs of his vodka and orange juice, pooling at the bottom of his glass. Dance music throbbed all around him, making it feel as if the percussion was engaged in an assault on Christopher's eyeballs, by way of the back of his skull. Smells of sweat, sick and sex hung immutably in the sweltering air.

This was Friday. Christopher had to repeat that to himself two or three times, because it scarcely seemed possible. It had been four days since Cecily had walked out of his life — or rather, since Cecily had politely but firmly requested that Christopher walk out of hers.

The rest of Monday had passed in a daze. Cecily had left the apartment to go get coffee, and to give Christopher time to pack his stuff. Somehow he had bundled his clothes and personal effects into a battered suitcase his parents had let him have, and piled his textbooks and notes into an old cardboard box he had found under the kitchen sink. The details of that day were no longer apparent to Christopher, but at some point he had stumbled across his parents' front doorstep, dropped the suitcase and the cardboard box at their startled and worried feet, clambered up the stairs to what had once been — and again was — his bedroom, and fallen into a fitful sleep.

Tuesday... Tuesday was lost in a haze of anger, fire-red and envy-green. Christopher found himself railing to whomever would listen — most often himself, reflected in the little mirror mounted atop his chest of drawers — against Cecily's infidelity, and her oh-so-casual dismissal of their nearly thirty months together. He could remember an invective-strewn tirade before his parents at the breakfast table (and even now, he felt that they were far more concerned with the loss of their potential daughter-in-law than with his own wellbeing). And at some point, there was a piteous telephone call to Craig Miller, the friend whose fiancée had hosted the ill-fated bachelorette party. It transpired that the fiancée had herself only a limited recollection of how Saturday night had unravelled, and furthermore was reticent to go into any great detail with Craig or with Christopher. Because of this, Christopher suffered with only a limited understanding of exactly what had led him, in such short order, to this sad and lonely state.

As Wednesday wore on, Christopher found his anger dissipating, almost despite himself. The coldly logical part of his brain was slowly making itself heard through the raging cacophony of his fragile psyche, and more and more he had to admit that, while the circumstances of his break-up with Cecily could undeniably have been kinder, the pair of them had been on a collision course with the act itself for months now.

On Thursday, Christopher tried to pick up the pieces and carry on as if nothing had happened — except for the small matter of everything in his life having changed irrevocably. He sent a short e-mail to his graduate supervisor (who already had concerns enough about Christopher's lethargic progress on his thesis and was now probably approaching a state of apoplectic fury) promising that his disappearance from the academic radar was unavoidable but short-term, and that he'd drop by his office after the weekend. He put his clothes and his books away, and was surprised at how easy it was to slip back into the routine he had known pre-Cecily. And he took in a movie — a comedy, in the hopes of lifting his spirits — and although he didn't laugh much, he convinced himself that this was probably mostly to do with the quality of the film. As he drifted off to sleep, he ardently resolved to go out and meet someone new, and put Cecily far behind him.

Of course, the only problem was that this was a classic example of something easier said than done. Though he desperately wished it were otherwise, Christopher was not very good at meeting new people, and had subconsciously geared his life towards avoiding meeting new people as much as possible. At university, his social circles consisted of the predominantly male graduate constituency of the Mathematics department. His hobbies tended to be solitary affairs in which actual interaction with others was rare and certainly didn't lead to hints of romance or the possibility of a date. And his friends were mostly married or in long-term relationships far more stable than his and Cecily's had turned out to be. As such, their parties tended to consist of the same people gathering together time and time again, and rarely were they interested in going out to a bar or anything similarly socially promising.

But Christopher had pledged to himself that he would meet someone new — or at least put in a valiant enough effort that he'd be able to respect himself in the morning. And so on Friday evening, having utterly failed to entice even one of his friends to go with him, Christopher coiffed himself as best as he could, swallowed deeply, and set out for the mecca of bars and taverns that was George Street.

He left his car beside the nearby waterfront to be eyed warily by the seagulls chanting raucously in the humid evening air, and made his uneasy way up to the strip, already thronging with the drunken masses of the northeast Avalon Peninsula. Looking about, Christopher quickly noted how most of the people were there in couples or in larger groups, and immediately felt his already shaky self-confidence start to deflate a little more.

Now, four hours later, he was sitting at the bar in a dance club halfway along George Street, forlornly stirring the ice cubes at the bottom of his glass with a straw. He had consumed several drinks already, in a failed attempt to prop up his flagging determination, and no longer remembered the name of the establishment. He was sure he had been here before on one of his rare previous excursions to the strip, but it had been called something different and been an Irish pub then. Of course, he reflected, the next time he passed this way, its name would probably have changed again, and it would be a jazz club or a karaoke bar or something else entirely.

"You know," said Christopher to the bartender, who wasn't listening, "you could have a really good pub crawl by staying at the same building and having a drink at each of its… incarnations through the years." He had been trying to put this sentence together in his head for nearly five minutes now, and feared that despite his best efforts he had slurred the word "incarnations" anyway. "Of course, then you'd need a time machine or something," he pointed out to himself. "Which would, admittedly, be a reason to celebrate." He chuckled to himself in a way that even he knew would look terribly sad, if anybody was paying attention. Which they weren't.

Christopher sighed, put down the glass and its half-melted ice cubes, and looked back at the dance floor. He swayed slightly as his equilibrium tried and nearly failed to make the half-turn with him. The hour was past one o'clock, but the bar was still crammed full of people, writhing and gyrating to the thunderous beat and the dizzying light show.

Christopher had tried, he honestly had. He was not a particularly good dancer, but he had sucked up his pride and made an effort, managing to convince a handful of girls to take a turn with him. But, no matter what he said or did, few wanted to stick around for a second dance, and none for a third. His hopes had been stirred slightly when one woman, raven-tressed and clad in what looked like an ultra-modern Japanese kimono, had allowed him to buy her a drink. But two sips into her rum and Coke, she was descended upon by a gaggle of girls in similar attire, and together they vanished across the bar like a high-pitched whirlwind, leaving Christopher behind in the dust.

He sighed heavily to himself. "Well," he told the bartender, who was not only not listening but was no longer even in

Christopher's line of sight, "at least I gave it a shot. Rome wasn't built in a day and…"

She was gorgeous.

At the sight of her, whatever other words of self-comfort Christopher was about to utter were not merely driven from his brain, but given a military escort across the border, beaten into the mud, and shot several times for good measure. He was left with his mouth hanging open like an imbecile as his brain tried to process the nigh-unfathomable information being supplied by his eyes. Getting to his feet in the hope of a better perspective, Christopher was blissfully unaware as his trailing hand upset his glass, spilling water and ice cubes onto the bartop.

It was a testament to her undeniable beauty that Christopher even noticed the woman, because she was actually halfway across the crowded bar, standing in profile against the right-hand wall. She was tall — Christopher guessed she would have rivalled his own six feet two inches — with a flowing mane of copper hair which seemed to almost float upon the sultry currents of the room. Her high cheekbones gave her a regal bearing, complemented by the almost proprietary look she gave as she surveyed the bedlam before her. It made Christopher think that she owned the bar — the city, the world! — and everyone in it, but in a way that was perfectly genuine, rather than haughty and arrogant.

If anything was odd about the woman, it was her clothing. Compared to the riotous colours and flesh-baring fashions worn by most of the bar's customers, she was dressed positively conservatively, in a plain grey blouse and dark slacks. Despite the relative warmth of the midsummer evening, a long blue overcoat was draped over her right arm; from what Christopher could tell, this was as featureless as the rest of the woman's garments. Truthfully, though, none of this really mattered to him: she was a creature who could make a burlap sack seem the height of chic if she so desired.

Christopher decided that "gorgeous" was too timid a word to describe the woman. He was trying to choose between "radiant", "transcendent" and "divine" when, with remarkable fluidity, she started to move.

If Christopher hadn't been utterly absorbed by the woman, he probably wouldn't even have noticed it. One moment, she stood gazing out across the undulating bodies, not so much looking for someone as simply absorbing the spectacle. The next, she had passed into the shadows at the edges of the dancefloor, almost out of sight in an instant.

And as she moved, Christopher saw, just out of the corner of his eye, something drop to the floor. A table was pressed up against the wall of the bar along the woman's path, and when she jerked her arm slightly to avoid colliding with it, her overcoat slid forward along her arm and something small and flat slipped out from amongst its folds.

It's true that Christopher was, at this stage, glum, tired and more than a little drunk. He was feeling slightly peckish, and he was beginning to suspect that the pulsations in his skull now had less to do with the house DJ than with an impending headache. And he was, self-confessedly, not exactly the quickest on the uptake when it came to matters involving the fairer sex, much though he bemoaned the fact and wished it weren't so.

But despite all these things, Christopher knew a golden opportunity when he saw one. This was the kind of conversation starter he always dreamed of: the gallant rescue and return of the fair damsel's bank card (or driver's license, or only surviving photo of a beloved childhood pet), leading to effusive thanks, leading to a late-night coffee, leading to... well, Christopher didn't want to get too far ahead of himself, though the possibilities were tantalising.

As quickly as his vodka-encumbered muscles would permit, Christopher stumbled around the dance floor — barely avoiding an unintentional right hook from one particularly energetic dancer, involved in what seemed to be a spastic reinvention of the Highland Fling — and staggered over to the table where the woman had dropped her belonging. In so doing, he tried his best to follow her movements: she appeared to be making for the ladies' washroom, which lay at the end of a short corridor leading out of the main room.

Christopher leaned against the table, which was strewn with label-shorn beer bottles and forgotten drinks at various stages of consumption, and scanned the floor. It was filthy, of course, the legacy of those who had managed to spill more of their drink than they had actually imbibed, and the haphazard lighting effects on the dance floor made it very difficult for him to clearly see anything at all.

He grimaced: he really didn't want to be seen rummaging along the floor of the bar like a vagrant, and his stomach was already more than a little queered by the thought of what he might be putting his hands in down there. But the woman was about to vanish around the corner leading to the bathroom, and the fear of losing his chance to meet someone so devastatingly lovely was all the motivation Christopher needed. Gritting his teeth, he knelt down and stuck his hand under the table. Immediately, he felt his fingers slide over something thin and smooth-textured. A giddy rush of adrenaline coursing through him, Christopher snatched it up and, without even looking at what he had recovered, ran at full pelt towards the washrooms.

He nearly collided with a small blonde girl — one of the kimono group, he realised faintly — as he spun round the corner leading to the short hallway. She glared daggers at him as he mumbled an apology, but he was already sprinting down the corridor, passing the entrance to the men's facilities which lay halfway along its length, and pulling up short in front of the door to the women's lavatory.

For the first time in at least thirty seconds, Christopher's thoughts managed to assemble themselves into some sense of coherency, as he realised that he couldn't just barge into the ladies' washroom. Quite apart from the fact that it wasn't likely to make a good impression on the red-headed beauty, it also risked getting him thrown out of the bar altogether, and that would almost certainly prove to be a rather monumental impediment to meeting the woman. He supposed he could politely knock on the door — though it mightn't be heard in the blaring din of the bar. Or he could just tarry until the woman came out, although this seemed entirely too long to wait for something which had suddenly achieved such looming importance in his life.

Christopher turned, about to pace the floor (as he often did when trying to make decisions under pressure). Suddenly, he was vaguely aware of a hint of movement in the corridor, and he realised that there was another door in the hallway he hadn't noticed before.

Unlike the doors to the two bathrooms, which were boldly coloured to ensure that no one — regardless of how incapacitated by drink they might be — could possibly miss them, this door was painted to blend in with its surroundings and had no signage on or near it. Christopher supposed it must be a janitorial closet — it made sense to have one so close to the lavatories after all — but then he remembered that the reason he had noticed it in the first place was because he had seen it shut closed, as if pushed from behind by a light gust of wind. And unless, as seemed unlikely, there was an open window in the broom closet, then this mightn't be a broom closet at all.

Christopher hesitated for just a moment. He always felt a trifle guilty and nervous about opening doors and going places he didn't think he was meant to. But if this was a back door — a guess which now appeared reasonable — then the woman may have used it as an egress, and that was potentially disastrous. He had to know for sure. All the same, he glanced down the hall to make sure nobody was coming before he reached out and turned the knob.

The door was indeed an exit from the bar, opening onto a back alleyway between the building on George Street and another which fronted onto Water Street. It passed along just one more edifice to Christopher's right before stopping at a chain link fence facing the sidewalk. It extended farther to his left, bordered by four or five buildings, stone or brick, on each side, before finally ending at the outside wall of another structure, which had no doors leading into the alley at all. It was in this direction that the red-headed woman was walking. She was softly reciting words in a strangely-accented language which tugged at Christopher's thoughts.

Christopher was about to shout out to her, but the exclamation died in his throat as he realised that the woman was not alone. Walking to one side and just a little behind her was a thickly-built figure, draped in an overcoat which looked as if it was a size or two too big for him. At least, Christopher assumed the person was male — the alley was cloaked in shadow, lit only fitfully by a handful of windows in the buildings which bounded it, and so it was difficult for him to perceive any distinguishing features. The figure's head was almost entirely bald but for a thatch or two of thin, scraggly hair, giving him little indication one way or the other.

Well, thought Christopher vaguely, so much for a nice one-on-one café latte. But, he still had the object the woman had dropped, and was not so heelish as to decline to return it simply because his hopes for a date were suddenly diminished. Again he started to call out to the woman and her companion, and again he stopped without uttering a word. For Christopher had realised that the pair had walked past the last door leading out of the alley. Instead, they actually seemed to be making for the wall which was the alley's eastern terminus, featureless but for a small bricked-up window on the upper storey.

Bewildered, Christopher started to wonder if perhaps these two were visitors to St John's and had lost their way. But no sooner had this thought occurred to him than the woman reached the wall and, without so much as hesitating, passed into it.

Despite himself, Christopher let out a small choking noise, and his eyed widened in disbelief. No portal had opened up in the wall; indeed, the stone surface appeared to be perfectly solid and unyielding. The woman had simply kept walking straight through it as though it wasn't even there.

The woman's companion, on the other hand, paused as he reached the wall and stood up straighter, as if alert for something. Feeling a little frightened now, Christopher slunk back into the shadows, pressing up against the wall of the bar. The person in the overcoat slowly pivoted his head to look back down the alley. Christopher was now desperately trying to make himself as small as possible and so was not committing himself to scrutinising the man's countenance. But even still, Christopher could not hope to miss the way the ambient light in the alley glinted gold and green off the figure's eyes in a manner not even remotely human. Christopher was more reminded of a lizard his friend Craig had briefly kept as a pet, and had to suppress a shiver.

The man — the creature — surveyed the alley for several seconds more before, apparently satisfied, he turned back to the wall. Like the woman before him, he passed impossibly out of sight.

Chapter Two
In which there is an Arrival at the airport

Though no wind blew down the confined space of the alley, Christopher found himself shivering. After several seconds of silence, broken only by the sounds of passing cars and the occasional hoot of drunken revellers in the distance, he stepped out of the shadows and peered at the wall through which the red-haired woman and her companion both seemed to have passed.

For a moment, he assumed he was imagining things — that the fog of alcohol had so clouded his brain that he had only believed he was watching two people walk through a solid stone wall, when in fact they had no doubt turned and exited through one of the doors at the far end of the alley. But, more than a little reluctantly, Christopher was forced to abandon this line of thinking. While that might explain the woman's disappearance, he knew that her vanishing had instantly dispelled any touch of inebriation from his mind, and as he had watched the man exit through the wall, he had been resolutely sober.

It was a trick, then, Christopher decided. There was a concealed door in the wall, one no doubt painted grey like its surroundings so that it only looked as though the alluring woman and her peculiar friend had passed through the stone itself. He chuckled quietly to himself, certain that he had hit upon the answer to this unexpected mystery, and to confirm it he marched boldly down the alley to the wall. He began prodding at its surface, looking for the tell-tale outline of a door, expecting to feel a change in the texture or a slight give in its resilience. But there was nothing — it was just one flat continuous expanse of stone, pocked here and there by the ravages of the Newfoundland climate.

Christopher stepped back from the wall, and shivered again. "It's not possible," he murmured to himself.

Once upon a time, when he was still in high school, Christopher, Craig and their friends had been avid role-players, staying up til all hours on a Saturday night to run through the latest scenario concocted by the endlessly inventive (and occasionally rather disturbing) mind of Ollie Gower. Christopher had eventually tired of such games, becoming bored of what he saw as a fantastical indulgence with no bearing on the real world. But he still remembered that one character he had played, a dwarf or a gnome or something, had the uncanny ability to pick out anything concealed in rock, no matter how well hidden: secret doors, cunning traps, all fell to the imaginary adventurer's keen stonetelling. Oh, how Christopher longed for that ability now, as he stood staring at a wall through which two people had disappeared, when his logical mind knew that no such passage could have occurred.

"It's not possible," he repeated, louder this time. He was aware that an edge of hysteria had crept into his voice, and was suddenly rather resentful of his newly sober state.

"Tis," came a voice.

Christopher was now more than a little on edge, so he had to consciously restrain himself from leaping a foot or two into the air at the unexpected sound. He forced himself to take three deep lungfuls of air, and then looked about the alley for the person who had spoken. But the narrow path was empty, except for a few pieces of litter lying forgotten on the ground and a rusted old garbage bin sitting forlornly against the chainlink fence.

"I'm... I'm sorry?" Christopher finally said, bewildered.

"Tis possible," came the voice immediately, as if its owner had been anticipating the question.

Christopher realised now that the words were carrying down from above him. He directed his gaze towards the upper floors of the tall, looming structures which lined the alley. None of the windows in these parts of the buildings betrayed any evidence of illumination. Indeed, Christopher was given to understand that most were used for storage or for office space for the businesses occupying the main levels, though he supposed some might be rented out as apartments.

"Um, what's possible?" Christopher asked, feeling a little disorientated.

"Are yer blind then, son? Do I have ter remind yeh of what yer just seen?"

Peering through the dinginess, Christopher thought he could see a dark shape half-hidden behind a drape in a window on the third storey of the building to his left. As far as he could tell, it was the only window cracked open against the mugginess of the night, so he assumed that this must be the location of his mysterious partner in conversation.

"Well," Christopher said, trying to collect his thoughts, "I'm honestly not sure what I've just seen."

"Ah," came the voice. It was aged and cracked, and sounded oddly diffuse as it rode the dense night air. Christopher wasn't entirely sure whether he was being addressed by a man or a woman. "Prolly fer the best, then. Let's juss go along wif that, then, an' we'll speak no more about it."

And Christopher thought he saw the dark shape move away from the drape.

"No!" he cried out, a little more loudly than he had intended. "Wait, please! I have something I need to return to the lady." And only then did he realise that he was still holding the object he had retrieved from under the table in the bar, holding it so tightly that the fingers of his left hand were starting to cramp. As if his statement needed supporting evidence, he waved it half-heartedly in the direction of the open window.

Silence returned to the alley for a few seconds, and Christopher felt his spirits sag. But then the drape fluttered almost imperceptibly, and the voice called out, "What hev yer got there, then?"

Christopher realised that he actually wasn't sure. Between his haste to catch up with the red-headed beauty and then the shock of... whatever had happened when she had disappeared from sight, he'd not really had a chance to pay it any attention.

"It's a... Er. Um." For Christopher was not entirely sure what he was holding. It was a small burgundy rectangle, about twice as long as it was high, and though it was very thin, Christopher found that he could not bend it. It was smooth and had a lustre like some kind of metal. One side of the rectangle was completely featureless, but upon the other side was written (or perhaps engraved, though Christopher could feel neither the raised ridges of a pen nor the crevices left by carving) one word: *Goibniu*. Beneath that was a peculiar symbol, like a stylised 'Y' enclosed in the curve of a bell. Christopher could see the word and the symbol because as his gaze fell upon the object, they seemed to draw in all the feeble light of the alley, taking on an ethereal life of their own.

"I think it's a message," he said finally. At first he was going to say 'letter' but he could tell that the rectangle did not actually contain anything within itself, nor did there seem to be any way to open it if it did.

"Aye," said the venerable speaker. "So it seems."

"'Goibniu,'" said Christopher. "Do you think that's the woman's name? It doesn't sound very feminine, but I wonder if she might be foreign. Or maybe she was intending to give this to somebody else..."

"Can't say as I know, son. It seems to me yer set on deliverin' that ter her, though."

Christopher felt himself blush a little. "Well... I'd hate to think that this was something important and she'd lost it. Especially if she is only visiting the city. I figure... I figure I ought to do what I can to return it to her." *It's not like I have anything better to do anyway,* he thought, a little miserably. "So, do you know where she went, her and... that other person? It looked like they actually walked right through that wall, but they couldn't have. Could they?"

"Already told yer that that was exackly what they done, did-n't I? Be yeh deaf now as well as blind?"

Despite himself, Christopher was getting more than a little frustrated with the meandering nature of the conversation, and was starting to feel rather patronised. "Look," he said, trying his best to maintain a civil tone, "could you just tell me where she went? She couldn't have just walked through the wall, there's no way through."

"Ah, but there was, son. Afore they put up thet great stone monstrosity what's at the end of th'alley now. Back in '51 thet was I reckon. I fink I et waffles the marnin they started work on the foundations. Afore that, peoples used ter use the alley as a thoroughfare all the time, specially fer bringin' goods ter the bidnesses. The fence went up at t'other end not long after, and since then th'alley hasn't hardly seen enny traffic goin' on fiffy years now. I finks most folk have plain fergotten it's even here."

"Okay," said Christopher, feeling no more enlightened than before the potted history lesson had begun, "but that was half a century ago. It still doesn't explain how two people could pass that way tonight!"

"But it do, me trout. Y'see, the cityfolk might not remember, but the city do. It remembers."

For several seconds, Christopher just stood there in the alley, trying to understand what he was being told. A bead of sweat wormed its way down his forehead. "So, you're telling me that because there used to be a way out of the alley where that building now stands, people can still walk out of here, no problem, even though there's a bloody enormous stone wall in the way?" He laughed nervously, and started to despair that the unseen person above was nothing more than a raving madman.

"Now yer understandin' me. I mean, it's a little more complicated than that, or else everybody an' their uncle would be doin' it, but yev got the right idea anyway."

"I'm sorry," Christopher said, starting to walk slowly back towards the door that led to the bar. "I just can't believe that. That's just... that's just nuts. It's crazy talk. People don't walk through buildings, and cities don't think."

"I didn't say the city thought, did I? No, I said it remembers, an' thass a different kettle o' fish entirely. Memory's a powerful thing, it binds all people an' places tergevver, an' if yer knows how, yer can make mighty use of it, boy."

Christopher had now reached the door, and his palm rested on the handle. One slight tug, and he would be returned to familiar if dissipiriting mundanity, and he could forget the lunacy of the last few minutes. He knew that he could simply walk back inside, order another drink or two, and spend the rest of the night glumly watching the happy couples on the dance floor until George Street closed down at the stroke of three. Then he'd head home (trying and likely failing to avoid rousing his parents), retire to his bed, and spend a drunken hour grieving the loss of Cecily and the dismal state of his existence before he finally passed into another restless sleep. By the time he woke up on Saturday morning (or, more likely, Saturday afternoon), these inexplicable events would have blurred into the background of his memories of the night, to trouble him no longer.

But he still had the rectangle — the card, the message, whatever it was — in his left hand. He paused, and idly ran his thumb over its weird, glossy surface. He pictured the woman who had dropped it, and the way she had moved through the room like an angel with a fiery halo. His right hand fell away from the door, and he slowly spun around. "So... can you help me?" he called out tentatively.

"I shouldn't be doin' this," the voice came to him from back down the alley. "But I kin see yer a well-intentioned sort, and yev seen enough already that a little more won't be the death of yer."

"You can show me... how to pass through the wall too?" Christopher asked. He had to admit that although the whole conversation was weird and a tad spooky, he was also feeling a little thrill of excitement. If what he was being told was actually possible...

"I'm a bit out of practise, but I think I kin get yer through. Jess start walkin' towards the end o' th'alley, jess as if there weren't no wall there at all, cause as far as yeh'll be concerned momentarily, there won't be. If yeh kin picture yerself in clothes from yer grandfolk's time, that might be a bit ev a help, too."

"I'll... I'll try," agreed Christopher. Why not? he thought to himself. It's not as though there was anybody here to witness him making a fool of himself, apart from the watcher in the window who was probably at least half-barmy as it was. At worst, he'd end up walking fairly gently into a wall, and he figured he could handle a bruised kneecap or a sore knuckle.

He took a deep breath, slipped the slender rectangle into his pocket for safekeeping, and started walking. The noise of the late-night downtown traffic seemed to fade as he focussed on his goal; even the sound of his shoes tapping on the asphalt of the alley no longer registered. Only the distant cawing of a crow, swooping low over the city, penetrated Christopher's concentration. But after two or three foul-tempered outbursts, the crow was gone.

And so was he.

"Drat," mumbled the voice in the window. "I prolly should've told him to close his eyes. I fink that might've been important."

* * *

St John's International Airport was a far different place than Donovan Chase remembered it. Recent renovations had transformed the former pallid, morose, colourless edifice into a dynamic and modern facility of glass and steel and unusual angles which pleasingly caught the eye. Where once disembarkation was a modest matter of turning a corner, it now involved a journey down a sweeping flight of stairs which created the illusion of a descent into the new and unexpected.

Chase was not a tall man, and he was easily lost amidst the sea of people at the arrivals gate. He appeared to be in his late fifties: his hair was grown long and wild in the back, but was thinning noticeably up top, and touches of grey were becoming predominant among the curly black thicket. Chase was not an ugly man, but nor was he particularly attractive; his lips were set in a subtle moue, his brow furrowed in a perpetual labyrinth of creases. His blue-green eyes, though, sparkled with a rare intensity. They surveyed the milling travellers and those who had come to the airport, to greet them or to welcome them home.

Unlike most of his fellow passengers, however, Chase made no move towards the luggage carousel. Instead, he took up his battered walking stick, made of a rich brown-red wood and carved with an intricate design that ran up and down the shaft like a snake, straightened the jacket of his black-and-white pinstripe suit, adjusted his silvery necktie, and made a beeline for the exit. As Chase moved towards the airport's glass doors, anybody observing him — and no one was — would have seen him dodge and dart around obstructions in his path with a dexterity belying his advancing years, occasionally doffing a non-existent hat in unheeded apology.

It was only as he extended his hand to open the door that Chase stopped. A keen wailing had arisen to his right, and he glanced over to see a young mother standing there, desperately trying to soothe her upset baby.

"Excuse me," said Chase, approaching the woman. His voice was rich and alive. He spoke in an English accent, underlined by the touch of a Scots burr. A slight gap between his two front teeth bestowed upon him a noticeable but not unpleasant lisp. "Mrs Holloway, isn't it?" She looked up at him warily, and he smiled kindly. "I overheard you on the plane."

"Oh," she grinned, relaxing a little. "I see. I'm sorry, I didn't notice you there. What can I do for you, Mister…?"

"Ah, actually, I thought I might be able to do something for you. I couldn't help but notice the little one's distress."

"My poor Alec," said Mrs Holloway, cradling the crying infant closer. "This was his very first flight — we've come home so his grandparents can meet him. I think his ears are hurting him."

"Perfectly understandable," replied the small British man. He leaned his walking stick against his leg and rubbed the sides of his head with both hands. "Mine aren't quite recovered yet, either."

The woman laughed lightly, but this only seemed to upset the baby further. She cooed softly to him, wiping his tiny eyes.

"I think all Alec needs is a little distraction, Mrs Holloway," Chase told her. "It's amazing what can happen if we let our mind wander just a little. May I?"

"At this stage, I'm willing to try anything," admitted Alec's mother. "Please, be my guest."

Chase reached into an inside pocket of his jacket. He groped around for far longer than would appear necessary, before finally withdrawing three small silver balls. These he transferred into his empty hand before retrieving two more balls. Then he uttered a meaningless sound which nonetheless captured the baby's attention, and with an uncommon adroitness, began juggling the balls in a complex pattern. As they arced through the air, the silver spheres caught and reflected the airport lights, casting dazzling beams of gold and green and vermilion in all directions. Little Alec was instantly entranced, his cries quickly giving way to a palpable glee. Within moments, he had passed into a gentle doze.

"There," Chase murmured, catching the five balls and deftly slipping them back into his coat. "That's better."

Mrs Holloway sighed with relief. "Thank you so much, sir."

"Don't mention it," said Chase. "Really." And without another word, he turned away, back towards the airport exit. His face darkened immediately, as though a shadow had passed across his features, erasing his smile in the bat of an eye.

"If only all my tasks were so easily accomplished," he muttered. Had anyone been listening, they could not have mistaken the bitter tang which had crept into his words.

Chase walked out of the airport into the sultry night. He knew that the St John's climate was frequently less temperate than much of the continent, but all the same was no stranger to sticky, sweaty evenings at the height of the summer. Despite this, no perspiration beaded the small man's brow, and he seemed to give no thought to removing his pinstripe jacket.

A row of taxis, each painted a sickly yellow, was lined up in front of the airport. A family pushed past Chase and clambered into the nearest, which zoomed off into the darkness. The remaining cabs advanced, and within seconds another taxi arrived at the rear of the queue.

Chase ignored all of these, however. He walked past the yellow cabs to the end of the sidewalk, where a dented green car awaited, sitting by itself in a pool of light cast by a streetlamp above. No one else was paying the green car any attention.

Without hesitation, Chase opened the car's rear door and clambered in, resting his walking stick on the floor across his feet. He was greeted by the anticipated smell of old leather and cheap cigars.

"Hello, Donovan," said the man behind the wheel. He did not turn around, but instead observed Chase in the rearview mirror. He was a grey-haired man with a thin moustache. An old scar crested the top of his rheumy right eye.

"Hello, Bannerman," Chase said mildly. "It's been quite a while."

The man inclined his head slightly. "Not since '63. Candlemas, as I recall. The night you sacrificed your other cane."

Chase smiled the ghost of a smile, and caressed the edge of his walking stick with the toe of one shoe. "Ah, so it was. It's hard to forget the sound of thirteen men screaming as the heavens erupt into life all around them." He snickered ruefully, then shook his head. "But I'd heard you'd returned to the old country. Was I misinformed?"

"No. I went back in the Seventies — retired, of a fashion. Until the Shoreditch... unpleasantness, in '88. After that, I had to get away. It seemed most sensible to take up here again."

"I understand," Chase murmured as the car pulled away from the airport. His eye slid to the empty seat next to him, where a small black valise lay. He picked it up and placed it in his lap.

"Did you have a nice flight?"

"Can't complain, Bannerman," the passenger responded as he played with the catches on the briefcase. "I had to make six or seven transitions to cut down on the travel time, but that's always the way when these matters arise so... urgently and unexpectedly. I did manage to spend seventeen minutes in first class. Everyone was speaking Dutch."

The man behind the wheel chuckled as Chase opened the valise. He reached in and withdrew a large, glossy photograph. It depicted a statuesque woman with flowing red hair, frozen in time with the hint of a smile touching her lips.

"Aislinn," said Donovan Chase. "At last."

The green car's engine rattled noisily as it sped away from the airport, towards the heart of the city.

*   *   *

Christopher felt as though he was walking in a completely new direction. Not forward nor backward, left nor right, up nor down, Christopher was moving in a way that was decidedly... other.

The stone wall was in front of him. He knew that, his eyes told him so, and as he reached it and extended his hand, he could feel the rough texture of the rock beneath his fingertips.

But at the same time, there was no wall. The asphalt beneath his feet was new, and the path continued on in front of him for several more yards, before emptying out into the street beyond. The sun beat down from above, newly revealed from behind grey stormclouds moving off to the east. Christopher walked through a puddle, felt the rainwater splash around his shoes and dampen the hem of his trousers. Everything was suffused with a bewitching golden glow.

A man walked towards him, dressed in a suit with a hat perched atop his closely-cropped hair. He wore thick-rimmed black glasses and was idly dangling a cigarette from his lower lip. He nodded to Christopher as he passed. Christopher could see himself reflected in the man's spectacles, but the image was like a double exposure: there he was as he had dressed for the evening, in his steely blue shirt with his dark brown hair moussed back, but at the same time Christopher could see himself dressed in the fashions of half a century past, with a conservative haircut and a handkerchief protruding neatly from his breast pocket. As near as Christopher could tell, though, the man observed nothing out of the ordinary about him.

But then, he knew, there was no man. And he was not walking through a narrow open street but through an empty room in the building at the end of the alley. Christopher felt a sharp stab of pain through his head as he tried to reconcile the two contradictory events being registered by his senses. He felt himself moving through another wall — down the last few feet of the path — into solid rock — and —

Christopher found himself on the other side of the building, leaning against the outer wall and panting audibly. The road was crowded with people passing to and from George Street, and several of them shot quizzical glances his way, evidently thinking he was either a poor soul having trouble holding his liquor, or else a freak well worth avoiding.

Trying desperately to catch his breath, Christopher looked left and right for the red-headed woman. He knew that he should be reeling in amazement at what he had just accomplished — that he should be either pumping his fists in excitement or shrieking in terror at the thought that he had just walked through a solid wall — but he tried to push that incredulity to the back of his head until his self-appointed duty was completed. His hand went to his pocket, and he was grateful to feel the strange, cool touch of the woman's lost object. His vision was swimming as he peered through the crowds, hoping for a telltale flash of that remarkable copper mane.

Then Christopher grimaced as realisation seized him: he had spent precious minutes in conversation back in the alley, minutes during which the woman and her companion would no doubt have vacated the area.

Staggering to one knee, clutching his pounding head, Christopher realised that his unlikely passage through the wall had been utterly in vain. The woman was gone, and he had no way of finding her again.

Christopher groaned in frustration as he felt his skull nearly split asunder. Explosions of colour filled his field of vision, and then an impenetrable darkness rushed in to enfold him.

He slumped to the pavement, unconscious.

Chapter Three
In which a Dark Shadow falls on George Street

Somebody was slapping Christopher's cheeks — three taps on the right in rapid succession, followed by three more on the left, and then the pattern repeated itself. Christopher wondered blearily how long this had been going on, and guessed by the slight burning sensation flushing his face that it had been a while now.

He groaned and flailed his arms outward, trying to shrug off whoever was treating him as a human telegraph. "Okay, okay, I'm up," he croaked. He coughed violently, and this jolted him back to his senses.

Christopher opened his eyes to find himself sprawled on the sidewalk. There were still plenty of people around — several of them were glancing in his direction and sniggering — so he guessed he hadn't passed out for an extraordinarily long time. The ache of the concrete pressing into his back, however, indicated that his unconsciousness had been more than just momentary.

He gradually became aware that there was a figure crouched over him. "Here, let me help," came a voice which was unmistakably feminine. Christopher hoped for a moment that this might be the mysterious red-headed woman, come back to reclaim the thing she had lost, but a lock of blonde hair caught his eye and the thought was swamped by a wave of disappointment.

The girl proffered a hand. Christopher clasped it and she dragged him to his feet. "Try and catch your breath," she told him, and he nodded, leaning against the wall and breathing deeply of the humid night air. The scent of roasting hot dogs and Polish sausages wafted down from George Street, reminding Christopher that he was now more than a little famished.

He took a moment to study the girl who had revived him. She was several inches shorter than Christopher, and her straight, shoulder-length blonde hair was so pale as to be almost white. She was dressed mundanely, in grey sweat pants and a plain green T-shirt dotted here and there with perspiration, implying that she was either not one of the downtown revellers, or else that she was the least fashion-conscious person Christopher had ever met. Instead of the expected look of bemusement at having assisted some poor pathetic drunk, the girl's face was brimming with curiosity, as though she was bottling up a million questions and they were all vying to be the first on her lips. He swallowed, and offered her his sincere thanks.

"That's okay," she said guardedly. Her deep blue eyes were trying to get the measure of him, every bit as much as Christopher was appraising her. The girl looked about nineteen or twenty, but those eyes could have belonged to a woman four times as old. "I'm Emma. Emma Rawlin." She spoke with a breathless abandon, like a person convinced that they had far more to say than their few years on this Earth would ever permit. She clearly had energy to spare for the both of them, though, and Christopher decided that he wouldn't be at all surprised if she had a penchant for jogging through the downtown streets at two o'clock on a Saturday morning.

He reached out and lightly shook Emma's hand. "I'm —"

"Christopher Prescott," she finished.

Christopher was instantly taken aback, the hairs on the nape of his neck rising. "How the h—"

Emma held up something in her left hand. It was small, black and square-shaped, and had a couple of twenties protruding from the top. "Wallet," she told him. "First thing I look for when I find a stiff lying on the ground."

"Really?" he scowled, and grabbed his pocketbook back from her. "And is that often?"

"You'd be surprised." She saw the look of suspicion in Christopher's eyes and sighed dramatically. "Oh, you can count your money if you want, I didn't take any. And yes, your cards are all there too. Jesus, if I wanted to steal something, I'd hardly have waited around until you woke up."

Fair enough, thought Christopher. He could always check through his wallet later: he knew the girl's name now anyway, assuming she hadn't been clever and handed him a pseudonym.

"Of course, if I was going to lift anything, it'd be that *fios* stone in your other pocket."

Christopher was about to ask her what she meant when he remembered the strange little object the red-haired woman had dropped. Instinctively, his hand went to his side, and he couldn't help but breathe a small sigh of relief to feel it still nestled beneath the fabric there.

Emma looked at him through narrowed eyes. "What I don't understand is... well, actually, there are two things I don't understand, Chris."

"Christopher."

"Whatever. First, I don't understand what you're doing with some powerful mojo like a *fios* stone. I mean, I've only ever seen them from a distance, and it's been a long time since my first Wandering Parliament. But what I also don't understand is what somebody like you, who I'm willing to bet has no idea what I'm even talking about, is doing passing through the Ways. Oh, wait... I bet you've never heard of the Ways either, have you?"

Christopher was trying desperately to hang onto the thread of the conversation, one-sided though it had now become. "The Ways... is that how I... walked through that building?" It sounded absurd as he heard himself say it, although he knew that that was exactly what he had done.

"In a manner of speaking, yes," Emma conceded cautiously.

"Look, there was a woman, with this amazing head of red hair. She came this way, a little before I did. I need to find her." Christopher knew he couldn't expect this total stranger to help him any more than she already had done — especially since she clearly thought there was something awry with him — so he tried to imbue his words with every ounce of sincerity and conviction he could muster.

Emma eyed him for a moment, then nodded as if making up her mind about something. She looked around: the crowd of people on the streets was starting to swell as more and more people decided to call it a night and head home. "Look, Chris, I think maybe we should find someplace a little less public to talk about this." She tapped her finger against her earlobe and waggled her slender eyebrows for emphasis. "You never know who might be listening."

*   *   *

Christopher was panting audibly by the time they reached Emma's lodgings. He lied to himself that it was just the night's previous exertions weighing on him, rather than an altogether far too sedentary lifestyle. Emma had insisted on jogging the length of George Street and beyond, all the way to Henry Street (assuring Christopher in an impressively serious tone of voice that he did not want to be responsible for interrupting her exercise regimen) and finally turned up a narrow lane, where she stopped in front of a tall brown residence that had clearly seen better days. Emma, who seemed none the worse for wear, led the labouring Christopher to a set of concrete stairs at the side, which provided access to a low-ceilinged basement apartment.

Emma's lodgings weren't much — a front room which gave onto a small kitchen area, a bedroom she warned Christopher he didn't want to see the inside of, and a bathroom she warned him he definitely didn't want to see the inside of — and a scent not unlike burnt toast hung unpleasantly in the air. The place was sparsely furnished and decorated, but an old beige couch looked comfortable enough and Christopher didn't hesitate to collapse wearily on top of it. His stomach was grumbling and he was tempted to ask for something to eat, but upon observing the rather barren nature of the apartment, he thought better of it and instead merely asked for a glass of water.

"So, what's your story, Chris?" Emma finally asked. She handed him a chipped mug filled half with water and half with ice cubes rescued from an enormous refrigerator which looked like a relic of the Fifties.

"Christopher," he mumbled between sips of water.

"Oh, okay, right, sorry. Christopher," returned Emma, exaggerating the last two syllables. She curled up on the room's only other piece of furniture, a big armchair whose crimson upholstery was ragged in places. A couple of springs protruded from the bottom.

Christopher drained his mug, then grinned sheepishly. "Sorry, it's just that most of my friends know to call me that, and most everyone else picks up on it from them. It's a bit odd to have to correct someone on it. Anyway, it's not a big deal. I was just never comfortable with contracting other people's names, so I guess people just started doing to the same to me. Now it's what I'm accustomed to."

Emma watched him for a moment as he chewed on an ice cube. "You're a little strange, aren't you, Christopher?" she finally said. Then she returned his smile. "That's okay, strange is good. As far as I'm concerned, the normal folks don't know what they're missing."

Christopher smiled sadly. "Cecily used to say much the same thing."

"Girlfriend?"

"Ex," he said, a little too quickly. The red-haired woman may have pushed Cecily to the back of Christopher's mind for a short while, but those thoughts had never left him completely, and now that the prospect of actually meeting the mystery lady seemed all too remote, they were back with a vengeance. "We, ah, split up a few days ago," he explained weakly.

"Right. Is she the redhead who gave you the *fios* stone?" Emma nodded in the general direction of his trouser pocket.

Christopher chuckled lightly. "Oh, no, Cecily wouldn't know anything about that. I found this, at a bar. A woman — the one with the red hair — she dropped it by accident." And Christopher briefly recounted the events that had culminated in Emma discovering his prone body by the side of the road. "I don't even know if I should be telling you this," he admitted. "I don't even know what 'this' is. Part of me just wants to go home, collapse into bed and forget that any of this happened. But I'd really like to return the stone... thing... to that woman. Especially if it's as important as you say."

"And, admit it, now that you know there are things going on around you that you never even suspected, you're a little intrigued. Aren't you?"

Christopher shrugged. "I don't know. I guess so, maybe a little."

Emma smiled, taking his now-empty mug and returning it to the kitchen sink. "It's how I got into the life. Well, sort of into it. I'm still unaffiliated, you see, so I'm a bit on the outside of all the big secrets. But I know enough to tell when somebody's using the Ways nearby — that's how I found you."

"Is that what I did, when I passed through the wall... through the building?"

"Yeah, more or less. That's one way to, er, use the Ways. If you'll pardon the pun. See, St John's is old, Christopher. Not as old as London or Paris or Rome, of course, but it beats out any other city on this continent. It's older than Toronto and New York, it's way older than Los Angeles. Hell, as far as cities go it makes Vegas look like it's barely out of diapers. And cities this old... they remember the paths people traversed in days gone by. There used to be an alley entrance where that building stands now, and the city remembers that. If you've got the know-how, you can tap into those memories… navigate them, I guess." Emma walked over to stand beside Christopher. Abruptly, she gave him a sharp swat on the back of the head. "But you gotta close your eyes, that's rule number one for novices. Otherwise, your brain thinks it's in two places — hell, worse, two times — at once, and that screws with your equilibrium something fierce."

Christopher cringed, both from the sting of Emma's smack and the memory of travelling out of the alleyway. "Yeah, I noticed that. Thanks." He rubbed the back of his head with one hand, and with the other he drew the mysterious object from his pocket. "So, this… this thing. What exactly is it again?"

"A *fios* stone," Emma told him, taking a seat on the chesterfield next to him. "I guess you could say it's a way to send messages."

"Wouldn't an envelope be easier?"

Emma laughed and shook her head. "I'm not talking messages like 'pick up a litre of milk for supper', Christopher. I'm talking… powerful messages. More than just words or images."

"Magic?" he asked, letting the word slip off his tongue with some reluctance.

Emma shrugged. "If you want. Most of us don't really like to put labels on such things — they are what they are, I guess you could say. But, yeah, since you're new to this game, I suppose it's fair to say that a *fios* stone transmits messages laden with… mystical undercurrents. Like I said to you back on George, it's some hefty mojo. If your ladyfriend lost this, she's gonna be pretty pissed off when she realises it's gone."

And so she should be awfully delighted with whoever returns it to her, mused Christopher with a rush of excitement. But he kept the thought to himself.

"Look," he said to Emma out loud, "you've already done an awful lot for me, and I hate to be any more of a pain, but could you do me a favour?"

"You want me to help you find Red."

"Well… yeah. Do you know her?"

Emma shrugged. "This is Newfoundland, Christopher. Red hair isn't exactly rare in these parts. From the way you described her buddy, though, it sounds like she's with the People of the Serpent."

"Serpents?" queried Christopher, a frown creasing his brow. "So is she not… good, then?"

Emma chuckled openly. "Christopher, pal, you've been reading too much *Harry Potter*. Well, or maybe the *Book of Genesis*. There's nothing inherently good or bad about serpents. That's just a fear that was drilled into our collective mindset back when mankind was still living in caves, and we were still learning that those itty snake bites could take out the burliest hunter-gatherer. Serpents are just animals, and there are good folk and bad folk amongst their People just like any of the Five Clans."

"Oh," said Christopher. "Okay. So, in that case… how do we find her? Does it help to know that she's with these snake-people?"

"It's the People of the Serpent, not the 'snake-people', Chris," Emma chided him, leaving a pregnant pause where the rest of his name should be. Christopher felt like he was back in a grade school classroom all of a sudden. "Names are important. If you're going to be meeting more of us, you're going to want to remember that. You're right to be fussy about your own name, as it happens — the way we choose to be called means a lot, not just to ourselves but to those observing us as well."

"Okay," said Christopher, nodding. "I get it. But that doesn't answer my question."

Emma thought for a minute, pressing her thumb against her chin. "It may help," she said finally, "but not with me. The People of the Serpent are an almost vanished kind — they've been the weakest of the Five Clans for centuries, far enough back that the histories become little more than myth. I've only met a handful of them, and none of them resemble the woman you're describing."

Christopher sighed in frustration. "So what do I do?"

Emma reached over and squeezed his arm. "It's what we do. You feel a responsibility to this lady? Well, to be honest, I feel a little responsible towards you now. I can't very well drop all these tantalising little hints and then kick you back out on the street. And, hell, the place for us to go is exactly where I was going to end up tonight anyway."

"Where's that?" asked Christopher, a little uncertainly.

"I mentioned it earlier: the Wandering Parliament."

* * *

All in all, Reggie Barter couldn't complain about life right now. Sure, maybe he lived in a broken-down old bungalow on the edge of the city's downtown area, whose ceiling leaked in eight places when it rained. And, yeah, his old lady's lawyer was still knocking on his door or ringing him on the phone, trying to get the money that old bag thought she had coming to her.

But as the city's seedier elements became a little bolder with each passing year, Reggie's services were more and more in demand, and these days he was kept as busy as he wanted to be. And what he couldn't quite afford through the proceeds of his little jobs, he could always acquire in other ways. The gorgeous widescreen plasma TV propped up against the wall of the bedroom was proof enough of that. Reggie glanced over at it admiringly.

A hand snaked under his unshaven chin. "Hey, Reggie, why are ya payin' attention to that when ya could be payin' attention to me?"

Reggie let his head be twisted to the left by the lanky creature with whom he was sharing his bed. He grinned and she giggled, shaking out-of-a-bottle blonde curls in his face.

"Sorry, Honey, I got distracted," Reggie told the girl. He reached over and tickled her in the narrow space between her breasts, his ministrations earning more infectious giggles. The girl thought Reggie called her "Honey" as a term of endearment; she may have been less delighted if she knew that it was actually just so that he wouldn't have to remember her name. As far as Reggie was concerned, "Honey" might as well be her real name. But frankly, he doubted she'd care much one way or the other as long as he took her out to dinner every Saturday, bought her something shiny once a month or so, and paid a minimal amount of attention to her in the sack.

"You're always gettin' distracted," Honey admonished him playfully, snaking her hand along Reggie's neck and down his chest.

Licking his lips, Reggie was leaning in for a closer inspection of the girl's rather impressive cleavage when he felt Honey's hand jerk against his stomach. The woman suddenly shrieked, high-pitched and ear-splitting, and pointed to a corner of the room.

Reggie had not come by what he had in life by being slow-witted or lazy. He knew Honey wasn't overreacting to whatever she had seen — she was dumb, yeah, but she was hardly delusional, even after half a bottle of wine — and he certainly had enough enemies who might want to break into his house, including a couple who'd be sick enough to stand around and watch him get it on with his woman instead of just jumping him while he was blissfully oblivious. A knife was taped to the side of his mattress, and in a flash Reggie was reaching for it, even as he spun around to face the room.

"Hello, Reginald. Remember me?" A small man sat on a wooden chair in the half-light of the room, his chin resting against his hand, which was perched atop his walking stick.

"Chase," spat Reggie. He quickly ran his palm back and forth along the mattress, feeling desperately for his knife. Had the damned thing fallen off during his and Honey's energetic play?

As Reggie glared at him, Donovan Chase held up his other hand to reveal the missing weapon. "Looking for this?" Chase chuckled.

Reggie grunted angrily. Behind him, he could feel Honey trying to cover her nakedness, though not as quickly as he might have expected. "What do you want, Chase?"

Chase rose to his feet and started to slowly pace around the bedroom, his walking stick tapping against the floorboards. "You've come up in the world, Reginald. You're not exactly living in the most lavish of residences, but it's rather nicer than the youth hostel you were inhabiting when we first met. When was that — 1985? '86?"

"Something like that. I can't say I keep track."

"Oh, Reginald." Chase tutted lightly. "You know I can't abide an insubordinate tone of voice." He lashed out suddenly with his walking stick, smashing it into the screen of Reggie's newly-acquired plasma television.

"Jesus Ch — what the hell do you think you're doing, Chase?" yelped Reggie.

Chase put both hands on the foot of the bed, staring at Reggie with steely eyes. "Call it encouragement, Reginald. I need to know that you'll give me your full cooperation."

"Who is this guy, Reggie?" whimpered Honey, who had nearly buried herself underneath the bedsheets.

"Shut up, Honey!" snapped Reggie. He looked across at Chase, tried to stare down the diminutive man, but finally gave up and lay back in bed. "Okay, Chase, I'll be good. What do you want?"

"I trust you still maintain your contacts amongst the... more secretive layers of society?"

Reggie didn't need to ask Chase to explain what he meant. Instead, he took a deep breath, and kept his response as cool as he was able, in case Chase decide to break something a little more personal. "Yeah," he grumbled. "I still got a few people who owe me some favours. You know what they say —

once you've put a foot in that world, there's no stepping back. Why?"

Chase fluttered something in one hand. It was a glossy photograph of a stunning red-headed woman. "Do you recognise her, Reginald?" Reggie shook his head. "She goes by the name of Aislinn," Chase told him, with a taint of venom. "I have to locate her with some urgency."

Reggie shrugged. "And I'm guessing I don't have any choice about helping you out." Chase simply smiled unpleasantly. "Okay, I'll talk to some people, see what turns up. If she's anybody important, I should able to track her down pretty quickly."

Chase nodded and tossed him the photograph. "Keep it. I have others."

"You, ah, you might wanna try the Wandering Parliament," Reggie suggested to Chase's retreating form.

Chase looked back at him. "There's one tonight? Now that is an interesting coincidence of timing. And you know, Reginald, I don't believe in coincidences. Thank you. I'll leave you to… finish up here before you 'talk to your people', as they say." And Chase left the room.

"Wait!" called Reggie after him, scrambling to sit up in bed. "How do I contact you, Chase? You got some sort of communication charm or something for me to use when I have something for you?"

Chase's head popped back around the corner, a bemused look on his face. "This is the twenty-first century, Reginald. Call me on my mobile phone. The number's on the back of the glossy."

And he was gone again.

* * *

The mood of euphoria in the dance club had crested and was now beginning to wane. The place was still bustling — though it was hardly as crowded as when Christopher Prescott had vanished out its back door — but the dancing was starting to feel less lively, as if the heat and the alcohol were no longer fuelling the partiers' high spirits but instead were beginning to leech them away. As the hour approached three o'clock, another Friday night on George Street was drawing to an exhausted close.

While most of the traffic was now leaving the bar, however, one figure was moving against the current. Those who noticed him — and there were precious few of these — saw a man of average build, with a plain face and brown hair brushed into an unassuming style. He was dressed in clothes which were neither fashionable nor ugly, but instead seemed selected to elicit the least amount of commentary possible, which in fact they were.

The man stood in front of the bar, studying the gaudy logo painted on a wooden sign above the door. Two burly bouncers stood beneath it, their arms folded forbiddingly, completely blocking off the way into the establishment. After a moment, the newcomer nodded almost imperceptibly to himself, and glanced at two women walking in opposite directions a little way down the strip.

Seconds later, the bouncers' attention became distracted by a scuffle which had broken out between the two young ladies, neither of whom had exchanged so much as a word nor even glanced in each other's direction until a moment before, when they had suddenly developed a deep and abiding hatred for one another. Advancing a few paces, the bouncers chortled as a well-placed fingernail pierced flesh and a spray of blood coated both girls' blouses. By this time, the plain-looking man had long since disappeared into the depths of the bar.

As he moved through the club, his gaze strayed to neither the slovenly-clad women still hanging around the dance floor, pining for one last chance at love (or at least something they could briefly fool themselves into thinking was love), nor the bar with its enticing racks of beer and liquor. Instead, the man made his way to the middle of the dance floor, the remaining revellers somehow managing to avoid him completely. He stopped there and seemed to sniff the humid air, his black eyes roaming back and forth.

Finally, the man's gaze fell to a table, pushed up against one wall of the bar. A chair had recently been dragged over to the table and a man now sat sprawled across its surface, moaning pitiably in his drunken stupor. A bottle of beer had fallen from his grasp and lay smashed at his feet, cream ale pooling around the soles of his sneakers.

The man in the middle of the dance floor stalked over to the table, his eyes alert for something. As he reached the side of the bar, his dispassionate expression changed for the first time since entering the place: he bared his teeth a little and let out a quiet hiss of aggravation. Why were his eyes not locating what he knew he should be able to find there?

The drunken man finally registered the presence of another person nearby and tried to sit up, though all he could manage was to raise his head slightly off the table and look in the other man's general direction. "Whass hap'nin'?" he slurred. "Izzit time t'go home?"

The plain-looking man regarded him as one might look upon a particularly loathsome insect. "Where is the *fios* stone?" he asked, in a tone of voice which practically defined neutrality.

"Wha?" was the most intelligent response the seated man could muster.

"I can... smell a *fios* stone. I must have it."

The drunken man giggled stupidly. "I don' have a fuckin' clue what yer talkinbout," he replied, resting his head back on the tabletop. "'Mgoin back to sleep."

The other man reached out, pulled open the drunkard's eyelid with one hand and, with a single finger of his other hand, casually punctured the eyeball thus revealed. As his victim began screaming uncontrollably, he grasped what remained of the ruined orb and plucked it from its socket. He popped it between his lips and began to slowly chew. After a few seconds he swallowed and shook his head. "No, Alvin Willicott. You have not seen the *fios* stone." He sniffed the air once more and picked up a faint scent of something. He nodded to himself again. "So it has moved elsewhere."

Alvin Willicott was flailing wildly in his seat, trying to get up and escape his attacker but too drunk and in too much pain to do so. Around them, the last few bar patrons danced on, or sucked thirstily on their final drinks of the night, or groped each other desperately in the bar's shadowed corners. No one seemed to notice the shrieking man at the table, nor the plain dark man standing over him.

Abandoning his attempts to stand, the one-eyed man began to sob, cradling his devastated face in his palms. The other man looked at him anew. "Shh," he said, and thrust his hand into Alvin's chest cavity, closing his fist around his heart until it had beaten its last.

Without even bothering to wipe the grisly detritus off his hand or arm, the man turned at once and padded slowly to the rear of the bar, towards the door to the alley.

Nobody noticed the body left lying in a growing pool of blood on the bar floor. Nobody noticed the bartender, an hour or so later, dragging the corpse out onto the street and depositing it in a dumpster (although his wife would admonish him the following morning for bloodstains on his trousers which he would never be able to satisfactorily explain). Nobody reported Alvin Willicott missing, or held a funeral for him.

In fact, across the dance floor, the woman who, seconds earlier, had been Alvin's girlfriend abruptly wondered why she had spent the past four months single and alone, ignoring the man who had been Alvin's best friend when he was so obviously fond of her. Acting on these feelings with a sudden and consuming impatience, she spent the rest of the night in his bed. The people who had been Alvin's parents woke up on Saturday morning to find themselves both pondering why they had kept an room full of junk in their house all these years, and quickly made plans to dispose of it. On Monday, a want ad went up for what had been Alvin's job at a local music store, and none of his coworkers could quite remember who had filled the position last.

For, in every way that mattered, Alvin Willicott had ceased to exist.

Chapter Four
In which there are Visitors to the Wandering Parliament

"Okay, exposition time." Emma's voice was only slightly muted by the thin wooden door to her bedroom, to which she had removed herself to get changed for the Wandering Parliament.

"I'm listening," Christopher called back.

"I've told you that there are five Clans, and I've already mentioned the People of the Serpent. I imagine a big boy like you can do the math and figure out how many that leaves."

"Well, yeah... now that you mention it, you've actually got a future Ph.D. in math standing in your living room."

There was a momentary pause from the other side of the door. "That's... very riveting of you, Christopher. And if I hear you say one word about logarithmic thingies or trigonometric... other-thingies... then I can guarantee you'll be going through yet another solid wall tonight, and this time without the "as if it wasn't there" part." Christopher scarcely had time to blink before Emma returned to her original train of thought. "Anyway, the other Clans are the People of the Cat, the People of the Caribou, the People of the Great Auk and the People of the Codfish."

Christopher barely suppressed a chuckle. "What, calling themselves the People of the Halibut would've sounded too flaky?"

Emma's door cracked ajar and she stuck her head through the opening, an annoyed expression on her face. "Hey! The codfish is a pretty integral animal in this part of the world. Don't make fun."

Christopher raised his hands in mock surrender. "I'm sorry, I'm sorry." Emma darted him one final dubious glare and then retreated back into her room. "So why those five? How come, I dunno, dogs and seagulls get short shrift?"

"That's a good question, actually. You're hardly the first to raise it. I don't know the answer; I'm not sure anyone does. The Clans have existed for as long as people have been on this island, back before John Cabot and the Vikings, and probably before the Beothucks and the Mikmaq too."

"I didn't think there was anybody in Newfoundland before them."

"Name a place and a people, and there'll always be somebody who lived there earlier, Christopher. Just because their names, and all traces of their existence, have been lost to the centuries doesn't mean they weren't there once. Go back two hundred or two thousand years and the Five Clans would already be around. Or so I'm told; it could all be a pack of lies."

Emma stepped out of the bedroom, now dressed in a black sleeveless top and long blue denim skirt. "So, do I look presentable?" she asked.

Christopher was still picking pebbles out of his shirt from his brief nap on the downtown sidewalk, and trying very hard not to think about a skirt Cecily owned which looked a lot like the one Emma was now wearing. "Well, you look better than I do," he offered.

She narrowed her eyes. "I suppose I'll have to take my chances that that's actually a compliment." She clapped her hands together. "Come on, we'd better be going. It doesn't pay to be too early or too late to a Parliament."

Christopher eased himself off the couch and followed Emma out the apartment door. "So where does this... Parliament happen, anyway? And how exactly does it wander?" Christopher had visions of a big house walking around on ostrich legs, like in the fairy tale about Baba Yaga he had read as a child.

"It's called the Wandering Parliament because it's run by a different Clan each time it's in session," Emma answered. "As for where it takes place, well, you'll see for yourself soon enough." A light breeze had arisen during the time the pair had spent in Emma's quarters, though it hardly diminished the night's increasingly oppressive humidity. As they strode towards the steeply-inclined sidewalk, it tugged at her fine blonde hair.

"Is it close enough to walk there?" Christopher wasn't going to complain, but he was sensitive to the fact that his feet were already a little sore from his ill-fated exertions in the dance club, and likely weren't up to an extended jaunt.

Emma grinned. "We could probably jog there before sunrise. But, no, I wouldn't do that to you, Christopher. And anyway, I'm hardly dressed for that anymore myself." She winked kindly. "We'll take a cab instead."

Christopher looked at her, perplexed. "A cab. What, is every taxi driver in the city part of... your people?"

They had reached the bottom of the hill and now stood on Henry Street once more. "Watch and be amazed," she told him. The only moving vehicle in sight was an old pickup truck, trundling away from them as it belched dark, noxious fumes into the air. Nonetheless, Emma put her fingers to her lips as if she was about to flag down a taxi passing directly by them.

Christopher expected the sort of piercing shriek he usually heard people use to attract attention — the kind he'd never been able to replicate himself, after childhood warnings about the rudeness of whistling left his development of the skill woefully neglected. Instead, Emma produced a complex, mellifluous trilling noise like a particularly sophisticated birdcall. And suddenly, Christopher realised that there was a car sitting at the kerb beside them with its engine running. It was dark in colour, and Christopher noticed that its windows were tinted so that you couldn't see inside. The familiar taxi light was mounted on the car's roof — and currently illuminated to indicate that the cabbie was seeking a fare — but it bore no company name or logo, and nor were there any other identifiable marks on the body of the vehicle.

Seemingly unruffled by the car's abrupt appearance, Emma was already clambering into the back seat. Halfway in, she realised that Christopher wasn't following and called back to him. "Come on, time's a-wasting!"

Christopher shrugged, deciding that this was likely the least of the strange phenomena he was going to experience tonight. He hopped into the taxi and closed the door.

The interior was clean and smelled faintly of caramel. The cabbie was a portly man with a big red nose and a few wisps of snow-white hair curling out from under a well-worn cap. This he tipped to Emma as he swivelled around in his seat. "Evenin', Miss Rawlin," he said to her. "Or I guess I should say, good mornin'."

"Good morning, Soloman," she replied, smiling warmly. Emma gestured to her companion. "This is Christopher Prescott. He's… new." Christopher grinned sheepishly.

"Well met, Mr Prescott," said Soloman, reaching over the seat and shaking the younger man's hand with enthusiasm.

"How's business been tonight?" Emma inquired.

The driver lifted his cap and scratched his balding pate. "A bit off tonight, actually, ma'am. I've heard talk that there might be somethin' amiss at the Parliament."

"Probably one of the Clan reps getting too aggressive, trying to recruit us independents," Emma chuckled. Christopher noticed a trace of concern underlying her casual words, though.

"Oh, no, ma'am, that'd be pretty much par for the course at a Parliament. I think this is somethin' a bit more worrisome than that, though I couldn't tell you more — can't go to the Parliament myself until I'm off duty, of course — and I don't mean to put you on edge afore you even get there. Anyway, we'll have you at the park in seconds."

"Thanks, Sol." Emma turned to Christopher. "We're going to be travelling the Ways now. This time, keep your eyes closed — I don't want you blacking out on me." Christopher nodded, feeling a bit like a dim student who has to be told not to eat the paste. Emma squeezed his hand. "Don't worry, we all go through this the first few times we pass through the Ways. It's only natural. We're not like some of the Clansfolk. We're only human — it takes a while for our systems to adjust to the, um… magic. You'll get used to it, believe me." She grinned supportively. "To be honest, I'm impressed that you didn't lose your lunch back on George."

"Thanks, Emma," Christopher murmured gratefully. He clamped his eyes tightly shut as he felt the taxi pull out into the street.

Christopher found the next few seconds oddly disjointed. The rhythm of the taxi's engine seemed to change at random intervals, and his stomach felt like it was somehow travelling uphill and downhill at the same time. It was not unlike that odd floating sensation you get in some elevators as they slow to a stop, right before the doors open — but repeated over and over again in rapid succession. A strangely melodic noise, like distant windchimes, floated through Christopher's hearing, and the pattern of light on his eyelids flickered unnaturally, as if someone was shining a strobe light on him. He briefly wondered if he had in fact fallen asleep back in the dance bar and the events since had been nothing more than a vodka-fuelled nightmare, but the soft application of the cab's brakes quickly put paid to that notion.

"You can open your eyes now, Christopher," Emma whispered in his ear. Tentatively, Christopher did as she suggested. Nothing seemed to have changed within the car — he noticed that Soloman had not bothered to turn the meter on, and wondered absently if it was just for show — and from the angle at which he sat, all he could see of the outdoors was darkness.

"Standard fee, Miss Rawlin," said Soloman over his shoulder. Emma reached into a pocket of her skirt and produced a couple of strangely-shaped coins which she passed over to the old man. "Keep the change, Sol. And thanks — for both the drive, and the warning. I'll be seeing you."

"Thank you, ma'am," the cabbie responded, tipping his hat to her once again. As Christopher and Emma climbed out of the vehicle, he called out, "You kids have a good night, now. Watch out for yourselves!" Emma shut the door and, before the noise of metal on metal had faded, Christopher realised that they were both standing in an empty car park.

He looked at Emma oddly. "What was that you paid with?"

"Money, obviously." Emma rolled her eyes, then darted a wry smirk in his direction.

"It's not any sort of money I've ever seen before," he protested. But Emma just winked enigmatically and set off across the parking lot. It was gradually dawning on Christopher that a lot of what he had once accepted as fact and taken for granted might be completely unreliable in this strange society he had stumbled upon. It was a most disconcerting, disorientating feeling.

Standing there, staring at Emma's retreating back, Christopher finally recognised where they were. The newly-terraced duck pond just visible beyond the lip of the car park was the giveaway, but Christopher would have known the place regardless, having visited it on numerous occasions and driven past it more times than he could possibly count.

"Bowring Park?" he asked in disbelief, as he jogged to catch up with Emma. "This Wandering Parliament of yours is in Bowring Park?"

"Sure," said Emma matter-of-factly. "Nice big open area, secluded from passers-by, closed after nightfall — it's perfect."

"But..." Christopher wracked his brain for some sort of reasonable objection. "Butbutbut I live just down the street from here. I can walk here from my house in, like, a quarter of an hour. This isn't possible!"

"Yeah, and you just travelled here from downtown in something under thirty seconds. I'd've thought you'd be getting used to all sorts of impossible things by now. No, actually, strike that. I enjoy the childlike sense of wonder. It's cute — keep it up."

"You're mocking me," Christopher accused.

"Now I can see why you're doing a Ph.D."

Christopher grunted deeply, then followed Emma down a short gravel pathway leading from the parking lot to the duck pond. The area was lit sporadically by streetlamps and by an illuminated fountain in the centre of the pond, and Christopher could make out dozens of ducks, of all sizes and colours, nesting on the grassy slopes around him. He kept a particular eye out for the park's notoriously ill-tempered swans, their mood made even more foul by the recent birth of several cygnets, but saw none. Behind him, Christopher heard a door slam and turned his head just in time to see another dark-coloured taxi — or maybe it was Soloman's again — vanish from sight. Three middle-aged women had evidently left the cab, and were now strolling across the car park, quietly gossiping in the dense nighttime air.

"So, just how did we get here so quickly?" Christopher asked Emma as they circled the duck pond. "I mean, usually that trip takes at least ten minutes, even by car — and that's assuming you don't hit any red lights."

"I told you, we travelled the Ways," she replied, carefully stepping over a mottled brown duck which had chosen to nap right in the middle of the trail. It turned an expressionless black eye to them and emitted a low, annoyed quack before returning to its slumber.

"Right, I heard you, but I still don't get it. I thought the Ways meant…" He gestured wildly with his hands, trying to choose his words so that they didn't sound completely absurd.

"… walking through buildings because once upon a time they weren't there… that sort of thing."

Emma shook her head. "No, no, you're missing the important part. Travelling the Ways is about tapping into the city's memory of the way it used to be, of the way it's always been. The city remembers an alleyway that existed for a century before a building was erected on the site. But it also remembers the millions of times over the past ninety years that people travelled from downtown to Bowring Park. And it remembers the jam-packed trains that used to run through the park — back when Newfoundland still had trains — and the station that once stood just a little way down the street from the parking lot where we were dropped off. There are paths in this city which are so well-trod that people who know how to navigate the Ways can flit along them in seconds, like a pebble on the surface of a pond."

Christopher just nodded, trying to take it all in. As he did so, he glanced ahead and saw that they were approaching the elegant bronze statue of Peter Pan which overlooked the duck pond. Christopher grinned despite himself. The statue always made him do that — made him feel as if he was still a four year-old boy who truly believed in a magical land where you might never grow up, who harboured no doubt that the sprites and fairies depicted at Peter's feet actually existed, just out of sight. Vaguely, he wondered how he could have let that heartfelt conviction trickle away over the years, especially now that he was discovering there really was more to the world than he ever would have imagined possible, just three hours earlier.

Emma noticed him looking up at the monument, and stopped. "What are you thinking?" she asked him.

"It's weird," Christopher said after a moment. "You know how things always seem so much bigger when you're a child than they do after you've grown up?" He gestured towards the eternal boy, perpetually sounding a note on his flute, a carefree expression permanently etched on his youthful countenance.

"Not Peter Pan, not for me. I still feel like I'm looking up to him in… in…"

"Curiosity?"

"Wonderment."

"Cool."

And after a minute, they turned right and continued their journey in a comfortable silence.

There were many paths through Bowring Park. Some were marked out in gravel and were well signposted; others existed only for those who knew them of old, or were brave (or foolhardy) enough to go looking for them. Only one path was paved, however. It began at the main entrance in the western end of the park, and lead over a concrete bridge which had spanned the railroad tracks in days gone by. There, it split into a giant loop extending as far as the park's eastern exit, a smaller bridge under which the Waterford River leisurely flowed into the duck pond.

Much to Christopher's surprise, it was onto this path that Emma steered him as they left the pond behind them. He was constantly expecting them to take one of the many side trails off the main track, to end up in some hidden grotto or clearing in the depths of Bowring Park. But they never did, and instead they followed the gentle arc of the roadway in silence as it ambled through the park's vastness.

Christopher's impatience and curiosity were about to get the better of him when suddenly, in the lulls between the gentle night breezes, he realised that he could hear a noise ahead of him quite unlike anything he had ever experienced in the park before. Moments later, the broad shape of the Bungalow came into view, floating against the darkness like a grey ghost, and Christopher understood their destination.

The Bungalow was as old as Bowing Park itself. Stately without seeming overblown, it was one of the few buildings standing within the boundaries of the park, and often played host to gatherings and receptions of all kinds. About the only thing which dwarfed the Bungalow was the great expanse of lawn it overlooked, the lush grass looking inviting even at this time of night. The lawn was ringed by mighty trees, many of them planted there by dignitaries who had visited Bowring Park through the years: here a red maple planted in the last decade by the Queen of Britain, there an English oak courtesy of a Governor General long since passed from office, and most famous of all, the weeping beech which had stood as a towering, mournful sentinel over the park since the days of the Great War.

Tonight, defying all logic, the Bungalow lawn was full of people.

Emma slapped him spiritedly on the back. "Christopher Prescott, welcome to the Wandering Parliament!"

Christopher had to consciously remind himself to close his mouth and not gape too obviously. Instead, he let his eyes slowly survey the scene before him, trying to take in every unlikely detail.

The lawn seemed to be divided into three sections. Closest to them, sheltering under the trees, were a number of booths and stalls. Most of them were made of wood, and appeared to have been hastily thrown together for the purposes of the evening. Each booth was manned by one or two people, who were shouting out enticements to those standing elsewhere on the lawn, as well as the newcomers arriving from both directions along the paved path or emerging from around the other side of the Bungalow. It quickly became apparent to Christopher that the wares and services being offered in these stalls were far from ordinary.

In one booth, a large, hairy man with an unkempt beard was holding small vials and tubes in his mammoth fists, waving them about. "Potions, ointments and salves here!" he bellowed in an impressive baritone. "Cure blindness, deafness, snoring and stuttering! Rid yourself of unwanted blemishes, scars and amputations!"

Next to him, a little old lady with enormous coke-bottle spectacles was exhorting a couple holding hands to purchase a small glass globe, one of dozens dangling from the walls of her stall. "Ooh, newlyweds are you?" she cackled delightedly. "Well, lovey, this one is perfect for you! It contains a tear of joy from Aonghus' right eye. D'you know of Aonghus then? It'll keep your love vibrant and new forevermore."

Elsewhere, people were hawking parchments and paintings, tattoos and trinkets, ornate jewellery and strikingly-coloured gemstones, and strange little machines which had no purpose Christopher could fathom. He noticed that, worked into the seemingly ramshackle design of all the booths, was an unusual sigil resembling twin antlers. He pointed it out to Emma.

"Tonight's Parliament is being hosted by the People of the Caribou," she told him. "Only merchants of the host Clan are permitted to ply their wares at the Parliament. It's one of the advantages of belonging."

Out of the corner of his eye, Christopher caught sight of the glow of a low fire at the back of one booth. Within, he noticed a young girl of no more than fourteen standing over an enormous cooking pot, carefully ladling a bubbling broth into an old wooden bowl. Moments later, an intoxicating aroma like the most succulent barbecued steak washed over Christopher, and his already malcontent stomach rumbled longingly. "Mmm, do you think we could stop and get something to eat?" he murmured to Emma.

"No way," she told him flatly. "I wouldn't trust any meal sold here. Hell, I wouldn't buy anything of any sort if I wasn't one hundred percent certain of what I was getting. The people of the Parliament are like any others, Christopher — a lot of them are kind and trustworthy, but there are plenty who would stab you in the back just as soon as look at you. I know Kian there," she said, gesturing to the hirsute man dealing in potions, "and maybe one or two others. But as for the rest... well, keep your wits about you."

Christopher nodded as Emma continued. "Anyway, I doubt your money's good with most of the stallholders. Not all of the people here are like me, Christopher — interacting both with the mundane world and with the world of the Five Clans. A number of them — more and more as the years go by, to be honest — keep themselves to their own kind."

Trying to ignore the wonderful smells of cooking coming from the market area, Christopher's gaze strayed to the centre of the Bungalow lawn. Surrounded by people, a simple stone sundial sat there. Despite the time of night, a gentle white light hovered above the clock face, and Christopher was astonished and impressed to see that this luminous apparition was giving the correct time.

This area seemed to be a sort of general meeting space, as all those standing there were simply engaged in conversation, in small circles of threes and fours and fives. It looked as though there was a regular rotation amongst the groups, as people drifted from one circle to the next and, in turn, inspired somebody else to leave for a different conversation. Christopher noticed that, every few seconds, heads would dart towards the entrance to the Bungalow, as if anticipating something.

"That's the meat of the Parliament," Emma indicated. "The gossip." The three middle-aged women who had arrived at the park behind them finally caught up, and Christopher watched as they made a beeline for a small clique whose chatter was dominated by a tall blond man with a roguish smile and a patch over his left eye. Emma appeared not to notice, her eyes scanning the crowd closer to the green-and-brown Bungalow itself. "Everybody getting caught up on what's transpired since the last Parliament," she was elaborating. "The schemes, the rivalries, the illicit love affairs. And, of course, the speculation over what pronouncements will be handed down by tonight's presiding Clan. That's always a hot topic."

Christopher pointed to the last area of the lawn, far to their left. "And what happens over there?" A number of small tents were set up on the slope at the edge of the lawn, their interiors hidden behind layers of what looked like black velvet. He noticed that the gossipers seemed to be giving the tents a wide and respectful berth.

"That's where the high muckety-mucks conduct their business. Dealmaking, power playing… politics, basically. Trust me when I say that you don't want to be involved."

Christopher rolled his eyes. "You don't have to tell me twice. I'm still not sure I want to be involved in any of this." But the slight yet unmistakable weight of the *fios* stone in his pocket belied his words.

The pair of them left the path and moved onto the lawn. Christopher was not ignorant of the fact that Emma detoured well away from the merchants, perhaps fearful that Christopher would be led astray by an unscrupulous stallholder.

Nonetheless, he couldn't help but glance across at the strange merchandise one last time as they passed. As he did so, his gaze fell on a small brown-haired boy of no more than five, standing behind the counter of a stall which, peculiarly, was bereft of any goods whatsoever. The countertop was far taller than the boy, and he appeared to be balancing himself precariously on something to allow him to peer out onto the grounds. As Christopher looked at the child, the boy's eyes shifted to return the stare, and Christopher felt an almost overwhelming tide of déjà vu wash over him.

"That boy," he started to say to Emma, but she cut him off.

"Soloman was right," she was muttering. "Something is wrong here." She was squinting at the sundial in the middle of the lawn, and her brow was furrowing in consternation.

"What?" asked Christopher, pushing the odd little boy to the back of his mind. "What is it?"

"It's nearly three thirty," Emma told him. "The Speech from the Throne should have started by now. I thought I'd timed our arrival just right — we'd hear the word from on high, then set to work finding Red for you. But something's happened."

Again Christopher saw the other folk gathered on the lawn glance frequently over at the Bungalow, and he became aware of an impatient undercurrent to the hushed chatter around him. Following Emma's gaze, he noticed for the first time that something large had been erected in the shadows of the verandah which ran around the perimeter of the Bungalow, though it was too dark to make out exactly what it was.

"Maybe they're just running a little behind schedule?" Christopher offered lamely, craning his neck forward to try to get a better look at the object.

"No, Christopher, that would be a major breach of etiquette. The Wandering Parliament is supposed to run flawlessly, like clockwork. It's been that way for... well, for long enough that it makes my head hurt to think about it. Any major problem would be a huge stain on the reputation of the People of the Caribou. I don't think —"

"Don't think what?" Christopher prompted. He turned back, curious as to what could have silenced his loquacious companion.

The glint of metal reflecting off the knife at her throat provided the answer.

Chapter Five
In which a Champion is Declared

Instinctively, Christopher jolted forward, fearful that there might be a second dagger heading towards his own neck. As he did so, he spun about to obtain a better view of Emma's attacker.

It was the blond man with the eyepatch he had spotted in conversation earlier. In addition to the knife held beneath Emma's chin, he had her right arm twisted roughly behind her. Two bald men flanked him — twins, Christopher thought — and all three wore arrogant smirks on their faces.

"Hello, Emmeline," the flaxen-haired man said, his lips almost pressed up against Emma's ear. His voice oozed false charm, like one of those smarmy low-rent lawyers Christopher sometimes saw advertising on late-night television. "It's been a while."

"Not long enough, Lochlann," Emma muttered angrily. She twisted against his hold as best she could without pushing her neck against his blade, and her face was contorted with a look of revulsion.

Christopher noticed that many of the people around them had stopped what they were doing and were now regarding the struggle in their midst. Oddly, though, a lot of them seemed to be doing less out of any concern that an assault was being committed, than out of boredom, as they awaited whatever was actually supposed to be transpiring here at the Wandering Parliament. He even saw a few people laughing amongst themselves, or rolling their eyes in a knowing manner.

"Woah," said Christopher, finally finding his voice. He held out his hands in a placatory gesture. "Calm down, guys. Let's talk about this like reasonable adults."

"Lochlann has never been a 'reasonable adult'," spat Emma.

The blond man, however, was appraising Christopher as if noticing him for the first time. "What have we here, Emmeline? Have you gone and found yourself a new champion?"

Unsure how to respond to this, Christopher looked quizzically towards Emma, who was sighing in frustration. "He's not my champion, Lochlann. We only met tonight and I'm doing him a favour."

The man with the eyepatch grinned nastily. "Then I shall be your champion once again, my darling. One way or another." And he whispered something in Emma's ear which made her curl up her face with disgust. The expression intensified as Lochlann began trailing lascivious kisses down the side of her neck.

Now, Christopher was at heart an old-fashioned kind of guy — not in his attitudes concerning the capabilities of women (frankly, he harboured little doubt that Emma would be able to take him in a fair fight without breaking a sweat) but in his opinions of how men should behave towards them. This was, he knew, part of the reason his night downtown had proved so unspectacular — at least until the moment the red-haired woman had appeared on the scene — as he simply felt uncomfortable making the kinds of aggressive moves which might lead to a drunken rendezvous on the dance floor and the beguiling possibility of much more afterward. Christopher sometimes resented this aspect of his character, but at the same time he felt a certain pride in it; and, ultimately, he knew that this was part of the very core of his being, and not likely to change any time soon.

So it really didn't matter that he had known Emma Rawlin for little more than an hour. It hardly even made a difference that she was going out of her way to help him in a matter which didn't remotely concern her. The only important thing was that Christopher was witnessing a woman clearly being mistreated in a most ungentlemanly way, and his temper, normally kept so well intact, began to flare in response. He felt his cheeks getting red and his placid demeanour melt away in an instant. Christopher took an assertive step towards Lochlann and Emma, and seethed, "Fine, jackass. If Emma needs a champion, I'll be her champion." He was inordinately grateful that his voice didn't crack, as it was unfortunately wont to do.

If Christopher had hoped to intimidate Lochlann, though, he appeared to have failed miserably. The man with the eyepatch looked up from where he was nuzzling the nape of Emma's neck, and chuckled in a way that made Christopher feel very small indeed.

Christopher cast his eye towards Emma, curious about her reaction. To his disappointment, he saw her staring back at him with a look that suggested that he had done entirely the wrong thing. "Oh, Christopher, no," she muttered in dismay.

Before he could say anything, Lochlann pulled his knife away, pushed Emma into Christopher (who, despite being caught off guard, managed to catch her after a moment's struggle), and threw himself into an exaggeratedly lavish bow. He straightened and, in a loud voice, proclaimed, "Let all those present at this Wandering Parliament attend! I was this woman's champion, but my devotion was spurned, my services —" his smirk became magnified at the word "— refused. Now my lady has found herself a new champion, albeit a somewhat ungainly and rather unattractive specimen." The crowd tittered, and Christopher felt even more blood rush to his head. "By the Standing Orders of the Wandering Parliament, I demand my right of satisfaction! Do you accept, champion?" Such was Lochlann's sneer as he uttered the last word that it seemed the basest insult ever devised.

Christopher smiled nervously. He mustered his most conciliatory tone of voice. "Okay, pal, you've had your fun. Enough's enough, let's not get carried away. I mean, you can't seriously be challenging me to a duel here!"

Then he saw that Lochlann's two bald friends were laughing uproariously behind the blond man, and his spirits sank like a dory in heavy seas. "As a matter of fact, that is exactly what I'm doing," Lochlann replied. "Do not try to dissuade me with idle prattle, newcomer, and do not make me ask you a third time: do you accept?"

Christopher glanced at Emma, who was now standing beside him, smoothing her skirt unnecessarily. He got the distinct impression that she was embarrassed by him, and was almost trying to ignore him. "What did I just do?" he asked out of the corner of his mouth, making an effort not to sound plaintive.

After a heartbeat, she looked up at him; a shadow had fallen over her pleasant features. "Just tell him no, Christopher. I'll suffer the consequences."

Christopher stared at her for a moment, nodded, and looked down at the soft grass of the Bungalow lawn. He could hear the murmurs of anticipation from the people around them, noticed that even the merchants had temporarily suspended their garrulous pleas for patronage as they awaited his response.

He thought of Lochlann, who wielded his dagger with a familiarity that most people these days reserved for their TV remote or the controller of their games console. He thought of himself, with his unfortunate tendency to get his lanky legs tangled up in things no matter how careful he tried to be, and who during grade school had always been the last to get chosen for anything remotely athletic, even when his own friends were doing the picking. He thought, inevitably, of Cecily, of the way that their life together had so easily slid into a too-comfortable pattern of routine and repetition, and how because of that, she had never pushed him to broaden his horizons, to become better as a person than he already was. And he thought of Emma, who had helped him discover more in an hour — albeit under pretty unusual circumstances — than he felt Cecily would have shown him in a lifetime together.

Christopher took a deep breath, and looked Lochlann straight in the eye. "You're on," he said. And his voice did break, just a little, but he put it out of his mind. The gathering seemed to be expecting something more, so he performed a grotesque parody of Lochlann's pretentious bow. This time, the snickers he heard appeared to favour him.

Still, the steely-eyed Lochlann was undeterred. "Good. You may have ten minutes to compose yourself, stranger — for as the Speech from the Throne is already tardy enough, I doubt our hosts will mind another slight delay." He began to turn away when he paused and added, "I'm sure this will be... most interesting." His tone of voice suggested that he expected quite the reverse; but to Christopher's modest relief, the grin that accompanied the statement did not seem quite as extraordinarily assured as before.

Lochlann retreated to his friends, who slapped him heartily on the back, clearly relishing the anticipation of the sport that was to come. Christopher turned his head to speak to Emma, but his words died on his lips: she was no longer standing beside him. He spun about, his eyes darting this way and that, and barely caught a glimpse of blonde hair and a swish of denim skirt disappearing around the corner of the Bungalow. For a moment, Christopher pondered whether he shouldn't just leave Emma by herself. But he quickly realised that he had little idea of what he'd committed himself to, and knew that she was the only person he could trust to give him any answers. He set off after her at a jog, inspiring some chuckling from onlookers who no doubt suspected he was fleeing from the imminent contest.

Christopher found Emma at the back of the Bungalow, standing in its shadows with her arms wrapped tightly about herself. He realised she was shivering, despite the oppressive mugginess of the night. He stopped behind her and, a little tentatively, put his hand on her shoulder and squeezed. Christopher had never been entirely comfortable making physical contact with women he'd only newly met, and the awkwardness of the situation just made him all the more unsure of the best way to approach her.

"I'm sorry," Emma said after a moment.

"For what?" he asked kindly.

"For the way I acted back there. For getting you into this in the first place." Still facing away from him, she nonetheless reached back and clasped the hand he had rested on her shoulder. "Christopher, Lochlann could really hurt you."

He felt his stomach quiver a little, but Christopher forced himself to not give in to panic. "Do you want to tell me about it?"

Emma laughed dismally. "I guess you deserve to know now." Still gripping his hand in hers, she led him over to a low stone wall and they sat. Christopher tugged at his shirt, trying to fan away some of the sweat that was making it cling to his body. He realised that the perspiration wasn't just from sheer nerves: the humidity pressing down on them had only swelled as the hours had worn on. A cloud passed across the crooked shape of the waxing moon and, glancing up, Christopher could see the silhouettes of more clouds massing behind it, just over the horizon. He couldn't be sure in the darkness, but he thought they looked like stormclouds. That the air was pregnant with moisture was no doubt just a harbinger of the weather to come.

"I guess you've figured out by now that Lochlann and I, um…"

"Have a past?" Christopher offered neutrally.

Emma nodded. "A past, right. You see, when I got into this life — and boy does that seem like a very long time ago — I was in trouble, Christopher. I think I might've been a little bit out of my mind… and considering what I'm like these days, that's saying a ton."

Despite the solemnity of the ordeal confronting him, Christopher grinned. "I've always thought that all the interesting people in the world are at least a little bit crazy."

"Well, Lochlann sort of… took me under his wing, I guess. Helped me survive, learn the ropes, that sort of thing. I won't deny it, I owed him a lot. And for a while, we were really happy together. Maybe as happy as I've ever been. Or, at least, that's what I thought at the time."

"So what happened?"

Emma waved her hand — the one that didn't have Christopher locked in a death-grip — in a gesture of frustration. "I was blind. I was so grateful to Lochlann, so over the moon that this hunky, silver-tongued, sword-swinging guy wanted to be with me, that I didn't realise for a long time that he's also a total ass."

"What did he do?"

Emma cringed as she cast her mind back. "Lochlann… he… he likes to get inside people's heads and… twist them around. And he's so good at it, too, because there's a part of him that really is that generous, charming guy I fell in love with, so it's easy to buy into the con. But really, he gets off on taking people and turning them into things that they aren't. I didn't realise he'd done it to me — no, it was a long time before I figured that one out — but I saw it happening to people around me, and when I finally understood what Lochlann was doing to them, it revolted me. And I guess there was just enough of who I really was left inside me that I was able to get away from him, hide away and undo all the knots he'd tied up in my head and my heart and my soul."

Christopher looked at Emma for what felt like a long while, even though it was probably only a matter of seconds. For the first time, he could see a vulnerability there in the wells of her blue eyes, buried deep beneath the surface. "I'm glad you did," he said finally. "I don't know if I could do what you did, in the same situation."

Emma shrugged. "I wouldn't be so quick to judge, Christopher. I think you might surprise yourself yet."

"Does that go for the duel too?" he asked her, hopefully. He knew that the ten minutes must be draining away, and his heart was now pounding in his chest like a massive metronome.

Emma, however, simply looked away, down at her sandaled feet in the dewy grass. "I'm sorry, Christopher. It's an ancient Parliament tradition. At least they haven't changed the weapon of choice in centuries, so you'll be fighting with swords instead of with guns or something. But I'm not sure if it'll really matter — Lochlann's a master with pretty much every weapon known to man, and probably a few that aren't."

"Oh." Christopher certainly didn't know what to say to that.

"It's why I wish you hadn't said anything about... being my champion. I mean, it was really very noble of you, Christopher, but this isn't the first time Lochlann's threatened me since I got away from him. Every time we're at a Wandering Parliament together, he pulls the same sort of stunt if I don't notice him first. He'd never go so far as to actually harm me — it'd hurt his popularity with the other ladies too badly. I'm used to it, really. But... what's done is done."

Christopher nodded and rose to his feet. "I'll... I'll do my best," he muttered lamely. "Look, will you be okay here by yourself? I've only got a couple more minutes, and I'd like to walk around and, um, breathe for a bit. While I still can."

Emma finally relinquished her grip on his hand. "Sure. Listen, there are two ways to win the duel — either incapacitate your opponent or knock the weapon out of his hand three times. Let Lochlann disarm you, okay? I don't want to see you hurt on my behalf."

"But what will happen to you if I lose?"

"Let me worry about that." And Emma turned her back to him, fixing her gaze on the dark trees surrounding the Bungalow.

Christopher strolled away across the lawn, making a brave but feeble effort at nonchalance. His pulse pounded in his ears, and he nearly choked when a dark shape sprang out of the shadows towards him. It was only when it had darted well past him, and his mind had finally processed the fact that it had just been a mangy-looking tabby cat, that he was able to swallow and continue on.

Part of him wanted to run screaming away from the Parliament and its peculiar attendees, away from Lochlann and his well-coiffed blond hair and his eyepatch and his apparently notorious swordfighting skills. But he couldn't leave Emma to face whatever consequences would follow, and he still needed to find the woman with the red hair and return to her the peculiar stone she had lost. So instead, Christopher angled his route towards the merchants, whose cacophonous pitches were once again ringing out across the Bungalow grounds. He was amazed that no one passing by on the street which bordered Bowring Park could hear them, so loudly did many of them holler, but he supposed there was some mechanism in place to address this.

Christopher felt many eyes upon him as he slowly paced the area around the stalls. The murmured conversations now were as much about the duel as about the continued absence of the representatives from the People of the Caribou who were meant to be hosting the Wandering Parliament. He could not fail to notice the exchange in some quarters of small orange-red coins which looked like teardrops made of flame, and wondered how long the odds had been set against the possibility of his winning the contest. Indeed, he rather strongly suspected that the betting was not on whether Lochlann would win, but simply on how long it would take him to do so.

Christopher passed a booth selling what looked like cheese of several dozen different varieties — his stomach rumbled for a moment at the sight, but he quickly recalled Emma's earlier admonition — and another whose wares consisted of nothing but small chunks of crumbling masonry, whom the hawk-nosed man behind the counter insisted were salvaged from the ruins of a place called Tir-na-Nog.

The next stall sold looking glasses of all shapes and sizes. Some were set in frames fashioned into terribly ornate forms, while others were plain and nondescript. Three men were examining the wares, and Christopher noticed with some bewilderment that the reflection in the mirrors they were holding were not their own. Or, rather, although they resembled the men, they appeared variously younger or older than their present ages. One man in his seventies, his skull crowned only by thin wisps of white hair, was depicted as having a full head of flowing ginger curls, and the liver spots which pocked his face were nowhere to be found. Another man, half the age of the first, was confronted with a rheumy-eyed version of himself, bald and sporting a hideously dishevelled beard instead of his neatly-trimmed goatee. The third patron laughed delightedly to see himself reflected as a giggling infant of no more than three or four months.

Desperate for some levity, Christopher stopped at the corner of the booth and picked up a small oval mirror, scarcely bigger than his hand, set in an ordinary brass frame. He held it up to his face, and staring back at him was a boy at about the right age for kindergarten. His dark brown hair was thin and unkempt — one fortunate side-effect of adolescence was that Christopher's hair had become much fuller, if no less unruly — and a hint of baby fat still lingered in his puffy cheeks. Christopher started to smile at the sight, but then gasped: he had laid eyes upon this face far more recently than two decades past.

He looked about for the empty stall he had earlier seen the five year-old boy manning, and realised that it was immediately adjacent to the booth with the looking glasses. Moreover, the boy was perched on the edge of his counter, his gaze fixed on Christopher. He reached over and plucked the mirror out of Christopher's grasp with his small fingers, then replaced it amongst the rest.

In the near distance, Christopher heard a voice which sounded like Lochlann's shout out, "Sixty seconds!" But he barely paid it any attention as he beheld a child who looked so like himself, once upon a time, scarcely older than the vision in the mirror.

"I've started to expect some pretty strange sights tonight," he told the boy, "but this goes beyond my wildest dreams."

The boy smiled elusively. "Dreams," he echoed in a quiet, faraway voice.

Christopher regarded him with puzzlement. "I'm sorry?"

"You dreamed of this night once," the boy told him, "or near enough anyway. Everybody had pointed ears and there were lions roaming the perimeter, but most everything else was the same."

"No, I —" Christopher began, for he remembered nothing of the sort.

"You did," the boy continued, undeterred. "You woke up in the morning and bounded out of bed full of enthusiasm, racing to get paper and pencil to write it all down. But by the time you'd sharpened the lead, the dream was already fading. As you sat to write the first words, your mother called you downstairs for breakfast… bacon and cereal and toast with strawberry jam. And by then, the dream had drifted away, like a summer cloud."

"You're right," Christopher said, straining to dredge up the memories from the very distant past. "There was a dream…" He could almost hear the roar of the lions guarding the lawn, even though he was pretty sure that Emma would have mentioned if such beasts were actually present.

The boy reached up and put his palms on either side of Christopher's face, brushing against the rough stubble which had started to grow there. "Remember the dream, Christopher," he chanted. His green eyes seemed to penetrate to the very core of Christopher's older, wearier pair. "Believe in the dream."

Christopher closed his eyes, trying to embrace the memory which now hung tantalisingly in the dimness just beyond the borders of his thoughts. "Believe the dream..." he mumbled.

Suddenly, a strong hand came down hard on his shoulder, shaking him out of his reverie. He looked back to see one of Lochlann's bald friends glaring at him menacingly. "Time to play, sunshine," he spat in a rough, gravelly voice.

Christopher glanced back to the young boy. But both he — and his empty booth — had vanished without a trace, leaving only a small avenue between the stalls of the market area.

* * *

In the deep shadows of the trees whose broad canopy sheltered the merchants, a figure sat watching the hustle and bustle of the Wandering Parliament in silence. He was barely conscious of the tall brown-haired man being led across the lawn by a bald-headed ruffian; or of the rogue with the eyepatch making a grand show of sharpening his sword whilst chatting with a gaggle of swooning admirers; or indeed of the blonde girl who also stood in the trees' reassuring embrace some feet away, unaware of the other observer's presence, a look of dire foreboding etched upon her pretty face.

Instead, the man's attention was concentrated upon the Bungalow itself — from which the hosts of the Wandering Parliament had been due to emerge some time before — and upon the bulky object which had been positioned on the verandah.

Dark thoughts billowing through his normally unflappable and inscrutable mind, Donovan Chase silently tapped his fingers against his lips, and waited, and watched.

Chapter Six
In which a Grisly Discovery is made

If Christopher had anything going for him at all, it was that at least tonight would not be the first time he'd held a sword. Of the friends with whom he had once engaged in fantasy role-playing games, Craig had gotten into the hobby a little more intensely than the others. At one point, he acquired a collection of broadswords which, fortunately, his parents forbade him to have sharpened. Nonetheless, for a brief time Craig was obsessed with challenging the others to mock duels with the blunt blades, and once or twice Christopher reluctantly caved in to his friend's insistent pleading, receiving his fair share of bruises in return for his indulgence.

Of course, the sword he now wielded was not blunt, and its twin — which Lochlann was arcing deftly through the air in a display clearly designed to intimidate him — would leave him with wounds far more grievous than a mere blemish. It was a plain weapon, its pommel unadorned with any finery. It was well-balanced, though — not that Christopher had much to judge it against — and fit snugly in his hand. He gave it a couple of practise waves in the air, and barely kept himself from overbalancing and falling flat on his face. He coughed to disguise the slip, but could see by the wry grins on some of the faces in the crowd around him that it had not gone completely unnoticed.

A stooped old man emerged from the surrounding throng, leaning heavily on a gnarled wooden cane. His long whiskers twitched violently as he reached the middle of the rough oval formed by the spectators, and he beckoned Christopher and Lochlann to approach.

"You both know the rules," he said in a quiet voice which sounded very, very ancient. Christopher was about to protest that he did not, but he thought better of it, and assumed that if there were any other important matters of which he ought to be aware, then Emma would have mentioned them. Right now, he just wanted to get this over with — for better or for worse.

"Of course I know the rules," Lochlann was saying in a bold tone, playing to the audience. "I am no mere neophyte in the duellist's arts!" A small cheer went up from the crowd and he smiled exultantly. Christopher simply nodded, and clutched his sword a little more tightly.

The old man sneezed, twice, and then rapped his cane against the ground before shuffling backward to the edge of the ring of spectators as fast as his aged legs would carry him. Christopher was still in the process of realising that this meant that the duel had begun when Lochlann rushed forward, his sword catching the silvery moonlight as it sliced towards him.

Christopher was hardly an athletic specimen, and it's true that his long legs tended to be more of a hindrance than anything else. But his reflexes were keen, and a sudden surge of adrenalin overcame any tiredness he might be feeling at such a late hour of the night. As Lochlann moved to the attack, Christopher dove to one side, and felt the sword whip past his left arm as he bolted.

It was immediately obvious, however, that Lochlann had not charged with all the quickness he could muster. Instead, he was approaching Christopher with a degree of caution, trying to gauge the younger man's skill. Christopher realised that while Lochlann had earlier assessed him as a novice with the blade, he could not be absolutely certain of his background, and so was taking no foolish chances. As much of a cad — or worse — as the man might be, he was evidently not an idiot.

Christopher knew he would not be able to match Lochlann's speed: even as the man with the eyepatch came at him again, his sword was whirling through the air like an airplane propeller and Christopher had to force himself not to be spellbound by the dexterity of his opponent's technique. He knew that his only chance was to stay on the defensive, and hope that Lochlann would make a mistake — an unintended opening, a slip on the grass, something which might allow Christopher to snake a lucky slice through.

But even as this rudimentary strategy began to form in his brain, Christopher realised that Lochlann was once again bringing his own sword to bear. He knew it was too late to dodge again, and with an audible curse, he tried to bring up his blade to parry the blow.

He was almost too late. But just at the last second, the edge of Christopher's sword nudged Lochlann's, pushing the blond man back a step. Christopher could not help but cry out at the painful vibration which shuddered up the shaft, and he dropped his blade as he would a hot iron. The crowd laughed, more mockingly than before, and he could bring himself to look nowhere but down at his feet.

"Come now, champion," sneered Lochlann. "Surely you're going to put up more of a fight than that? Or does fair Emmeline's honour mean so little to you?" Christopher glared at him, baring his teeth, but said nothing in response; instead, he just grappled with breathing, in short desperate gasps.

Lochlann reached down with his sword and prodded Christopher's weapon, flipping it up into the air with practised ease. Christopher caught it, albeit clumsily. "Ready?" Lochlann looked over to the old man, who again pounded his cane against the dirt.

Unlike Lochlann, Christopher did not avert his gaze. Instead, he listened carefully for the sound of the heavy wooden stick hitting the earth and then moved as quickly as he could, swinging his blade two-handed towards Lochlann's swordarm. But the other man almost seemed to have anticipated this move: he brought his weapon up easily, turning aside Christopher's blow in a fluid motion. "Good!" he yelled boisterously. "We'll give this crowd something to remember about this particularly tedious Parliament yet!"

Then he was once more on the attack, backing Christopher up again and again, his sword snaking ever closer to the brown-haired man's chest. Unlike his opponent, Lochlann held his blade in but a single hand, and occasionally used the free one to wave arrogantly to a cheering woman in the crowd or gesture confidently to one of his bald friends. Finally, one strike got past Christopher's meagre defenses and scored a searing blow against his upper leg, ripping through his trousers and slicing deeply into his flesh. Christopher fell back and rolled away to the edge of the crowd. He was coated in dew and dirt and sweat, and he clenched his eyes closed against the pain, waiting for the killing blow to come.

Then a voice floated to him through the darkness and the haze of his wound. "Please, Christopher, get up. I... I believe in you."

And suddenly Christopher was five years old again, asleep in bed on a cold January night with the sleet pounding against his bedroom window. He had been dreaming about school — he didn't really like kindergarten, he felt out of place, as though all the other kids had been given lessons on what to do and how to behave, but he'd somehow missed out — and in his dream, Mrs Bonaventure had asked him to do something very very important. But Christopher hadn't been able to understand the words she had spoken to him, and so now he was wandering around the school, fervently praying that whatever he was supposed to be doing would miraculously become obvious to him.

He crept down the stairs to the main floor of the primary school, past a classroom in which all the first-graders appeared to be swimming between the desks, and it seemed perfectly reasonable to Christopher that the water would not seep out under the door. Then he turned a corner and found himself in The Park.

At age five, Christopher vaguely knew that The Park was really called Bowring Park, and he had even visited one or two other parks in different parts of the city. But this was the only park which really mattered and so, as far as the young boy was concerned, this was simply The Park.

He walked around the duck pond, which was peculiarly bereft of waterfowl of any sort, and frolicked briefly amongst the flowers surrounding the wonderful, magical Peter Pan statue. This, of course, was years before they had reterraced the duck pond and surrounded the statue with cobblestones rather than the beautiful multi-hued flowers which seemed to suit it so much better.

Then he walked away from the statue and, with the kind of suddenness one never questions in dreams, found himself on the lawn of the Bungalow. He nodded to a lion which was keeping watch for bullies at the edge of the lawn, and the big cat smiled toothily at him and tipped the wide fedora hat he was wearing with one massive paw. Christopher tried to wave back, but he was holding a huge sword now, one so big that he needed both of his small hands to carry it.

The Bungalow lawn was full of people. Many of them had pointed ears, and Christopher thought a few of them had beautiful gossamer wings sprouting from their backs. He leaned forward to get a closer look, but as he did so, the sword he was dragging caught on something in the moist grass, and he found himself sprawling on the ground.

And this was bad. This was very bad, because there was a man there with a sword as big as Christopher's and the man wanted to fight and the man was swinging his sword towards Christopher and…

"I remember!" Christopher — the real, grown-up Christopher — cried aloud, in a voice rather stronger than he had intended. And even before he opened his eyes, he brought his sword up sharply. Lochlann's coup de grace was unexpectedly stymied, steel clanging resoundingly against steel. Christopher strained to push him away, throwing the other man back a few paces.

Christopher sprang to his feet, ignoring the stinging pain in his leg. As he rose, he spied Emma out of the corner of his eye: she had made her way through the crowd as he and Lochlann had battled, and it had been her words which had touched him moments before. He smiled at her in what he hoped was a reassuring way.

Because he did remember the dream now, in all its glorious, impossible detail. No, he didn't just remember the dream — he remembered the way he had felt for those scant moments upon rising the next morning, the way that the dream had seemed like the grandest, most wonderful thing ever, before it faded away in the face of the mundanity of the real world. It had been a long time since Christopher had experienced a dream which so inspired him to... believe. But, for brief minutes on that snowy January, he had believed in that dream.

And now he believed in it again.

Lochlann came back at Christopher, growling like a wild beast. But Christopher was no longer surprised by the other man's tactics. It's not that he consciously knew what was coming. Instead, he simply let his muscles respond instinctively, while he looked on in exactly the way we watch ourselves in dreams.

Lochlann struck, three times in rapid succession. Twice, Christopher parried the thrust, and the third time he simply twisted away, letting the sword cut the air harmlessly to his right. His eyes met Lochlann's, and for the first time he saw the blond man's cocky expression falter just a little. The murmurs from the spectators became slightly more discordant, as a few of them began to suspect that perhaps the outcome of the duel was no longer the ironclad certainty they had been expecting.

Of course, Lochlann was still both stronger and more agile than Christopher. But that no longer seemed quite so intimidating: as with so much in life, a single intelligently-conceived, well-executed swing of the sword was far more potent than any number of fast and heavy blows.

And so, as Lochlann stepped towards him yet again, in his dreamlike fugue Christopher recognised that his opponent was feinting, appearing to be striking to the left when in fact he was preparing to bring his sword around for a thrust directly to the midsection. But this meant that Lochlann was in an awkward position to defend his right side, and without hesitation, Christopher struck.

Again, it bears emphasising that Lochlann was no idiot. While he could scarcely have expected Christopher to take advantage of the feint's vulnerability, he certainly knew that that vulnerability existed, and was prepared to make the appropriate response to such a counterattack. What he did not anticipate, however, was that not only did Christopher try to take advantage of the vulnerability, but he did not make the obvious move of striking, hard and swift, at Lochlann's exposed side. Instead, Christopher's swing was softer and more angled, and as Lochlann shifted his weight to evade the blow, he left Christopher capable of pursuing him with his weapon without losing momentum. Momentarily thrown by the unexpected tactic, Lochlann leaned too far, stumbled, and dropped to one knee.

Without missing a beat, Christopher reached down and slapped Lochlann between the shoulder blades with the flat of his sword, overbalancing the blond man and forcing him face-down into the grass. Planting his own knee against the small of Lochlann's back, Christopher rested his sword against the fallen man's neck. Just like he remembered saying in a dream more than twenty years earlier, he murmured, "Do you yield?" The masses surrounding them had fallen utterly silent.

Lochlann struggled for a moment, but Christopher pressed the blade harder against his neck, drawing a thin line of blood.

"Do you yield?" he asked again, louder, more confident this time.

Lochlann grunted and tried to spit out a garbled curse before, finally, he fell silent. He breathed deeply three times and then, in the tone of a man who has had his entire life's work stolen away from him, answered, "Yes."

Shocked whispers arose from the crowd as the old man who had been presiding over the duel stepped forward once again and thumped his cane three times against the dirt. "The contest is finished," he announced, "and the lady and her champion are the victors." There was a polite smattering of applause: Christopher thought that the lack of enthusiasm wasn't so much because the onlookers didn't want him to beat Lochlann, as that they were shocked that he had accomplished it. Well, he considered, maybe those who had bet money on the outcome were justifiably subdued.

Emma stepped forward and curtsied before the old man. "My lady," he addressed her, "the challenger is now indebted to you, and your champion, for one favour each, to be fulfilled at any time and in any place of your choosing."

He reached into his breast pocket and withdrew two small, bent metal discs, dull grey in colour. Then he ambled over to where Lochlann was slowly picking himself up off the lawn. The man with the eyepatch looked at the elderly figure sullenly and, without a word, extended his hands, palms turned upward. The old man placed one disc in each palm, and then nodded severely. Gritting his teeth, Lochlann closed his fists tightly around the little circles of metal. He cringed, and Christopher thought he could see a little tear escape from the corner of the man's good eye. Then he opened his hands, and the old man took back the two discs; the plan grey of their surfaces was now run through with streaks of vivid red. He tottered back to Emma and presented her with one of the discs. As Christopher moved over to stand beside her, the old man pressed the other disc into his hand. Lochlann's evident discomfort still fresh in his mind, Christopher winced slightly despite himself, but the disc simply sat upon his palm, the red slashes seeming to pulsate ever so slightly.

Emma saw Christopher looking in puzzlement at the object. "Any time you want to call in your favour from Lochlann, just grip the disc in your fist and picture him."

"Oh," came Christopher's simple reply. He was not sure if he wanted to extract a favour from the man, let alone spend time envisioning his cocky features. But he put the disc in his pocket all the same, and felt it nestle there against the red-headed woman's strange possession.

Lochlann, meanwhile, had sulkily made his way over to his two bald friends. Everybody else in the crowd now appeared to be pointedly ignoring him. His companions' faces were flushed and riddled with panic, and one of them seemed almost on the verge of weeping. Christopher wanted nothing further to do with the blond man — felt he'd already had far more involvement with him than his life could ever possibly require — but walked over to him all the same, extending his hand in as sportsmanlike a manner as he could summon. "Good, ah, match," he said, knowing that the words sounded stupid. "I think I got a bit lucky there, that's all."

"Yes, you did," retorted Lochlann. He eyed Christopher's proffered hand. "But you still beat me. And that is worthy of some little respect." And he shook Christopher's hand — not for very long and not particularly vigorously, but it was clear that he meant what he said. "Tell Emma that I'll leave her be from now on." Then the arrogant grin returned to his face. "She has come to bore me, anyway." He made a great show of suppressing a yawn. Then, as one, he and his two friends turned their backs on Christopher, and walked away into the shadows.

"I'm impressed."

Christopher spun around to find Emma approaching him. He smiled. "Oh, it was nothing. My parents always taught me not to be a sore winner."

The blonde girl sighed. "Not that, you twerp — the duel. There aren't many people around who can beat Lochlann in a fight — not even by sheer chance." She arched her eyebrow coyly.

"Sheer chance?" Christopher spluttered theatrically. "Why, I'll have you know that that was one hundred per cent pure Prescott prowess, that was."

"Really? Was it pure Prescott prowess that landed you on your posterior just before the end there?"

"Oh, that?" Christopher grinned. "Just letting Lochlann build up a false sense of security. Yay for tactics!" Emma rolled her eyes in response, and Christopher's smile became all the jollier. He breathed deeply, letting the heady aroma of the dozens of different varieties of flowers in the park, buoyant upon the night air, sweep over him.

"Seriously, though," he said after a moment, "what you said back there, when I was down for the count... it meant a lot. Really, I think it might've made the difference."

Emma shrugged. "I just didn't want you thinking that nobody out there was cheering for you. A little bit of confidence goes a long way. Still, how exactly did you —"

But Emma's question was cut off by a horrified scream coming from the direction of the Bungalow. Heads began turning towards the source of the noise like a wave washing towards the seashore. "Oh no," Emma muttered under her breath. She turned and raced away in the direction of the steps which led up onto the verandah of the wide building. Christopher paused for only a moment before he followed her, pushing past Parliament attendees who had only just begun to resume the conversations they had been conducting before the duel, and were now finding them interrupted once again.

As he approached the Bungalow, Christopher could finally get a better view of the object which stood upon the verandah, the one he knew did not normally belong there in the light of day. He realised that part of the reason why he had had difficulty discerning the thing's shape before was that it had been covered by a large brown tarpaulin, which now lay discarded on the deck to one side.

What it had concealed was a chair. No, not a chair, Christopher realised: a throne. He remembered the passing references he had heard to a now-belated Speech from the Throne, and realised that this was meant quite literally. The throne was a high-backed affair, carved out of what looked to be a very lustrous and expensive wood. Plush wine-coloured cushions adorned the seat, the back and the armrests, and carved high up on the throne were stylised representations of five animals: a fish, an odd-looking bird, a cat, a caribou and a snake. As Christopher watched, the icons seemed to writhe and shift before his eyes, giving the impression that the animals were chasing each other. One moment, the cat stood leftmost; the next, the caribou had charged over to displace it farther to the right. Christopher would no doubt have been bemused by these antics, were it not for the shape which lay sprawled across the throne. Even from a distance, Christopher had dire suspicions as to what this shape might be, and as he ran up the stairs in Emma's wake, these were horribly realised.

Once upon a time, the thing on the throne had been human, Christopher thought, although the hair which covered its blood-spattered arms was unusually curly and plentiful. But there was very little left of the body now: the man — or perhaps woman, it was very difficult to tell — was twisted into unnatural shapes. There were great rents along its form, limbs were wrenched wildly out of alignment and bent in ways that seemed almost geometrically impossible, and some parts just appeared to be missing. Terrible gouges marred the person's face, obliterating the nose and one eye, twisting its lips into an obscene rictus. A massive cavity was opened along its chest, and Christopher tried to avert his gaze from the things he could see poking up out of the crevice. Blood still dripped from a dozen different places, pooling on the throne and the verandah below.

A tall, thin man stood to one side of the body, obsessively cleaning his half-moon spectacles with a hand which shook like a jackhammer. "I-I-I was getting im-im-impatient," he stuttered, though his eyes were unfocussed and Christopher wasn't sure that he was addressing anyone in particular. "I th-th-thought I'd give my own... my own Speech from the Throne. It was meant to be a j-j-joke." And he began sobbing, nearly dropping his glasses. A heavy-set woman about Christopher's age moved over to comfort him, stepping carefully around the blood and gore as she did so.

Looking upon the morbid scene, Christopher barely fought down the urge to gag, and was suddenly very grateful that he'd had nothing to eat for several hours now. He was a little surprised to see Emma examining the body almost stoically, showing little of the revulsion he knew must be painted across his own countenance.

"Soloman was right," she murmured. "Something was very wrong here tonight." She turned to him, a look of deadly seriousness brimming in her eyes. "Christopher, I've told you before that I'm not familiar with all the bigwigs in the Five Clans. But this guy I do... did know. I actually shared a brew with him once, at a Wandering Parliament not long ago. His name was Davin of the People of the Caribou. He was supposed to be tonight's Speaker."

"Would he have been the only, ah, representative of the People of the Caribou?" Christopher asked, still only vaguely understanding the protocols and procedures of the Wandering Parliament.

Emma shook her head vehemently. "No, their delegation would be at least a dozen men and women strong. You need that many for all the pomp and circumstance that's supposed to go on. And for all the political wheeling and dealing, of course."

"So what's happened to the rest of them?" asked somebody standing next to Christopher and Emma.

The eyes of all those who had gathered on the verandah turned to the door of the Bungalow, and the dark interior beyond.

*   *   *

There were, of course, other people in Bowring Park that night besides those attending the Wandering Parliament. Although the park closed officially at ten o'clock, as posted in red letters on a big white sign at both entrances, this was really just an invitation to a clientele quite unlike the families and pedestrians attracted to the park during the daytime. After ten on many nights, Bowring Park played host to a small horde of teenagers, and adults who still acted as though they were teenagers. It was only thanks to certain efforts on the part of the Wandering Parliament that the Clansfolk remained undisturbed by, and unknown to, these other denizens of the park.

The duck pond at the eastern end of Bowring Park was fed by two rivers: the Waterford River, which wended its way just a little north of the Bungalow, and the South Brook River, which coursed through an area of the park which had long been neglected, only recently undergoing any sort of serious maintenance and development. Of course, this made it perfect for Bowring Park's late-night visitors, especially since — just a short walk up from the remains of the old stone dam which, in days long gone by, had helped to turn a portion of the South Brook River into the park's swimming hole — there stood a broad clearing, perfect for nocturnal carousing. The many scorch marks on the ground there were testament to the antics of literally generations of young people up to very little good.

Seamus Cochrane was one such young person. He had been introduced to the Bowring Park scene by his best friend, Max, and now spent every night he could there, gorging himself on whatever he could smuggle out of his parents' liquor cabinet or skive off one of the others in the clearing. Tonight, he and

Max had been lucky: Max's new girlfriend, Tanya, had come across a drifter passed out in the trees carrying half a case of beer and nearly a full bottle of rum, plus a few hits of ecstasy tucked into a pocket.

Most of Seamus' night thereafter had passed in a blur. He could vaguely remember trying to put the moves on a girl Tanya had introduced him to, and remembered getting absolutely nowhere with her. But he wasn't sure and, at this point, was too blissfully and mindlessly out of it to care.

Looking about, Seamus realised that he wasn't in the clearing anymore: he was following Max and Tanya out of the park. They were entwined in each other's arms and were exchanging bawdy whispers, glancing back at Seamus occasionally as if they really wished he wasn't there.

The three of them were walking along the gravel trail which had once been the route of the railway, and Seamus had to be careful not to stumble on the loose stones. The sky overhead was just showing the slightest glimmer of predawn grey, and Seamus supposed that this must be why they had left the park — either that, or all the prospects of more chemical stimulation had well and truly dried up.

They trudged along for some time in the dark, their surroundings almost hidden by the tall foliage which grew up on either side of the path. Vaguely, in the distance beyond Max and Tanya, Seamus thought he could see a shape walking towards them, though he supposed this might just be an alcohol-induced figment of his imagination.

As he stared at the gradually approaching figure, Seamus became aware that Max and Tanya were no longer speaking in hushed tones but instead were barking at each other in short, angry-sounding bursts. Abruptly, Tanya pushed Max away from her and, with an incendiary glare, Max started walking faster, putting some distance between himself and his two companions.

Christ, thought Seamus, he's such an asshole. He wondered what it would be like to pull out the switchblade hidden in his jacket pocket and throw it at the back of Max's head, what sound it would make as it impacted with the other man's brain. Very little of Seamus' mind was suspicious as to where this suddenly homicidal hostility towards his best friend had come from.

He was further distracted by the sight of Tanya right in front of him. Her jeans had slipped down a little, baring the top of a black thong. Seamus started to grin lasciviously, realising that Tanya had just rejected Max. Since he was pretty sure he had been spurned earlier in the evening, Seamus saw his chance to finally get lucky tonight.

He moved up behind Tanya and grabbed her roughly, cupping her ample breasts in both hands. Her reactions dulled by the night's indulgences, Tanya didn't react at first, giving Seamus a chance to start suckling her bare neck. Thoughts of the stud Tanya wore through her tongue only spurred his eagerness.

"Jesus, Seamus, what the fuck —" the girl finally began to screech, struggling to get away from the unwanted attention. Seamus just smirked all the more and began grinding himself against her.

* * *

Max, now some distance ahead, heard Tanya's exhortation and turned around. Even in his extremely inebriated condition, he felt a surge of rage as he saw Seamus forcing himself onto his girlfriend. "You motherfucker!" he screamed, and he began to run back towards them. He was dizzy and off-balance, though, and his foot slid on the gravel path, pitching him heavily to the ground.

As he picked himself back up, cursing the blood that was seeping from the palms of both hands, Max was stunned to see Tanya's attitude had abruptly changed. Not only was she not trying to get away from Seamus, but now she was actively responding to his affections. She grabbed one of his hands and pulled it up under her tank top. Max could imagine Seamus rolling her engorged nipple between his fingers as Tanya's face lit up in ecstasy. "Mmmm, Max," she cooed, "why didn't you tell me Seamus was so much better at this than you are?" And she reached behind her and started fumbling with Seamus' belt buckle.

Max was overcome with a blinding fury. Almost without even thinking, he reached down and tugged a switchblade — a twin to Seamus' — from his pocket. Flicking the button, he lunged towards Tanya and Seamus, a guttural roar escaping his lips. As he did so, Seamus pushed Tanya towards Max and went for his own knife.

Moments later, a plain-looking man walked past a dying girl and two men bleeding profusely from a number of vicious slashes to the face and upper torso. He sniffed the air as he walked, and a hint of something that could almost be described as anticipation touched his lips.

The two men were now down on all fours, growling at each other, foam flecking their lips like rabid dogs. Still they lunged with their knives, and they would not stop their bestial combat until they both lay, dead and disfigured, on the gravel path. By this time, the strange man would have long since passed out of sight in the darkness.

None of the three teenagers would be mourned, or even remembered.

Chapter Seven
In which an Investigation is conducted

Christopher was trying very hard not to think about the obscenely mutilated body lying not ten feet away from him. He was also trying not to think about the yet-untreated sword wound to his leg, which was still bleeding and had begun to throb rather painfully. Unfortunately, because he was actively trying not to think about two things simultaneously, the net effect was that he was thinking about them both very much, and in the eerie silence which had descended upon the Wandering Parliament, he was wishing fervently that somebody would say or do something to distract him from his unpleasant thoughts.

It was Emma who finally broke the horrified hush. "We have to get in there," she said, nodding towards the Bungalow door. "We need to find out what's happened to the rest of them." But she was toying nervously with a lock of her blonde hair, brushing it again and again behind her right ear, and Christopher could tell that she was as frightened as the rest of them.

At that moment, Christopher was shocked to realise that part of his brain was actually going along with Emma's proposal, was trying to work up the nerve to go over to the Bungalow door and discover what lay beyond. It dawned on him that part of him had gotten swept up in this strange new world of cities with memories and Wandering Parliaments and dreams that were more than just dreams. But despite his romantic nature, Christopher's adult life had made a pragmatist out of him, and so he pushed these thoughts to one side. "Go in there?" he questioned, filling his voice with wariness. "Shouldn't we be calling the police?"

Emma shook her head vehemently. "This is Five Clans business, Christopher. It would be against all protocol and tradition to bring... normal laws into this. And I can't even imagine what kind of powers would have to be wielded to let the Constabulary in here without having the entire city descend on us. It would be disastrous, just disastrous." She took his hand and peered at him with her deep blue eyes. "You do understand, don't you?"

Christopher stared back for several seconds, his mouth going dry at what she was asking him to do. Somewhere nearby, a cat wailed mournfully. "I... I guess so," he finally answered, though the tone in his voice was more than a little dubious.

Abruptly, Emma pulled him into a tentative hug. "Oh, Christopher, I can't believe what I've gotten you into tonight. Go home. Forget everything you've seen, as best you can. All of this will get dealt with, somehow. You don't need to be involved. I'll make sure that you're left alone."

He would have been lying if he'd claimed that the offer wasn't tempting. But...

"No," he said quickly — a little more quickly than he'd intended. "Forgetting about this isn't an option anymore. And we haven't even started on what we came here for in the first place, remember? I can't let that go unresolved." Christopher took a very deep breath. "I'm part of this, for the time being, whether I like it or not. Okay?"

Emma stepped back and gave a furtive nod. "Okay."

All around them, the silence was still palpable, as the Clansfolk waited for someone to step forward and take charge. Christopher knew that that person couldn't be him — if nothing else, he was far too much of a stranger to this society to claim that role — but he figured he could at least get things moving forward. So he swallowed twice and then raised his quivering voice to the loudest volume he could manage: "Has, ah, anybody seen any of the, um... Caribou people. Er, People of the Caribou," he corrected himself, recalling Emma's earlier rebuke. "The ones you've... we've... been waiting on. Maybe in those... tent things?" he suggested weakly, pointing at the structures erected on one side of the lawn.

A few moments passed in uneasy silence. Then a nasally-voiced man acknowledged in a tremulous voice, "I was supposed to meet with Muireann. She didn't appear, but that's hardly unusual — we all know that sometimes the Parliament hosts are otherwise detained." A couple of others nodded their heads and offered similar comments.

"Oh," said Christopher. "Well, I guess that doesn't really tell us anything, then..." His gaze drifted back to the Bungalow door. "I suppose somebody's going to have to go inside then. Has anybody tried just knocking?"

Light, nervous laughter arose briefly from the crowd, dying away just as quickly. Seeing that nobody was actually following through with his suggestion — which seemed eminently sensible to Christopher — he steeled himself, crossed over to the door, and rapped sharply, three times, on its wooden frame.

A minute passed, with no response.

Christopher strained to hear inside the building, but it was deathly quiet. He looked to Emma, who had moved beside him, wondering what should be done next. "Isn't there somebody who should be handling this?" he whispered to her. "Somebody in authority?"

"Not really. The people in charge are the People of the Caribou. Everybody else basically has the same standing here as you or me... well, as me, anyway."

"What about the merchants? Didn't you tell me that they were all People of the Caribou?"

Emma nodded. "But they're just commonfolk; none of them are members of the Cabinet of the People, and that's who we've been waiting for."

"Davin was in this Cabinet?"

"Right."

Christopher wiped his brow, trying to think clearly. "So, each of the Five Clans has a... Cabinet that governs it?"

"That's the basic idea, yeah."

"Well, what about the Cabinets for the other four Clans? Shouldn't they be the nominal bosses now?"

Emma shrugged. "Maybe. But look around you, Christopher — these people are scared shitless." And it was plainly so — the crowd of about two hundred was, almost to a man, just standing around now, appearing frightened and confused. A few folk were talking in low voices, but most just looked about themselves in silence, waiting for somebody to tell them what to do. "The Wandering Parliament is supposed to be a sanctuary of sorts, Christopher. It's not in any of our best interests to disrupt its workings. The duels are usually the most bloodthirsty aspect, and they've been happening for so long that they're practically *de rigueur*. As far as I know, nothing remotely tragic has happened at a Wandering Parliament since..."

"The Great War, dearie," murmured an old woman with tremendously thick spectacles, perched to Emma's left. Christopher remembered her as the merchant who was selling the peculiar glass globes. "There was a... disagreement over politics at the Parliament one night, and at the next, one of the participants in said disagreement murdered t'other in cold blood. A sad night, that was, but it pales compared with this." She shook her head, setting her mop of curly grey hair bouncing gently, and clucked her tongue.

"There you go," Emma said to Christopher. "It's been quite a while. So you can understand why this is so shocking."

Christopher nodded. "Then I guess it's up to us. I mean, I know I really shouldn't even be here, but since I am, I can't just... do nothing."

Emma squeezed his arm lightly. "I know. I feel the same." She smiled a little. "This selfless streak is going to get me into trouble, you know." Christopher returned her grin, knowing that she was referring as much to her efforts on his behalf as to uncovering the fate of the Cabinet of the People of the Caribou. Once again he fished his hand into his trouser pocket to make sure that the *fios* stone was still there. He was beginning to wonder if he would ever have a chance to track down the mysterious red-headed woman who owned it.

Christopher breathed deeply and reached for the door handle. The silence around him deepened further, as anticipation became mingled with the tangible sense of fear. He swallowed hard and twisted the knob.

"Locked," he revealed after a moment. "Um, does anybody have a key?" The prolonged suspense was becoming unbearable.

To his surprise, Emma gently pushed him out of the way. "Not necessary," she told him. And without elaboration, she reached forward and rested her fingers against the lock. Christopher noticed that her eyes were closed, and she appeared to be concentrating very intently. After a few seconds, Emma stepped back. "Try it now," she said to him, gesturing towards the door. When Christopher looked at her quizzically, she merely shrugged and quipped, "We all have our talents."

Once again, Christopher tried to turn the knob, and this time it yielded. Feeling his heart beating a little faster, he pushed the door open and quietly stepped into the darkened room beyond.

The entrance gave directly onto a large room, often used for receptions and banquets. Even in the gloom, Christopher could see that, tonight, it most closely resembled an abattoir. Bodies — and, even worse, pieces of bodies — lay everywhere: on the floor, draped over chairs, hanging across the large wooden table in the centre of the room. Areas of the chamber not occupied by cadavers were thick with blood and ichor; bodily fluids still dripped to the floor all over the room, creating a morbid timpani which was impossible to tune out. All about the place hung the smell of death; it washed over him like a foetid tide. This time, Christopher could not help but be sick, right there to the side of the doorway, though he was merely contributing to what was already a grisly and grotesque tableau. Behind him, Emma was leaning against the door frame and coughing violently, no doubt trying to settle the bile rising in her own throat.

Christopher closed his eyes for a few seconds to blot out the terrible scene. He swallowed down large gulps of air through his mouth and tried as best as he could to steady himself. He cast his mind back to the slasher flicks and war movies he'd seen, films filled with blood and guts and gore and death, and attempted to view the devastation before him in the same light, to divorce himself from the reality of what he was confronting. Finally, he opened his eyes again, and cast a stoic eye about the scene. Outside, he could hear people wailing audibly as word of what had happened to the People of the Caribou filtered out to the crowd.

Suddenly, the room was bathed in red-flecked light as somebody — Emma, he realised — found the switch. Christopher almost wished she hadn't: the carnage was all the more gruesome in full colour. "Who could have done this?" he asked in a strained voice.

"I can think of a few Clansfolk who have the ability," she told him in a voice that was studiedly neutral. "What I can't figure out is why. All these people…"

Christopher stepped further into the room, looking about for any clue that might be found amidst the rent and twisted bodies, though really he had no idea of what he should be looking for. It occurred to him that the murderer or murderers (surely, it would take more than one individual to slaughter this many?) might still be in the building — there were more rooms leading off of this main one — and so he nearly jumped when something slapped wetly against the nape of his neck.

Slowly, Christopher reached back and wiped at the stickiness he could now sense there. A bloody scarlet smear came away onto his fingers. "How could —"

"Christopher." He turned and saw Emma staring up at the ceiling above him. He followed her gaze.

There was another body on the ceiling, fifteen feet above their heads. It was pinioned there, spread-eagled, enormous nails having been driven through both hands, both feet, and the stomach. Blood was pooling around the five wounds and slowly dripping downward to the floor. Other than that, Christopher noticed, the feminine body was in a conspicuously different condition from the others: no other wound was apparent, but the skin bore a strange grey sheen, and the woman's face was shrivelled slightly, like a grape that had been left in the sun too long. It was hard to tell for sure, though, because her long, greying brown hair hung down about her cheeks, obscuring her countenance.

"Who is she?" Christopher asked Emma.

"I don't know," Emma replied. "I don't think I recognise her. But, like I told you, I hardly know everybody…"

"Her name was Eachna," said a strong, clear voice behind them. Christopher and Emma turned as one, to behold a short man with greying hair, dressed in a black and white pinstripe suit. His lined face was studying them darkly from where he stood in the doorway, his eyes constantly roving about like a hyperactive child. Christopher was a little surprised to hear the man's crisp British accent — like most Newfoundlanders, the people he had thus far heard speak at the Wandering Parliament tended to have accents that were mixtures, to varying degrees, of the more neutral Mainland drawl and a gentle Irish lilt.

Emma stared at the newcomer strangely. "Eachna? Not a chance. I knew Eachna — she was only a couple of years older than me. Definitely younger than Christopher here."

The man shrugged. "I don't disagree, Miss…"

"Rawlin," came the response after a moment's wary hesitation. "Emma Rawlin."

"Christopher Prescott," Christopher offered politely, gesturing towards himself.

"Donovan Chase," said the man. He made as if to doff a hat, but then realised that he wasn't wearing one, and turned the motion into a sort of wave instead. "And yes, Miss Rawlin, one is indeed left to wonder how a woman in her early twenties could become the desiccated, seemingly ancient corpse now dangling above us. What did transpire in this room, on this night? What does it all mean? And what are you doing here?"

Christopher was mulling over Chase's first two questions before it dawned on him that the third was fired in his direction. "Excuse me?" he asked, caught a little off guard.

Chase strode forward and beat his elaborately-decorated walking stick lightly off Christopher's chest. "You don't belong here, Mr... Prescott, was it? I can tell. You're too... normal."

"Wow," muttered Christopher. "I think that's the first time anybody's ever accused me of being normal."

"He's here with me, Mr Chase," Emma interjected. "And you're right, he's not one of us. He's here by accident, and once he's done what he's come here to do, he'll be going back to the regular world."

"And just what are you here to do, Mr Prescott?" Chase inquired as he began walking in a seemingly random pattern around the room, scrutinising a shorn arm here, a smattering of blood there.

"I'm, ah... looking for a woman, actually," Christopher told him sheepishly, realising how foolish it sounded to say out loud.

"Aren't we all," murmured Chase. "At least two hours, I should think," he said abruptly.

"Excuse me?" said Christopher, confused at the apparent *non sequitur*.

Chase gestured towards a body which was almost split in half like a wishbone, splayed across the arm of a chair. "That's how long they've been dead, unless I miss my guess. Which is exceedingly rare," he added, lest there be any doubt.

Christopher eyed the people outside the door. No one else yet seemed willing to enter the Bungalow, though each new utterance from those within was clearly being passed along to the fearful masses by the brave few who still lingered on the verandah. "Do you know who did this, Mr Chase?"

Chase thought on the question for a moment before responding with a clearly-enunciated, "No. But I'm as curious as any of you to find out."

"And why exactly is that?" Emma asked him. "You're clearly not from around here, I've never seen you at a Wandering Parliament before. You've got to admit, your sudden appearance here seems a little suspicious."

If Emma was expecting a well-reasoned rebuttal, she didn't get it. "Yes, doesn't it?" was Chase's simple response. As he uttered the words, he smiled an enigmatic smile which Christopher thought was tinged with just a hint of something unsettling — malice or simply grimness, he couldn't quite tell.

"It seems this is the night for newcomers here, then," Christopher suggested. He could see Emma's temper beginning to fray, and wanted to head off a confrontation between the two — at least until they were able to ascertain whether or not this peculiar little man could help them. "Do you have any… ideas, Mr Chase?"

"Several, and none of them pleasant. But we need more information before even I would be willing to hazard an educated guess."

"And just how do we get that information?" Emma asked, plainly put off by the stranger's elusive manner.

"We ask her," Chase replied, pointing at the corpse nailed to the ceiling.

Christopher looked between the pair with some bewilderment. "But she's, um, dead," he noted — rather unnecessarily, he felt. "You guys can't speak to the dead… can you?" He had now come to terms with the fact that there were powers in the world he had previously thought relegated to the pages of fairy tales, but the ability to commune with the deceased was too fantastical all the same.

"No, we can't, Christopher," Emma told him. "Even the *Gan Aireachtáil* can't use their foul powers on the dead, thank god."

"The what now?"

"The… Unnoticed, they're sometimes called. Believe me when I say that you never want to run into one."

"They can relive a person's experiences by… digesting certain body parts," Chase explained. "Amongst other baleful abilities."

"Oh," said Christopher. "I don't think I wanted to know that."

Heedless, though, Chase continued on. "But I'm afraid you're mistaken, Miss Rawlin. The dead can still tell us their tales, if we act quickly enough."

Obstinately, Emma folded her arms. "No way, pal, you're the one who's wrong."

It would be misleading to say that Chase marched over to Emma; his movements were far too nonchalant for so aggressive a description. But, in thinking back on the moment, Christopher would later be unable to recollect it in any other way, such was the forcefulness of the little man's bearing. He stood before Emma and glowered at her with an almost palpable disdain. Though they were virtually the same height, Chase seemed to somehow tower over the girl, to envelop her in the long, dark shadow his small form cast.

"How long have you been part of this life, Miss Rawlin?" Chase demanded, rolling the 'R'. "Ten years? A dozen? You certainly weren't born into the Five Clans, I can tell that much. And do you really think that in that brief moment of time, a mere mote on the face of eternity, that you have learned all there is to know about this realm?" He paused, perhaps to give Emma a chance to retort, but she stood there close-lipped, her arms folded, just staring back at him with an unfathomable expression. "No, Miss Rawlin, there are deep secrets buried beneath the fabric of every society, both his —" he gestured over his shoulder to Christopher "— and ours. And that which may seem impossible even to our kind may yet be achieved, if we make haste."

Emma eyed Chase for what seemed to Christopher like forever before she finally spoke. "Fine," she said at last. "I think you're probably full of it, but I guess we don't have anything to lose. Frankly, I don't know what else to do with this mess anyway."

Chase smiled graciously. "I shall endeavour to justify the enormity of the faith you display in me." Emma grunted. "Now, we need to get Eachna's body down from the ceiling."

"How are we going to do that?" Christopher wondered. "We'd need a pretty big ladder to reach it, and I don't know where we'd find one, especially at this hour of the night… morning… whatever."

Emma nodded in agreement. "Somebody outside probably has a talent which would let them do it, but it doesn't look like anyone else has the slightest inclination to come in here. Honestly, I don't know how they're going to get everything cleaned up in time to abandon the park…"

Chase, though, was shaking his head and grinning that elusive grin of his. "Don't worry, we don't require outside assistance of any sort. Mr Prescott, would you agree that a person being nailed to the ceiling represents a rather unstable system?"

"Sure," Christopher concurred, his mind effortlessly slipping back to his studies of math and physics.

"And all it would likely take would be for one of those nails to come loose, and the whole would give way?"

"Sure," the other man said again. "But how…?"

"Vibrations, like Tiggers, are wonderful things," Chase declared. "Induce a vibration of sufficient intensity, propagating with a suitable frequency and wavelength, and you can shatter even the most solid of structures, isn't that true?"

"Yes…"

"And in this case, all we need do is shift the plaster of the ceiling just sufficiently to dislodge one of those nails."

"Right, but I don't..."

"Observe." Chase studied the room for the briefest of moments, glancing once or twice to the corpse suspended above them, and then moved to one side of the chamber, near a wide archway leading into the kitchens. He casually kicked away what looked like the shredded remains of a leg, and then placed his walking stick upon the wooden floor. Chase steadied himself, concentrated vigorously, and then rapped the stick against the floor, twice in rapid succession and then three more times at slightly lengthier intervals.

For a few seconds, nothing happened. But then Christopher, who was still standing directly below the body, once again felt something trickle onto the back of his neck: plaster dust. He looked up just in time to see the nail driven through Eachna's right arm slide awkwardly to one side, then drop heavily to the floor beside him. Her arm swayed wildly, and Christopher could see the other nails, unable to bear the strain of the sudden torque and shift of weight, begin to come loose.

"Show-off," muttered Emma, just loud enough for Christopher to hear.

"Get ready to catch, Mr Prescott," Chase murmured. No sooner were the words out of the little man's mouth than two more nails broke free, one glancing off Christopher's shoulder, and then Eachna's corpse was plummeting downward. Christopher reacted as quickly as he could, and was barely able to position himself in time to cradle the body in his arms — a task made easier by the unexpected and unnatural levity of the cadaver. Gently, he lowered Eachna's remains to the floor, trying to avoid any of the more extensive puddles of blood and other fluids.

Emma knelt opposite Christopher and reached out to brush Eachna's limp, bedraggled hair away from her face. She was indeed emaciated — like a very old person deprived of food for weeks on end. Her flesh was wrinkled and papery, and

Christopher found it hard to believe that death could have come as recently as a couple of hours earlier. The orbs of her eyes seemed to have exploded in her skull, leaving only gaping black pits behind. Something odd appeared to have been carved into the centre of her forehead, though it was difficult to discern the shape given the withered nature of the corpse.

"It's like she wasn't just killed," said Emma tonelessly. "It's as though all the life were… sucked out of her."

"I'm very much afraid that that's exactly what happened, Miss Rawlin," Chase informed her as he strolled back over to them. "Her life, her knowledge, her memories, her soul… her very essence, drained away, leaving behind only this desiccated husk."

"But why?"

"That is what we need to find out," Chase said with conviction. Then his eyes narrowed and he reached out, placing his hands on either side of the body's forehead. He carefully stretched the skin, smoothing out the area between. "Look. What do we have here?"

Now Christopher had a better view of the shape imprinted into Eachna's skull. He realised that it wasn't so much carved there as somehow burnt, the flesh seared away to form a vaguely bell-shaped symbol, enclosing a rough 'Y'.

"Is it a message? A signature? A mark of the means used to slay Eachna?" Chase wondered aloud. "Have either of you seen it before?"

Both Christopher and Emma shook their heads emphatically. But they were looking at each other furtively, knowing that they had indeed laid eyes on that symbol, or one very much like it, barely an hour earlier.

It was the same symbol as the one adorning the *fios* stone sitting in Christopher's pocket.

Chapter Eight
In which Voices speak from Dark Places

Christopher and Emma emerged from the Bungalow into the darkling dawn of a Saturday morning.

Immediately, Christopher noticed that the lawn was far less crowded than when the two of them had arrived. The bustling atmosphere which had greeted them had given way to one of paranoia, suspicion and fear. Some of the merchants' stalls had vanished completely — no trace of their construction now lingered upon the grass — and those vendors who soldiered on were hawking their wares with far less gusto than had previously been the case. The black tents on the opposite side of the area had been dismantled: clearly, no one had any desire to talk politics for what little remained of this night.

Chase remained in the building. When Christopher had last seen the little man, he had been moving in the direction of a fireman's axe, and neither he nor Emma had any inclination to stay behind to observe how Chase intended to use it. Chase had told them that he would rejoin them shortly, and they had made all haste for the exit.

It was not yet light enough for the world about him to have blossomed back into colour, but Christopher could tell that sunrise was now not far off. The blackness of the sky above was infused with a subtle light — the night fighting a losing battle against the oncoming day. And the first gentle trills of waking birds lilted down from the treetops, a strikingly serene contrast to the grisly sights he had been witness to in the past few minutes. He breathed deeply of the early morning air, filling his lungs with the freshness of a day too newborn to yet be sullied.

"We need to get that leg of yours taken care of," Emma said to him softly. Christopher noticed that almost everybody was whispering now. It wasn't just because people were cowed by the tragic events which had marred this Wandering Parliament: the oncoming dawn seemed to practically demand such reverence. He smiled at Emma gently. In truth, he had forgotten about the wound Lochlann had delivered during their duel. (Was that really less than an hour ago? Did he really see the red-headed woman pass through the bar less than three hours ago?) It had stopped bleeding at some point during their investigations in the Bungalow, but now that he was reminded of it, it began to throb rather painfully.

Emma walked away, towards one of the remaining merchants. Christopher took a look around him, noticing that Davin's corpse, and indeed the Throne over which it had been sprawled, were gone, and nothing remained to suggest that either had ever been there. He figured that, if the Wandering Parliament was indeed a regular occurrence in Bowring Park, then the Five Clans must be rather adept at hiding any trace of their gathering, even traces as bloodcurdling as a murdered man.

Christopher shook his head at the thought: for years, these meetings had been transpiring just a short drive down the street from where he had lived his entire life. Not just for years — for decades, apparently. He remembered the old woman's mention of the Great War, around which time the park would have been newly opened. Was the Wandering Parliament held here back then too, or was Bowring Park just the latest in a series of locales down through history? He supposed it must be, and tried to imagine where else the gatherings might have been held in the past.

He wondered now how he could ever return to his normal life. Would he be able to go back to the world of academia and movies and bad reality television, knowing that all this... this magic or whatever it was, was happening just out of sight? Would he be allowed to become part of this existence, like it seemed Emma had done as a young girl? Did he even want that?

Christopher thought back to the moment in the bar when he had laid eyes upon that red-haired beauty. If she was half as lovely in manner as she was in appearance, he could certainly imagine wanting to stay in this life with her. But then, what did it mean that the symbol on the *fios* stone she had lost was the same as the symbol burned into Eachna's forehead? Was the red-headed woman in trouble? Or should he be drawing darker conclusions? Christopher tried to push this last thought out of his head.

Emma returned, carrying both a small jar whose bottom was coated with a viscous, pinkish slime, and a pair of old, rusted scissors. "What are those for?" he asked her.

"This is *ungadh*," Emma told him, holding up the container. "It's a salve that should help your injury close up quickly, and lessen the pain. Just smear it all around the wound, and it should work in a few minutes." She passed Christopher the jar and he unscrewed the top. A foul odour wafted out; it reminded Christopher unpleasantly of a gym bag his friend Ollie had left at the bottom of his locker for nearly an entire school year. He wrinkled his nose in disgust and quickly shut the container once more. "Sorry about the smell," said Emma belatedly. "It'll go away pretty quickly once it's been applied."

"I hope so," replied Christopher, still grimacing. "What are the scissors for?"

Emma gestured to his trousers. "I figured those are pretty much ruined, so I thought you might want to cut off the legs and turn them into shorts. Sorry about that... I hope they weren't expensive."

Christopher took the scissors from her and began to cut away the material from where Lochlann's sword had sliced into his garment. "Nah, I'm not much one for pricey clothes," he assured her. "It's a good thing Cecily isn't here, though — she bought me these for my birthday last year. I doubt she'd be too pleased if she saw what's happened to them."

"Cecily… Your ex-girlfriend, right?"

"Yeah. We broke up pretty recently," Christopher mumbled as he finished his makeshift tailoring. The words still sounded odd and unnatural in his mouth.

"I'm sorry," Emma told him, and she meant it.

"Don't be. It wasn't pretty, but… I think it was inevitable anyway. If it hadn't happened now, in the way it did, then it would have happened sooner or later, somehow."

"Does that make it feel any better?"

"Sometimes," Christopher said with a shrug. He could see in Emma's eyes that she understood; there was no need for further elaboration. "Anyway, we had a couple of great years, but now I need to move on."

"To a certain mystery woman with red hair?"

"Maybe," said Christopher, a little more sheepishly than he would have liked. He toyed absently with a loose thread dangling from the rough edge of one of his now-abbreviated trouser legs. "This doesn't look too bad." He pinwheeled his arms about: the greyness now touching the sky had done nothing to dispel the oppressive humidity that hung there, and indeed the air was further encumbered by a dewy heaviness. "Looks like shorts are going to be a good idea today anyway, and who knows when I'll get home to change."

"You know you can leave whenever you want. There's nothing keeping you here, Christopher."

"I know." But both of them were well aware that he was long past the point where that was true.

"Hopefully this business with Eachna's… um… with Eachna won't take long. And then we can get back to finding you the woman of your dreams."

A part of Christopher wished Emma hadn't used the word 'dreams', because it reminded him of the fact that it was now well past the hour when he should have been asleep, and the adrenaline which had been driving him onward would not last forever. He was a little grateful that he had spent so much time convalescing in bed over the past week; otherwise, he felt sure that his eyelids would already be drooping with exhaustion.

Emma left Christopher then to apply the evil-smelling pink solution to the deep cut on his upper thigh. She seemed to be making an effort to chat briefly with those few Clansfolk remaining at the Wandering Parliament, for a short while taking solace in what ought to have been the night's primary activity. All about them, people were slowly drifting away into the early morning, down the asphalt paths or behind the Bungalow, presumably returning to waiting taxis and whatever other means of transport were available to and from the park.

Christopher had just finished applying the ointment — and was marvelling at how quickly the sensation of being stuck through the leg by a hot poker was dwindling — when he felt a presence beside him. It was Donovan Chase, now clutching something wrapped in an old blanket beneath one arm. Christopher noted that the object in the blanket was roughly the size of a human head, and realised that he did not need to inquire as to what Chase had needed the axe for.

"Are we ready to go?" the little man asked him briskly.

Christopher nodded. He saw that Emma had noticed Chase's emergence from the Bungalow, and was now making her way back towards them. "What is our destination, exactly?" Christopher inquired.

Chase merely waggled his eyebrows, rather infuriatingly. "You'll see soon enough, my boy." Emma sighed. "Have you used the Ways before, Mr Prescott?" the British man asked, and Christopher responded in the affirmative. "Good. Where we're heading can be accessed only by the Ways, you see."

"There are such places?" Emma asked. Christopher noticed that she seemed a bit shaken by how much more Chase appeared to know about these things than she did. In a sense, Christopher was better prepared for this than Emma — he had already accepted how little he knew.

"There are a few," Chase confirmed. "They're well-guarded secrets, even amongst our kind. And for good reason."

"What reason is that?" Christopher wondered, a feeling of trepidation welling up inside him. He had developed an instinctive trust in Emma and yet had been wary enough when she had led him out of her house and into the unknown, earlier that night. He had no such faith in Donovan Chase, and feared that they might end up in a place much worse than even the scene of carnage within the Bungalow. That Chase again refused to answer his question — this time not even with a vaguely-worded sidestep — did nothing to alleviate his misgivings.

"You said time was short," Emma reminded Chase. "Can we get on with this? If we can help figure out who killed all those people, I want to get the word around as quickly as possible."

"Of course," Chase agreed. "Come with me, both of you." And he led them across the lawn along the paved path which Christopher and Emma had followed upon their arrival in the park.

There are, it bears repeating, many paths through Bowring Park. There are the obvious routes, such as the asphalt roadway which joins the most popular facilities. There are also well-groomed gravel trails which snake through much of the park, following the course of the Waterford and South Brook Rivers, or briefly darting through a wooded copse or past a secluded flower bed, giving one the fleeting sensation of not being in the midst of a city at all, but rather adrift somewhere in the untamed wilds.

Then there are the routes which would not appear on any tourist's map of Bowring Park, but which are well-enough known all the same, and obvious to all but the most casual of observers. These are dirt paths, often crisscrossed by a labyrinth of protruding tree roots, created and maintained not by park staff but by the passage through the years of many curious feet. Some of these trails are merely shortcuts between the park's myriad attractions, while others are most often used by lovers in search of a few moments' torrid privacy, or by mischief-makers trying to evade the eyes of parents or park officials.

But then there are the other paths — those known to just a select few, that might be stumbled upon only by the most outrageous of chances. Most passers-by would not see a path at all: merely a narrow corridor between two bushes, or a low tunnel beneath the bending trees, no doubt leading quickly to a dead end or to a part of the park far more conveniently reached by other means. Most would walk right past these trails without a second thought, blissfully unaware that there was even a trail there to be explored.

Donovan Chase knew of such paths, however, or at least of one such path. Walking at a sprightly pace, he led Christopher and Emma across the concrete bridge which overlooked the route followed by the trains which had ambled through Bowring Park in days gone by, itself now a broad trail. They passed what many people still thought of as the "new" swimming pool (even though it had stood on the spot for decades now) and the burgeoning playground which seemed so much more impressive than when Christopher had cavorted there as a child.

Looking beyond the swings and see-saws, Christopher could now see the first glimmers of yellow-white light touching the Southside Hills, which rose mightily in the near distance to their left. The innumerable fir trees which bedecked their slopes were still visible as little more than a solid black mass, but Christopher thought he could make out a hint of green now, as the monochrome of night gradually faded.

Finally, just past the western entrance to Bowring Park, Chase turned onto a wide gravel path and navigated around a barrier erected to impede the passage of cars. Christopher was familiar with the route, having strolled along it occasionally in the past. To their immediate left was now a plunging wooded ravine, leading eventually down to the banks of the South Brook River. At the point where the descent was steepest, a warning sign stood forlornly, warning passers-by to keep well clear of the crumbling edge. As they reached it, Chase extended his arm and grasped the slender metal post upon which the sign was erected.

"Here we are," he murmured.

"Um... here where?" Christopher asked, looking about. The trail continued on for quite a while ahead of them, and to their right was a densely forested area.

Chase extended his walking stick, pointing down the precarious incline. "This is our route," he told them.

"Are you serious?" retorted Emma. She was standing at the edge of the precipice. Loose dirt and gravel skittered down the hill into the river valley below.

"Usually," returned Chase. "Be very careful," he warned. ("You don't say," muttered Christopher.) "Tread only where I tread, until we join the Ways. Even then, follow close behind — we travel along dark and lonely avenues, and the going may be more dangerous than you're accustomed to." And with that, he readjusted his grip on the morbid package he carried under his arm, and stepped over the edge.

"I guess I'd better keep my eyes open then," Christopher whispered to Emma.

She smiled at him comfortingly. "Are you up for it?"

"He'd better be!" Chase declared without turning around.

Christopher decided that the worst part of the walk down the slope was not the dizzying angle of the ravine but the vertigo it induced. He tried desperately to just look at his feet, but his vision was drawn inexorably to the shallow river, which could be glimpsed in flashes through the gnarled and twisted trees which hugged the hillside, and he kept feeling as though the ground beneath his feet would give way at any moment, sending him careening downward.

Fortunately, though, Chase seemed to know exactly where to step as they went — the earth was as solid and stable as if the invisible path they followed had been paved with flagstones. Only when Christopher did not follow Chase's lead precisely, stepping a few inches too far to the right or extending his stride to a length greater than the smaller man could muster, did his footing feel at all precarious. He noticed that Emma, walking between Chase and himself, was having no difficulties at all in treading exactly where she was meant to.

Chase lead them along a frustratingly circuitous route, sometimes moving almost perpendicular to the incline, sometimes bounding virtually straight downhill, and sometimes even doubling back and ascending once more towards the gravel path they had left behind. On one occasion, Christopher found himself circling a dying maple tree not once but twice, and he began to wonder if Chase wasn't playing him and Emma for fools after all.

He wiped his brow, now damp with sweat as the emerging day renewed the ferocity of the heat and humidity. The sun had finally cleared the top of the Southside Hills, although it was barely visible through the lowering grey clouds which filled the sky from horizon to horizon. Christopher could sense the promise of rain in the air, but it was pent up, like an obstinate piñata which refuses to burst.

As they continued on their wandering hike, Christopher became a little surprised that Emma had not protested at the seeming randomness of their route. Indeed, she had been completely placid for the whole of the journey, apparently doing nothing more than concentrate on where next to place her foot.

And suddenly, Christopher realised why this was.

The world around him had become a little darker. At first, he thought the sun had disappeared behind a cloud, before he remembered that the sun had been masked by the clouds ever since its rising. Looking about, Christopher realised that it wasn't the quality of the light that had changed — it was the resolution of their surroundings. Everything had suddenly become a little blurrier, a little murkier — the leaves on the trees lost their definition, the sparse grass on the ground faded into a morass of green on brown and grey. And with each step he took, following Emma following Chase, the phenomenon became more pronounced.

"Hold my hand, Christopher," Emma instructed. She reached back, though she did not take her eyes off Chase. Christopher obeyed without question.

"What's happening?" he whispered.

"We're moving onto the Ways," Chase called back; Christopher was surprised the man had even heard his comment. "Though this is a seldom-used part of them indeed. Remember, Mr Prescott, you must keep moving unless you wish to be cast out of the Ways. The places you might wind up from here would likely be... forbidding indeed."

Now Christopher found himself walking through a darkened void. He wasn't even sure what he was placing his feet on: it certainly didn't feel like dirt or rock, and he could no longer detect the steep incline of the hillside. Ahead of him, Emma and Chase floated in his field of vision, pallid and distorted, like images in an old photograph that had blurred down through the years.

The noise of birdsong and the smells of midsummer flora had vanished too. They were replaced only by a faintly echoing rushing noise and a scent like a closet filled with mothballs, one that has just been opened for the first time in years.

"This isn't what it was like the first time I passed along the Ways," Christopher said to Emma.

"This isn't what it was like any of the times I've used them either, Christopher," she told him in an uneasy tone. "The Ways are usually brimming with energy. This road... it feels almost dead..."

"Very apt, Miss Rawlin, as you'll shortly see," Chase murmured. "Now, be quiet, both of you. We don't want to attract any… undesirable attention down here. And keep treading close behind me — this is not a place you want to become lost in."

Christopher gulped, wondering what Chase meant by 'down here'. Somewhere, impossibly far away, he thought he heard a mournful wail, and a noise like the ocean crashing against rocks on the shoreline. Occasionally, he thought he could make out vague shapes in the dark, a deeper black moving against the blackness to his right and left. He tried to ignore these passing apparitions, and the low, insistent whispering that seemed to arise in their wake.

Once again Christopher reached up to mop his brow, and run his hand through his matted hair. The quality of the heat had changed — it was no longer a cloying humidity, but instead an aggressive warmth, like that which infested the furnace room in his parents' basement. To make matters worse, no wind blew along this road — the air was stagnant and lifeless.

After what seemed like an eternity (but was probably closer to fifteen minutes), Christopher felt something change. He couldn't put his finger on what exactly was different, but he was gripped all of a sudden by a sensation of dislocation — it was still dark and hot, but in a way that was subtly altered from what he had been walking through just seconds earlier. He felt his stomach churn and spots flared in front of his eyes. He staggered and Emma, who had been maintaining a steady grip on his hand the entire time, did her best to steady him.

"It's okay," she whispered soothingly. "We've moved off the Ways. We've arrived at our destination… wherever that might be."

Christopher nodded, trying to steady himself. This trip hadn't been as bad as that first time he had traversed the Ways back on George Street, but he knew that his body was still far from accustomed to the experience.

He tried to take a deep breath, and instantly regretted it. The stale air was now laden with something even more unpleasant: it was the odour of death. Not the kind of recent, pervasive death which had assaulted him in the Bungalow; this was the scent of old death, of corpse dust and of bones denuded of their flesh, of mouldering shrouds and of coffin wood long rotten beneath the earth. It was the smell that lingered long after the life has fled a mortal vessel.

"Where are we, Chase?" Emma demanded, in a voice she barely kept from shaking.

Chase's head was slowly panning from left to right, though Christopher had no idea what the man could possibly see in the darkness. Then he nodded and turned to them. He appeared to be fumbling in the pockets of his jacket — Christopher couldn't be too certain, because the weak, spectral illumination which had allowed him to see his companions during their trip was slowly fading, like a flashlight whose batteries have run low. After a moment, Chase found whatever he was looking for and the smell of sulphur briefly assailed Christopher's nostrils as a match was lit, the sudden light dazzling before his eyes. He blinked furiously to try to clear his vision, and as detail returned to him he realised that Chase had, rather absurdly, produced a stubby tallow candle — complete with a tarnished silver holder — from somewhere, and was using this to shed light on their surroundings.

"Where… are we?" Emma asked again, but this time her impatient tone had given way to one of incredulity.

"The city of St John's," said Donovan Chase, "has existed in one form or another for nearly five centuries. As the popular history books have it, it has endured savage frost, searing fire and terrible pestilence; and it has experienced far worse things you'll find in none of those histories. Through the years, it has been built and rebuilt, it has expanded and absorbed, and many things have become lost in the process."

He turned around again and held the candle out before him. Though the light it provided was not strong, Christopher could see that they stood in a cavern of some sort: the walls, ceiling and floor were all formed of rock and hard-packed earth, leading off into the stygian gloom. Tree roots, ancient and gnarled, protruded from the dirt, but so too did other things, and it was these that arrested Christopher's attention. For exploding outward at intervals from the walls and floor and ceiling, at every possible angle, were coffins — or at least the remains of coffins, such was their unimaginable age.

"This is the Forgotten Cemetery," Chase intoned funereally.

"We're underground?" Christopher asked timorously. Emma still hadn't let go of his hand and he could tell that she was more than a little anxious; and that, in turn, was having a deleterious effect on his own frayed nerves.

"So it would seem," Chase acknowledged. "Popular rumour has it that we're somewhere uphill from St John's Harbour, below a parking lot or a business centre or even the catacombs of a church. But I tend to have little faith in popular rumour." Christopher imagined the number of people who probably walked over this spot every single day, without giving the barest of thoughts to what might lie just a handful of yards beneath their feet. For all he knew, he could well have been one of those people, once or even hundreds of times.

"I've heard of this place," Emma said softly, almost reverently. She was thinking of whispers she had heard during her time amongst the Five Clans — mentions in barely-remembered stories, allusions in the ravings of the old and infirm. "I always thought it was just a legend."

Chase shook his head. "No, Miss Rawlin. We live amongst folk who can live for a hundred years without aging a day, people with the eyes and senses of a great bird, men and women who can skim the surface of your thoughts as easily as a shallow pond. We don't have legends, we merely have things which have passed out of the common culture — things which have been hidden or misplaced or suppressed as our society dwindles towards inevitable obscurity." The last words were spoken with a mixture of bitterness and melancholy, unanticipated emotion from a man who seemed stoic almost as a rule. Christopher wanted to ask Emma what he meant, but decided to wait until they were back in the open air.

Chase handed Emma the candle and then pulled the bundle out from under his arm, holding it gingerly in both hands. "Now," he said, "we mustn't tarry here too long. Let's be about our business and away."

"Okay," mumbled Christopher, not entirely sure what he was meant to be doing. Emma merely nodded.

Chase looked around, his neck straining forward as if he were trying to penetrate the dark shadows around them without having to take another step deeper into the Forgotten Cemetery. After a moment he motioned to Christopher and Emma to move closer, and as they did so, the light from the candle caught something large and oblong resting on the ground a few feet away. "Ah," said Chase, and together they approached the object.

Unlike the other visible caskets, which were all made of wood of varying quality, this was a stone bier, of such venerability that it almost seemed to be a part of the cavern rather than a man-made object. Writing — or perhaps iconography — was carved upon the lid, but it had long since faded into illegibility. At some point down through the years, the sealant around the lid had weakened and the slab had shifted slightly, exposing a narrow aperture. It was before this that Chase halted. He placed his swaddled burden on top of the bier and said in a clear voice, "You know why we have come?"

Although Christopher could not see anybody else in the cavern, he had no doubt whatsoever that Chase was not addressing him or Emma. He shivered a little despite himself, and he and Emma squeezed their hands together more tightly.

"You know why we have come?" Chase repeated, more forcefully this time. Suddenly, the candle Emma was holding flickered — although there was no movement of air in the Forgotten Cemetery — casting strange and unnatural shadows onto the earthen walls. Then, all around him,

Christopher could hear a susurrant noise like the earth settling. In the silences, more subtly but more disturbingly, was another sound which he could describe only as dry bone scraping against rotted wood. And in the conjunction of these noises, Christopher realised that he could make out words, low and mournful:

... *You come seeking knowledge from beyond the veil...*

"Yes!" declared Chase. "Vital knowledge, knowledge which may impact the very survival of the Five Clans!"

... *But you are not of the Five Clans. You are apart...*

"I have their interests at heart nonetheless," the little man muttered. "I represent them. As does this girl." And he gestured towards Emma, who shuddered involuntarily.

... *And what of the other?...*

Christopher realised the voice was referring to him. "A tagalong," shrugged Chase. "I needed a third, and he was willing."

... *Let him speak for himself...*

"I... I just want to help," Christopher offered lamely. "I'm sorry, I know I shouldn't be here."

... *No. You alone are welcome in this place, Christopher Prescott...*

Chase crooked an eyebrow. "Really?" he murmured. But the sepulchral voice continued unabated.

... *For you, we will abide by the precepts of the ancient rite. He who calls himself Donovan Chase may proceed...*

"Very well. We three have come, as tradition demands, *céad*, *déanach*, and *idir*. We bear the candle made from a condemned man's hand —" Christopher blanched at the statement, and was amazed that Emma hardly flinched, but continued to hold the candle steadily aloft in her free hand "— and the mouth of the departed we wish to hear speak once more."

... *Yes. The ritual is satisfied. Ask your questions, Donovan Chase. But do not try our patience...*

"I wouldn't dream of it," Chase responded straight-facedly. "Eachna of the People of the Caribou," he called out in an imperious tone of voice, "tell me how death befell you." Christopher realised that Chase was speaking directly to the blanket-shrouded form he had placed atop the bier.

The candle flickered once more, and it looked to Christopher as if all the shadows in the cavern were converging on the ancient stone coffin. He watched with widening eyes as the object within the blanket appeared to move, almost imperceptibly — a small, jerky motion, like a mouth opening and closing against the folds of the cloth. And then another voice was heard in that place, one which seemed to come from impossibly far away and yet which also emanated from the shape enfolded within the blanket. "In life… I was Eachna…" said the voice, and it was followed by a piteous howl, brimming with rage and sorrow and regret.

"Does that sound like her?" Christopher whispered to Emma. His companion nodded curtly.

Chase shot Christopher a brief but unambiguous glare. "Please, you must answer my question," he ordered the swaddled form, in a voice which was respectful while brooking no argument.

After a moment, the wailing ceased, and Eachna's voice could be heard again. "I remember… we had arrived at the Wandering Parliament. We knew there was something wrong… we had been followed along the Ways… But it was a feint, a diversion — they were already waiting for us. They fell upon us in a swarm, tearing and rending and killing. They took such… perverse glee in the way they mutilated us. They were so many…

"Davin was the last to fall, apart from me. They were aware that he was Speaker and I was First Minister, though how they came by this knowledge, I cannot say. They made me watch as they tortured him, and then left him on the Throne for others to find once they'd departed. Then they surrounded me, and conducted a fell ceremony the likes of which were new to me… and I remember no more. Please, how long has it been? How many years have passed since I was murdered?"

"It was only earlier tonight, Eachna," Emma said in a choked voice.

"Oh… it seemed as though I had already passed many years in the dark, alone."

"Eachna, tell me what the purpose of the ritual was," demanded Chase.

"The *eochair*, the Waykey, was in my possession. They sundered my very soul and claimed it as I died." Christopher wanted very badly to ask Emma what a Waykey was, but once again forced himself to hold his tongue.

"Eachna, who did this? Who killed you, and stole the *eochair*?"

There was a lengthy pause. Then the answer came, as if ripped from Eachna's dead throat: "The Sixth Clan. It was the Sixth Clan!"

Chapter Nine
In which there is a Parting of the Ways

The candle Emma was holding guttered and died as Eachna's final words echoed mournfully about the Forgotten Cemetery. The cavern was plunged into absolute darkness — not even the strange glow which had illuminated the three travellers when they first arrived was in evidence now. Christopher heard what remained of the candle fall to the earthen floor, followed by the sound of footsteps marching towards him: Chase. "We have to go. Now!" he breathed.

Christopher wondered momentarily what the hurry was. Then he began to discern more noises in the air around him: things moving, things rising, things which had not stirred in many, many years. He gulped and followed swiftly in Chase's wake.

… You do not need to leave us, Christopher Prescott. You are welcome in our cold embrace. Stay…

"Um, no, sorry," Christopher called out. Feeling a perverse need to explain himself, he stopped and turned back the way he had come. Emma brushed quickly past him. "I have something I need to do," he said. "Something I need to return to a certain red-haired woman."

"Come on, Christopher!" Emma called out from up ahead.

… Stay or go, it makes no difference. This is where you belong…

Christopher tried to summon a witty retort, but then he felt something jagged and stiff and cold grasp at his arm. He lashed out with his other arm and jumped back, pointing himself in the direction that Chase and Emma had taken and then running as fast as he could, his shoes pounding against the dirt and rock beneath his feet.

"Hurry!" It was Chase's voice, seemingly a very long distance away. Christopher, never a particularly swift sprinter at the best of times, found it somewhere within himself to put on an extra burst of speed, just as something wispy and ephemeral like a spider's web brushed the back of his neck.

... Fare thee well, Christopher Prescott. Until we meet again...

Suddenly, Christopher could tell that he was no longer in the Forgotten Cemetery. He was once again treading through the empty void of this forgotten avenue of the Ways. Through the gloom, Chase and Emma became visible ahead, once again illuminated, phantom-like, by a palsied white glow.

"Come on and catch up with us, Christopher!" Emma shouted. "Remember, we can't stop moving!"

Under normal circumstances, Christopher probably could have reached his companions without too much difficulty. But he was famished and frightened, and he was exhausted — not just from the lateness of the hour, but from the emotional misery he had endured for the past week, and the disorientation of all that had transpired over the last hours. And because of all this, just as he closed the gap between himself and Emma to no more than two dozen feet, Christopher stumbled and fell awkwardly to the side of the path, outside the trail marked by Chase's passage. He heard Emma cry out, Chase curse, and two pairs of feet rushing towards him.

As he lay on the nothingness that was serving as the ground, trying desperately to catch his breath and get moving again, Christopher realised that he could hear a rustling in the shadows around him. Abruptly, it felt as though he were being swallowed by something terrible and enormous and so very hungry. The inky darkness seemed to writhe around him. He felt an involuntary scream well up in his throat…

And suddenly, Christopher was sprawled not upon some black road of night but upon a freshly-polished floor. Lights shone brightly down from the ceiling above, hurting his eyes. After a moment, he felt strong arms pulling him to his feet.

"You young fool." It was Chase. "Where have you sent us?"

"Leave him be, Chase," Emma grumbled. "Are you okay, Christopher?"

"I think so, thanks," he replied, appreciative of her kindness but feeling guilty at his clumsiness nonetheless.

With a sigh, Christopher rubbed his eyes and looked around. He was shocked to find their surroundings familiar. They were in a long corridor, dotted periodically with doors bearing painted three-digit numbers. Most of the wallspace in-between was occupied by tall grey lockers, sparkling new with barely a dent or a hint of mistreatment. When Christopher had attended this high school, the hallway had looked much the same, but the lockers were battered, battle-scarred after decades of abuse, and the paint on the doors was chipped and worn in places. "This isn't possible," he muttered, though part of his brain wondered when he'd finally be forced to abandon that expression once and for all.

"We're not where we seem to be," Emma murmured, wrapping her arms about herself. "This is a trap."

"I told you to be careful!" Chase berated Christopher. "Always keep to the path, don't you know anything?"

Weary and downtrodden, Christopher felt his patience slipping away. "No, I guess I don't!" he retorted. "All I wanted to do was return this —" he pulled the *fios* stone out of his pocket and waved it under Chase's nose before returning it to safekeeping "— to its rightful owner. I didn't ask to be dragged halfway across St John's. I didn't ask to be a witness to a wholesale slaughter. I didn't ask to be dragged to some godforsaken graveyard and —"

"Hello."

Three teenaged girls stood in the corridor, which had been empty just moments earlier. Christopher realised that they had uttered the greeting together, in three curious, strangely melodic voices which mingled and merged into an eerie harmony. They were dressed in the white blouses and conservative dark skirts which had been the uniform dress at Christopher's high school in the days when it had been an all-girls Catholic institution. Oddly, though their features were different, all three girls stood exactly the same height.

"What do you want?" Chase asked, his eyes narrowing.

"We wanted," said the girl on the left, who had long blonde hair and wore glasses.

"To welcome you," said the middle girl, her hair curly and auburn, her face freckled.

"To our home," said the girl on the right, her short hair midnight-black. High cheekbones and a slender nose lent her a regal bearing.

"Um, thanks," offered Christopher.

"Don't talk to them," Chase growled, standing beside him.

"Why not?" asked the blonde girl.

"Don't you think you're being rather rude?" asked the brunette.

"Have you not learned proper manners?" asked the dark-haired girl.

"Please, just let us continue our journey along the Ways," Emma said diffidently. "We got a little lost, that's all."

"Oh yes."

"You are lost, Emma Rawlin."

"More than you could possibly know."

Emma arched one eyebrow. "And what exactly is that supposed to mean?"

But the three girls had turned to confer with one another.

"Note their pleasing symmetry."

"Maiden, mother and crone."

"The original trinity."

Christopher looked at his companions with some confusion, wondering which of them was supposed to be which. He wasn't quite sure how any of the three descriptions could apply to himself or to Chase. But the girls were still chatting gaily.

"And see: one has betrayed them."

"One will betray them."

"And one will slay another."

"Delicious," all three girls said in unison, and they giggled impishly.

"What is going on here?" Christopher muttered to Chase.

"Lies and misdirection," Chase replied under his breath. But the girls had evidently overheard his comment: as one, their heads snapped in his direction.

"Oh no, there are no lies here, Solitary Traveller."

"Only true tellings of the times to come."

"Begone."

And Chase was no longer standing next to Christopher. There was no movement, no sense of the shorter man vanishing: one second he stood there, glowering at the three uniformed girls, and the next he simply… was not.

"Where did he go?" Emma demanded, her pretence of timidity evaporating. She walked over to stand beside Christopher, opposite the space vacated by Chase. "What are you people?"

"Look at them," sighed the girl on the left. "They do make an attractive couple."

"Oh yes," sighed the girl in the middle. "Complementary of form and complementary of spirit."

"It's true," sighed the girl on the right. "And while he is rather older by the measure of years, she is rather older by the measure of life."

"Shame then."

"That it cannot come to pass."

"Not in this life."

Christopher thought that Emma was about ready to offer some response — probably to dismiss the rather absurd notion that they might have a relationship extending beyond the current predicament — when abruptly, she was gone, just like Chase before her. Christopher was left alone in the school hallway with the three mysterious girls.

"So... what now, then?" Christopher asked apprehensively as six eyes — two green, two blue, two brown — converged on him. He wanted to ask after Emma and Chase, but knew the question would be a waste of breath.

"Darkness."

"Fear."

"Pain."

"I've had all three of those already," Christopher suggested, trying to keep his tone light.

But the girls were smiling at him now, and he could see that their teeth were just a little too pointed, their stare just slightly too predatory. He felt shadows wash over him, though the light in the corridor did not change. Christopher tried to back away from the strange trio, but his legs were unresponsive. Worse yet, he was suddenly standing right in front of them, even though neither he nor the girls seemed to have moved. They reached forward and caressed his face with fingernails that were too long, too crooked.

"You shouldn't have ventured away from the fields you know, Christopher Prescott."

"The woods are ancient and wild, and full of hidden terrors."

"You learned this in your dreams once, long ago, but those dreams are forgotten these many years."

Christopher tried to flinch, tried to shake off the girls' discomfiting touch, but only his mouth still seemed to function. "My dreams again," he murmured, feeling his mouth go dry. He was thinking back to the little boy sitting amongst the merchants' stalls on the Bungalow lawn. "Why this obsession with my dreams and my childhood all of a sudden?"

"There is power and wisdom."

"In dreams."

"And in nightmares."

Then the girls grinned slyly at one another, as their faces turned papery and ragged, their lips crumbled to dust and their eyeballs became withered and opaque. With a low hiss, they leaned forward to pull Christopher into a hideous embrace…

And darkness overwhelmed him.

*   *   *

Emma awoke to find herself lying on her couch, one arm dangling downward onto the threadbare carpet of the floor. A staccato rhythm was pounding behind her eyes and her mouth tasted foul. "Must've been quite the Parliament," she moaned, shielding her eyes with one hand.

She couldn't remember a thing about the night before — couldn't remember much since she had left the house for a jog around the downtown, actually. She wondered if Davin had gotten her started on that wicked home brew of his again — convinced her to have a pint or two to celebrate his rousing performance as Speaker, and then sat back and watched as a couple of pints turned into nine or ten. Emma groaned miserably, grateful only that she had at least made it back to her own apartment, somehow or other.

Groggily, she pulled herself up off the couch and rose unsteadily to her feet. "This'll be a day t'spend in bed," she told herself and nodded, though she instantly regretted the abrupt motion. "Yep, def'nitely."

With great deliberation, Emma staggered to her bedroom door, pulling off her blouse and randomly tossing it behind her. Her bed, old and lumpy though it may be, looked incredibly inviting, and she almost tripped in her haste to slip off her skirt and collapse onto the blankets, the weather being far too stifling to climb beneath them. As her skirt hit the floor, she was vaguely aware of something small, round and metallic falling out of the pocket and skittering away into a corner, but she really didn't care.

By the time her head hit the pillow, Emma was already fast asleep.

*   *   *

Donovan Chase looked around. He was slumped over a wooden bench in the middle of a brightly-lit mall, just beginning to teem with Saturday morning shoppers. His walking stick was lying across his legs and he seized it gratefully, using it to push himself upright. He supposed he must have shown up at the mall early, probably to take advantage of some bargain or other before his vacation ended and he had to return to Brit—

"No." Chase gripped his walking stick even harder and shut his eyes tightly. He could feel phantom memories clouding his brain, but breathed deeply and, with a mental cry of rage and indignity, shouldered them aside. "I am not so easily fooled," he muttered angrily, earning bemused glances from a gaggle of teenagers who were sauntering past. Chase ignored them and rested his chin on his walking stick.

"Now," he said to himself. "What next?" He felt something shift in one of his jacket pockets, and remembered instantly what he had acquired. Chase beamed grimly. "Ah yes…"

*   *   *

A plain man stood along a dark and lonely road in the midst of a twilight void. He had been standing in the same spot, cloaked in a shadow of his own creation, for hours now and had not moved — not to shift his weight, not to stretch his legs, not even to blink.

The man had followed the scent this far, and knew that the object of his search had passed by this way, and so must lie up ahead. But the man also knew that this path was a terminal one, and that his quarry had to return to this point on the way back to the bright, comforting light of day.

Except that hadn't happened.

Finally, the ordinary-looking man made a decision: if those he sought had not yet come back — and after this much time, he doubted that they would — then they must have taken the only other route available to them, into the sinister lands which bordered this part of the Ways. He knew that his prey could only suffer for the experience, and while this meant that it might take him more time to track them down again, they would be all the easier to deal with once they had been located anew.

The glimmer of a smile creased the man's face, just for an instant. It was not a smile which harboured anything remotely resembling human joy.

Soundlessly, the man spun on his heels and walked away.

* * *

Hard rock was sending shivers of pain up and down Christopher's spine when he finally awoke. He wondered briefly if he might be able to suffer the discomfort and rest a while longer, but then his stomach got into the act, radiating pangs of hunger which wracked him to the point that he could barely think straight. Finally, he reached a deal with his body: eat first, then more sleeping — possibly hibernation, if he could get away with it. Oh, and hopefully figure out where he was at some stage too.

Christopher opened his eyes to see a solid ceiling of thick, grey cloud looming far above him. Although it was not easy to tell, the sun seemed to be very high in the sky, and he wondered how long he had been lying on the ground.

Ignoring the cramps which were torturing his back, he sat up and looked around. He was in the midst of a cracked and broken stretch of land, virtually bereft of grass. There were great mounds of dirt and rock all around him; in the distance, he could hear the faint noise of construction, though it was obscured as the land rose uphill in almost all directions. He stood at the bottom of a bowl-shaped depression. Only ahead of him was the ground mostly flat, and he could faintly see trees, several minutes' walk away.

A tantalising image of long red hair flashed through Christopher's mind.

"Oh shit," he yelped, as the events of the previous night came rushing back to him. Just for an instant, he wondered if it could all have been a dream, but his trousers were indeed cut short, and he could still see a tiny smear of pink on his thigh, immersing a fading scar. His face felt like it was full of paper cuts, and Christopher shuddered as he recalled the three girls' warped fingers stroking his cheeks and chin.

"Definitely not a dream, then," he told himself. He looked about, wondering what had happened to Emma and Chase — perhaps they were just up over the incline? Even if they weren't, he could always head back to Emma's apartment and hopefully meet her there. Then they could resume their search for the *fios* stone's alluring owner. He slid his hand into his pocket, anticipating the comforting and now familiar solidity of the strange little object.

But the stone was gone: his hand closed only about the little metal disc he had received after winning the duel with Lochlann.

Christopher swore. Frantically, his eyes roved the ground where he had awakened, hoping against hope that the *fios* stone had merely slipped out of his pocket while he slumbered.

As he searched, a shadow fell across the ground in front of him.

"Well, well, well. What do I see?" The voice was guttural and sounded almost effortlessly nasty. Christopher peered up to see one of the bald men who had accompanied Lochlann to the Wandering Parliament. He was standing at the crest of the rise, silhouetted against the overcast sky. His arms were folded and his cramped face twisted into a leer.

Christopher was about to respond when he heard a foot crunch on the rocky ground behind him. Looking back, he saw that the other bald man had appeared at the top of the depression as well. He crouched down and studied Christopher for a moment. "I think you sees exactly what I sees," he concluded, and kicked some loose pebbles in Christopher's direction. The expression on his piggy features was almost identical to the other man's; Christopher wondered if they were twins, as he had first suspected, or had just spent so much time together that they'd lost all trace of individuality.

"Um, hey guys," Christopher offered weakly. "How did you find me?"

"We has a certain gift," said the second bald man, standing upright again.

"A talent, as they say," agreed the other.

"Oh. Cool. Ah, listen, you haven't seen a strange little stone around, have you? It's rectangular, about so big..." Christopher gestured appropriately, but the bald men didn't seem to be paying any attention.

"You shafted us royally last night, bud," one of them told him.

"That you did. We had a good thing goin' with Loch."

"Yup. All the chicks loved 'im, and the ones he didn't want settled for us."

"Or we got to play with 'em after Loch finished with 'em. After he had 'em all bent out of shape and they didn't even realise it."

"Did we ever have that little blonde honey our matey here was with?"

"I don't remember. Maybe we'll have to take a run by her place and get to know her better." The two men chuckled cruelly.

Despite being incredibly fatigued and famished, Christopher's temper was reaching its boiling point and he stepped towards the man who had spoken last, his fists clenched tightly. "Hang on a minute, guys, I don't like the way you're talking about…"

The first man jumped down next to Christopher, forcing him to take a step back. The bald man's body smelled sweaty and rank. "I don't remember askin' you."

Christopher, though, was not to be so easily intimidated, even if common sense dictated that he ought to find a peaceable way out of the encounter. "I'm telling you anyway," he growled. "Nobody talks that way about a friend of mine."

"Is that so? Oh, the stories we could tell about little Emmeline!"

"I'm serious," hissed Christopher. "I beat your buddy Lochlann, I'll take my chances against you morons."

"Loch ain't our buddy anymore. He ain't no good to us after you kicked his arse. 'Sides, there's one big difference between us and Loch."

"What's that?" Christopher asked, eyeing the bald man warily.

"Loch fights fair," said a voice behind him. It was the second bald man, who had taken advantage of the conversation to clamber stealthily down the slope and manoeuvre himself behind Christopher. Before Christopher could even start to turn around, he felt a massive fist pound into his kidneys. He cried out despite himself, and fell against the other man.

"Never could figure out why he did that," the first man confessed, pushing Christopher off of himself and then landing a solid kick to his groin. Christopher felt his stomach heave and tears well up in his eyes as he collapsed to the ground.

Before Christopher could even think about crawling away or crying out for help, one of the men was on top of him, his bulk pressing into his chest and pinning him to the rocky, uneven ground. The thug started whaling away at Christopher's face, punch after punch landing squarely.

Christopher, who had never suffered so much as a twisted ankle in his life, felt his nose shatter in the wake of one well-placed blow. His eyes were soon swollen shut under the constant battering. He tried to get his arms up to protect himself, but the other man was on him in an instant, pinning them to the ground and then grinding them against the stones with his knees, tearing the flesh and popping one wrist wildly out of joint. At some point, Christopher started screaming, but the two men just laughed.

Eventually, he was too weak to mount a defense and so one man moved to work on his bare legs and stomach, raining down a series of kicks which plummeted Christopher into as-yet unexplored realms of agony. The other man had become tired of his incessant punches and had resorted to pulling roughly on Christopher's short hair, punctuated occasionally by a punishing slap across his bloodied cheeks.

This time, Christopher welcomed the blackness of unconsciousness when it finally, mercifully, embraced him. The last image which floated through his mind as awareness fled was of the woman with the red hair. He despaired to think that he had failed her, and now he would never have the chance to find her…

Chapter Ten
In which an horrific Devolution occurs

Flash:

Christopher couldn't open his eyes. Colours swam violently across his field of vision, and he felt a whispered moan escape his swollen and blood-encrusted lips. Through a fog of pain, he could feel broken rock underneath him, and he thought he must still be lying on the barren stretch of land where the bald men had attacked him.

He tried to shift his body, vaguely considering crawling out of the depression and attempting to make his way to the sounds of construction which now seemed so very far away. But at the slightest movement, new agonies from a dozen different injuries coursed through his frame, and he slid back into oblivion.

* * *

Flash:

A wind was blowing over his prone form, but it offered no succour: Christopher thought that the humidity had only intensified since his last fleeting glimpse of awareness, and the breeze was merely moving the heavy heat around, pummelling it against his body.

Once again he tried to open his eyes, and this time he barely managed to crack one open, though it stung as though it had been ravaged by a nest of wasps. For a moment, all was still and quiet around him. But then Christopher caught an impression of something moving, just at the edge of sight — something small and furry and lithe and fanged.

And again he passed out.

*   *   *

Flash:

Christopher could tell that he was moving, though he was still sprawled out flat on his back. The quality of the light behind his sealed eyelids kept shifting subtly. He tried to speak but his throat was too parched to emit even the most primitive of sounds.

It gradually dawned on him that something was sitting on his chest. Again he barely managed to open one eye, and was greeted by the disorientating shimmer of a curtain of gold all around him. The Ways, he thought, I'm travelling the Ways again.

Something slender but solid and sharp pressed against his chin, and he tried to angle his good eye downward to get a look at what was pinning him in place. He registered a sharp claw and a glowing green eye with a black, crescent-shaped pupil fixed upon him.

Then he knew no more.

*   *   *

Emma groggily pulled herself out of a dreamless sleep. Straightening an errant bra strap, she glanced towards the window; through the threadbare blue drapes, she could see that twilight had fallen over downtown St John's once more.

"Dear God, how long was I out?" she moaned. Whatever she had imbibed last night, it must have been seriously strong stuff to lay her low like this!

She reached over to her ancient alarm clock. Its digital readout consisted, as usual, of just a couple of random red lines, but after Emma had pounded on it a few times, the rest of the display sprang grudgingly into life, and she saw that it was nearly nine o'clock at night. "So much for Saturday," she sighed remorsefully.

After briefly contemplating staying in bed until morning, Emma finally caved in to the part of her that was aghast at the thought of wasting an entire day, and dragged herself out of bed. She shed her underwear and padded down the hallway to the cramped little bathroom, where she spoiled herself with an extra-long shower — albeit one that wasn't quite as scalding-hot as she normally liked it, a concession to the unbearable stickiness that had infested the city. Finally, she returned to her room and dressed herself in a tank top and shorts.

While her memory of the previous night was still a blank, Emma was glad that she had at least managed to evade any symptoms of a hangover. In fact, she was now feeling ravenously hungry, so she went out to the kitchen and, after assessing the meagre contents of her fridge and cupboards, managed to scramble together enough ingredients for a sizeable omelette. She prepared it, cooked it, devoured it eagerly, and in short order placed the dirty dishes in the sink.

As she did so, Emma's eyes fell on a strange dark stain next to the front door. It started on the carpet and extended all the way to the wall, and then actually rose up the wall for several feet. If she didn't know better, she would have thought that it was the shadow of a man — except that she was the only person in the apartment, and indeed she had not had a visitor since her landlady, Dina, had stopped by on Tuesday to pick up the overdue rent. Of course, Emma knew of a few individuals who were able to mask themselves from the sight of others, so she stepped over to where such a person would have to be standing. The dark patch did not shift, and she windmilled her arms around to confirm that nobody could possibly be there.

Emma stood next to the mysterious stain, rubbing her chin in thought. She considered that perhaps this was the end result of something she had gotten up to the night before, but largely discarded the notion: even drunk, she was mostly sensible these days, and there was nothing remotely sensible about defacing her own apartment. Dina was not going to like this.

So instead, she thought hard to remember if she knew of anybody — be it an individual person or type of creature — whose shadow could literally burn itself into the fabric of a room, like she had heard happened to people in Japan when the nuclear bombs had been dropped. And suddenly, Emma realised that she did know of such a being. "Oh shit," she muttered, her jaw dropping. "There was a *Gan Aireachtáil* here." In her shock, she didn't notice her bare foot slide a little to the right, onto the patch of eerily blackened carpet.

Immediately, Emma's body was flooded with an unnatural coldness. She tried to cry out, but the sound died in her throat. Her eyes went wide, but as they did so, her pupils flared and expanded, blotting out the blue of her irises and then the white surrounding them. She tried to run, but her foot was held fast to the spot. And before she knew it, Emma Rawlin had fallen under shadow.

* * *

Emma felt lips against her own, and a tongue playfully roaming her mouth. Her eyes snapped open with a start and she pulled away.

"Emmeline, dear, whatever is the matter?"

Emma blinked furiously, trying to focus. She realised that she was sitting on somebody's knee... No, not somebody — Lochlann. Who else? She smiled shyly at him. "Nothing, Loch. I'm sorry. I think I forgot where I was for a moment." And she simpered girlishly, in just the way Loch liked. He kissed the nape of her neck, his blond goatee tickling her almost unbearably.

"Probably had a bit too much booze," suggested one of Loch's bald-headed friends.

"Or not enough!" guffawed the other, aggressively slapping his companion on the shoulder.

Emma — Emmeline — looked around her. She was in her apartment… No, wait, that was silly. She lived with Loch in his house; there was no way he'd ever let her move out on her own. And no way she'd ever want to. Leave Loch? It was too frightening to even consider. No, this place must belong to one of Loch's friends. That made sense. He liked to take her along to parties — to show her off, and to enjoy the pleasures of her company.

But then, why did it all seem so familiar — the battered couch, the big comfortable-looking red chair, even down to the layout of living room, kitchen and doors leading off? Emmeline didn't want to think about it; it made her head hurt. Seeking distraction, she turned back to Loch and cradled his head in her hands, pulling him into a heated and energetic embrace.

As Emmeline pressed herself against Loch, heedless of the wanton stares of the two bald men and anyone else who might be in the room (Emmeline thought that there were others hovering about, but she knew that if they were important, Loch would introduce them), she was remotely aware of the door opening. Suddenly, Loch was pushing her forcefully away from him. She tried to resist — she wanted to stay lost in the oblivion of his attentions forever if she could — but Loch was too strong. She looked down at her weak and too-skinny body as he manhandled her onto the couch. She remembered when she used to exercise regularly, when she was younger, but Loch liked his girls thin and not too muscled, and she wanted very badly to please him in every possible way.

"Where are you going?" she whined at his retreating back. She hoped she sounded pathetic enough that Loch would drop whatever he was planning to do and come back to her.

But Lochlann had already walked across the room to stand next to the person who had come through the door. Emmeline couldn't see the figure very well, but it was a woman, and she knew instinctively that the woman was extraordinarily beautiful. Emmeline had always thought that she was Loch's ideal, but with a hollow sinking sensation, she realised that this newcomer was everything she was and so much more. And without even responding, the suave man with the eyepatch had glided out the door, his perfect woman — far, far more perfect than Emmeline — on his arm. She knew with dread certainty that he would not be coming back.

"No!" wailed Emmeline. She started to get up from the couch to run after Loch, to beg him not to do this to her.

But one of the bald men had moved over to sit beside her and he now held her down with his massive paw-like hands. "It's okay, love," he said. "Lochlann said we can have you now that he's done with you."

The second bald man sat on Emmeline's other side, and started running his hand up her bare thigh. "We've both wanted you for a long time," he drooled. His friend was trailing one hand through her flaxen hair.

Emmeline sank back into the couch, prepared to let them do what they liked with her. If this was what Loch wanted, who was she to question his decisions? She closed her eyes as one of the men began tugging up the bottom of her tank top. It didn't matter anymore... Loch was done with her... Loch had found somebody else... Life wasn't worth living... Wasn't. Worth. Living.

Emmeline screamed, momentarily startling the two thugs, who had already become lost in their lust. She took the opportunity to spring off the couch, and ran for the kitchen area. Before either of the men — their senses dulled by alcohol and who knew what else — could react, she had thrown open a drawer. Emmeline wasn't sure how, but she knew that this was where she could find what she was looking for.

She turned back to the men, brandishing the largest and sharpest knife she could find. "If Loch doesn't want me," she sobbed, tears running down her cheeks and staining her mascara, "then my life isn't worth living!"

"Woah, come on, we're only havin' a bit of fun," protested one of the bald men. The other just sat there and watched the drama unfold, a feral grin slashing across his features.

Emmeline shook her head and held the knife out in front of her, the blade aimed at her heart. "I need Loch," she moaned wretchedly. "I'm nothing without him. He's my whole life. Now I just want to… to…" Her words choked off as her eyes widened in grim determination.

"Look, you're not even strong enough to do what you're tryin' to do! You're just gonna hurt yourself and damage those hot little —"

"Shut up!" Emmeline screamed. "Just shut up!" And she clutched the handle of the knife as tightly as she could, so tightly that she could feel her knuckles turning white.

(And Emma sat on the low stone wall behind the Bungalow and clutched the hand of a man with brown hair until her knuckles turned white.)

"What?" she said aloud, to no one in particular.

"I thought you wanted us to shut up," chortled the bald man who had been silent to this point, content merely to leer at her.

"I said you're not strong enough to do that," the other told her, ignoring his friend.

"But I am," she replied. "I exercise all the time. I do aerobics, I weight train, I…"

"You?" laughed one of the men. "Lochlann likes you weak and docile. He'd never let you work out."

(Emma jogged through the downtown night, heedless of the drunken revellers spilling down from George Street. Out of the corner of her eye, she saw a figure emerge from a solid grey wall.)

These thoughts… were they hers? Where were they coming from? If it was possible, her grip on the knife actually intensified.

(Emma walked through the darkened void, a figure trailing behind her, their hands firmly clasped like a lifeline through the shadows.)

Without Emmeline even realising it, the arm holding the blade drooped downward. She was staring into the middle distance, trying to make sense of the images darting through her mind. Emmeline — Emma — stifled a sniffle, and the knife clattered to the floor.

In an instant, the man who had been keeping up a dialogue with her was on his feet, pounding across the room to her. Had he seen the smile of wonderment which lit up Emma's face, he might have been stopped dead in his tracks. "This is all a fiction…" she murmured, and knew it was true. As the bald man loomed over her, she let fly a torrid punch which caught him right under his massive chin.

As if Emma had put her fist through a stained-glass window, the man shattered into a hundred multicoloured pieces. All around her, the room shattered into a thousand more. Emma was screaming again, but now it was a scream of triumph.

*　　*　　*

At some point, the world around Emma stopped fragmenting and cascading. She put out a hand and steadied herself on the kitchen counter, breathing in deep lungfuls of air, not caring about how muggy and cloying it tasted. Her mind was a whirl of images and feelings and impressions, many of them dredged up from the most unpleasant corners of her past.

"I will never be that person again," she told herself fervently. "Never again."

After a while, Emma forced herself to calm down. She bent over and, with some deliberation, picked up the knife she had nearly used to pierce her own breast. She replaced it in its drawer, which she slammed shut with a satisfying thud.

The apartment was as it had been — there were no bald men, no Lochlann, no other vaguely-glimpsed onlookers. Nor was there any trace of their presence, because of course they had never been there in the first place. Even the shadow of the *Gan Aireachtáil* had all but vanished, leaving behind just a few gossamer tracings of blackness which withered and blew away like dust as Emma watched.

A *Gan Aireachtáil*... Emma had no idea how one of the Unnoticed would come to be standing in her apartment, nor why it would remain long enough for its terrible shadow to linger in its wake. She almost didn't even want to hazard a guess. She just considered herself fortunate at having survived the deleterious effects the shadow had on a mortal being — and at not having had to face the far more deadly proposition of encountering the *Gan Aireachtáil* itself.

She just wished she could remember how she had managed to emerge from darkness, to sunder the terrible illusions which had nearly caused her to take her own life...

Emma sighed, and decided that maybe spending the rest of the night away from her apartment was the wiser course of action after all. She didn't know what she would do if the Unnoticed returned; in the morning she could try to find somebody who might be able to help her. She went back into her room, flipping on the light switch as she entered, and sat on the bed, trying to catch her breath before she packed up a few essentials and got out of there.

Something on the floor, half-buried beneath a pile of dirty laundry, caught a stray beam of light from the bare bulb overhead and reflected it back at her.

Curious as to what it might be — an extra twonie certainly wouldn't go astray — Emma knelt down on the floor and crawled over to the heap of clothes, being careful not to take her eyes off the glimmering object. She reached forward, and plucked out a small grey disc, run through with veins of vivid red. Where had this...?

Emma gasped, her hand covering her mouth as memories flooded back to her.

"Christopher!"

* * *

Beyond the deep wells of his unconsciousness, Christopher could hear somebody calling his name. He wanted to resist the impulse to respond — feared the thought of life flooding back into his crippled and tortured body, because excruciating pain would surely follow swiftly in its wake — but the lure of the waking world was too strong, and he felt awareness floating back to the surface of his mind.

Something was licking Christopher's left cheek.

"What...?" he groaned, trying to open his eyes. To his surprise, he managed to drag both of them about halfway open and felt far less pain in the process than he had been anticipating.

He realised that he was lying on his back on something soft and yielding. A small white figure hovered to one side of him; though his vision was still swimming, he could not help but notice the small pink tongue which was lapping at his face. He was momentarily overwhelmed by a strange, musty smell, but it was so pervasive that he quickly found himself able to let it wash over him, to the point that he could almost ignore it.

"Welcome back, Christopher Prescott," said a mellifluous voice from somewhere beside his head. "You are Christopher Prescott, aren't you?"

"Yeah," Christopher wheezed. His ribs still hurt from the pounding they had taken, but he could have sworn that the bald men had cracked at least two or three before he'd blacked out, and the blaze of pain he would have expected was oddly — though pleasantly — absent. Instead, it merely felt as if he'd pulled a couple of muscles in his chest, and even that sensation was fading with every breath he took.

"We thought as much," the voice said proudly. "My late uncle Osric spoke very highly of you."

"Osric?" mumbled Christopher. "The only Osric I know was my cat and I..." It was roughly then that realisation struck.

Despite the discomfort it sent surging through his frame, Christopher rolled over and stared at his partner in conversation.

She was a small, lithe cat with fur the colour of newly fallen snow. Two clear blue eyes matched his startled stare with one of supreme confidence. The cat was seated at the edge of the water bed Christopher now realised he had been lying on, her thin tail flicking gently behind it.

"Cats can talk," he finally muttered after a prolonged silence.

The white cat nodded. "You're a quick study. Good. You might survive your ordeal yet."

Christopher shifted his head and saw another feline sitting to his left. This cat was also white, but his fur was dirtier and thinned in patches. He was rather larger than the speaker — mostly thanks to a well-fed belly which dangled pendulously as he stood on all four paws regarding Christopher — and his eyes were different colours, one blue and one green. Christopher assumed that this was the creature that had been licking him; now the feline seemed confused as to whether he should continue to attend to Christopher in this way, or lie down on one of the pillows and have a nap. After a few seconds, he opted for the nap.

"Cats can talk," Christopher repeated to himself.

The thinner cat rolled her eyes. "Oh dear, and here I thought we were making progress."

"No no," Christopher assured her, carefully pulling himself up onto his elbows. "I've seen enough crazy stuff the past little while that it's not such a shock to my system anymore. It's just that this is the first time it's actually made sense. Cats can talk… it's obvious when you think about it."

"Oh," said the cat. "You are a bright one. I can see why Osric took a shine to you. I'm Spot, by the way." Christopher's eyes scanned her unblemished white fur and his face crinkled in consternation (and not a little bemusement). The cat seemed to sigh knowingly, as if she'd been through this before. "Look, I'm a cat," she told him. "I don't choose my name, my name chooses me. Anyway, there used to be a black patch in the middle of my forehead. I grew out of it. Honest."

"If you say so," Christopher grinned. "I guess I have you to thank for the fact that I'm not squealing in agony right now."

Spot chuckled. "You have us to thank for the fact that you didn't bleed to death on the ground. But yes, Frankenstein there has a talent for healing. That's why he was licking you when you woke up; he was working on the injuries to your face."

It was like that ointment Emma had given him, mused Christopher, but a hundred times more potent and not nearly as smelly. Then another thought occurred to him. "How did you manage to heal up my broken bones and cracked ribs — all the internal injuries?"

Spot regarded him for a moment and then murmured, "Don't ask. Just be glad you were asleep while Frank was doing it."

Christopher nodded, noting that that probably explained the taste of pureed chicken in the back of his throat. He tried to follow Spot's advice and not dwell on it.

"Look," said Spot, "why don't you lie back and let Frankenstein finish his work. You'll feel a million times better, I'm sure. We can chat a bit while he clues up."

Christopher concurred and rested his head on one of the big puffy pillows next to the dormant feline. "Oh, nudge him to wake him up, will you?" asked Spot, clearly content to remain where she had settled herself on the bed. "The poor guy is as deaf as a board." Christopher reached over and scratched Frankenstein behind one ear. After a moment, the big cat opened an eye, and Christopher gestured apologetically towards his battered face.

Frank grunted sleepily, but grudgingly rose to his feet and padded over to Christopher to resume his ministrations. Christopher tried to ignore the ticklish feeling this produced.

"So how did you find me?" Christopher asked Spot.

"How do cats find anything?" came the reply. "We smelled you. Or, more precisely, my friend Gadget smelled the *ungadh* you'd coated your thigh with. We always get it confused with tunafish, it's really irritating. But anyway, once Gadget had found you, she knew something was up — it's not often that you find a Clansfolk bleeding to death in the middle of nowhere at the height of a summer's day. So Gadget called in one of the elders, wild-eyed fellow name of Faraday, and Faraday recognised you from Osric's descriptions."

"Hang on... the stray I took in two years ago is important in... kitty society?"

Spot made a noise that could have been a splutter — or maybe a furball, Christopher wasn't sure which. Either way, her voice sounded more than a little affronted. "'Important' is an understatement. And I'll ignore that 'kitty' crack. Actually, Osric was half-brother to the First Minister, the lady Rose."

"Huh? First Minister?"

"Right. The First Minister of the Cabinet of the People of the Cat. You can see why I prefer to stick with 'First Minister' — saying the word 'of' too many times in a row makes my whiskers twitch uncontrollably."

"I'm confused," admitted Christopher. "I thought the Five Clans were all... well... people."

"Excuse me?" said Spot indignantly. She brought one paw up to lick it, and Christopher noticed that her claws were protruding slightly. "Tell me you're not suggesting cats aren't people."

"Sorry," he said hastily. He started to lean forward placatingly, only to elicit an impatient growl from Frankenstein, who was still trying to finish his work. "I wasn't trying to offend you, Spot. What I meant was that I thought everyone in the Five Clans was human."

"Dear me, no. What would be the fun in that? You have more to learn about our world than I thought. Look, Christopher, we're a society that can perform feats of illusion and conjuration and prestidigitation that normal folks think are utterly impossible. Do you really believe that everyone in the Five Clans conforms to your notion of 'human'? No, some of us are human, and a few are lycanthropes — half-breeds, I guess you could call them." Christopher remembered the strange, scaly figure accompanying the red-haired woman. A feeling of despair washed over him as he recalled the loss of the *fios* stone he had been carrying with such care. "But the best of us are... well, look at me," Spot had continued loftily.

"Spot," Christopher interjected, "when your, um, friends found me, did they happen to also find a..."

"A *fios* stone?" Spot finished for him. "No. We could smell its presence in your pocket, but it was nowhere to be found when we got to you. And we searched, believe me — the last thing we need is one of those getting into the hands of the normals. No offense."

"Damn," Christopher murmured, crestfallen.

"Damn indeed," agreed Spot. Her voice was suddenly very sober. "In all honesty, Christopher, we really need to know what you were doing with that *fios* stone in the first place."

Frankenstein, meanwhile, ran his rough tongue over the edge of Christopher's jaw for a final time. Then he snorted proudly, nodded once in Spot's direction, and collapsed back onto a pillow, already fast asleep.

"Let's go, Christopher," purred Spot. "You have to come with me."

"Where to?" Christopher asked warily, tentatively sitting himself up. He was amazed at the improvement in his condition — he was still sore in places, and his eyes felt a bit red and raw, but otherwise it was as if his beating at the hands of the two bald men was nothing but a bad dream.

"Just upstairs," Spot told him. "You have an audience with the First Minister herself."

Chapter Eleven
In which there is an Audience with the First Minister

Christopher wasn't sure whether he should feel awe, trepidation or simple bemusement at Spot's statement, but finally nodded and rose unsteadily to his feet.

For the first time, he took a careful look at the room in which he had awoken. It appeared to be a bedroom of reasonable size, but one which lacked many of the usual trappings. For instance, while the bed upon which he had lain was large and very comfortable, there was no bureau, and the open closet door revealed a space devoid of clothes but instead piled to a depth of a foot or so with blankets. There were two windows in the room, and both had window sills which seemed unusually wide. Most amusingly, the floor was littered with scratching posts, toy mice and other uniquely feline accoutrements. Christopher's friend Ollie had once tried to rear an entire litter of kittens, in addition to the four cats he and his family already owned, and Christopher realised that the overpowering odour he had sensed upon awakening was much the same as the smell which had infested Ollie's house for those months.

"This is your room, is it?" Christopher asked Spot, who had hopped down from the bed to walk in front of him, her tail held proudly erect.

"Excuse me?" said Spot, looking back at him.

"You cats — this is where you sleep?"

Spot emitted a rough approximation of a chuckle. "No, Christopher," she replied. "This isn't our room. This is our house." She trotted over to a door opposite the closet and slid smoothly through a small swinging hatch set close to its base. Christopher was relegated to turning the handle, and he heard the hinges squeal as the door swung open, suggesting that the traditional human means of egress was rarely employed.

Christopher emerged into a wide hallway, with several other doors leading off of it. He noticed that all of these doors had a built-in hatch as well. Cats were everywhere — entering and exiting rooms, chatting lazily with other felines, grooming themselves or, most often, simply dozing on one of the many pillows, blankets and other sundry perches made available for that very purpose. One small black-and-white kitten was even sprawled out in the middle of a potted fern in a corner of the hallway, his lean belly coated in a layer of rich brown soil. Spot tutted at the sight. "Nigel's going to have that plant killed before the week is through," she muttered resignedly.

The door opposite the one through which Christopher had passed was slightly ajar, and through it he could see a sizeable bathroom, which appeared to contain all the expected amenities. But the toilet seat was completely missing, and the taps in both the faucet and the bathtub were running at a steady if not torrid pace. He watched as a tawny Siamese sauntered into the bathroom, his head swivelling back and forth between the sink and the toilet. After a brief hesitation, the cat finally sprang up onto the counter and began lapping greedily at the water spilling from the tap.

"Hang on," said Christopher, still trying to come to grips with all of this. "You cats occupy the entire house?"

"Oh yes," answered Spot. "We've owned the place since the last human First Minister passed away in... oh, 1926 or thereabouts. Sorry I can't be more exact with my dates — 1926 seems a lot further away for a cat than it does for your species."

"So not all of the Clans are run by the... appropriate animal?" Christopher asked. "No, wait, they can't be — the

People of the Caribou had a human First Minister…" And he tried unsuccessfully to push the image of Eachna's shrivelled corpse to the back of his mind.

"No, it's mostly humans who run the show. They've got numbers on their side — only a precious few of us cats have embraced the mysteries of the Five Clans. Besides, can you seriously imagine an entire Clan run by a great shaggy thing with antlers, or a big dumb bird which nearly got itself made extinct? Cats are, of course, the only one of the five totem animals with the wherewithal to handle their own affairs."

"Of course," agreed Christopher, smiling placatingly. "But this is a big house… nobody's noticed that no humans live here?"

Spot shook her head. "It's amazing what your species willingly chooses to ignore, Christopher. And anyway, we have cleaning staff and delivery people come by pretty often — the few humans who do suspect that something's amiss probably assume one of them lives here."

By now the cat had led Christopher some distance down the hall, to the bottom of an elegant spiral staircase. A mammoth ginger tabby was sound asleep upon the balustrade. Spot nimbly hopped up the steps, taking them two at a time, and Christopher had to hurry to keep up.

The staircase brought them to a small antechamber, where a number of cats stood milling about, speaking in voices too low for Christopher to hear. The room was largely empty but for a set of gauzy drapes at the opposite end, beyond which he thought he could see a door.

As he tried to get a better view, the crowd parted to allow two of their number through to confront Spot and Christopher. Both of the newcomers were relatively small cats — one all black but for a small snowy tuft under his chin, one striped orange and white — but they somehow exuded an imposing aura which left no question that Christopher had best watch his step around them.

"Christopher, these are Shadow and Esther — they're the lady Rose's most trusted advisers and bodyguards."

"Hi," said Christopher, waving half-heartedly. He noticed both cats tense momentarily at the abrupt gesture, their ears bending aggressively backward. He made a mental note to be very deliberate with his actions as long as he remained in their presence.

"He is the one Osric adopted?" Shadow asked Spot. Christopher got the impression that the cat's choice of phrasing was not remotely accidental.

"This is Christopher Prescott, yes."

Esther spat noisily. "Silly human names. To think that they choose them themselves, rather than learning their true name in the proper fashion. No wonder they make such a mess of everything they do."

"You know that Rose believes that Christopher has already discovered his true name, Esther," chided Spot. "He just doesn't realise it yet."

"Um, am I meant to understand what this is all about?" Christopher inquired, feeling rather as if he'd missed a memo somewhere along the way.

"When you understand, you will understand," Shadow told him in a low, penetrating tone.

"Oh. Thanks." Christopher couldn't help but roll his eyes at the byzantine statement.

"Frankenstein has healed his injuries?" Esther queried.

"Well enough, anyway," Spot confirmed. "Is Rose ready to see him?"

"Yes," Esther said primly. Her yellow eyes glared at Christopher. "Be on your best behaviour, human. You're about to meet the leader of the People of the Cat. Don't give us reason to use our claws and our fangs."

Spot rubbed gently against Christopher's leg. "He's been well-mannered so far, Esther. I don't see any reason why that should change in Rose's presence." She looked up at Christopher as she twined herself around his right shoe.

"Don't use baby talk, don't steal her crunchies, and don't touch her hind paws. Beyond that, you should be fine." And with that, Spot settled herself on the floor and starting washing behind her small triangular ears.

"I'll do my best." Christopher looked disdainfully down at his attire: he was still dressed in the clothes he had worn downtown, now frayed and torn, and laden with sweat, grime and blood. "Um, do I look decent enough to appear in front of your First Minister?"

Spot looked up from where she was preening her tail. "Christopher, we're cats. Unless you think you can grow a healthy coat of fur in the next twenty seconds, it's all going to look the same to us. You can go in naked for all Rose will care."

"Enough of this idle chitchat," Shadow intoned in a voice which suggested urgency more than irritation. "Come with us, Christopher Prescott." As one, Shadow and Esther turned. The small sea of felines fell back again to allow them through, followed by a wary and tentative Christopher.

The two guardcats led him beyond the gauzy drapes to a thick wooden door. Esther slipped through the now-familiar hatchway into the room beyond, while Shadow stopped and looked up at Christopher. "Enter," he said simply, nodding towards the door.

Feeling surprisingly timorous, Christopher twisted the brass doorknob and eased open the door, careful not to inadvertently swing it into Shadow or any of the many cats packed into the antechamber. More curtains were hung on the other side of the door, and Christopher picked his way through these, followed by Shadow. Christopher noticed that while the black cat did not dog his heels, he remained within easy springing distance.

Christopher found himself emerging into a lavish penthouse suite. It was dominated by a gargantuan white four-poster bed placed in its very centre. About this were arrayed various blankets and cushions; Christopher was bewildered to note that one of the blankets was set out with bowlfuls of fresh fruit and vegetables, baskets of thickly-sliced bread, and a covered metal platter from which the succulent scent of roast chicken was undulating seductively. Christopher's stomach rumbled tortuously, and he became instantly aware that while the cats had healed most of his wounds, he had still not eaten in about twenty-four hours.

Farther away from the bed, against one wall, sat an old couch whose upholstery seemed to have been systematically shredded over an extensive period of time. Just beyond this, a corner of the room was sectioned off with velvet drapes — perhaps that was where the kitty litter was kept, Christopher pondered, more soberly than he would have thought possible just hours before.

Most impressive about the penthouse, however, were the walls and ceiling, all of which were made of glass. In the daytime, this would have afforded an amazing panorama of the entire neighbourhood. Or perhaps the view would be limited to sprawling grounds, Christopher thought: if this house was as palatial as it seemed from the inside, he doubted it sat right on the sidewalk. Indeed, through the darkness Christopher thought he could make out tall trees swaying, concealing the house from easy view from the street. It concerned him a bit that it was already nighttime — he had clearly been unconscious for more than half a day.

The glass forming the walls was divided into regular panels, some of which could swing open to allow a flow of air through the room. Christopher expected that, normally, this would create a rather pleasantly cool atmosphere in the penthouse, but tonight the air which blew into the room was sluggish and heavy, the humidity clearly having done nothing but worsen during his convalescence. To account for this, electric fans had been set up at intervals all around the room, and these were furiously trying to combat the interminable midsummer heat.

As Christopher cast a curious — and rather impressed — eye over his surroundings, his attention was drawn to Esther, who was standing next to the four-poster bed. As Shadow entered the room behind him, the red cat seized the corner of the bed curtain facing Christopher in her mouth and tugged it open with practised ease.

Seated on the bed, her two front paws extended before her in a quietly majestic pose, was a black cat with more than a hint of Persian in her features. Unlike Shadow, this cat's fur was fluffy, and tinged with a hint of brown. Most striking were her eyes: they glowed an almost preternatural green-gold, and radiated with a rare and precious wisdom.

"This is Christopher Prescott, my lady Rose," Shadow said formally. He remained sitting on his haunches to Christopher's rear. "He is the human whose coming Osric foretold."

The black cat on the bed blinked a couple of times and regarded Christopher intently. He felt as if she was attempting to peer straight through to his very soul. "Greetings, Christopher Prescott," Rose finally said, in a proud and noble voice. "Our half-brother Osric spoke very highly of you and your ladyfriend. We rather expected that when we met, she would be accompanying you."

Christopher realised that Rose was referring to Cecily: she had played almost as much of a role in Osric's care as himself. "She, ah… she's not my ladyfriend anymore," he said softly.

"Our condolences," Rose offered demurely, not appearing remotely thrown by the revelation. "It hardly matters, though. You are the one Osric thought important." She shook her head absently. "Oh, but where are our manners? Please, seat yourself and enjoy the food. You must be famished after your recent trials."

Christopher nodded, a little sheepishly. He tried to maintain his sense of decorum and sidle patiently over to the veritable feast, but in retrospect he feared he had virtually raced over to the blanket on the floor and begun gobbling up the delectable offerings. It wasn't long before the smouldering chicken had been revealed and he was cutting vigorously away at it with the provided cutlery. Truth be told, he was half-tempted to just tear into it with his hands. He figured that cats probably wouldn't mind such a breach of human etiquette, but finally came to the conclusion that he shouldn't take any chances at offending the First Minister, especially not with Esther and Shadow subtly but unmistakably watching his every move. Nonetheless, the food tasted heavenly, and Christopher barely concerned himself with the question of who had actually prepared it. As he wolfed down the nourishment, Rose waited patiently on the bed, purring softly.

"I apologise for being so ravenous, First Minister," Christopher finally said, as he tried to lick grease off his fingers. "It's just that you were right, it's been a rough couple of days, and I can't remember the last time I had something to eat."

"Don't fret, Christopher," Rose told him pleasantly. "In return for the services you rendered unto Osric, it is our pleasure."

"I'm a little confused, actually," Christopher mused as he snatched up a handkerchief and began dabbing at his chin. "How do you know Osric?"

"We told you, Christopher, he is our half-brother."

"Right, but we named him Osric — Cecily and I. I don't know what he was called before we found him, but I doubt it was that!"

Esther sniffed contemptuously. Rose, however, merely shook her head lightly. "No, Christopher, Osric was called Osric because that was his name. We cats seek out our true names; we do not assume meaningless sobriquets based purely on personal preference or random whim. And it is by our true names that we permit humans to refer to us."

"So you're saying that it's sheer coincidence that my girlf — um, ex-girlfriend — studies English lit and has a major Shakespeare fixation. That he would've ended up being called Osric even if... I don't know... if she'd been studying the air-speed velocity of the unladen swallow."

Rose said nothing, but just sat there and purred a while longer.

"Fine," Christopher sighed resignedly. "Answer me this, then, please: how could Osric have told you about me when we never let him outside the front door for the entire eight months he lived with me?"

Another snort from Esther. "We cats have methods of communication which are… non-verbal," Rose told him.

"And not the kind that involves obsessively sniffing your friend's posterior, like certain other forms of four-legged life I could mention," Esther added, earning a slightly reproving look from Rose.

"Suffice it to say, Christopher, that Osric was in frequent contact with us. And what he reported was both very wonderful and very frightening."

"Before you were brought here," Shadow noted, "there was some debate as to whether we should return you to the bloom of health, or finish the job that your attackers had begun."

Christopher noticed that Rose wasn't purring any longer.

"Osric," she said, "had a gift — one that was not uncommon in times gone by, but has become exceedingly rare in these declining days. Osric was… we believe 'prescient' is the closest word that you would understand, Christopher."

"He could see the future?"

Rose appeared to consider this, then nodded. "Of a fashion. Although it was an ability which had more to do with his sense of smell than with his eyesight.

"Osric had been living in the wilds somewhere on the Southside Hills when one day, some years ago, he caught scent of something… unexpected on the breeze. To this point, his predictions had been of relatively mundane events — a developing ploy by the People of the Serpent to advantage themselves in the manufacture of certain unguents, a park patrolman who would soon accidentally find his way past the enchantments which protect the Wandering Parliament, that sort of thing. Important, but scarcely earthshattering."

"And this was different?"

"This was the end of our world."

"Oh."

"Osric thought that what he was foretelling was the utter destruction of our culture — and whether something new and better would emerge from its ashes, or whether that would be the final end of the Five Clans, he could not say. But he set about pursuing the source of this wind of change."

"And did he find it?"

"He did." And Christopher realised that Rose's eyes — and, for that matter, those of Esther and Shadow — were fixed directly upon him.

"Me?" Christopher exclaimed, flabbergasted.

"You, Christopher Prescott. A normal man, ignorant of our ways and customs and history. And yet, here you are. In the past twenty-four hours, you've travelled the Ways, you've attended the Wandering Parliament, you've even touched the unfathomable potency of a *fios* stone. You've uncovered the massacre of the Cabinet of the People of the Caribou. And, if our nose is still as reliable as it was in our youth, we believe you've visited places of old power which have been forgotten even by many of our kin. Your presence here, Christopher, could be the harbinger of our doom — the final stage of our descent into obscurity, or perhaps something far more cataclysmic."

"But I'm only here by accident," Christopher protested. "I was just trying to do someone a favour."

"And yet, it is as Osric foretold."

"Now the question becomes, what do we do with you?" Shadow murmured.

Christopher felt his mouth go dry; was it his imagination, or was there now a distinct tint of malice in the cats' glowing eyes?

"Look, there's something I don't understand," he spluttered, as much to redirect the conversation as anything else. "Actually, there are several somethings I don't understand, but here's one of them. You've said it here, First Minister, and I've heard it mentioned before, that this… hidden society of yours is waning. I guess that's the right word, anyway. But what do you mean by that?"

Rose answered his question with one of her own. "How many people were at last night's Wandering Parliament, Christopher?"

"I don't know… maybe a couple of hundred?"

"Some of the elders speak of a time, before the Wandering Parliament was located at Bowring Park, when it would be teeming with a thousand or more of our kind. And this was an age in which the Parliament met with far greater frequency than in the modern day. Now, two hundred Clansfolk is seen as a successful crowd. Talents which once were commonplace reveal themselves no more. Crucial knowledge is lost, to the point that even the memory of us having once held that knowledge slips away. Whole avenues of the Ways grow dark and fade through disuse and neglect, and as remembrances of how things once were pass so utterly from the public consciousness that even the city begins to forget."

Rose hung her head forlornly, her tail drooping in kind. "In days past, Christopher, even you normal folk adhered to a degree of belief in what you would term 'magic'. Superstition was still rampant among your kind; folk tales were lent a credibility which, while perhaps not acknowledged aloud, nonetheless ran deep in the hearts of many. That environment allowed our kind to thrive, meant that we did not have to maintain nearly the level of secrecy and even paranoia which now grips the Five Clans."

Esther picked up the thread. "Once, long ago, the Wandering Parliament was held in a clearing in the woods off what is now Thorburn Road. No charms and glamours were needed to keep the prying eyes of your people away; the merest hint of a rumour of eldritch goings-on was more than enough. And those bold few who did venture out to spy on us were, to a man, ideal candidates for acceptance into our society. Those days, however, are long dead. And, inevitably, so too will the Five Clans die. Perhaps sooner than we would once have believed."

"Six Clans," Christopher muttered, almost under his breath.

"Pardon?" said Rose.

"The ones who murdered the People of the Caribou at the Wandering Parliament — they were called the Sixth Clan."

Shadow emitted a low, sinister hiss. Esther bared her fangs angrily. "Don't be ridiculous, idiot human," she snorted. "There are only five Clans. There have always only been five Clans."

Christopher shrugged. "Hey, I'm just repeating what I was told."

Rose had remained silent throughout this exchange; she simply sat there with her eyes narrowed, appraising Christopher. Finally, she spoke in a voice that rang out through the room like a bell on a clear day. "Christopher may not be incorrect."

"What?" spat Esther, incredulously. Shadow arched his back, but did not challenge the First Minister.

"There have been whispers in the dark, little Esther..." Rose said distantly. "Events which have gone unexplained... A sixth Clan... Could it truly be possible?"

"I think the human merely seeks to stave off his own death," Esther sneered. Then she seemed to realise the temerity of her words. "Assuming that is the course of action which has been decided upon, of course, my lady."

"No, Esther," replied Rose, sounding suddenly very old and weary. "Christopher Prescott shall not die. Not by feline paws, anyway."

"Oh, thank god," Christopher sighed with relief.

"Do you know why the Cabinet of the People of the Caribou — and in particular, Eachna, our counterpart amongst them — were slaughtered, Christopher?"

Christopher wondered if he should relate his journey to the Forgotten Cemetery, but thought that perhaps it was best not to go into details about that experience. The parting words of the sepulchral voice in that place still sent morbid shivers through his bones. "I... I think it was to get something called the Waykey. Whatever that is."

"The *eochair*," confirmed Rose. "Or, more precisely, an *eochair*. There are five Waykeys, you see, Christopher. Or five pieces to the single Waykey; the distinction is effectively irrelevant."

"And what does a... a Waykey do, exactly?"

"You have travelled the Ways, Christopher. You know that in doing so, you are riding the memory of the land, of the city."

Christopher nodded — he'd gathered that much from Emma (and oh, how he wished she were here with him now). "Right," he said. "That's how you can get from place to place so quickly."

"But the Ways are more than just a means of transportation, Christopher. Think about it — access to the collective, ancient consciousness of an entire city. All the thoughts and deeds of every person who lives there and has ever lived there. The Ways could be used to obtain immeasurable power, both in our world and in yours."

Christopher nodded, his mind filling with hazy but irrefutable suspicions as to what Rose was alluding. "These Waykeys prevent that, then?" he asked.

"The *eochair* control the Ways and what can be done within them, Christopher. Aeons past, one *eochair* was given to each Clan for safekeeping, to ensure that no one faction could gain supremacy over the Ways, and thereby over the rest of our kind."

"And now somebody has stolen the Waykey belonging to the People of the Caribou."

"So we had deduced. And we cannot fathom why anybody would steal one of the *eochair* without having designs on procuring the rest as well."

"Oh. Crap." Christopher's face suddenly wrinkled in consternation. "But what does all this have to do with me? I mean, yeah, I found the bodies of the People of the Caribou, but I certainly didn't have any involvement in their deaths!"

"No," agreed Rose. "You possess neither the knowledge nor the means to wreak the devastation that befell the People of the Caribou. It is on this point that we are most confused as well. Osric believed that you would be involved in events of such import, but he could not say in what fashion." Abruptly, the black cat rose to her feet. "So we will involve you in a manner which we do understand."

"Excuse me?" said Christopher, taken aback.

Rose glared at him, her green-gold eyes boring into his own. "Step towards us, Christopher Prescott. Step towards us and bow your head to within our reach."

Shadow darted forward suddenly, clearly alarmed. "Rose, what do you think you're doing?" Christopher could tell from the male's tone that he strongly suspected exactly what Rose's intentions were — but Christopher himself had not the slightest clue.

"What we must, Shadow," Rose sighed. "Christopher Prescott will bear the *eochair* belonging to the People of the Cat."

Esther seethed in fury. "This is madness! He is a human, and not even a member of our Clan! Is the rest of the Cabinet in agreement on this matter?"

Rose drew herself up, making herself look as large and as imperious as possible. "The feline elders will do as we tell them, Esther. The human members of the Cabinet, for their part, will continue to be content with what little political power we permit them. This is what must occur."

Christopher found himself agreeing with Esther. "But why? Why me? What good will that do?"

"If some power — be it a sixth Clan or some other person or group — is truly determined to obtain the five Waykeys, what better place to hide ours than with a non-aligned human? Even better, a human with only the most tenuous and recent of connections with our society?"

"But can we trust him, First Minister?" Shadow asked. He was keeping his voice level, but it was clear that he had grave misgivings about this plan. "How do we know he won't just seek out this unknown enemy and hand over the *eochair* for some ephemeral reward?"

Rose sighed. "Osric described you as loyal, honest and dependable, Christopher. In short, as a good person, especially in these dismal days of selfishness, deceit and untrustworthiness. And, much though we appreciate the advice of the elders and of Shadow and Esther, there has never been anyone whose opinion we respected more than our half-brother. This is why we know you will not betray us.

"But we are no fool. We know that even the most reliable of judges can be misled, and that even the best of men can be corrupted and seduced. And we do not embark upon this plan without according it much consideration.

"The Waykey is — for want of a description you will better understand, Christopher — a magical essence. It can be kept in many different vessels; like Eachna of the People of the Caribou, we have chosen to store that essence within ourself, and so it shall be with you. But we will not merely impart the *eochair* unto your mortal spirit, Christopher: we will bind it there, such that if it should ever be removed without our approval, the act will mean your own death." Rose's eyes slid over to regard Shadow. "Is this acceptable to you?"

Shadow stared back at her in silence for several seconds. "Yes, my lady."

"Esther?"

"If you truly believe that this is the best course of action, First Minister… I have faith in your judgment." But the ginger feline had her ears bent low, and it was clear that she was anything but happy.

"Thank you, little one," Rose said kindly. She turned back to Christopher. "Now, human. Approach. The hour grows late, and we grow weary."

Christopher breathed deeply, scarcely able to fathom what he had gotten himself into now. But he could tell that Rose was determined to execute her plan, dubious though it seemed to him, and he guessed that she would not refrain from forcing him to comply if he resisted. His heart beating urgently within his breast, Christopher stepped forward and lowered his head until it was almost level with the black cat's own.

Before Christopher knew what was happening, Rose lunged forward and sank her fangs deep into the side of his neck. He tried to cry out in shock and in pain, but the sound died in his throat. His flesh burned where Rose had penetrated it, as though it had been set alight.

And, indeed, Christopher could suddenly see a bright, hazy, red-orange glow out of the corner of his eye. It flared and flickered just like flame, but no heat emanated from it — instead, it felt as though the fire was surging into his veins, turning his blood molten and searing through his entire body. A manic pounding started to echo through his skull. He placed his hands on the bed to steady himself, and they curled into tight fists as he tried to hang on to consciousness. His vision grew indistinct as the brilliant light show washed across his field of view, making him feel as if he were swimming in an ocean of red and orange.

Distantly, Christopher could hear words — or at least something approximating words, though no human larynx could produce such sounds. They were a mix of shrill whines, guttural yowls, and sibilant hisses, but chanted with a rhythm and complexity that left no doubt that they contained meaning. As the invocation reached a feverish crescendo, Christopher felt his heart beat faster and faster, to the point that he feared it might burst.

And then it was over: Rose slid her fangs out of his flesh and stepped back. Christopher collapsed onto the bed. His first instinct was to rub the spot on his neck where the black cat had punctured his skin, and he was astonished — though not quite as much as he once would have been — to find that not even the slightest of lacerations remained to indicate anything had happened at all. In fact, Christopher no longer suffered any pain or discomfort whatsoever from the ritual. On the contrary, all his body's energy was replenished — and then some — as if he had slept for a week and only just awoken.

Christopher looked over at Rose, and immediately saw a marked change in the black cat's demeanour. She had curled up into a ball, her eyes had lost their dazzling lustre, and she was struggling just to keep them open. "Go now, Christopher Prescott," she mumbled sleepily. "It is best if we don't meet again. At least... not until all of this is over, one way or... another." And with that, Rose fell into a deep repose.

Shadow hopped gently up onto the bed next to Christopher. "Leave now," he said, softly but firmly. "Spot will escort you outside."

Christopher nodded and, with a last look back at the dormant Rose, stepped through the curtains and out the door.

* * *

Donovan Chase strolled through the humid air of the newly fallen night. He was whistling a mournful old lullaby which had last been heard in St John's on that summer day in 1892 when much of the city core had burned to the ground. Chase's lone concession to the stifling mugginess was the removal of his jacket, which was now slung over his arm, brushing against his walking stick as he moved along.

Eventually, he reached a white picket fence which gave onto a short flagstone path. Chase turned and followed it to a charming two-storey bed and breakfast, its clapboard freshly painted in blue and brown. Wind chimes hanging next to the front door tinkled pleasantly as he entered.

Chase nodded politely to his landlady, who was sitting in the front room watching television, but did not stop to chat. Instead, he made directly for the stairs, mounted them, and passed through the door at the very end of the second-floor hallway.

The room beyond was small but attractively furnished in a manner which skilfully trod the line between tastefulness and kitsch. There was a chest of drawers, surmounted by a tall oval mirror, a narrow desk, and a bed which Chase thought looked quite cozy, though he had yet to find an opportunity to test this theory. Nonetheless, he sank gratefully onto it, dropping his jacket and walking stick atop the pillow to his left.

Chase had endured a fruitless day, following up a variety of potential leads without success as he tried to locate the whereabouts of the red-headed Aislinn. He had also kept his ears open for a hint of the fates of Christopher Prescott or Emma Rawlin, but nothing had reached him. No word had yet come from Reggie Barter, either, though he was confident that his recalcitrant cohort was not sparing any effort on his behalf. Fortunately, Chase still had at least one more approach to take.

He reached over and slipped his hand into his jacket, fumbling around in one of the interior pockets. After a moment, he found what he was looking for, and smiled.

"Now, let's see what you can tell me," he whispered as he withdrew the *fios* stone Christopher Prescott had so accommodatingly, and inadvertently, provided for him.

Chapter Twelve
In which certain Inquiries bear Strange Fruit

The cats milling about the antechamber leading to the First Minister's room were far more subdued as Christopher passed through the doorway. He noticed that neither Shadow nor Esther followed him out of the penthouse, and hoped fervently that the strain of what had just happened had done nothing worse than exhaust Rose.

"So how did that go?" came a tentative voice by his feet. Christopher looked down to see Spot there, staring anxiously up at him.

"I'm... not sure," Christopher admitted.

"Well, look at it this way: at least you're not going to be part of the Meat Puree Surprise that's on the menu tomorrow." Christopher couldn't tell if Spot was joking, or if she was actually aware that Rose had contemplated doing away with him, rather than risk the apocalypse he may or may not bring down upon them — however the hell he was supposed to manage that.

Christopher mopped his brow and shook his head, trying to rid himself of the small pinpricks of red and orange light which were still exploding intermittently in front of his eyes. "Can you just show me the way out, please, Spot?" he asked. "You guys have done an awful lot for me —" maybe more than I would have preferred, he thought ruefully "— but I really shouldn't impose any longer. I'll be on my way."

Spot nodded and she and Christopher threaded their way through the crowd of felines, most of whom were eyeing the human suspiciously. They went back down the spiral staircase, walked along the hall, and then descended another set of steps, a wide and imposing main staircase which bridged the first and second storeys of the house. This led to a circular foyer from which a number of doors radiated — all marked by the now-ubiquitous cat hatchway, Christopher noted idly. Straight ahead of them was a long porch with a spacious closet on one side and coathooks and benches on the other. The front door was at its far end.

"There you go," said Spot. "Just follow the path through the trees to the gate and you'll be off."

"Thanks, Spot. And thank Frankenstein, too, for fixing me up."

The cat sat on her back paws and shrugged. "Aw, old Frank's probably already forgotten he did anything other than eat, sleep and take a leak today. But you're welcome all the same. Where will you go now?"

Christopher shrugged. "I can't go back to my regular life, not yet. I still have a woman to find, even if the reason I wanted to find her has become kind of moot now. But I should still explain, I think."

"And I'm assuming that whatever you and the lady Rose talked about is going to get in the way of normalcy, too? Not that I'm prying or anything — that's between you and her."

Christopher smiled half-heartedly. "Yeah, probably. I guess so. I suppose we'll have to see. But I figure the only person — well, the only human — I really know in your world is a girl who helped me last night, so the sensible plan is probably to track her down again."

"Sure. Good luck with it all, Christopher. Maybe I'll see you sometime when I'm out on the prowl."

Christopher felt like he should be shaking Spot's hand, but settled for a scratch behind the ears and a gentle tug on her slender tail. "Bye, Spot."

And with that, Christopher departed through the door of the cats' home. The only thought now running through his mind was of finding Emma — he was praying that she'd have some idea about what was going on, and what he should do next.

*   *   *

Emma had to figure out what was going on, and what she should do next. "Think think think," she told herself as she sat on her bed. The disc she had received in the aftermath of Christopher's duel with Lochlann was still clenched between her thumb and forefinger, as though it might help focus her mind.

"Okay, let's break this down into manageable chunks. Exhibit A: there was a *Gan Aireachtáil* in my apartment. Exhibit B: I've learned that the First Minister of the People of the Caribou has been murdered and their *eochair* stolen. Exhibit C: the culprits were apparently some heretofore unknown sixth Clan. Exhibit A might be completely unrelated to Exhibits B and C… but my faith in coincidence isn't that strong.

"Analysis: Well, I don't think anybody wants to assassinate me, so the *Gan Aireachtáil* must have been tracking somebody. But the only other person who's been here in ages was Christopher last night. Christopher's not a member of the Five Clans, he's not even unaffiliated, he just stumbled into this world when he found… Oh, shit. Exhibit D: the *fios* stone. And maybe the *fios* stone contains information related to the murder of the People of the Caribou.

"Conclusion: The *Gan Aireachtáil* is tracking the *fios* stone Christopher's mysterious red-headed woman dropped. Could be it's working for this Sixth Clan, though that's not necessarily the case. So maybe Red dropped it on purpose — got rid of it to throw the Unnoticed off the track, so that she wouldn't be another one of their never-remembered victims. Or maybe she really did just lose it, and doesn't even know that she was being stalked. In which case, she may still be in danger. Which means I'd better get hold of her.

"Complication: Based on what Christopher told me, Red is probably a member of the People of the Serpent, and I'm hardly on a first-name basis with any of them." Well, except for a few from back in the Lochlann days, Emma thought to herself morosely; she knew she certainly didn't want to speak with any of them again. "So who do I know who might be able to help me out?" She tapped her fingers restlessly against the bedsheets as she feverishly wracked her brain.

The image of Donovan Chase swam briefly through her thoughts, but she dismissed it immediately. Not only had she no idea where he might be now, but she found herself consumed with mistrust for the man. She could not shake the impression that Chase had been anything but forthcoming with herself and Christopher, and wondered what games the little man was really playing.

The dull glistening of the disc in her hand caught Emma's attention once more, stirring unpleasant memories of the appalling illusion conjured by the shadow of the *Gan Aireachtáil* — and of life with Lochlann as it had actually been, which was scarcely better. But it also gave her an idea.

It was true that virtually none of the people she had consorted with during her time in Lochlann's thrall were worth remembering, let alone worth renewing an acquaintance with. But, as with all rules, there had been exceptions to this one, and the most notable had been a man in late middle age who was confined to a wheelchair. He went by the name of Turlach, of the People of the Codfish, yet seemed very well-connected with folk from outside of his own Clan.

Turlach had been solemn and pensive while most of Lochlann's crowd was rambunctious and boisterous, and he had never treated Emma with the derision and cruelty evinced by others. Indeed, some of his quietly-delivered words of encouragement had helped to fan the flames of Emma's independence, and imbued in her the conviction to leave Lochlann behind forever. And on that last day before she had escaped her tortured existence, he alone had somehow sensed what she was planning, and he had slipped her…

"Where is it?" Emma gasped. She stuck the disc into her pocket and dove over to the boxes which were jammed into a corner of the small room, half-buried beneath clothes and books. Contained therein were the few remnants of her life with Lochlann (and the even fewer remnants of her life before that). Heedless of the anarchy she was wreaking in her already messy room, Emma started pulling things out of the boxes and tossing them over her shoulder.

Finally, towards the bottom of one box, she found a cracked cassette case. Once it had held a Tori Amos tape she had long since worn out; now it contained just a yellowing slip of folded paper. Emma yanked the case open, pulled out the note and prised the two halves apart to reveal a seven-digit number written in a shaky hand. Then she ran to the living room and grabbed the phone out of its cradle, dialling as she plunked herself into the old red chair.

Five rings trilled out unanswered, and Emma's spirits started to flag: maybe Turlach had moved since her time with Lochlann, maybe he had even passed away. But just as she was anticipating the sixth ring, there came the sound of a receiver being carefully lifted up and a voice — worn and diffident but still laced with a distantly familiar tinge of kindliness — said, "Who is this, please?"

"Turlach? Is that you? This is… god, you probably won't even remember me, but my name is Emma Rawlin. We knew each other… what seems like a very long time ago."

"Emma Rawlin… Emma Rawlin… blonde girl, too thin, used to spend all her time perched on Lochlann's knee?"

Emma coughed. "Well, I'm not too thin anymore, and you'd catch me dead sooner than on that bastard's knee. But yes, Turlach, it's me. And I really need your help again."

"Well, my dear, I'm not sure that I ever did lend you much assistance in the past, but I could never refuse such a charming young creature as yourself. It's not a man again, is it?"

"No. Actually, it's not really even my problem, Turlach, it's... well, it's kind of hard to explain. But I think it could have ramifications across the Five Clans."

There was a moment of silence at the other end of the line. Then: "In that case, Emma, perhaps we had better meet in person. This sounds grave indeed."

* * *

The street outside Donovan Chase's bed and breakfast was devoid of pedestrians, and any normal person strolling past the edifice wouldn't have noticed anything amiss at any rate. Those rare few whose senses were attuned to more unusual wavelengths, however, would have perceived a sudden and violent eruption of energy through the open window of a room at one end of the building.

Within, Donovan Chase was perched upon his bed, one hand crooked in a warding gesture which had barely saved his life moments before. In the other hand, he still clutched the *fios* stone, although it was now quite warm to the touch and blazed with an angry colour which was very slowly fading back to the stone's original state.

"Mmmm, fine then," he muttered petulantly, addressing the mysterious artefact. "You are too tough a nut to crack. But fortunately, not all of your secrets are concealed within." And he gently traced the mysterious bell-shaped symbol and eyed the word *Goibniu* which surmounted it — a word whose significance he knew all too well.

Chase sat there motionless for some time before he finally rose from the bed, abruptly full of animation once more. He tugged his jacket back on and slipped the *fios* stone into a pocket again.

He was about to leave his room when his eyes fell on the open window. The humidity had built throughout the Saturday, and the lowering cloud cover was becoming more and more ominous in the heavens above; it was only a matter of time before the inevitable storm broke upon the city. Chase was not a man who took unnecessary chances, even when it came to something as mundane as the weather, and so he crossed the little room to shut the window.

As he did so, his eyes looked out onto the empty street below. Not even a solitary car was to be seen…

But wait: that wasn't true, he realised. Just at the edge of his vision, where this road intersected another, he caught the barest hint of movement. Wary, Chase leaned forward out of the window to get a better view. No, there was nothing there — perhaps he was imagining things, or perhaps the gentle swaying of a tree in the hot, burgeoning breeze had played tricks on his perception.

No! There it was again — a little closer this time. His eyes kept sliding off the source of the movement, so he focussed his mind and stared intently at the seemingly barren sidewalk.

There was definitely a man there. Plain, undistinguished, he was making no effort to keep out of Chase's sight yet still managed to lose himself in the darknesses between the pools of light cast by the streetlamps.

His emotionless eyes were fixed upon Donovan Chase.

"*Gan Aireachtáil*," Chase gasped, taken uncharacteristically aback. And there was no doubt in his mind that the creature was coming for him.

*   *   *

Christopher had quickly recognised the part of town in which he found himself after leaving the cats' residence. He was actually not too far from the downtown, in an area that in times past had come to be known as the land "above the hill". The heart of old St John's had been ravaged by more than one inferno over the decades, though it had been the one in 1892 which echoed most resoundingly down through history. It was in the wake of the Great Fire of 1846, however, that many of the city's merchants had chosen to cease the practise of living over their shops on Water Street and Duckworth Street, and had instead built stately new homes on the brow of the gentle slope which lead inexorably to St John's Harbour. Many of these houses were now more than a century old, and every time he passed through this neighbourhood, Christopher could feel the weight of the ages: there was a sense here of neglected glory, of an almost Ozymandian relegation of old power, money and influence to the dust of seasons.

Fortunately, this meant that he was not a great distance away from Emma's apartment: a walk of no more than half an hour, and all of that downhill. And despite the heady pace and disconcerting events of the past day, he at least found his energy reinvigorated thanks to his experiences in the house of the cats.

It was perhaps because of this resurgence of vitality that Christopher realised, after ten minutes or so, that he was being followed. Part of him just wanted to keep walking — to let whoever was behind him do whatever they wanted. It would probably just blend in with all the other agonies he had suffered already. But he knew that Rose had invested him with no small degree of responsibility and, even though he had not asked for that burden, he felt obliged to do what he could to live up to it.

He stopped abruptly, and heard footsteps behind him shuffle awkwardly before they fell silent. "Is there anything I can do for you?" Christopher asked over his shoulder.

He looked back then, to see a man in late middle age standing in the shadows of a tall fence at the edge of the sidewalk. His greying hair and beard were long and unkempt, and his face, while not grimy, was dusky in a manner which implied an existence filled with hardships. The man's clothes were old and frayed, but the same could not be said for the spirit glimmering in his beady brown eyes. If first impressions were anything to go by, Christopher thought, this was a man who had suffered some of the worst life could throw at him, but still soldiered on. He looked like an old wolf who had endured many harsh winters while others of his pack had fallen to the snows.

"Sorry," said the man after a moment's hesitation. One of his teeth was chipped, and so he whistled slightly when spoke. "Din't mean to startle ye, young feller. 'Sjust I saw ye comin' outta the cats' place, an' ye piqued me int'rest as dey say. Not too many normals come an' go from dere."

"Spend a lot of time watching their house, do you?" Christopher queried sceptically.

The man shrugged. "More 'n I ought, prolly. But it fills de day, and I likes cats anyways. If'n I had me time back, I prolly would've joined der Clan back when. De People o' de Great Auk din't suit me as well as I'd 'oped. But den, all de Clans've 'ad more downs den ups dese days."

"So I've heard it said," Christopher acknowledged. "Although the cats seem to be doing pretty well for themselves."

Again the man shrugged. "Dey're cats, ain't dey? Cats'll always get by, it's in der nature. Plus I've 'eard it said dat der First Min'ster's a cat an' lives dere. An' trust me, b'y, de Five Clans're just like yer reg'lar politics — de guys at de top enjoys der position. It's de little folks dat do de suffrin'. I'm Faolan, by de way." He extended his hand. Christopher clasped it, and endured a strong, vigorous, and rather painful handshake.

"Christopher Prescott," he returned. "Is it that obvious that I'm, um, a normal?"

Faolan chuckled. "Oh, ye don't get to be my age widdout knowin' how to tell de Clansfolk from de rest o' de world, Christopher. Ye must be a pretty important normal if ye found welcome wid de cats, dough."

Christopher shook his head. "No, I'm nobody important, Faolan. Just a guy who got mixed up in your world by complete accident. To be honest with you, I'm still trying to come to grips with it all."

The older man nodded. "I unnerstand. Dese days, most o' de Clansfolk're born dat way — recruits used to be a big parta our society, but not no more. But dere's still a few, an' more often den not, for a goodly while dey feels exactly de way I expect you do right now, specially if all ye've been talkin' to is de high-falutin' types. Look, 'ave ye got a few minutes? I c'n take ye to where ye can meet a few reg'lar joes like meself. Maybe it'll give you a clearer perspective on our life."

Christopher mulled over the offer. He really wanted to track down Emma — and he figured that she qualified as a "regular joe" in this mysterious and enchanted society. But then again, he supposed that there was no true urgency to find her — at least, not so much that he couldn't spare a brief moment of time — and maybe it wouldn't be such a bad idea to get a broader view of the Five Clans. Most of all, though, he recognised another opportunity to ask after the red-haired woman.

"Sure," he finally said to Faolan with a grateful smile. "Lead the way."

* * *

Turlach lived on the top floor of a rickety three-storey building in the Quidi Vidi Village district of St John's, a rustic fishing community swallowed up but never consumed by the larger city. The house had seen better days: the yellowish paint was chipped and faded, and a window shutter on the second floor dangled forlornly above the weed-choked lawn below. The structure loomed over the narrow roadway as if it might collapse onto the asphalt at any minute.

It had been a simple matter to travel the Ways to the vicinity of Turlach's residence: just minutes away was idyllic and historic Quidi Vidi Lake. While the shores of the pond were all but deserted now — Emma had seen only two or three strollers in the distance, ambling along through the humid night air — in just a couple of weeks they would be teeming with crowds from all over the Avalon Peninsula as the lake played host to the annual running of the Royal St John's Regatta. The Regatta had been a fixture on the city calendar for nearly two centuries according to the history books; Emma had heard whispers amongst the Clansfolk that their kind had been running contests on the pond for much, much longer. Either way, the annual pilgrimage to Quidi Vidi Lake had created an enormously strong impression on the memory of the city, and the Ways to the area were amongst the brightest and most rapid she had experienced.

Emma entered the decrepit house. Passing a rickety elevator concealed behind a locked gate in the foyer, she ascended a precarious set of stairs to Turlach's floor. On the way, she urgently tried to compose in her head the clearest, most concise way to tell the man what she had learned and experienced over the past twenty-four hours. She was, after all, a virtual stranger to him. Even if he had heard of the massacre of the People of the Caribou at the Wandering Parliament — and Emma had little doubt that word would have spread far and wide by now — he had no reason to believe her wild tales. Frankly, were she in his position, Emma wasn't sure that she'd lend herself much credence either.

She finally reached the apex of the long climb and found herself confronted with a thin-looking wooden door. She rapped thrice upon it, and after a few seconds heard a shuffling inside. The door opened to reveal the wheelchair-bound form of Turlach, looking much as she remembered him. He was a pale and sickly fellow, his legs invisible beneath a thick plaid blanket despite the incredible mugginess of the evening. His brown hair was thin and sparse; he seemed to have abandoned any hope of it ever covering his scalp again. His chin was weak and shuddered spasmodically, but a familiar smile — tender and welcoming if tinged with perennial nervousness — touched Turlach's thin, pallid lips.

"Well, don't just stand there," he said, wheeling backward. "Come in, come in. I've made us a pot of tea."

Emma returned the smile and entered his lodgings, softly shutting the door behind herself. Turlach's floor seemed to consist of just a handful of small rooms. A kitchen was located to her left, and down a short hallway ahead of her were two sealed doors — one of them presumably Turlach's sleeping quarters. She followed Turlach down the hall, which turned left and lead into a living room; she noticed that entrance could also be gained by passing directly through the kitchen. A small dining table sat in the corner of the room nearest this second entrance, while the rest was furnished with just a couple of chairs and an end table. Plants — clearly suffering from the extremity of the recent weather — depended from hooks all over the room, casting a vague smell of rot into the air. Through the foliage, Emma could see unusual paintings hanging on the walls. They were in some sort of abstract post-modern style, and she tried not to look too closely at them because although she couldn't perceive any definite shapes, she found them vaguely unsettling all the same. There was a window in the wall to her left, but the long drapes were drawn shut against the night, making the little room feel dark and claustrophobic.

Turlach bade Emma sit in one of the chairs while he trundled over to the dining table. Upon it sat a tea service, the tarnished silver kettle steaming quietly.

"Milk? Sugar?" he asked her mildly.

"Yes, please, to both, and make it three lumps if you don't mind." She didn't really want the tea — her anxiety and the weather hardly made a hot beverage desirable — but she decided it was best to be polite.

"Of course, of course. Sweet tea for such a sweet girl." Turlach began fussing over the cups. As he poured and stirred, he called back, "Why don't you tell me more about what's brought you here?"

Emma sighed. "You're probably gonna think I'm nuts."

Turlach laughed lightly. "Emma, I used to participate in the rather sordid lifestyle of your former lover. I have seen madness, and survived to tell of it." He trundled over to face her, carefully clutching two cups without letting his fingers break the surface of her tea. Emma quickly took her mug from him and sipped the beverage. It was competently-brewed and she could even detect a hint of something that tasted like almonds, but it was definitely not what she wanted to be drinking now. She mimed taking bigger mouthfuls for the sake of appearances. "My dear, I hardly think anything you can tell me will come as much of a shock," Turlach was saying.

"Okay," she said dubiously, setting her mug on the end table. "Here goes, then." Turlach relaxed back into his ancient wheelchair to listen.

"I found a guy on the street last night. A regular guy, not a member of the Five Clans or an unaffiliated like me. But somehow, he had come into possession of a *fios* stone."

The man in the wheelchair swallowed down a cough. "Unusual," he croaked. "But it is not unheard of for one of our relics to accidentally pass into the hands of the mundanes — even something as powerful as a *fios* stone."

"Sure. He said it had been dropped by some lady and he wanted to get it back to her. I was heading to the Wandering Parliament anyway, so I figured I'd give him a hand — he seemed nice and genuine enough. But… I'm guessing you heard what happened at the Parliament?"

Turlach nodded. "A great tragedy," he murmured through pursed lips.

"Right, well, here's where things get complicated. To make a long story short, I found out — or at least, I think I found out — who murdered the People of the Caribou."

Turlach's eyes widened a little. "Now that is news to me. I had heard that the killers were still unidentified."

Emma shrugged. "Yeah, well, I haven't had a chance to tell anybody about it, and I doubt that any of the people who were with me have, either."

"And who was you with?" Turlach asked, draining the last of his tea.

Emma waved her hand dismissively — the last subject she wanted to bring up was the oh-so-enigmatic Donovan Chase. "Doesn't matter," she said. "I'm trying to keep this brief, remember. Anyway, I finally got back to my apartment today... and I'd had a visitor. A *Gan Aireachtáil*."

Turlach's eyebrows rose upon his forehead. "And yet you're here to tell the tale?"

"I got lucky, I suppose — it had already been and gone. Its shadow still lingered, but I... got through that."

"Then you have indeed enriched your spirit since the last time we met, Emma. I'm proud of you. I take it the *Gan Aireachtáil* was in search of the *fios* stone?"

"That's what I figure, yeah." Emma sipped again at her tea, wondering if she might distract Turlach long enough to drain the steaming mug into one of his big, leafy plants.

"And where is the *fios* stone now?"

"I guess Christopher still has it. I doubt he'd let it get away from him, he really wants to give it back to the lady who lost it."

Turlach considered this. "How noble. Christopher... who, did you say?"

Emma furrowed her brow. "I didn't. Um, Prescott is his last name, I think."

"And where is this Christopher Prescott now?"

"I don't know — we got split up early this morning. To be honest with you, I'm a little surprised that he hasn't tried to contact me yet. A little worried too, actually."

"But you think that he will try to contact you?"

"Yeah, probably, I don't know how he's going to return the stone otherwise. Hey, listen, why the sudden interest in Christopher? You haven't even asked me why the People of the Caribou were killed, or who did it. That's what's important here."

Turlach ran a finger along his thin, dry lips. "Oh, I'm afraid I already know the answers to those questions, my dear."

Emma shrank back a little in her chair. "But you said nobody knew yet…"

"A puzzle, isn't it?" Turlach agreed. Emma noticed his eyes dart to the cup of tea sitting on the end table next to her. She thought again of the unexpected taste of almonds, and a dawning horror started to creep across her mind. She was suddenly very grateful that, from where he sat, Turlach could not see how little of the tea she'd actually drunk. "In fact, my dear, I already know that those poor souls had to die so that their *eochair* could fall into the hands of the Sixth Clan."

Suddenly, Emma became aware of a faint sound coming from all around her — a chittering sound that made her shiver despite herself. Nonetheless, she forced herself to listen to Turlach as he continued to speak.

"You see, I was once entrusted with the care of the *eochair* belonging to my Clan, the formerly-mighty People of the Codfish, now brought so appallingly low." He shook his head. "In fact, I possessed two — because what very few Clansfolk know is that once, some years past when my Clan was the most powerful of the Five, the People of the Great Auk bartered their *eochair* to us in exchange for certain… favours. The People of the Great Auk have been teetering on the edge of oblivion for so long, you see, that they had been reduced to trading away their most potent treasures. Sad." He wiggled the fingers of his left hand at Emma, and she noticed he wore two rings, set with simply-cut but very beautiful stones: one a vibrant green, the other a vivid blue. If she looked closely enough, she thought she could see patterns moving about within the stones. But her attention was constantly diverted by the strange noises in the room, which seemed to be growing louder. Something was very wrong here, but she had to stay and hear Turlach out — the information he was imparting was too valuable to miss.

"So now," the man in the wheelchair continued, "only two Waykeys remain at large. And that is why we brought you here, Emma. Once we learned of your rather suspicious questions and company at the Wandering Parliament, we knew that you would be invaluable to our cause."

Now Emma was truly confused. "But... but I came here of my own volition. I telephoned you!"

Turlach shook his head, as if he was talking to a very small, very stupid child. "No, my dear. Why do you think that, tonight of all nights, you recalled a poor, ugly old cripple you had utterly dismissed from your memories? For that matter, why do you think Lochlann tolerated my unappealing presence for all those years?"

Emma stifled a gasp. "You're a thoughtcaster."

Turlach arched an eyebrow. "Ah, still reasoning with a clear head, I see. A thoughtcaster I am indeed — one of a precious few the last century has produced. So you see why Lochlann adored me. In the presence of a person suitably intoxicated or otherwise of diminished capacity, I could tie strings around their mind and have them dancing like a puppet after just an hour or two. It made Lochlann's little games so much easier to play. But even from miles away, with enough concentration, I can still implant impressions in the mind of someone I have encountered before."

She nodded in grim understanding. "Enough to dredge up an old memory, and steer someone to consider a certain course of action." The chittering sound now seemed to be burrowing into Emma's brain; she didn't know how much more of this she could stand. Then something else occurred to her, and she was barely able to keep her jaw from dropping at the realisation. "And enough to suppress what I learned at the Parliament, to lure me here with the promise of discovering it all over again."

"Quite. So you see, I was most pleased when my phone rang and your melodious voice emanated from my receiver."

Emma shook her head disgustedly. "Mindrape," she spat. "And why? Why are the People of the Codfish helping this... this Sixth Clan, whatever it is?"

Turlach tutted. "Perhaps I have given you the wrong impression. You see, while it is true that I was, until recently, a member of the People of the Codfish, that is no longer the case. That Clan is obsolete. Its time has passed — as it has for all the Five Clans, truly. I received... a better offer."

Suddenly, shapes erupted all around Emma: from the hanging plants, from behind the paintings, from the ceiling tiles and up through the carpeted floor.

They were bugs. Hundreds, if not thousands, of writhing, swarming, undulating bugs.

"Now I have joined the People of the Insect!" Turlach roared, as the black horde closed in.

Chapter Thirteen
In which glasses clink at the Matthew's Rest

For just a moment, Emma felt as though she were a small child again, shivering beneath the bed covers as some bogeyman — real or imagined — cavorted around her.

But only for a moment.

With a cry — not of fear, but of rage — Emma grabbed the nearly-full mug of steaming tea off the end table and hurled its contents at Turlach. He threw his hands up to protect himself, but too late — he had expected Emma to be quiescent by now, suffering the effects of whatever he had slipped into her drink or simply cowering in terror as the creeping army of bugs swarmed around her. The hot tea caught him full in the face and chest, and he went toppling backward out of his wheelchair, shrieking pitiably. The old metal vehicle crashed noisily onto its side.

Without pausing for so much as a breath, Emma tore out of her chair, just as a crawling wall of insects rose over the back like a surging black tidal wave. As she passed Turlach's writhing, mewling form, she saw that the blanket which had concealed his legs had fallen to one side.

What was uncovered was not remotely human.

From the thighs down, Turlach's legs were thin and grey, jointed far too many times and covered in coarse fur which excreted a noxious-smelling pus. He had no feet to speak of —

just small sets of claws which snatched at the air, seemingly of their own volition. They were, simply put, the legs of a bug.

Turlach caught Emma's look, even as she went streaking by him. "You see, Emma? There are advantages in joining the Sixth Clan!" And as he vanished out of her peripheral vision, she could hear the sound of rending, blistering flesh.

Emma crossed the living room in an instant. She briefly considered taking a shortcut through the kitchen, but a quick glance through the archway which led therein immediately put this idea out of her mind. Insects were boiling out of the kitchen cupboards, had pushed open the stove door, were even bubbling up out of the sink drain.

Instead, she headed back the way she had come in, down the small hallway. But as she reached the right-angled turn where the two closed doors were located, she realised that the one directly in front of her had creaked partly open. In the darkness beyond, she could see that the air was alive with a tempest of buzzing bugs. They seemed to recognise that she was coming towards them in the very same moment. The whirling mass suddenly erupted out of the doorway. Worse yet, the insects in the kitchen appeared to have deduced her plan of escape and were emerging from the archway closest to the door out of the apartment.

Reacting almost on instinct, Emma reached for the only other means of egress: the remaining sealed door, which lay to her left. She desperately wrenched at the knob.

Though she had hoped she might be proved wrong, she was hardly surprised to find it locked.

Like most people who were indoctrinated into the culture of the Clansfolk, rather than being born to Five Clans parents, Emma did not possess inherent talents like Turlach's thought-casting. But she had not been lax in picking up what skills she could, and her life with Lochlann had exposed her to certain abilities frowned upon in more polite company. One of these was now her only hope of surviving more than a few seconds longer.

Keeping her hand pressed tightly against the doorknob, Emma concentrated with all her might on releasing the lock. Usually, this exercise took patience — even simple locks needed the application of several seconds' calm and consideration. But Emma didn't have several seconds — already the droning in the air was becoming almost intolerable — and so she channelled all her will power into the lock, demanding that it pop open for her.

And then the door was swinging inward. Emma swooned, just for an instant, as a backlash of power rushed through her brain, but she forced herself to dive into the room beyond and shut the door behind her as forcefully as she could.

Kneeling on the floor, Emma allowed herself exactly three seconds to catch her breath. Already, insects were creeping through the spaces between the door and its frame, and she could feel a massive weight pressing against the thin wood.

She looked around herself quickly, trying to absorb as much information as possible in such a short amount of time. This room was virtually empty. A desk shoved into a corner next to the lone, bare window, one of its legs tilted at a dramatic angle, suggested that this might once have been employed as Turlach's study. Now he seemed to use it only as a dumping ground for the last fragments of his human existence: stacked upon the desk were a photo album, some yellowing correspondence, and a few meaningless trinkets and knickknacks. In a cardboard box pushed up against the desk Emma could see a pile of trousers, shorts and underwear — none of which the metamorphosing Turlach would need now, she knew. But Emma could spot nothing that would help her leave this place alive. Rising to her feet, she began stomping furiously at insects as they appeared from under the door, but she knew that such efforts could only delay the inevitable, and for a desperately short time at that.

Wait! Had she seen...? Emma turned to regard the desk again. Then, with narrowing eyes, she dove over to it, reappraising the junk which lay in a clutter upon its surface. She ignored the old letters and the photo album, instead letting her eyes rove through the jumble of mementos.

Emma smiled coldly as she snatched up an old, beat-up box of matches. Its label was faded, but she could still make out the image of a woman with improbably gigantic breasts gesturing salaciously. Half-expecting the worst, Emma shook the box nervously, and breathed a sigh of tremendous relief as she heard a faint rustling from within. She popped it open and saw three lonely red-headed matches.

"Emma!" Turlach's voice called from out in the hallway. His formerly kindly tones were distorted, both by his evident mania and, thought Emma, something even more obscene. "You can't escape us, Emma. You will become like us, whether you want to or not… but life will be so much easier for you if you do it willingly!" Emma thought she could hear Turlach dragging himself along the hallway — it seemed his new insectoid legs weren't actually any more mobile than his human ones had been, but perhaps that was because his transformation was not yet complete.

"Go to hell, Turlach," Emma shouted defiantly. "And here's something to help you get there!" She plucked the first match out of the box, striking it emphatically. It flared into incandescent life as the scent of brimstone assailed her nostrils. With grim satisfaction, she touched the match to the frail wood at the bottom of the door, and watched as it immediately caught light. The fire lapped at the insects which were trying to push into the room, and these were quickly reduced to smouldering ash.

Emma wasted no time, though — she lit the other two matches and set the room ablaze in opposite corners, then tossed the box into the blossoming flames. Already, a wave of heat was rolling through the little chamber, one far more dry and intense than the moist humidity already present there. Emma nodded curtly at her handiwork, even as she covered her mouth against the acrid smoke filling the room.

And then the handle of the burning door began, slowly but inexorably, to turn.

"Time for the mad getaway," Emma told herself, feeling her gut wrench. She only prayed that she'd assessed the layout of Turlach's lodgings properly.

She went immediately to the window, a square pane of glass about three feet on a side. She cursed as she realised that it was permanently sealed — but then she thought again and shrugged, knowing that this really didn't matter anyway. Emma moved back over to the desk and grabbed another of Turlach's kitschy heirlooms — a statuette of a particularly ugly and disproportioned dog, carved out of dark, solid wood — and hurled it at the window. The glass shattered on impact, and she could hear the shards raining down upon the ground far below.

The fires were already kissing the plaster ceiling and slowly advancing along the hardwood floor as she stood in front of the aperture where the window had been. Emma looked down. She let out an uneasy breath she didn't realise she'd been holding as she saw, one floor below, the dangling shutter she'd noticed on her way here.

Behind her, the door suddenly flew open, revealing that the corridor beyond was already awash with flame. Hundreds of insects lay curled up, dead or dying, in the sea of fire, but thousands more still crept along the walls or hung in the air, chittering angrily.

And in their centre was Turlach. Or, more precisely, the creature that had once been Turlach.

He was still crouched on the floor, his useless legs trailing behind him. But now the parts of him that had been human — his face, chest and midsection — were hideously changed. His skin seemed to be melting away, dripping off him and over the remains of his shirt like ice cream left out in the sun. Between the undulating strings of flesh and tissue, Emma could see something that looked like an oversized, underdeveloped insect — huge multifaceted eyes, small twitching antennae, and hideously quivering mandibles, but all slightly ill-defined and immature in appearance. It was as if some crazed sculptor had set about carving the likeness of a man-sized bug, but abandoned his project before its completion. Emma was reminded of Jeff Goldblum's metamorphosis in *The Fly* in the worst possible way.

Turlach was flailing about, trying to stamp out the flames with the stumpy, clawed remains of his arms. But it was no use — the fire had caught too quickly, the brittle wood of the old house was feeding it too well. "This is your fault," he slavered in a voice that was becoming more and more inhuman. "My change… has come too soon. You'll regret this, child!"

"Gotta catch me first," Emma retorted, and vaulted through the window.

For the briefest of instants, all of Emma's worries fled from her mind as she fell through the sultry summer air. She could forget her troubles — the Unnoticed, the People of the Insect, the loss of three Waykeys into sinister hands, even Christopher's abrupt arrival (and equally sudden departure) from her life — and just enjoy the rush of the wind as she arced downward. Even the traumas which burdened her past were lifted from her shoulders in the sensation of virtual weightlessness.

But just as part of Emma felt like giving in to the serenity and letting gravity have its way, she suddenly stuck both arms out in front of herself, and grabbed onto the protruding shutter as she fell. For a moment it felt as though her fingers might slip on the edge of the thin wooden rectangle, but Emma gritted her teeth and hung on.

As she dangled there, swaying in midair, she was able to look through the second-floor window. The room beyond, like those above, was alive with moving insects — they seemed to notice her almost instantly, and quickly pressed themselves up against the glass. If anyone else was living in that house, Emma knew, the conflagration she had started was hardly their concern now.

Abruptly, there came the sound of groaning metal, and Emma felt the shutter shake alarmingly as its last remaining hinge began to prise itself loose from the house under the added encumbrance of her weight. She took a deep breath and adjusted her grip so that she was suspended from the bottom of the shutter rather than the top. She looked down momentarily: the drop was still significant, but now only about half of what she would have faced had she fallen straight down from the top-storey window. Emma gulped audibly as the shutter gave way, and she plummeted to the ground.

Bending her knees and bracing for the impact as best she could, Emma still felt a crippling shock scorch through her body as she hit the earth. She collapsed onto the grass and lay there insensate for several seconds, just trying to force herself to breathe. Her vision dimmed ominously, and she fought hard to stay conscious.

Then an unearthly screech above her shook her instantly back to her senses. Rolling onto her back, Emma glanced up to see that Turlach had flung himself out of the window and was falling straight down towards her. Just as it looked like he would slam directly on top of her, a hideous ripping sound filled the air. Giant, papery grey wings suddenly pushed out from Turlach's back, tearing through what was left of his shirt, and with a jerk of these new appendages, the hybrid creature's fall was arrested. He hung there, hovering in midair, those awful wings flapping noisily.

"There is no escape from the People of the Insect," Turlach wheezed. "We are everywhere!" And then he dove downward, his claws and mandibles outstretched, grasping towards Emma.

Out of the corner of her eye, Emma saw something bulky lying in the grass just a few feet to her right. Her gaze not flinching from Turlach, she flailed her arm out wildly, trying desperately to grab hold of whatever it was. Straining, she felt her fingers brush against it: the heavy wooden dog she had thrown through the window.

Almost without thinking, Emma grabbed the statuette and swung it mightily in front of herself, just as Turlach reached the climax of his descent. The wooden dog slammed with a sickening thud into the side of the man's head with a tremendous crack. The insectoid body was flung to one side, rolling violently across the ground and onto the street. Emma could see green ichor oozing from the cavity she had torn in the side of Turlach's face, and he lay on the ground, motionless.

For a moment, all was silent.

Then a droning cacophony arose above her head. Emma looked up to see a thick swarm of bugs emerging from the dense, dark-grey smoke rolling out of the shattered third-floor window. The insects seemed less focussed than before, but Emma knew it was matter of seconds until they spotted her and renewed their attack. There was no way she could fight a horde of bugs — she had to get out of here, return to the Ways and find help.

Hurling herself to her feet, Emma took off like a shot, stepping carefully around Turlach's body. But with improbable speed, the man's claw-like hand lashed out and snared Emma's ankle in a vice-like grip. "We... are... endless..." he whispered. "We... are... supreme!"

Before Turlach's tirade could continue, Emma aimed a savage kick at his arm with her free foot, forcing him to relinquish his hold. But even as she turned to run once more, she could hear Turlach stirring, injured but still very much alive. Bugs continued to pour out of the house, which was now visibly aflame, and she pushed her legs as fast as they would carry her, now more grateful than she could ever imagine for her late-night jogging routine.

After what felt like an eternity, Turlach's terrible home was just a memory behind her, and Emma finally found herself racing down the shimmering golden avenues of the Ways. The distant chittering of thousands upon thousands of insects faded mercifully into nothingness. As she ran, Emma reviewed her options and quickly came to the realisation that, with time clearly running out on the Five Clans, only one choice really remained open to her.

It was a recourse she had hoped she would never need to fall back on. But now that she remembered the essential piece of knowledge that Turlach had made her forget, it was all she had left.

*   *   *

Christopher was pleasantly surprised that Faolan actually led him in the direction he had originally been heading, descending towards the downtown core. Whereas Emma's apartment was located a little north of the centre of the area, however, Faolan kept to its more easterly outskirts, leading Christopher to an old stone building which seemed to date practically from the rebuilding of the downtown in the wake of the last Great Fire. Faolan lead Christopher around the side of the structure to a small laneway in the back.

Tucked away almost out of sight there behind a row of sickly bushes was a set of concrete steps leading down to an imposing oak door. Faolan rapped three times on the door, paused, then added two more beats at a slower pace than the original burst. "Little secret knock, just t'be on de safe side," he told Christopher with a wink as the door swung slowly open.

Christopher wasn't sure what to expect as he passed through the entrance — but it probably wasn't the old-time pub in which he found himself. He stood in a fairly long room, panelled in a deep, rich brown-red wood. Round tables sat in an erratic formation all around the tavern; these were made of a slightly more yellowish wood, as were the chairs which surrounded them. The bar, to his left, was carved from yet another type of wood, this one so dark as to be almost black. A phenomenal array of bottles and flasks, a myriad of different colours and shapes, sat upon narrow shelves behind the bar.

"Welcome to de Matthew's Rest," said Faolan with a sweep of his arm. "Established... oh, round abouts 1700, wasn't it, Feaver?"

The man behind the bar looked up from where he had been polishing its countertop with a worn old rag. He was a burly fellow nearly as broad as he was tall, and his face was practically buried behind a mop of long, curly black hair and an equally unruly beard. "Something like that, Faolan," he chuckled. "You know I never did have much luck remembering dates."

"No, nor much luck askin' for 'em in de first place," riposted Faolan with a wheezy but congenial laugh.

Christopher's brow creased with perplexity. "But this place can't have been open since 1700... this whole part of St John's was decimated in the Great Fire."

Faolan shrugged. "Well, de Matthew's Rest has more stayin' power den dat — it'll take more den a few licks o' flame t'bring dis place down."

Christopher decided, as he had now become accustomed to doing, that the best course of action was just to accept such statements at face value. He didn't even want to think what it meant that the building above, while certainly a century or so old, was nonetheless apparently far younger than the tavern housed in its cellar.

"C'n I buy ye a beer?" Faolan asked Christopher. The younger man appraised him tentatively, eyeing the shabby condition of Faolan's clothes and the man's generally rather destitute appearance. "Oh, I knows what yer thinkin'," he said with a shake of his head. "But yer normal money's no good 'ere, an' my tab'll hold fer a while longer, right, Feaver?"

The barman glowered at Faolan, but nodded reluctantly, setting his thick hair and beard bouncing rhythmically. "I suppose so, Faolan, for a while longer. The usual? Pint of Guinness?"

"But o' course. An' fer you, Christopher?"

Christopher had never really acquired a taste for beer — he could stomach it when he had to, but it was never his beverage of choice if there was another option. "Screwdriver?" he suggested with a shrug.

Faolan gave him a wry look. "Guinness'll put 'airs on yer chest. But, whatever wets yer whistle."

As their drinks were being prepared, Christopher described the owner of the missing *fios* stone in as much detail as he could offer. But to his heavy-hearted disappointment, neither Faolan nor Feaver appeared to recognise her. "I'll ask around for you, though," the barman offered, sliding their drinks across the counter to them. Christopher smiled his thanks as Faolan led him to a table tucked away in one corner. The pub's few other customers — three elderly men sitting in stony silence at one table, and a middle-aged man and woman chatting idly at another — eyed Christopher with some apprehension as they passed.

"'Tis a bloody shame," mumbled Faolan as they sank into their seats. He idly clinked his mug of beer heavily against Christopher's glass, and the other man briefly cringed for fear that both might shatter.

"What is?" Christopher asked, once it was apparent that both vessels would remain intact.

"T'see de Matthew so empty on a Saturday night. Dere was a time when dis place'd be packed to de gills, Christopher. But not no more." Faolan sighed heavily and seemed to retreat from the world as he guzzled the thick, dark beer.

As his companion sat in melancholy silence, Christopher took the opportunity to have a closer look at the pub. The walls, he noticed, were dotted with framed photographs, all depicting scenes from the tavern at various moments down through the years. A few were in colour — the most recent he could spot dated from about thirty years ago — but most were monochrome. A number of the pictures were so old that they had lost some of their original clarity, and were taking on that hazy, indistinct look Christopher had seen in history books.

He glanced up at the photo hung on the wall immediately next to his table. It certainly depicted the Matthew's Rest in a more crowded state than it could now claim. The pub appeared to be bursting at the seams with dozens of revellers, all laughing and smiling and knocking back frothing mugs of ale. A plate pinned below the picture read: "Taken on the occasion of the Hunt of the Kelligrews Hobgoblin, 19th August 1926." The garments worn by the men and women in the photo bore out the date. There was no doubt about it, thought Christopher — this was an old place, like the Forgotten Cemetery had been. Even without the photographic evidence, he could feel the weight of history which had seeped into the wood of the walls and tables and chairs. He was sitting where thousands, where tens of thousands of people had sat before him, and each and every one of them had left an invisible yet palpable mark on the site.

"Me ma," Faolan muttered abruptly.

"I'm sorry?" said Christopher, turning back to him.

Faolan stuck out his arm and, with one grubby finger, tapped the glass covering the picture. He was pointing to a young woman with curly hair, smiling warmly as she clung to the arm of a well-built man smoking a cigar. "Dat's me ma." He paused, staring, then chuckled. "But dat ain't me pa, mind."

"Oh."

"Look, Christopher, I'm sorry I drifted off dere for a few minutes. It gets me down, is all, seein' all dese pictures o' de Matthew in better times, an' den lookin' around at de empty tables 'n chairs. But I guess dat's what I brung ye here t'show ye, innit?"

"You tell me. The cats gave me some idea of what's been happening to your society but... well, I'd like to hear it from somebody a little more... normal, I guess."

"I t'ink dat might be de first time anybody's ever called me normal," Faolan guffawed, and Christopher could not help but recall uttering a similar sentiment, not too long ago.

"Cause I'm not, y'know, Christopher. Not compared to ye. I'm of de Five Clans, have been goin' back eight or nine gen'rations. Course, most o' de Clansfolk have long hist'ries dese days."

"That wasn't always the way?"

Faolan shook his head. "Nah, used t'be we'd get lots o' recruits from yer crowd. Folks who'd heard de legends, de folktales — who'd gotten intrigued an' wanted to know more. Most o' de ones who actually managed t'find us, dey were de types who didn't want to go away again. So dey stuck around, gave up dere normal lives. Some of 'em joined a Clan right away, some stayed unaffiliated for a while or even fer good, like Feaver o'er dere — didn't matter much. Just havin' em among us was de most important t'ing in our world."

"Why's that?" Christopher asked, genuinely curious, as he drained the last of his drink.

"Cause dere's a price to be paid fer what we can do, Christopher. Dere's always a price, remember dat. An' more of'en den not, for us, dat price is… barrenness, I t'ink is de word. I was me ma's only child, an' her an' me pa tried for so long to have me dat dey was almost afraid to try any more, fer me ma's health."

"So you need normal folk like me to come into your world… or else you'll die out."

"Got it in one, me b'y, got it in one." Faolan slammed down his empty mug, belched noisily, and hollered to Feaver to bring him another.

"But that's not happening anymore?"

"Oh, it 'appens ev'ry now an' den." Christopher thought of Emma, and nodded. "But not like it used to. See, yer kind… dey don't believe no more. Dey don't come chasin' us down, spyin' on our meetin' places, lookin' fer magic an' baubles an' potions an' charms."

"Couldn't you just make yourselves easier to find? Relax some of… whatever you do to keep people like me away from the Wandering Parliament, or whatever?"

"It's been discussed," said Feaver, depositing another pint of Guinness in front of Faolan. He tugged painfully on his thicket-like beard. "But it would contravene certain... compacts. And besides, it would only attract the wrong types from your culture. And that would be worse than what's happening to us already." He sighed forlornly. "The Five Clans... we live in the margins of the Book of Days, and that is both our blessing and our curse."

"What 'e said," agreed Faolan.

"No luck with the other customers, by the way," Feaver noted regretfully. "None of them know who your mystery woman might be, either. Sorry."

Christopher nodded gratefully all the same. "I appreciate the effort, Feaver."

As the barman retreated across the pub, Faolan resumed his discourse. "Bear in mind, Christopher, I'm not averse t'change. I t'ink it's as necessary as breathin', and maybe my crowd... maybe we have been a little too reluctant t'embrace change in de past. But sometimes de old ways are de best ways, and dat's de case here. Dis time, it's yer bunch dat's changed, fer de worse. Yer folk — dey don't b'lieve in de simple mysteries no more. Dey've fergotten dat der might be wonders out dere dey've only imagined before. I 'ates to use de word, Christopher, but basic'ly, dey've lost de magic. I mean, did you b'lieve in magic, before ye stumbled into our world?"

Christopher thought long and hard, staring off into space. He remembered the young boy who lay in bed at night, images of beautiful fairies and dashing heroes cavorting through his slumbering mind. He remembered the teenager who, though would he never ever admit it, still found solace in fantasy books and role-playing games because they let him cling to those fertile imaginary lands of his childhood. And he remembered how every passing year had made him a little more of a cynic, a little less of a dreamer; how he had, almost unconsciously, put away childish things and embraced the cold, stark world of adulthood, in which dragons and wizards and giants were just embarrassing trifles to be mocked or ignored. He remembered how nothing seemed meant to be in this world — not even true love, the love he had once thought he shared with Cecily, which had withered on the vine like so much else.

"I did once," Christopher finally murmured. "And then, for a long time, I didn't." His mind flashed back over the events of the past two days, and kept returning again and again to the strange little boy in Bowring Park, the one who looked so much like himself as a child, whose simple words had inspired his improbable swordfighting prowess. Christopher smiled. "But you know, I think I'm ready to believe in it again." He recalled the tremendous burden of responsibility placed on him by the cats, and the debt he had assumed towards the mysterious red-headed woman, and he chuckled wistfully. "Come what may."

Faolan looked across at him through narrowed eyes for a very long time. Then he took a sip of his beer and nodded, once. "Per'aps dere's hope yet, den."

Christopher glanced down at his wristwatch, which was miraculously still ticking away despite everything he — and it — had been forced to endure recently. "I should go," he told Faolan. "I need to find a friend of mine, and I don't want to leave it too long."

"Course, b'y," Faolan said. "I 'preciates de comp'ny while I drank me brew."

"And I appreciate the insight," Christopher returned.

Faolan reached his hand across the table and Christopher took it, shaking it as earnestly as Faolan had done when they had first met on the street. "Best o' luck to ye, Christopher."

"You too, Faolan." And Christopher stood to go.

"Wait a sec!" Faolan suddenly exclaimed, gesturing to the younger man. Christopher paused and Faolan snapped his fingers. Suddenly, in his other hand lay a dagger, sheathed in an ancient leather pouch. Curious symbols were marked on the pouch, now faded and barely legible. "I'd like ye t'have dis,

Christopher. Tis a fam'ly heirloom. I could ne'er bear to barter it away, despite being tempted to on occasion, but it'd do me 'eart good if ye'd take it."

"But Faolan, we've only just met," Christopher stammered. "I can't accept this!"

"Ye can and ye will," Faolan barked. "Christopher, I'm ne'er gonna have a son or daughter o' me own, and I must say, ye're a good kid. I've taken a shinin' to ye, b'y — and not in no creepy type way neither, mind ye."

Christopher chuckled. "That's good to know."

"Please, look, if I e'er change me mind, I'll come lookin' for you to get it back, okay?"

Christopher hesitated, staring at the gift. "Okay," he sighed reluctantly. He picked up the weapon and tugged it out of its sheath. It was a simple dagger with a smooth pommel which felt comfortable in his palm. Despite the blade's obvious antiquity — there was more than one notch in its edge — it was still exceedingly sharp: Faolan had clearly kept very good care of it.

"Now, bear in mind, dere's nothin' special 'bout the knife, exceptin' how old it is," Faolan said, wagging his finger. "It's de pouch dat's a little... unusual. Put de blade back in an' snap yer fingers." Christopher did as he was bade. Sheath and dagger vanished in the blink of an eye. "And again." The weapon reappeared in Christopher's left hand. "A simple trick," Faolan noted dismissively, "but useful at times."

Christopher snapped his fingers one more time, to send the knife away. "I'm really very grateful," he said genuinely. "I'll keep it sharp."

"I knows ye will," grunted Faolan. "Now go on an' find yer girlfriend while I convinces Feaver t'let me have anudder." And he hoisted his empty flagon optimistically.

"She's not my..." Christopher began, but shook his head at Faolan's wolfish smile. "Never mind," he chuckled. He turned and left the pub, waving at Feaver on the way out.

"Come again — if you ever get any proper money," the bartender called out jovially.

Christopher passed through the door to the Matthew's Rest, and emerged back into the stifling night air. Somewhere in the distance, he could hear the wail of a siren from a fire truck travelling east. Christopher headed in the opposite direction, intent on finding Emma and — with her help — hopefully getting to the bottom of things once and for all.

* * *

Emma nearly collapsed through the door to her apartment. She leaned back against it as she slammed it closed, breathing heavily, trying to keep her thoughts in order. Now that she had escaped from the People of the Insect, armed with knowledge about their intentions and how far their plans had progressed to date, she knew that she wasn't even remotely safe here. To make matters worse, the Sixth Clan would probably now move up their timetable, meaning that every second was suddenly more precious than ever.

Emma took a quick look around her home. She had been hoping against hope that Christopher might have shown up while she was out confronting Turlach, but it appeared that, once again, luck had not favoured her. A shame, too — she had a feeling that that *fios* stone of his was somehow important to the entire matter. And besides, she would have appreciated his company in what she was about to do. As it was, she would have to soldier on regardless.

Emma dropped onto the worn yet comfortable chair in the living room. She closed her eyes and forced herself to relax for a full minute, steeling her nerves and her resolve. Then she reached into her pocket and plucked out the dull metal disc. Emma grimaced — she had been hoping to save Lochlann's indentured favour until she had come up with something really embarrassing to make him do. After all, he deserved no better. But now the disc had taken on a new importance.

Emma placed it in the palm of her hand and squeezed tightly. Then she cringed, and forced herself to bring to mind Lochlann's smarmy mug — the eyepatch, the neatly-trimmed blond goatee, the grin like a Cheshire cat she had once thought was so disarming and now found so repugnant.

The disc abruptly felt warm in her palm, and she could sense the solid metal liquefying in seconds. She let rivulets of grey and red run down the sides of her hand and pool on the floor in front of her until her palm was dry. Then the puddle suddenly rose up and assumed a vaguely human form. As Emma stared, the rough shape rapidly became infused with colour and detail. Then Lochlann stood before her, dressed in a silk shirt with far too many buttons undone, and matching trousers.

"Well," he said, his lips crooking into a smug grin, "I would've expected your noble champion to call in his favour long before you'd deign to do so, Emmeline."

The blonde girl leapt to her feet to confront him, her blue eyes holding his glare. "It's Emma, Lochlann. Emma. Emmeline was your foul creation, and I'm not her anymore. Remember that."

Lochlann yawned wearily and lazily traced the outline of his eyepatch with one finger. "Is that your grand favour, Emmeline — sorry, Emma? To call you by such a mundane name rather than the far more dignified epithet I devised for you?"

"No," she hissed, "you'll do that or I'll kick your bony ass all over this goddamned room." Lochlann merely stood there and smiled contemptuously. Emma forced herself to remain calm. "Your two bald friends," she began.

"Ah ah, not my friends any longer," Lochlann corrected her. "Your champion saw to that. It seems I've... lost my appeal to the ladies of the Wandering Parliament — temporarily, of course — and so those two dullards wanted nothing more to do with me." He shrugged. "I was bored of them anyway."

Emma waved her hand in an effort to silence the man's prattling. "Look, whatever, I don't care. But they were top-notch trackers, right? That was their big shtick?"

Lochlann shrugged. "That was one of their talents, yes. You know as well as I do that I only keep people around me for two reasons: because they're beautiful, or because they're useful. And I fully expect that even the mother who shat them out found those morons as ugly as sin."

Emma sighed, wondering if Lochlann had always felt compelled to answer a question in fifty words when five would have sufficed. "Then would I be correct in assuming that you... picked up some of that know-how?" she asked impatiently.

"I have been known to keep my eye open to see what new tricks I might learn, yes. Why?"

Emma took a deep breath. "In that case, then, in fulfillment of the favour which you are bound to perform for me, I want you to lead me to a member of the People of the Serpent."

"There are still more than a few of those lingering about, Emma. Does this individual have a name?"

Emma nodded. "Aislinn," she told him. "Her name is Aislinn."

Chapter Fourteen
In which a Betrayal is revealed

Stop for a moment and think: no matter where you are, no matter what city or town you live in, not far away there are people doing things. Lots of people, each going about their own lives, occasionally intersecting with the lives of others, all carving out their own tiny niche in history at the exact same time as you read these pages. It doesn't matter if it's the middle of the afternoon and you're riding home on the bus after a long day of classes, or if it's late on a winter's evening and you're curled up in front of a fire roaring in the hearth. It might even be the small hours of the morning, and you're squinting to read these words by lantern light in a tent somewhere out in the middle of a vast campground.

No matter who you are, no matter where you are, they're out there, nearby. And you can't even begin to imagine all the stories that are unfolding around you.

For example, consider one hot and humid St John's night in late July. A brisk wind tugs at the treetops, skirts along the emptying streets. But it brings no relief from the heat and humidity which have been steadily building for two days now. Electric fans and air conditioning units churn madly, but meet with scarcely more success. Distant car horns blare and frustrated shouting echoes along the roadways as tempers fray and snap. The dark clouds in the sky above have massed like mighty armies, and now they hang poised above the city, as if awaiting something. A hush of wary anticipation settles onto a weary, bedraggled city.

*   *   *

Emma Rawlin paces reluctantly behind Lochlann as they leave her apartment. Her skin bristles just being near the man, and she wishes fervently that she had some other way to accomplish what she's doing. But fate has seen fit to throw them together once more — for the last time, Emma prays — and she's determined that their association will at least be productive on this occasion.

Emma's heart is heavy with regret at not having had the chance to tell Christopher that she had learned the red-headed woman's name back at the Wandering Parliament. One of the merchants, an old acquaintance whose lover was a member of the People of the Serpent, had recognised her description, and divulged it after some cajoling on Emma's part. But she was too leery of Donovan Chase to reveal this discovery in his presence, and had not enjoyed another moment alone with Christopher before they were split up. And then, between the eerie schoolgirls' fogging of her mind and Turlach's baleful influence on her memories, what she had learned had become hidden to her... Emma cringes involuntarily at the thought of the insect-man wriggling through her brain, finding solace only in the fact that the veils were finally lifted.

Lochlann stalks breezily ahead of her, looking for all the world as if he's out for a late-night stroll. He's humming a bittersweet old dirge, wandering incessantly in and out of key. Emma assumes that it's something to do with his hunting method, although for all she knows he might just be doing it to get on her nerves.

Three times, Lochlann pulls up abruptly and doubles back to take an alternate route through the downtown streets. Emma begins to get a little frustrated, fearful that maybe Lochlann hasn't really learned the tracking technique from his brainless bald flunkies and is just putting on a good show to live up to his end of the bargain. But the third time, Lochlann suddenly accelerates his stride, and Emma can see a more serious aspect emerge to subdue his perennially cocky expression.

Soon, the two of them are travelling the Ways once again, and Emma starts to steel herself for the confrontation to come.

*   *   *

In an affluent neighbourhood in the city's east end, Naomi Holloway sits on the bed in her old room. She cradles the crying baby Alec in her arms, and begins to wonder if the child will ever be silent again. She vaguely wishes that nice man from the airport — whatever his name was — was here again, as he had crafted a rapport with the infant in mere seconds which she has been unable to cultivate in months of trying.

Naomi sighs forlornly, looking about the room, feeling a flood of half-forgotten memories wash over her. This is not how she had envisaged her life, she thinks to herself.

She had travelled to England right after high school to make a name for herself in London's East End — to become the greatest theatrical actress St John's has ever produced... or near enough, anyway. Instead, the best she managed was an unflattering role as Luce in what the *Times* had dubbed "the first production of *The Comedy of Errors* in history to truly deserve the title." And even that came about purely by virtue of a passionless and soul-throttling affair with the director, which nine months later left her a mother and a partner in a loveless marriage, one which ended in divorce scant weeks after Alec's birth. Naomi vaguely remembers telling the kindly man at the airport that she was only home so that her baby could meet his grandparents; she wonders when she's going to admit to herself that that was a monumental lie, that she's really fled home in a desperate search for meaning and direction and hope, and that her dreams of dramatic stardom have never seemed more fleeting.

Alec's wails intensify, and Naomi feels like joining him. She presses the child to her breast and rubs his back soothingly. In her mind's eye, she's remembering herself at age nine, bouncing animatedly upon this bed, pretending to be Juliet or Sarah Brown or the Witch from *Into the Woods*.

More than anything, Naomi Holloway thinks as she stares out the open window at the ominous clouds above, she wishes she could be that nine year-old girl again.

*   *   *

Above the grounds of Memorial University, nestled in that part of St John's where the old city gives way to the new, a clock tower stands — a grey granite pillar looming above the institution. The campus below is a study in contrasts: the gleaming glass and metal of the more recent buildings clash harshly with the crumbling stone facades of the original structures, now more than half a century old. Memorial has tried to rush into the future while neglecting its past, a dichotomy made manifest throughout its grounds.

In the long, deep shadows cast by the clock tower, Reggie Barter stands motionless, trying to silence even the rasp of his breathing. Beads of sweat — borne of both the stifling night and the tension in his gut — run down the side of his face, and he forces himself to suppress the urge to wipe them away.

Reggie is watching a figure wrapped in a heavy overcoat despite the closeness of the weather. The person is trudging carefully across the open area in front of the sparkling new student centre which sits by the base of the clock tower, the red and white tiles of the plaza now bereft of academics at such a late hour on a midsummer Saturday night. Every now and then, the figure veers, unknowingly, a little too close to the overhanging lamp posts, and in the brief burst of illumination, Reggie can see green-grey skin, scaled like a reptile's.

Reggie has spent more than a day following up leads — pursuing red herrings, running into blind alleys, finding his path twisting back on itself. Finally, earlier this evening, Reggie's keen ears caught wind of a whispered conversation in the food court of the city's largest shopping mall and, acting a little out of intuition and more than a little out of sheer desperation, those half-heard words have lead him here. And, at long last, it appears his work for Mr Donovan Chase is nearing fruition.

Reggie thinks of Honey, and wishes the perspiration beading all over his body was being brought on by her wild, frenzied ministrations. He wonders what she's doing now — whether she's angrily given up waiting for him to take her for their weekly evening out, or if she's sitting at home, as eager for his return as he is to get back to her passionate embrace.

Reggie squeezes his eyes shut and pushes the thoughts out of his head. He has to remain professional for a little while longer — one slip now and he might never have the chance to caress Honey's tantalising curves again.

He waits a few seconds more and then sets off in the direction the creature in the overcoat was heading, his shoes padding soundlessly along the ground.

* * *

In a modest but well-kept house not far from Bowring Park, Christopher Prescott's mother stands fearfully in the doorway to his bedroom. The sounds of the television waft up from the living room below, where her husband is falling asleep in front of the late-night news. She wonders how the man can be so calm in the face of their son's abrupt disappearance. He's sure that Christopher is just having a good time somewhere, that he passed out at a friend's house last night and is probably enjoying an equally torrid Saturday night. Mr Prescott claims that he did much the same himself during his college days (though Mrs Prescott finds this claim more than a little dubious), and has assured his wife that Christopher will show up before the weekend is out, none the worse for wear and hopefully with a renewed sense of optimism after the devastation of what happened with Cecily a week ago.

But Mrs Prescott cannot bring herself to share her husband's casual dismissal of Christopher's absence. She knows her son better than she knows herself — she's sure that, even if he was just having an uncharacteristically rowdy weekend, he'd still find a moment to call home and reassure her that he's okay.

Something has happened to Christopher, something she cannot even begin to envisage. Her chin trembles as she starts to wonder if she'll ever see her only son alive again.

* * *

Rose stirs in her restless sleep, meowing mournfully but not waking. Esther sits next to her, a relentless sentinel, but despite her resolute demeanour the worry is plain to see on the ginger cat's countenance. It is good that Rose has survived the tremendous toll she placed on her body, Esther knows, but she worries that the People of the Cat are going to need their leader in perfect health to guide them through the events to come, and she feels certain that that time is approaching far, far too quickly. Briefly, she considers summoning Frankenstein to attend to Rose, but she knows the effort would be fruitless: the strain the First Minister endured is not physical, and so Frankenstein, though he would no doubt have the best of intentions and try his utmost, could do nothing for her. Like healing truly mortal wounds, it is simply beyond the limits of his abilities.

As Esther maintains her almost motionless stance beside Rose, Shadow silently paces around the room, his eyes being drawn constantly to the window. He is not gifted with the foretelling that made Osric so treasured, but even still he can scent something unusual on the warm wind — a sense of expectation, yes, but underlying that a pervasive fear of what is on its way. Shadow suddenly finds his thoughts being cast back to his father, who was a most trusted advisor to Rose's predecessor; and to his grandmother, who held a similar position at the ear of another First Minister; and on and on back through the generations — even back to the times when humans still held the most powerful position in the Cabinet of the People of the Cat. He finds himself overwhelmed with pride at the faith which has been invested in his family over the decades, and especially in the way they have lived up to that faith. Shadow realises that he wishes very much to father a litter, one of whose number might some day carry on that tradition.

Shadow barely tilts his head as Spot sidles into the room through the hatch in the door. The impatient young cat has made frequent visits to the penthouse, to check on Rose's status and keep the rest of the house updated. Now she catches Shadow's gloomy mood and steps timidly over to the black cat. Shadow stands there for a minute, appraising her, and then, with an almost imperceptible gesture, invites her to nuzzle against his well-groomed mane. Finding comfort in each other's company, the two cats gaze apprehensively through the glass walls at the heavy night sky.

*   *   *

Faolan still sits in his usual spot in the Matthew's Rest. He's nursing his third Guinness because he's pretty sure Feaver won't permit him a fourth, and he doesn't want to push his luck and get tossed out of the pub (not for the first time, either). The Matthew's Rest is busier tonight than he's seen it in many a year — at least half a dozen people have entered in the quarter-hour since Christopher Prescott departed, and none of those already present show any signs of leaving. Faolan knows it's because everybody can feel the electricity in the air — knows that something's happening, even if nobody can possibly guess at what that might be.

Faolan sits back in his chair and begins to hum a bittersweet ballad he once heard, wafting out onto the street from the open door of a boutique on Water Street. He cannot remember the words, but the melody catches everyone's attention, and all eyes turn to him. It is a tune which speaks of lost love, ancient memories, and old ways now faded and gone.

A round of applause erupts from the tavern faithful, unintentionally heralding the arrival of even more Clansfolk. Ribald laughter soon rings out from one corner of the pub. A rapturous (and more than a little embellished) tale of times gone by unspools in another. Faolan can't stop himself from grinning. Maybe, just for one last night, things can be as once they were — the way they will never be again.

*   *   *

If you happened to be strolling through Bowring Park late on this night, and if you were quick-witted and keen-eyed and lucky, you might spy a small child skipping gaily down one of the dirt paths which follow the course of the Waterford River. Look once, and the child is a young boy of eight summers with a mop of curly red hair. Look again, and she's a ten year-old girl, her blonde pigtails bouncing merrily as she goes. Look once more, and you might see a five year-old boy with dark brown hair who dreams of guardian lions and noble duels.

The child stops beside the shadow pools, which perfectly reflect her angelic countenance, untouched by cynicism, untroubled by fear and doubt. In the depths of the shadow pools, the child can see the upside-down clouds press closer together, and he giggles excitedly.

He moves along, dancing around the gallant statue of the Fighting Newfoundlander, straining to see fish pass under the pink granite bridge spanning the South Brook River. She enjoys a pretend game of tennis with herself on the deserted courts, and stares wondrously up at Peter Pan playing his pipe.

If you happened to be strolling through Bowring Park late on this night, you might see a small child frolicking with the carefree, heedless abandon of youth, the embodiment of the spirit of every young boy or girl who found delight and laughter and wonderment in the park.

Or you might just see the wind ruffling the long grass, and think of it no more.

*   *   *

Christopher Prescott walks urgently along Henry Street. He is eager to see Emma again, and with her help to hopefully figure out just what is going on — what to do about the missing *fios* stone, about finding his red-haired mystery woman, about the Waykey now embedded within him. A little short of breath, he nonetheless jogs up Emma's street when he reaches it, and is practically running as he heads along the side of her building towards the steps which lead to her apartment.

He stops abruptly when he sees who is waiting for him at the top of the stairs.

"Chase."

"Hello, Christopher," says the small British man as he steps out of the shadows. "I'm afraid you've missed Miss Rawlin — nobody's home."

"Oh," Christopher mutters, crestfallen. "Well, I guess I can always wait here for her with you."

But Chase has not taken his eyes off Christopher, has hardly appeared to blink. "I'm not waiting for Emma, Mr Prescott. I'm waiting for you. I gambled that you'd find your way here eventually, and it seems once again I have been proven correct."

Christopher frowns in consternation. "But how did you know where she lived?"

Chase smiles in a way that makes Christopher feel more than a little uncomfortable. "I have my ways and means," is the extent of his reply.

"Okay... then can you tell me why you're looking for me?"

Christopher notices for the first time that Chase is holding something in his hand. It catches the distant light of the nearest streetlamp. "I wanted to return something to you," Chase tells him, and hands the object over.

It is the *fios* stone Christopher had thought lost forever.

And suddenly, words come unbidden into his head: one of the cryptic remarks made by the three schoolgirls in the eerie parody of his old high school. *One has betrayed them, one will betray them, and one of them will slay another.*

"You son of a bitch!" Christopher exclaims angrily. He defiantly snatches the *fios* stone out of Chase's fingers and stuffs it back into his pocket. "You fucking stole this from me!"

Unperturbed, Chase merely shrugs. "It may have inadvertently slipped into my pocket when I was standing alongside you in that mockery of reality you lead us into."

Christopher just stands there, shaking his head. "You're some piece of work, you are — all enigma and misdirection. What are you playing at, Chase? I'm amazed you're even bothering to give the damn stone back to me."

"Ah, well, there is a reason for that," Chase admits. "You see, it seems there's a... monster of sorts following that particular relic. A *Gan Aireachtáil*, to use the vernacular. One of the Unnoticed."

"How do you know that?" queries Christopher, a touch of dread starting to creep over him.

"Because it found me, in my current abode. I was fortunate enough to spot it before it got too close, and slipped away in the nick of time."

Christopher breathes a sigh of relief. "So you lost it?"

But Chase's countenance remains inscrutable, emotionless. "Oh no, Christopher. The *Gan Aireachtáil* are not put off the scent so easily. Look behind you."

Christopher spins around. Standing on the sidewalk in front of Emma's house is a very ordinary looking man — the sort your eyes would just slide right over if you saw him in a crowd.

But now Christopher's gaze is locked on the strange man's, as he takes one step forward, and then another. Christopher tries to run, tries to cry out, tries to scream in defiance.

But he can't move. He can't speak. He can't even think. And a darkness descends upon Christopher Prescott which is deeper and more impenetrable than even the blackest of nights.

*   *   *

In the skies above St John's, the clouds stare remorselessly down upon the sweltering city — at Reggie Barter and Naomi Holloway, at Rose and Mrs Prescott and a little child running through Bowring Park. The wind lashes down upon the houses, whipping violently around the homes and office buildings, curling around traffic lights and power lines.

Then, for just a brief second, the gale dies away, and everything is as silent as the grave.

And suddenly, the low rumble of thunder rolls over the Southside Hills, followed by a second peal, and a third. The first droplets of rain splash down on the wharf at St John's Harbour. Tendrils of lightning thread violently through the ocean of cloud.

The storm which has been building for a night and a day and a night has finally begun.

Chapter Fifteen
In which Dark Thoughts are made manifest

*S*urrender *your soul to me, Christopher Prescott.*

Surrender your soul willingly, and the pain will merely be excruciating. Struggle... and you will know torture beyond the boundaries of your fragile imagination. For I will claim your soul, Christopher Prescott, and there is nothing you can do to prevent it. None live who can resist the Gan Aireachtáil *for long.*

Which is it to be?

The struggle?

As you wish...

*   *   *

Christopher wiped his hand across his face and breathed deeply, trying to clear the cobwebs from his mind. Where was he? What had he been doing?

There were people around him, rushing past him, to and fro. They seemed hazy and indistinct, but maybe he was just tired... The smell of burnt popcorn invaded his nostrils, made his stomach curdle a little. The movies? Is that what he had been doing? Quivering in the dark, watching vapid celluloid fantasies play out before him, trying to hide both body and mind from the pain and hopeless of the past week...

Yes, that must be it. He was in the mall, he was fairly certain of that. Now that he thought about it, looked more closely, he could make out the too-bright illumination and the chintzy storefronts, half-glimpsed between passing figures. There was a far-off droning that might have been the loudspeaker system. He should leave, though — he was clearly exhausted, still drained from splitting up with Cecily, from the fear that all the light in his life had just gone out.

Christopher trudged away from the gaping mouth of the cineplex entrance, doing his best not to stumble into other shoppers. He wondered briefly what time of day it was — he felt so drained that he figured it must be nighttime, but there was an unusual number of patrons in the mall if that was the case. Maybe there was some sort of "midnight madness" sale happening?

He was trying to scan his surroundings, to solve this minor mystery and to just generally ensure that he was headed in the right direction, when he caught a glimpse of long, lustrous black hair, held in check by a bright red clip, just the way Cecily liked to style herself. Christopher shook his head dismally — he had to stop letting every little thing in the world remind himself of her. He kept walking, hoping that he'd reach the exit soon.

"Just going to ignore me, are you?" came a voice. It sounded an awful lot like Cecily's. Christopher stopped and peered about, straining to see where the question had come from.

Suddenly, one patch of the broad corridor seemed to come into focus, to be lit in an entirely different manner from the rest of the mall. Standing there were five people, and Christopher recognised each of them.

Positioned slightly ahead of the others was indeed Cecily Bond, dark-haired and green-eyed. She wore a blouse Christopher had bought her for her birthday the year before, but he noticed that the silver necklace which he had given her to commemorate their first year together, and which had become a fixture around her slender neck ever since (even when it didn't quite suit her outfit) was no longer in evidence. Cecily had her arms folded contemptuously across her chest, and was regarding him with an undisguised mix of disgust and pity. Christopher felt like he was shrivelling under her gaze. Behind Cecily stood her tall, muscular brother Marcus; her supercilious best friend Angelica; her mother, small and quiet, her lips pursed in unvoiced distaste; and worst of all her father, an enormous bull of a man, red-faced and possessing a voice which could cut across a football stadium.

"Oh, hi," Christopher mumbled meekly. "I'm sorry, I didn't see you there."

Angelica snorted disbelievingly. Cecily merely shook her head. "Whatever, Christopher. How have you been the past week?"

Christopher shrugged. "Well, it hasn't been the best, you know. But I suppose I'm getting by. How about you?"

Cecily smiled, and it wasn't an expression of kindness. "Fantastic, actually," she told him sincerely. "Dumping your ass was the best thing I ever did for myself." Marcus guffawed loudly, as if this was the funniest thing he had ever heard.

Christopher stared at Cecily. "Excuse me?" he said, trying and failing to keep a waver out of his words. "What are you saying?"

"I'm saying that I can't believe I wasted two and a half years with you, Christopher. What the hell was I thinking? I could have been doing so much better for myself!"

Christopher felt his mouth go dry. "But... but we had so many good times. I mean, yeah, obviously things didn't work out in the end... but that doesn't mean I wish we'd never gotten together. Do you?"

Cecily nodded vigorously. "You better believe it, Christopher. You're really kind of pathetic, you know that? So meek, so mild, so... so frigging boring. God! Being with you was like dating a cardboard box."

"I don't understand," Christopher told her. "I thought we had fun together."

Angelica stepped forward to stand beside Cecily. "She was just fooling herself, Christopher. For whatever reason, for a little while Cecily went nuts and actually thought your relationship was a good thing. Thank god she smartened up. I always knew you were beneath her; we all did, all Cecily's friends. Janie said she saw you walking down the sidewalk yesterday — she wanted to veer across the street and mow you down with her car rather than have to look at you a moment longer. But frankly, you're not worth getting the dents fixed."

"I wouldn't mind kicking your ass right here and right now," Marcus sneered, slamming his fist repeatedly against the palm of his other hand. "Give you the beating you deserve."

Cecily shrugged mockingly. "It's all true, Christopher. You know, for a little while there I actually felt bad about the way we broke up… But then the commercial ended and I realised that, really, it was all your fault anyway."

Christopher's face screwed up in confusion. "What do you mean? What are you telling me?"

"Does she have to spell it out for you, boy?" Mr Bond roared. He charged forward and stuck his huge red face right into Christopher's own. "You're a sad, ridiculous excuse for a human being. You're dull as dishwater. Your work ethic is laughable, so you're never going to amount to anything. You're an ugly, weak little toad who couldn't do a push-up to save his life. You're naïve as a two-month-old baby, people walk all over you and you're too stupid to realise it. You're so clueless as to how to live in the real world that if you ever moved out of your parents' house, you probably wouldn't last ten minutes. And while I'm not really keen on hearing about this sort of thing from my only daughter, I understand you're a lousy lay, too." Behind the huge man, Christopher could see his wife silently nodding as Mr Bond enumerated each of Christopher's many deficiencies.

"You can say that again, Daddy," Cecily agreed matter-of-factly. "Seriously, Christopher, in the highly unlikely event that you ever get another girl to go out with you — did I mention how highly unlikely that is? — I may have to tell her what an abysmal lover you are, just as a public service. Nobody should have to endure what I've gone through for the past couple of years."

Christopher could hardly believe the verbal assault. His mouth twitched soundlessly, and he felt salty tears stinging the backs of his eyes. Angelica was laughing delightedly. A huge, feral grin was spreading across Marcus' dimpled face. And Cecily appeared to be revelling in the moment — each nail she drove into him, each dagger she twisted in his gut, seeming to bring her to ever-greater heights of joy and exultation.

With a groan, Christopher sank to his knees before her upon the mall's white tiled floor.

"Pathetic, just like you said, sis," Marcus was chuckling. "Can't even stand up for himself. What a man."

"Christopher's hardly a man," Mr Bond spat. "I'd call him a mouse, but that would be an insult to the vermin."

Christopher peered up at Cecily, hoping to find some trace of compassion in her cold sea-green eyes. But there was none. "Let's face it, Christopher," she told him, "I was your one and only chance at happiness, and you let me get away. You're never going to find somebody as good as me — not anyone as smart, not anyone as attractive, and certainly not anyone who'll turn a blind eye to your massive list of flaws. You're going to live alone, you're going to grow old alone, and you're going to die alone. Alone, forgotten, and especially, unloved. You might as well just slit your wrists right here and now, and save yourself a lifetime of pain."

Christopher held his wrists out in front of himself, his eyes wandering back and forth between them. He could feel the rhythmic pulsing of the blood coursing through his veins, just below the surface. It would be so simple, he knew: just a couple of deep slices with a knife, and in minutes it would all just fade away. He wouldn't have to worry about being alone forever... He wouldn't have to worry about watching every woman he ever became attracted to find happiness in the arms of other men… He wouldn't have to endure mocking whispers just at the edge of his hearing, reminding him of how he could never hope to fit in…

Everything grew quiet. Even the sound of the shoppers in the mall faded away to a faint background buzz before vanishing altogether. Only Angelica's mocking laughter still echoed about the walls.

And then, almost imperceptibly, a whisper: "No."

Cecily arched an eyebrow. "Excuse me?"

"No," Christopher repeated, more loudly, slapping the palms of his hands against the floor.

"'No' what?" Mr Bond demanded.

"No, I will not accept what you're telling me." Christopher's voice rose, and he rose to his feet with it. "Maybe you're right, Cecily. Maybe you're all right. Maybe I am sad and pathetic, maybe I'll die without ever again being in love with somebody who loves me back. Maybe I will be alone and lonely forever and ever." He swallowed, and a steely smile crept onto his lips. "But I'll take my chances. I'd rather go through the rest of my life looking for love and companionship without ever finding it, than to give up right here and now and brick up my heart. Maybe my way is more painful, maybe I'll end up with a hundred sleepless, tear-stained nights. But just the chance of one day meeting somebody I care for and who cares for me back… that makes all that hurt worthwhile."

Christopher stepped right up to Cecily, and looked her straight in the eye. "I will never give up hope."

Cecily began to scream, a shrill, inhuman noise. Then, one by one, Angelica, Marcus, Mr Bond, and finally Mrs Bond joined in, emitting a rising, howling cacophony. Christopher was forced to cover his ears to try to block out the piercing sound, and even that had little effect. He shut his eyes tightly against the pain…

* * *

Ah, despair is such a simple tool, and yet so often effective. But it means nothing that you can rise above despair, Christopher Prescott. There are far more insidious means to bring you low. And then you will wish that you had succumbed to mere despair.

*   *   *

The first throbbing beats of a new song emanating from all around him made Christopher open his eyes and sit up. Where was he? A bar… yes, that certainly seemed to be a fair guess. But hadn't he just been at the mall? He had a fleeting impression of standing outside the movie theatres there, but it faded in the hollow glow of the alcohol he had been imbibing.

He was seated on a stool pushed up against a round table. In his hand he held an empty glass with traces of something neon-blue puddled amongst the half-melted ice cubes at the bottom. The room was hot and dark. A bar was an unusual location for Christopher to find himself in, but he vaguely recalled wanting to come downtown. He had hoped that maybe he could meet somebody nice to take his mind off Cecily… and, failing that, several rounds of booze should do the trick quite nicely, if somewhat less pleasantly come the next morning. There was no woman seated opposite him — nobody at all, in fact, so obviously Christopher had been forced to resort to option number two. He struggled to recall how many drinks he'd downed so far tonight.

His gaze wandered up from the tabletop towards the dance floor which dominated the room. Figures writhed and shook beneath flashing, multi-coloured lights. They seemed to be dancing so quickly that Christopher couldn't make out their faces: they were just blurs before his eyes, and even the rest of their bodies were ill-defined.

No, that wasn't entirely true, he realised. His eyes were drawn towards the centre of the dance floor, where three people were dancing very close together. A permanent light shone on the trio, and Christopher thought there was something very familiar about the person in the middle. Although they did not seem to be nearly as hazy to the eye as the other bar patrons, he still couldn't see them clearly through the juddering forms which passed between them. So he eased himself carefully down off his stool and, his head swimming unkindly, he lurched onto the dance floor to get a better look.

It was soon obvious what was going on. Two handsome men were dancing on either side of a woman who was clearly very drunk. She was dressed obscenely even for the downtown scene, her outfit consisting of a very brief black top with a plunging neckline and a ludicrously short red skirt which scarcely covered any of her long, toned legs. The girl was locked in a passionate kiss with the man on her right, whose hands clutched enthusiastically at the rear of her skirt. The other man, apparently unperturbed by the attention she was giving to his friend, was pressed up against her back, his hands entwined about the woman and pawing greedily at her breasts. He seemed to be trying to slip one hand down the open front of her blouse, and was failing only because of the spasmodic gyrations she was performing, trying vaguely to keep to the rhythm of the music even as her mouth was filled with the first man's tongue.

Christopher shook his head, wondering at how anyone could behave so shamelessly in public. Then her head tilted as she finally broke the soul kiss, and he could see that the girl's styled black hair was held in place by a vivid red clip.

His jaw dropped. "Cecily?" he breathed.

He thought he had merely whispered the name, but suddenly the girl looked sideways and spotted him standing there. She smiled lewdly. "Hi, Christopher," she called out to him playfully, with more than a touch of a slur lacing her speech. The two men simply stared at him, not sure what to make of this interloper on their licentious revelry.

"Cecily, what the hell do you think you're doing?" Christopher demanded, aghast.

Cecily shrugged, trailing her hand down the chest of one of the men — the one she hadn't been kissing, Christopher noted vaguely. "Having fun," she said. "What do you care? It's not like we're together anymore."

"Butbutbut," Christopher stammered, casting about frantically for the right words to say. "Cecily, that doesn't mean I don't still care about you — worry about you! Look at you, you're piss-loaded drunk and you never get more than a little buzzed when you're downtown. You're… the way you're dressed…"

Cecily grinned. "Do you like it? These guys do, don't you, boys?" And she gave both men kisses on the nape of their necks. Her hand snaked down and begin massaging one man's groin, much to his obvious satisfaction. Cecily giggled at the reaction.

Christopher thought he was going to throw up. "What's happened to you?" he asked hoarsely, so quietly he wasn't certain any sound had actually come out.

"Do you remember last weekend, when I went on the staggette and I got with that guy?"

Christopher felt his face go even paler than it had already become. "How could I forget?"

"Well, it felt so good, to just go downtown and pick up some man! It made me feel wild, sexy, amazing… And I decided I didn't want that feeling to go away, Christopher. So I've been back down here every night this week, getting with as many guys as I can." She closed her eyes and smiled dreamily. "I think I've already lost track of how many men I've been with this week, let alone the number I've gone down on. One boy just took me right on the middle of the dance floor, just hoisted me up and had his way with me. All the people around us were cheering us on… It was incredible!"

Christopher narrowed his eyes. "This is bullshit."

Cecily staggered forward, falling against him. "This is the new me." She ran one finger along the line of his jaw. "I love being a slut, Christopher. And I never want to go back to the way I was." She snuggled against him and licked his earlobe salaciously.

"I can't believe that's true, Cecily," Christopher murmured, his face now flushing with anger and fear and — though he almost couldn't admit it to himself — a touch of arousal. "Nobody changes that much, that quickly."

"Believe it, baby," Cecily whispered. She grabbed his right hand and pressed it up underneath her blouse. "No bra," she giggled. Her breast was sweaty with exertion, her nipple swollen against his fingers. She grabbed Christopher's other hand and slid it up under her skirt. "Nothing down there either," she moaned as she rubbed him against herself. "This is me now. This is what splitting up with you has made me become. Mmmm. But even though we've broken up, I'll still let you have me one more time. I bet I've learned some new tricks since the last time we fucked. What do you say?"

Christopher felt blood pounding in his ears, his heart beating a mile a minute in his chest. It would serve Cecily right if he did have sex with her one more time, even in this depraved condition into which she had let herself descend. He deserved one more taste…

Abruptly, Christopher shoved Cecily away, sending her stumbling backward into the two men she had been dancing with. "I don't think so," he told her stolidly.

"But why not?" she whined. She grabbed the hem of her blouse and pulled it up, lewdly shaking her breasts at him. "Don't you miss playing with these? Don't I turn you on anymore?"

Christopher shook his head sadly. "I was turned on by the girl I fell in love with, once upon a time. If this is you now, Cecily, if this is what truly makes you happy… then you're not that girl anymore. So you can do whatever you want, with whomever you want. It doesn't mean anything to me now." With no small degree of reluctance, he turned his back on her. "Goodbye."

As he walked away across the dance floor, Christopher's senses were assailed by a hideous wailing from behind him. His head pounding interminably, he clapped his hands over his face to shut it out.

*   *   *

What does it take to make you crack, youngling? What will make you betray yourself, and fall forever under my shadow? If a change of approach is required, then so be it…

*   *   *

"Christopher?"

His eyes opened. Everything was pitch black.

Then, suddenly, it was as if a spotlight had been turned on, somewhere very high above him. He was bathed in a circle of cold, pitiless white light. And he was not alone.

"Cecily?" She stood opposite him, wringing her hands, tears staining her cheeks. Images danced in front of Christopher's eyes — Cecily laughing at him scornfully, a half-naked Cecily letting strange hands roam over every inch of her body — but they vanished quickly, like the mist at sunrise on a spring morning. "Cecily, what are you doing here? What's wrong?"

She hugged herself forlornly. "Christopher, I… I don't know how to say this." And she began to cry disconsolately. Automatically, Christopher crossed the pool of light and took her in his arms, burying her face against his chest, the red clip which held her dark hair in place filling his vision. He felt her body shudder with great, heaving sobs and she pulled him even more tightly against herself.

Finally, Cecily raised her head back to look up at him. "I was so, so wrong," she whispered between sniffles. "You meant the world to me… you mean the world to me… and I just tossed you aside like… like spoiled leftovers. Oh god, that's a horrible analogy."

Christopher smiled at her tenderly. "It's okay. After all, you're only an English major." And Cecily returned his smile with one full of warmth, one that reminded him so much of the grins they had once shared, never thinking that there might come a day when those exchanges would begin to fade into dim and distant memory. "But, Cec... what are you trying to say to me, exactly?"

She took a deep breath. "Last weekend... I had too much to drink, I wasn't thinking straight, and I let things go too far with some guy I met. It was entirely my fault, and I'm so incredibly sorry about that. And then... well, I guess I panicked, Christopher. I'd never done anything like that before, never hurt somebody as much as I hurt you, and so I overreacted."

"By breaking up with me?"

"By breaking up with you. Christopher, I love you more than words could ever describe — English major or no. Going through the rest of my life without you... it makes me sick to my stomach just thinking about it. The idea of you going out and meeting somebody new and falling in love with her... I don't know if I could handle that. I try to live my life without regrets, Christopher, but if we're apart then I'll spend every moment from here til eternity cursing the day I stepped foot in a downtown bar. And I will never, ever stop wondering what magic I lost by losing you." Cecily paused, and cupped his cheek in her hand. "Please please please, Christopher, can you find it in your heart to forgive me for everything I did? Will you take me back?"

Christopher looked deep into those beautiful green eyes, still brimming with tears. All the wonderful times they'd shared together passed through his mind — laughing spiritedly in the park, twining hands at the movies, pressing their naked bodies together against the chill of a frosty February night, and so much more. And to think, all of that was in just two years and change; how much more happiness would unfold over the course of a lifetime together? It would be so easy to slip back into the comfortable skin of their relationship, to pretend that the past week was just a bad, frightening dream...

Christopher swallowed hard, and then whispered, "Yes."

Cecily sagged with relief, and hugged him close. "Oh thank you, Christopher, thank you. You don't know how afraid I was that —"

"Yes, I forgive you," Christopher interrupted.

"Excuse me?" Cecily drew back a little, frightened by the frosty tone which had suddenly entered her lover's voice.

"I forgive you for what happened downtown, Cecily. It stung me like nothing's ever hurt me before, it'll still haunt my dreams for a long time to come... but we're all only human, and we all make our share of mistakes. And I love you; I always have loved you, and a little part of me always will love you. You're a brilliant, beautiful, incredible person. So of course I forgive you.

"But I don't want to be your boyfriend again, Cecily. Because as painful as the circumstances of our split were, that doesn't make it any less right that we did break up. I know it in my heart, Cec... We were great together, you're right, and I'll never ever deny that or regret our being together for two awesome years. But I need to broaden my horizons before I can settle down with somebody forever, and you need to figure out just who you are as a person, beyond 'Christopher Prescott's girlfriend'. We could get back together, and I doubt we'd be unhappy. But it still wouldn't be right. As hard as it is for me to say — and believe me, it's tearing my guts out right now — being apart... that's what's right. I know it with every fibre of my being; with all my heart, and all my soul. Even though a really big part of me wishes that I'm wrong."

Cecily was choking back tears. "Then you never want us to be together again?"

He shook his head, and smiled a bittersweet smile. "Maybe in another time... another life."

Cecily stepped back, a look of abject fear marring her lovely features. "You can't mean this, Christopher. You can't!"

Christopher sighed, as certain memories came seeping back into his consciousness. "I can, and I do. And if I ever get out of this situation I've stumbled into in the real world, maybe I'll get a chance to say that to the genuine Cecily Bond someday." For want of anywhere else to look, Christopher pulled his head back and stared without flinching up into the faraway source of the white light. "Do you hear that? Are we finished with this game yet? Or do you have another angle to throw at me? Another nightmare to torture me with? Cause I'm sick of this! Sick! Of! This!"

*   *   *

Donovan Chase stood motionless by the steps leading down to Emma's apartment. He was silently mouthing a mantra in a language long forgotten by all but a handful of people on the face of the Earth. It was the only thing keeping the *Gan Aireachtáil* from taking notice of him and drawing him into whatever sordid illusions he was tormenting Christopher with. He knew that if the Unnoticed hadn't been so fixated on Christopher and the *fios* stone, even this diversion wouldn't have worked. And he was all too aware that his becoming embroiled in those terrible fantasies would only make the boy's trials all the more unbearable.

Out of the corner of his eye, Chase watched the *Gan Aireachtáil* as it slowly circled Christopher's body, which lay curled into a foetal ball upon the ground. The plain-looking man had been pacing the same route for several minutes now, with no change in his bland, emotionless expression. Chase began to feel the first pangs of fear that perhaps he had miscalculated, that the creature would succeed in corrupting the young man as it had so many other victims before.

Then, suddenly, an almost imperceptible light flickered into being around Christopher's still form. Before Chase could even begin to think what it might mean, the light erupted into an incandescent glow, so intense that it enveloped Christopher's shape.

Only then did the Unnoticed's face betray an emotion. And that emotion was fear.

The luminescence grew stronger, reaching out and engulfing the *Gan Aireachtáil*. The creature screamed a shrill, high-pitched scream, discordant and terrible to behold, full of hate and anguish and suffering. It was the first sound of true emotion ever to emanate from its hellspawned maw. And as Chase watched, the Unnoticed's body grew thin and transparent under the intensity of the pure white light — withering away until, finally, it was as if no being had ever stood there to begin with.

The light winked out as abruptly as it had manifested. At the same moment, Christopher stirred, groaning miserably. Chase ceased his chanting immediately and knelt down beside the boy, turning him over and fanning his pale face. In the sky above, lightning arced across the sky, pursued swiftly by the sonorous rumble of thunder.

"Wh — what happened?" Christopher mumbled. Rain began pelting down all around them and he opened his mouth, gratefully letting a few drops of water splash against his tongue.

"You did it, Mr Prescott. You defeated the *Gan Aireachtáil*, as I knew you would."

Christopher grunted dubiously and struggled to sit upright. "How did I manage that?"

Chase tapped his finger against his lips before responding. "The Unnoticed prey through corruption. Even physical contact is impossible until a person has been befouled. If their victim is weak-willed or in a state of diminished mental capacity, this is straightforward and virtually instantaneous. But for those of strong character — like you, Christopher — the process is not so easy. I imagine the *Gan Aireachtáil* projected various scenarios into your mind, to try to trick you into betraying who you are, the very core of your being. Had you done that, you would have become its thrall. And I would have done you a favour by killing you."

"But it didn't succeed?"

"No," Chase confirmed with a smile. "You held true to yourself, Christopher, time and time again, no matter what it subjected you to. The Unnoticed couldn't handle that — and so you destroyed it."

"Oh," said Christopher. "Good for me." Coughing up a mouthful of phlegm, he rose uneasily to his feet, shoving away Chase's attempts to assist him. "Don't think I've forgotten that you were the one who stole the *fios* stone and lead that monster to me in the first place," he snarled.

"But Christopher, I did that precisely because I knew you could beat it. I sensed the good in you from the moment we met. You see, had I been in possession of the stone when it caught up to me..." Chase shook his head, a funereal expression falling across his features. "There are things in my past the *Gan Aireachtáil* could have played upon to destroy me utterly. I am many things, Mr Prescott, but I am not the man that you are. And I am sorry that I had to put you through that. If there had been another way..."

Christopher started to say something else, but he was interrupted by an electronic warbling coming from one of Chase's inner jacket pockets. He ran his fingers through his sodden hair as Chase retrieved a slim mobile phone and answered the call.

"Hello?... Ah, Reginald, I was beginning to worry that you'd unwisely forgotten about me... Is that so?... Yes, I know the place... Very good, Reginald, thank you. I'll be in touch." Chase terminated the call and slipped the phone back to its resting place.

"What was that all about?" Christopher asked warily.

"Your mysterious red-headed woman, Mr Prescott. Would you like to finally meet her?"

Chapter Sixteen
In which a Long-Awaited meeting takes place

The light but steady rainfall pelting against the street and sidewalk and nearby buildings sounded like timpani as Christopher absorbed Chase's question. It had been posed in such an off-hand manner, so lackadaisically and out of the blue, that he wondered for a moment if he had misheard. "Do I want to what?" he finally responded, weakly.

"I know where she is, Christopher," the little man replied with a rather self-satisfied grin. "That was an… acquaintance of mine on the phone, finally reporting in. Frankly, I had expected to hear from him long before now but, as they say, good help is so hard to come by in this day and age."

"But I barely even mentioned her to you. How could you know enough to have somebody track her down?"

"Ah, a good question," Chase admitted. He tapped his finger against his lips pensively. "Actually, I have to confess that I was looking for her for some time before you and I first met. I didn't even realise you were seeking her too until a while later, when you first showed me the *fios* stone and made passing reference to her. Her name is Aislinn, if you're curious. And I imagine you are."

Christopher furrowed his brow in irritation. "Then why didn't you mention this earlier?"

"What purpose would that have served?"

"What purpose?" Christopher exclaimed, frustration urging the level of his voice towards shouting. "Maybe we could have,

I don't know, pooled information or something? Found her even quicker? If nothing else, it just would have been bloody courteous, and a hell of a weight off my mind!" He shook his head and smiled deprecatingly. "You're ridiculous, Chase. I've never met a man so mistrustful of others, and who inspires so little trust himself."

Chase's countenance darkened. "You should trust me because I know what I'm doing," he growled.

"So you say," Christopher scoffed. "Tell me this, then: I know why I'm looking for... Aislinn, or whatever her name is. Why are you looking for her?"

"Because I was commissioned to do so."

"That's not much of an answer. Commissioned by who? To what purpose?"

Chase glared at him as the rainshower intensified, the individual spatterings of each droplet on the ground mixing and merging together to form a continuous thrumming. "I can't tell you these things, Mr Prescott. I guard my secrets jealously, yes, but for good reason!"

"I think you're nothing but secrets, Chase. I think if you ever gave them all away, you'd just curl up and vanish, like a puff of smoke."

Chase seethed in silence. "I can say this much," he finally muttered through gritted teeth. "Aislinn has something to do with what's been going on. With that *Gan Aireachtáil*, obviously. With the slaughter of the Cabinet of the People of the Caribou last night." And, therefore, with why he had been granted the burden of the People of the Cat's *eochair*, Christopher thought to himself. "I need to find out what her involvement is," Chase continued. "And I'm convinced that that *fios* stone is the key." He held out his hand, palm upward. "May I have it back, please?"

Christopher looked down at him incredulously. "You pickpocketed it from me once, and now you expect me to just hand it back over on your say-so? I don't think so, Chase. Let's go to wherever Aislinn is and find out from her what's on the go. The *fios* stone can stay with me. You might think I should trust you, but I'm finding that pretty damn difficult right now."

Chase kept his palm extended for several more seconds, until so much rainwater had collected there that it started to run down the sides of his hand. "Fine," he spat at last. Then he spun about, and started heading back towards the road. "We'll take the Ways, it'll be quickest. Do you think your body is up to the challenge yet?"

Christopher was thinking back to the flash of red locks he had glimpsed in the bar the night before, and to the heavenly creature from whose head that hair spilled in copper waves. He could barely suppress a grin of anticipation. "Yeah," he nodded. "I think I'm ready."

Chase, though, had scarcely waited for a response, and indeed was moving at a rapid pace down Emma's street. Christopher had to jog to catch up with him. "Fortunately, the downtown area is riddled with accesses to the well-travelled high roads of the Ways," Chase told him without turning his head. "We'll be at our destination in no time."

"Good."

Chase was true to his word; less than a hundred paces later, the little man began muttering something under his breath. Christopher had heard similar words before, what seemed like a very long time ago, floating down from a window in an alley behind a bar, and he realised that they were almost starting to make sense to him, that he was on the verge of perceiving a pattern in their exotic and elusive construction.

Then the world around him seemed to change — imperceptibly at first, but then faster and faster, like water bursting through a dam. His surroundings didn't fade — quite the reverse, in fact. Everything suddenly became much sharper and brighter, new detail becoming evident in places where he didn't even realise he was missing any. Christopher had worn glasses once — a necessity since obviated through the wonders of modern laser eye surgery — and he remembered the first time he had slipped those spectacles onto his face while he looked at the view of the Southside Hills through his kitchen window. Suddenly he had been able to distinguish the forest which covered the side of the hills: a great swathe of amorphous green was transformed into a vast collection of individual trees. This felt much the same, but the effect was far more pronounced.

At some point, a golden glow infused everything around him, and from that moment on, each step propelled Christopher into an entirely new set of surroundings. From the small, cloistered houses of the city centre, he abruptly found himself amidst the statelier homes above the hill, with their great gated gardens frequently choked with weeds and overgrown flora. He thought he might have caught a glimpse of the cats' house, just for a second, hidden behind dense foliage; but it might as easily have been his imagination.

Another few steps, and he was amidst farmland. Christopher didn't recognise the region at first — the city's agricultural areas were now largely confined to Brookfield Road in the south-west or towards the northern rim of the municipality along Mount Scio Road. But as he looked more closely, he could make out the vague impression of familiar homes and buildings overlaid upon the fields and pastures — structures he could identify so easily because he passed them almost every day on his way to and from his office at the University.

And sure enough, as Chase halted in his strides (and Christopher nearly ran right into him, such was his distraction), the golden glow faded away, accompanied by the richness of the detail, and Christopher found himself standing along Elizabeth Avenue, gazing across the street at the sprawling southern half of the Memorial University campus.

"Did your contact tell you exactly where Aislinn was? The University is a big place," Christopher murmured.

"Oh yes. Reginald was quite explicit."

Chase led Christopher across the empty road, avoiding the puddles which now dotted the pavement. Christopher realised that he couldn't recall if it had been precipitating or not as he travelled the Ways; in some bizarre manner, it was as if it had been both raining and not raining, at precisely the same time. As he passed, the pools of water practically sizzled in the oppressive heat of the night.

Chase turned onto the arcing driveway which led past the Administration Building, and shortly thereafter the rectangular beige shape of the Mathematics Building appeared through the rain to their right. It was a place Christopher knew well — he had spent an almost immeasurable amount of time closeted within those walls, be it in a classroom or the computer lab or the cramped little office he shared with another grad student. It was perhaps the most normal, mundane place he knew — apart from the more colourful and eccentric members of the faculty — and he was certain that nothing even remotely unusual or supernatural transpired therein.

So Christopher was more than a little taken aback when Chase stopped, peered at the Mathematics Building, and turned sharply to approach it. "This is it," he muttered.

Christopher couldn't help himself: he started laughing. He knew it was laughter tinged with hysteria, but it erupted out of him uncontrollably. Only a loud peal of thunder, unaccompanied by lightning, drowned him out and coaxed him back to calm. "You have got to be kidding me," he chuckled. "I have spent nearly the last decade slaving away in that building. And the mystery woman I've been chasing around St John's for the past two nights is holed up, what, just down the hall from my office? I'm sorry, Chase, I've become ready to accept some pretty outlandish things, but that's still way too much of a coincidence." But Chase just kept walking towards the building, and once again Christopher found himself racing to catch up.

"Do you know what this structure was before it housed the Department of Mathematics and Statistics?" Chase asked as soon as Christopher was back within earshot.

Christopher was caught a little off guard by the question, but he quickly recovered and replied, "Yeah, um, it was the library. Until the big new one was built back in my parents' day." It was true: the cramped and claustrophobic facility had been the original home of the University library, a collection which eventually threatened to erupt through the building's thin walls. The thousands of books were finally moved into a more spacious home just a short walk across campus, but many alumni still thought of the Mathematics Building in its ancient context, with tales of streakers running through the halls and risqué behaviour amongst the stacks proliferating down through the generations of students.

"Indeed. And though it is not widely known, the Memorial library includes tomes which... do not appear on any course syllabus, shall we say. At least, not for any courses the University will admit to offering. These are tomes which hold some of the history and the power of the Five Clans."

"Clearly I shouldn't have been wasting my time looking through the differential equations tracts in the math section," Christopher quipped.

Chase looked at him impassively. "Oh, these volumes can't be found on the library shelves, nor even amongst the restricted titles below stairs."

Christopher sighed wearily, wondering how they had wandered off onto this tangent, especially when his goal was apparently so near at hand. "Is there a point you're trying to make here, Chase?"

"These books can be accessed only via a secret stair. And while, as with the mundane texts, this more potent collection has migrated to the new library, that hidden way to their former place of concealment still exists."

"And that's where Aislinn is?"

"So Reginald tells me."

Christopher looked around. They were now standing in the small parking lot which abutted the Mathematics Building. The door to the basement was to their left, while to the right was a patch of parched, yellowed grass, clearly lapping up the downpour of rain. A twisting stone staircase lead up a storey, an unusual emergency exit which Christopher had always thought was out of place with the architecture of the structure. The main entrance was on the opposite side of the structure, facing a small plaza which separated several University buildings. Right now, the entire area was deserted, save for the occasional car speeding down Elizabeth Avenue through the driving rain. "Where is your lackey, anyway?"

Chase smiled grimly. "Oh, I imagine Reginald absconded the moment his duty to me was fulfilled."

"Well then, why don't we get on with this?" Christopher was consumed with impatience, the *fios* stone burning a metaphorical hole in his pocket. His hand was constantly flitting to his side to ensure that its slim bulk was still nestled there, and he kept a safe distance from Chase, just to make sure the man didn't perform another feat of legerdemain and make off with it again. He was determined to return the stone to Aislinn himself, and without further delay.

"All right," Chase conceded. He sounded wary for some reason, but Christopher put this down to the man's apparently innate state of paranoia. "Be very careful, Mr Prescott. Don't relinquish the *fios* stone for any reason. Remember how powerful it is."

Christopher nodded, although he could barely suppress a grimace at the covetous tone which had crept into Chase's words. He wanted to tell the little man that he was crazy if he thought Christopher was going to keep the artefact for him rather than return it to Aislinn, but decided it was best to brook no further arguments at this stage.

Chase had approached the stone staircase and was beginning to ascend. Christopher followed, uncomprehending. "Um, Chase, I hate to break it to you but this just leads up to the part of the building run by the Computing Services group. And the door'll be locked now anyway."

Chase ignored the comment. "Pay close attention, my boy. At the seventh step, place your foot not on the horizontal flat of the stairs, but on the vertical," he commanded.

Christopher was about to protest at the impossibility of the feat, citing the obvious problem of gravity not working that way. But the objection died in his throat. In Chase's society, he realised, even gravity was just a toy, to be obeyed or ignored as circumstance dictated. And, indeed, as he watched, Chase put one foot against the damp, upright side of the seventh stair, and continued to ascend in that manner, now oriented perpendicularly to Christopher even though all the laws of physics were screaming at the young man that this shouldn't be possible. To silence them, Christopher followed Chase's example, and was astonished at how natural and easy it seemed as he climbed the stairs, the rain pattering down right into his face and eyes.

And then, it wasn't raining any longer.

Christopher blinked and looked around. Now he was in a narrow, musty stairwell, standing upright, surrounded on all sides by grey rock laced through with a filigree of tiny cracks. Cobwebs hugged the corners, and the lingering smell of ancient books wafted down from an archway ahead of him, through which Donovan Chase was about to pass. Christopher looked back over his shoulder to see nothing but an endless series of steps, spiralling away into the darkness and out of sight.

Christopher completed his ascent, and paused behind Chase, who stood before the archway. From within, he could hear the sound of somebody shuffling heavily along a flagstoned floor. Chase looked back at him, seemingly about to mutter some comment. But instead he tugged on the lapels of his pinstriped jacket, letting rainwater drip silently onto the carved rock, and then stepped through the archway.

As Christopher watched, Chase's form was lit up by a brilliant burst of electricity, emanating from the archway all around him. His body contorted painfully, his features were gurning in agony, and a tormented scream was wrenched from his throat. Before Christopher could even react, the tortuous flares died away, and the little man slumped, insensate, to the flagstones.

Not even thinking that the same fate might befall him, Christopher dashed over to Chase's immobile figure. He rolled him over onto his back, and began feverishly feeling for a pulse.

"He'll be fine after a little while," came a woman's voice.

Christopher looked up. He was in an enormous room, supported by granite pillars at regular intervals, each of which was adorned with a flickering torch set into a bronze sconce. The floor was thick with dust, although it was run through with footprints — some recent, some not so. Christopher could vaguely see, in places, long rectangular outlines where the dust was slightly less deep than its surroundings, presumably marking where a bookcase had once stood.

At the far end of the room was a raised area accessible via a series of semicircular steps. More torches were bracketed to the wall behind it. A woman lay there, reclining on a fluffy purple blanket. As she rose into the torchlight, Christopher could see her majestic features, framed by long, sinuous red hair. She now wore a flowing green velvet dress which left her shoulders bare, instead of the grey blouse and dark slacks of the night before — although the unseasonable blue overcoat was balled up at the foot of the blanket. But she was unmistakably the woman he had seen walking through the bar. The woman who had dropped the *fios* stone. The woman who had taken his breath away then, and was stealing it away again now. Aislinn.

"Ummm… hi," Christopher mumbled, feeling for all the world like he was fifteen years old again, trying to ask Kelsey Pennywell out on a date.

The woman smiled disarmingly. "Hi yourself," she said, descending the steps from her podium. Christopher felt his heart beat a little faster as he realised how her dress hugged the attractive curves of her tall, lithe frame. It made her, if anything, even more wondrous a sight to behold than the first time he had laid his eyes upon her. "I'm really sorry about your friend. I've been... hiding out here for a while now, and that ward has really been my only protection. Actually, I'm surprised it didn't catch you too — it's not supposed to be a one-shot deal."

Christopher stood up and patted himself down, miming checking for injuries. "Nope, looks like I got through unscathed. You're... Aislinn?"

She narrowed her eyes warily and halted halfway across the musty chamber. "I'm afraid you've got the better of me, sir."

Christopher blushed, realising how impolite that must have sounded. "Oh, I'm sorry. I'm Christopher Prescott. My, erm, companion here —" he gestured at the unconscious Donovan Chase, pointedly avoiding Aislinn's use of the word 'friend' "— told me your name. He's been sort of helping me find you."

"Has he now?" Aislinn said. She at least seemed vaguely mollified by Christopher's congenial tone, although he could tell that she was still on her guard. Nonetheless, she crossed the rest of the way over to him, standing opposite him across Chase's prone body.

"So... who exactly have you been hiding from, if you don't mind my asking? Is it the, um... the Unnoticed?"

Aislinn nodded vigorously. "Yes! How did you know about that?"

Christopher grinned proudly despite himself. "I ran into him... it... whatever... earlier tonight. I think I actually managed to, um, destroy it."

Aislinn's eyes went wide. "You did what?" Then she shook her head. "No, never mind, it's not important. But... why did the *Gan Aireachtáil* seek you out? Unless I miss my guess, you're not even of the Five Clans, though I presume your... companion here is."

Christopher shrugged. "I think he's more of a free agent, actually. But to answer your question, I think that, ah, creature came after me because I found this." He slipped his hand into his pocket, and withdrew the object hidden therein.

The red-headed woman gasped. "My *fios* stone! So that's why the ward didn't affect you — I had specifically designed it so that anyone bearing this would be allowed through. But how did you..."

"I saw you drop it in a bar downtown last night. I figured it must be important, so I retrieved it and went after you. But you disappeared before I could catch up. So, well, I guess I've been looking for you ever since." He wasn't sure if that made himself sound incredibly noble or incredibly pathetic. Probably a bit of both, he decided.

But Aislinn's elegant features were touched by an impressed smile. "You've sacrificed more than a day of your time, just looking for me?"

"More or less, yeah. It... seemed like the right thing to do."

Aislinn lowered her eyes bashfully. "That's more than most men would do," she told him, making him smile sheepishly. Beneath them, Chase stirred slightly, though he did not awaken. "I think I shall have to find a way to reward you handsomely, Christopher Prescott."

Christopher's mouth went dry — this was the moment he had been dreaming of for what felt like an eternity now, even if it really had only been about twenty-four hours. This was the culmination of this entire bizarre, wondrous, painful, unlikely adventure. Aislinn reached over and ran the tips of her slender fingers along the back of the hand holding the *fios* stone. "May I have it back, please?" she asked him demurely.

"Of... of course," Christopher whispered, relishing the grace and tenderness of her touch. He looked deeply into her dazzling emerald-green eyes, and gently placed the *fios* stone into the palm of her waiting hand. Chase's earlier warning, already viewed with such skepticism, had utterly been forgotten. "There you go."

Aislinn cradled the stone for a moment, then smoothly tucked it up one of the long sleeves of her dress. Christopher was surprised to see her wearing such a stifling garment in this weather, but then noted that the chamber was actually rather cool, despite the absence of any obvious form of air conditioning. "Thank you," the woman said to him primly.

Chase sat bolt upright on the floor. "Christopher, no!" he howled. Surprised, both Christopher and Aislinn jumped back away from him.

And only then did Christopher realise that there had been somebody creeping up behind him the entire time he had been conversing with Aislinn. He determined this purely by virtue of stumbling backward into the solid figure, who seized Christopher's arms tightly. To the young man's horror, he noticed that the hands which clutched him were not human: they were thick, green and scaly, bearing only three digits which terminated in hideously large grey claws. Struggling uselessly, Christopher was at least able to angle his head back to get a better look at his attacker. He caught a glimpse of a feral reptilian head, inset with slitted green-gold eyes. The face had only small black holes where a nose and ears should be, and his mouth was filled with an obscene number of small but very pointy teeth, over which a thin forked tongue slavered eagerly. Christopher knew that this was the cloaked individual who had accompanied Aislinn in the bar, and remembered the unsettling way his eyes had glinted in the light of the alley.

"Too late, Donovan," Aislinn laughed haughtily, backing away from him a few paces more.

"What's going on?" yelled Christopher in abject bewilderment. "How do you know Chase's name?" He grunted as the creature holding him increased the pressure on his arms. "And will you tell your pal here to… urgh… let go of me?"

Aislinn sighed dramatically. "I'm so sorry, Christopher. You're a really sweet guy, and it's delightful how smitten with me you are." In an instant, her expression darkened, a sneer casting a sinister pall over her beautiful face. "But you're also a fool. Chasing all over town looking for a woman you've only glimpsed from a distance, thinking that an act of kindness might be the first step towards winning her heart? What kind of dream world do you live in?"

Christopher had stopped struggling, and just hung limply in the reptile-man's steel grip. "Butbutbut... I figured... it couldn't do any harm," he uttered lamentably. "And I thought I was doing you a favour..."

Aislinn snorted contemptuously. "A favour? The *fios* stone was left in the bar on purpose, you idiot! Did you even stop to consider that? The *Gan Aireachtáil* went there to collect it! It should have all worked out so simply: an innocuous location no Clansfolk observer would suspect, a contact I never even had to lay eyes on... But no, you had to go and stick your philanthropic nose in where it didn't belong. So because of you, I've had to stay holed up in this dusty tomb waiting for the stone to turn up again, in case my erstwhile employers suspect I'm going to do a runner on them!"

Christopher was speechless. It felt as if all the breath had fled his lungs; he just wanted to curl up somewhere and sleep for an age.

But Aislinn's tirade was not finished. "Well, at least you weren't only dumb enough to take the *fios* stone in the first place... you were so stupid that you actually delivered it right back into my hands. So for your unerring mental deficiency, I do thank you, Christopher." She curtsied mockingly. "Now kill him, Iollan, and then we can finish this once and for all."

The reptile-man's grip on Christopher's arms tightened painfully. He could feel his shoulder straining agonisingly, on the verge of dislocating. Out of the corner of his eye, Christopher could see that maw full of teeth flash towards his neck with a sibilant hiss. And this time, there was nothing he could do to save himself.

Chapter Seventeen
In which the Stone gives up its Secret

Christopher could feel hot breath against his neck and a rank odour assail his nostrils as Iollan, the reptile-man, moved to sink his myriad teeth into his flesh. He remembered how unpleasant Rose's puncturing of his skin in that same area had been — was it really just a few hours earlier? — and knew that this would be much, much worse. He closed his eyes tightly and waited for the excruciating pain, and then the oblivion that would inevitably follow.

"No!" a voice rang out.

Christopher's eyes opened. Iollan paused reflexively. Aislinn snarled in annoyance. And everyone realised simultaneously that they had forgotten all about Donovan Chase.

The little man had leapt nimbly to his feet, and held his walking stick out before himself as though it was a sword, swinging it back and forth between Aislinn and Iollan. "Leave the boy alone," he commanded, and Christopher could feel the reptile-man automatically shrink back a little. Chase's blue-green irises appeared to spark with an unnatural electricity. And though he was the smallest person in the room, to Christopher's eyes he seemed to dwarf the rest of them. The hairs on the back of his neck bristled at the sight.

Chase turned to Aislinn, whose confident swagger had abruptly vanished. "Submit to me, Aislinn of the People of the

Serpent," Chase intoned. "And tell your lackey to stand down. Do not make me demonstrate to you why mine is a name feared all across this sphere, and beyond."

Aislinn snorted, absentmindedly smoothing down her velvet dress. "You don't scare me, little man. Your reputation is built on tall tales and parlour tricks. As soon as Iollan is finished with my would-be paramour, he'll deal with you just as easily. You'll make a nice after-dinner treat."

"Is that so?" Chase glowered at the red-haired woman. And suddenly, his arm snaked out, and he struck Iollan in the shoulder with his walking stick. Except it wasn't a walking stick anymore: now Chase held a long, thin blade which Christopher thought looked incredibly sharp — and given how close the sword had come to hitting him, he was at a fairly good vantage point from which to judge. The blade sank deeply into the reptile-man's scaly flesh, and Iollan immediately released Christopher. He tossed his head back and hissed a cry of unbridled agony, his long forked tongue quivering in the air.

On his hands and knees, Christopher shuffled over towards one of the pillars, fully aware that there was nothing he could do to help Chase. The older man seemed consumed by rage: he tugged the sword from Iollan's shoulder and adjusted his footing quickly, appearing ready to strike another blow before the reptile-man, reeling from the pain of the first injury, could even move to defend himself.

"Wait!" Aislinn's imperious voice rang out above the fray.

Chase glanced over his shoulder and spat, "What?"

"Do you really think I'm so shortsighted that I don't have an ace up my sleeve?" She mimed drawing something from the folds of the same arm in which she had secreted the *fios* stone, then smiled haughtily. "I believe you're missing a friend of yours... blonde girl, hair about shoulder-length, a little shorter than myself? Attractive, I suppose, in a very low-rent sort of way."

Christopher emerged from around the pillar, having clambered angrily to his feet. "Emma!" he cried. "What have you done to her?" And his heart ached at the realisation that he had scarcely thought of her since Chase had learned of Aislinn's whereabouts. He was indeed an idiot and a fool, he thought to himself bitterly. Aislinn was right about that.

The red-haired woman grinned predatorily. "She came here, a little while before yourselves — she and a man with an eye-patch, although he promptly disappeared. I have no idea how they knew where to find me, but find me they did. Silly little bint put up quite a fight as a matter of fact, but between us, Iollan and I subdued her. That's how I knew to set up the ward over the archway, in fact."

"Where is she now, Aislinn?" Chase demanded.

"Oh, I didn't have her killed, if that's what you're wondering. That would be a tragic waste of a good hostage. No, she's safe somewhere, and if you and Christopher are good boys and let us go on our way, we'll release her... eventually."

"How can we trust you?" Christopher asked, disgust dripping from his words. He could scarcely believe that this was the creature he had been swooning over, whose half-glimpsed face had been so indelibly etched onto his thoughts. So, so, stupid...

Aislinn shrugged coyly. "I guess you're just going to have to. Because believe me, if word gets out that anything happened to me, she'll endure a death more appalling than anything you could ever conceive of. That's not a threat, Donovan, that's just a statement of fact."

Chase stood there, simmering with fury, as Christopher looked on helplessly. Behind Chase, Iollan stood with one hand grasping his ravaged shoulder, green ichor spilling down between his claws onto the black overcoat he wore. Panting heavily, he too was watching Aislinn, awaiting a signal to indicate whether or not he should renew his attack.

"Very well," Chase muttered in a low, dangerous voice. "Leave this place. But if you harm Emma Rawlin, Aislinn, I will hunt you to the end of the world, to the ends of all worlds, to avenge her. Are we understood?"

Despite herself, Aislinn blanched at the intensity of Chase's warning. "We are," she finally said through lips that were just a slip away from trembling. She spent a moment composing herself, then swept past Chase. "Come, Iollan. Leave them. We have somewhere else to be." The reptile-man nodded curtly and, with one last, ugly hiss aimed at Chase, he shuffled after the woman.

As soon as they had disappeared through the archway, Chase slumped heavily onto his walking stick, which had once again assumed its original form. Christopher approached him tremulously. "Are you okay?" he asked, breaking the sepulchral hush which had fallen over the dust-laden chamber.

"You idiot," Chase seethed, not turning about.

"Excuse me?"

This time, the British man did spin around to face him. "You unmitigated gormless simpleton! Why did you just hand over the *fios* stone? It was the worst thing you could have done! Why didn't you listen to me?"

Christopher raised his hands defensively. "Hey, hang on now, you're the one who brought me here, and I thought the whole idea was that it was so I could give the damn thing back to her."

Chase wrung his hands in frustration. "I wanted Aislinn to know that you possessed it, yes, but only so I could discover what it contained! Because believe me, Mr Prescott, that knowledge may be the key to unlocking this entire chain of events!"

"Oh," Christopher muttered weakly.

"Now, not only do we no longer have the *fios* stone, but we've lost Emma to the enemy, and we don't even know where Aislinn is making for!"

"We could follow them," suggested Christopher gamely.

"No," Chase said dismissively. "We'd run the risk of being spotted; Aislinn is no fool. And I don't wish to endanger Miss Rawlin's life any further."

"Then what do we do?" pleaded Christopher.

"I don't know!" howled Chase. "This was all falling into place so perfectly, until you children confounded my plans!"

Between Aislinn and now Chase, Christopher had had his fill of put-downs for one night. "That's enough!" he roared, momentarily startling the other man. "If you had let me in on everything from the start, we wouldn't be in this predicament. But, no, once again it's you and your bloody secrets. We just had this conversation outside Emma's house an hour ago, and you clearly didn't listen to a goddamned word I said! If we're going to save Emma and stop Aislinn, you can't hold anything back from me, Chase. Full disclosure, starting now!"

"'We', Mr Prescott? Your role in this has played out — you've found your mystery woman, even if she did not turn out to be all you'd hoped. You should go home, go back to your own world and your own people. Forget about everything you've seen and heard and experienced these past two nights."

"'We'," Christopher avowed, in a manner that brooked no argument. "I'm up to my neck in this thing, I'm not going to turn away now. Anyway, it's my fault Emma got wrapped up in all of this. I owe it to her to try to get her to safety, and there's nothing you can say to discourage me."

Chase glared at him for what felt like a very long time. Finally, he whispered, "Fine."

"And full disclosure?"

"Yes, all right! You now know virtually everything that I do, anyway. Certain… powers within the Five Clans, and specifically within the People of the Serpent, had become suspicious of Aislinn — whom, as you may have surmised, I know of old. And no, don't ask me how — it's not relevant to the current affair anyway.

"At any rate, I think Aislinn was a member of their Cabinet, and the People of the Serpent are particularly secretive when it comes to their leaders. That would have made her extraordinarily difficult to identify — were it not for our past history together — let alone locate. Although Emma managed it, somehow... she's resourceful, that one. But, be that as it may, these powers believed that Aislinn was planning to share dangerous knowledge with some unknown entity — another person, a faction, they weren't sure."

"Presumably it's this mysterious Sixth Clan that Eachna mentioned, in the Forgotten Cemetery. And I guess whatever information she stole, that's what's contained in the *fios* stone?"

"Yes... but Aislinn slipped through their fingers before her Clan could try to stop her, and so they contacted me to hunt her down and deal with her. And here we are."

"And you have no idea what the 'dangerous knowledge' might be?"

"No," Chase sulked. "I suppose I could have just given the *fios* stone back to the People of the Serpent once I'd... acquired it from you, Mr Prescott. But then we'd be no closer to identifying Aislinn's confederates, and the threat would still be out there."

"Besides which, your curiosity wouldn't let you just walk away from things that easily," Christopher said pointedly.

Chase glared at him, but did not disagree. "One assumes that Emma must have uncovered something, though," he murmured. "Why else would she be in such a hurry to come here?" He gritted his teeth. "I wish she had gotten in touch with me, rather than just heading to this place unprepared!" Christopher shot him a knowing look. "Yes, yes, I know... I hardly gave her reason to confide in me."

"Much less a means of contacting you."

"Quite." Chase sighed in frustration.

And then a thought struck Christopher. "Hang on a minute... Aislinn said that when Emma first arrived here, she was accompanied by a man."

"Yes, a man with an eyepatch or some such. What of it?"

"I don't know what she'd be doing with him, but that has to be Lochlann."

"The man you bested in the duel on Miss Rawlin's behalf, at the Wandering Parliament?"

"The same. They... used to be involved, I think, a long time ago. Maybe he's a part of whatever Aislinn's up to, too?"

Chase shrugged. "It's a possibility, but Aislinn didn't seem to know him. And she did say that he suddenly disappeared after accompanying Miss Rawlin here."

Christopher nodded vigorously. "Yeah, I've been thinking about that... Lochlann has a couple of friends. I had an... unfortunate run-in with them earlier today, and I gather they found me because they have a knack for locating people really easily. By magic, if you don't mind my using the term." Chase motioned for him to continue. "Well, what if Lochlann has the same ability... and what if Emma used the favour she earned from the duel to get Lochlann to lead her to Aislinn?"

Chase thought this through. "It's a sound enough theory," he admitted grudgingly. "Do you propose we go find this Lochlann and ask him?"

Christopher smiled, glad that he could finally contribute to this whole mindboggling mess. "Even better." He reached into his pocket and pulled out his own grey-and-red disc. "I propose we summon him here and ask him ourselves. And if I'm right, maybe he can lead us to wherever Emma is."

Chase nodded, seeing where this was leading. "Which, chances are, is also where Aislinn will be." He grinned. "For a newcomer to our culture, Mr Prescott, I believe you're learning rather swiftly."

"I try," Christopher offered in humble response.

At a silent gesture from Chase, Christopher placed the disc in the palm of his hand and squeezed it tightly, as he reticently summoned the image of Lochlann to his mind. In moments, the disc had liquefied, flowed onto the flagstones, and began the process of forming into the shape of a man. Just twenty-four hours earlier, such a sight would probably have stupefied and frightened Christopher. Now, he merely watched calmly, appreciating the wonder and spectacle of the transformation — even if the figure who soon stood before him was hardly a man he had any particular desire to meet again.

"For god's sake," Lochlann groaned as his one good eye met Christopher's. "Don't you people have any patience at all? You're like children with a new toy — you can't wait to get it out of the box and play with it. What do you want?"

"So I was right," Christopher noted. "Emma did use her favour earlier tonight. What did she have you do, Lochlann?"

"And is obtaining that knowledge the favour you wish to ask of me?"

Christopher glared at the blond man. "No, that's just a question I'm hoping you'll answer of your own free will." Christopher sighed heavily. "Look, I think Emma's in trouble, Lochlann. Big trouble. Of the legitimately life-endangering kind. I know the two of you have a past, and she can't stand you, and I'm guessing you probably don't think much of her anymore, either. But if you ever truly loved her, if there was ever even a shred of genuine affection buried deep within you, please help us out."

Lochlann stared spitefully back at Christopher. "For the embarrassment and indignity you've wrought on my person, I should deliver you a beating so fierce that your own mother wouldn't recognise the bloody pulp I'd leave behind." Christopher felt his breath quicken as he readied for an attack. To one side, Chase merely watched the exchange with a curious expression on his face. Lochlann sighed dramatically. "But, alas, I am bound by the compacts of the Wandering Parliament to render no harm unto your person while I am in your debt. So I suppose, in the absence of something better to do, I might as well answer your query.

"Yes, Emmel — Emma expended her favour this night. She had me use my not inconsiderable tracking skills to lead her to some woman named Aislinn, though in truth I have no idea why. I did as she bade me, and I lead her..." He looked around at his musty surroundings for the first time, and his eye widened in surprise. "Oh. I lead her here. Where is she?"

"That's the problem," Christopher told him. "Aislinn captured her, took her someplace. We need to find her and rescue her."

"How insufferably heroic," Lochlann muttered dryly. "But, it's your dime, as they say. Do you want to use your favour to have me lead you to Emma?"

"I do," Christopher said, with conviction.

"Then follow me."

* * *

Aislinn stepped off the Ways, Iollan quick on her heels. With theatrical flair, three jagged bolts of lightning rent the heavens above her in quick succession, accompanied by the sonorous boom of furious thunder. Sheets of rain were cascading down all around her; she flicked her wrist in irritation, muttered, "*Scáth*," and the precipitation was suddenly repelled away from Aislinn, like magnets of the same polarity. Even the puddles proliferating on the pavement shrank away from her feet as she strode forward.

"You're sure this is where we're supposed to meet?" Aislinn asked Iollan as she surveyed the vicinity. Iollan nodded and breathed a guttural hiss. "Figures," Aislinn pouted. "Some people never check the weather forecast."

The pair stood at the entrance to a car park high atop Signal Hill. The promontory loomed above St John's, which sprawled to the north and west, marking the gateway to the Atlantic Ocean. To her right, huddled on the cliff face, Aislinn could see the tiny, storm-tossed houses of the Battery, so named because of the neighbourhood's proximity to the mighty guns which once guarded St John's Harbour from invasion. In the opposite direction, just past a low stone wall, the wide open sea vanished into the darkness of night. Its surface frothed violently in the thunderstorm, the raging of the waves audible even over the incessant drumming of the downpour. In front of Aislinn and Iollan stood Cabot Tower, a large sandstone structure whose cubic symmetry was broken only by an octagonal turret in one corner. Built more than a century earlier to commemorate both the four-hundredth anniversary of the discovery of Newfoundland by the Italian explorer Giovanni Caboto and the sixtieth year of Queen Victoria's reign, it was now most famous as the site of the first wireless transatlantic communication, courtesy of another Italian, Guglielmo Marconi. To Aislinn, however, it was merely a familiar and irrelevant sight: her eyes were focussed on the parking lot, scanning it for the person she was supposed to meet.

Three cars were stopped atop Signal Hill. In each of them, Aislinn could see couples, avidly watching the electrical display in the skies above. Her contact did not seem to be amongst them; they were just obstructions, to be dealt with as quickly and efficiently as possible. Extending both her hands, she made a series of intricate gestures and intoned in a sultry, seductive voice, "*Ainmhian... paisean... gnéas...*"

Within moments, all three cars had fled, their occupants stirred into an urgent, almost mindless frenzy to head home and make wild, passionate love. Aislinn nodded in appreciation of her handiwork, grateful that none of the stormwatchers had become so aroused that they'd simply decided to throw propriety to the wind and satisfied their lusts right there in the seat of their car.

Aislinn strode to the centre of the now-vacant parking lot, hands on hips. "Where is he?" she demanded of Iollan, who was still cradling his wounded shoulder. "It's bad enough that this has gone on a day longer than I'd planned... Now that I've finally got the damn stone back, he decides to procrastinate. Wonderful!" Her humour was not improved as droplets of water occasionally penetrated her protective enchantment, running down her bare shoulders onto the front of her velvet dress. "Well," she muttered spitefully, "if I've got to endure this effrontery, then little Miss Blondie can come out and drown too."

Aislinn reached into one of her sleeves and withdrew a small square of parchment. It was brown and brittle, and looked very old. On one side of the parchment, a simple painting was etched in the Renaissance style, depicting a young woman with flaxen hair. It seemed as if the artist had attempted to do something with her hairstyle to make it more appropriate to the apparent age of the painting, but had finally given up and left it looking distinctly and anachronistically modern. The same could not be said of the girl's clothes, which consisted of a flowing cream gown, decorated with an intricate burgundy pattern running vertically from the shoulders to the waist, and arcing just above her breasts. Though the portrait was very small, it was still possible to perceive the expression of anger and indignity which marred the young woman's clean and pleasant features.

Aislinn regarded her monstrous companion. "Are you well enough to assist me, or am I going to have to do this all by myself?" she grunted. Iollan drew himself up to his full height, hissing aggressively. Nonetheless, green pus still oozed from where Chase's blade had ruined his arm. Aislinn arched her slim eyebrow. "I suppose we'll have to make do, then. Be ready."

And with one fluid motion, she tore the parchment down the middle.

* * *

There was a momentary blaze of light, more dazzling even than the spectacle occurring in the cloud-covered skies, and Emma Rawlin suddenly stood awkwardly before Aislinn. Recognising her surroundings and remembering what had happened to her, Emma tried to swerve quickly to one side and get away from Aislinn and Iollan. But her muscles were unprepared for the sudden motion, and she fell heavily to the sodden ground. Aislinn snapped her fingers and her reptilian lackey was upon Emma in an instant, dragging her to her feet and holding her roughly in place.

Emma closed her eyes and let the driving rain wash soothingly over her face. "What the hell have you done to my clothes, you bitch?" she finally asked, matter-of-factly.

"My apologies, dear," Aislinn returned coolly. "It's a side-effect of the imprisonment artefact. If it helps, that dress is probably worth a hundred times what those natty regular clothes of yours cost. Once you've got it properly cleaned, anyway — you seem to have made it rather filthy."

"Well, aren't I the ungrateful one?" Emma quipped, her voice dripping with sarcasm. She strained against Iollan's vise-like grip, but while his hold on her was weakened because of his injury, she still found she could scarcely budge an inch.

"Enough of this," snapped Aislinn. "Bind her, Iollan." She waved at the stone wall overlooking the ocean, and murmured, "*Srian.*" A pair of handcuffs, firmly affixed to the wall, suddenly materialised out of nowhere. Iollan dragged the struggling Emma over to them, and slapped the irons about her wrists, painfully tightly.

Over the reptile-man's shoulder, Emma could see Aislinn swoon momentarily. For a few seconds, the rain pelted down upon her undeterred. Then she steadied herself, wiped a manicured hand across her face, and breathed deeply. Once again, the water steered clear of her.

"*Overtaxing yourself, Aislinn?*"

The red-haired woman spun about, looking for the source of the eerie, sibilant voice which carried easily across the car park to Emma.

"*We thought you stronger than that.*"

Once more the voice came from somewhere around her. Aislinn again peered about for the speaker — now rejoined by Iollan, who had finished cuffing Emma to the wall. With mounting dread, Emma realised that the words sounded as if they were coming not from a human throat at all, but rather were formed from the susurrating beating of small wings, the high-pitched grinding of miniscule legs, the noisome chittering of little mouths.

And then she saw it: without her even being aware of it, the car park had become covered with an advancing carpet of insects. They blotted out the yellow lines dividing the parking spaces, they crept down the walls which protected sightseers from the sheer cliff face, they crawled across the message boards tracing Signal Hill's lengthy military and maritime history.

"Oh god," Emma groaned, "not again." She held herself as far away from the wall as the handcuffs would permit, and cursed the fact that Aislinn's portrait prison had left her wearing flimsy sandals instead of the sneakers she could have used to crush as many of the bugs as possible. She knew that doing so wouldn't put even the slightest of dents in the unimaginable numbers now blanketing the summit, but at least she would have felt as if she were offering some resistance, no matter how insignificant.

Then a dark shape passed over Emma's head, and something winged but vaguely man-shaped alighted in front of Aislinn. Emma knew at once that it was Turlach. Although it was certainly possible that other humans had allowed themselves to become abominations in the service of the People of the Insect, the festering wound which slashed across one side of the creature's face made it clear that this was the man who had already come close to killing her once this night. And now she had fallen into his clutches for a second time.

"Who the hell are you?" Aislinn demanded, clearly repulsed by Turlach's monstrous new form. Emma noticed that he seemed to have grown an extra set of limbs, erupting outward from his torso, since their last meeting. These now writhed and clutched about in the air, like newborn babes lashing out at the too-bright world. Turlach's legs still appeared to be useless, however: while he kept himself at ground level, his wings continued to beat furiously at the air, and every now and then an updraft would cause him to levitate an inch or two above the pavement.

The insect-man regarded Aislinn with what Emma thought could only be arrogance and disdain. "Once, I was called Turlach of the People of the Codfish. But now, I am the first of a new breed... an Adam, if you will, for a race which will devour the old and take its rightful place atop the hierarchy of souls."

Aislinn, though uneasy, seemed less than impressed. "That's really fantastic, Turlach, or Adam, or whatever name you're going by these days. But I thought I was supposed to meet the top dog, if you'll excuse the poor choice of words, of the People of the Insect here. And I'm guessing you're not him."

"*But we have already met, Aislinn of the People of the Serpent.*"

Aislinn looked all around her, but no other figures were in evidence atop Signal Hill. "Okay, who is doing that?"

Turlach chuckled disturbingly. "That is the voice of our leader, Aislinn."

"And where is he?"

Turlach spread his four arms widely. "All around you, closed-minded flesh bag," he cackled.

Aislinn looked down at the seemingly endless swarm of bugs which surrounded her.

"*Yes, Aislinn. We are the People of the Insect, and we are its government. We are legion, and we are one. And soon all the Five Clans will be one Clan, will be our Clan, will be us. We are... inevitable.*"

"Is that a fact?" said Aislinn. "Well, I'd prefer to keep my individuality for as long as possible, if it's all the same to you."

Turlach drifted closer to her, caressing the two rings he now wore on a rough chain around his neck. "Do you have it?"

"The merchandise? Yes, it's right here," Aislinn told him. She reached up the sleeve of her dress and withdrew the *fios* stone. "Sorry about the delay. Your pet *Gan Aireachtáil* was too late arriving at the rendezvous point. Some idiot normal accidentally picked it up and took off with it, although I'm guessing that you already knew something about that. He's been dealt with, obviously."

Emma's eyes went wide as she realised that Aislinn could only be referring to Christopher. She was overcome with remorse at the thought of him falling prey to the insidious powers of an Unnoticed… and all due to the fact that she had let him tag along after her in his search for Aislinn, because she saw in him the spark of a kindred spirit — the same *joie de vivre* buried beneath disappointment and misfortune, the same tenacity and determination to persevere even in the face of unbearable misery, the same rare verve that not even life's worst tidings could steal away. And now… who knew what fate had befallen him? She grimaced at the appalling thought.

Turlach, meanwhile, had made to grab the *fios* stone away from Aislinn, but she pulled it back dextrously. "Ah ah ah, payment first. Friday night I was prepared to wait a day or so to get what's coming to me… But let's just say that my patience has worn a tad thin since then."

"Of course," chirruped Turlach. He reached into the tattered remains of the shirt he still wore and tossed something to Aislinn. Through the hammering rain, Emma caught a glimpse of crystal glistening in the glow of a lightning bolt streaking across the sky. Aislinn held her reward in both hands for a few seconds, studying it intently. Although she kept it out of Emma's line of sight, the expression of rapturous avarice and delight which had consumed the red-haired woman's features was plain to behold. Emma thought that she was practically on the verge of drooling.

Finally, Aislinn slipped her prize up her sleeve and then grudgingly passed the *fios* stone over to the slavering bug-man. Turlach drew it greedily towards himself, turning the small rectangle over and over again in his inhuman hands.

"*Does it bear the ancient seal, and the true name of the First Minister of the People of the Serpent?*"

"Yes," Turlach breathed ecstatically.

"You've already acquired the opening rune?" Aislinn asked off-handedly.

"Oh yes," Turlach giggled. "This night has been well prepared for."

"Well then, gents… cockroaches, earwigs, arachnids, whatever… it seems my work here is done. You've got what you want, and I've certainly got what I want. You'll pardon me if I don't stick around, but quite frankly, on my list of places to be right now, this one ranks pretty much at the bottom."

"*We could consume you now, Aislinn. Or overwhelm you until you became like us.*"

Aislinn froze for a moment, caught off-guard by the unanticipated threat. "You could," she finally conceded, in a tone suddenly brimming with menace. "But I'm no lightweight. Try it, and I guarantee you'll regret it."

"*Go, then. We will come for you in time. None of your kind will elude us for much longer.*"

"I'll take my chances," Aislinn opined, and started to walk away across the car park, the thick forest of bugs clearing a narrow path for her. Iollan followed in her wake, darting suspicious glances at the teeming insectoid mass.

"Hey, what about me?" Emma demanded.

"Oh yes," said Aislinn, looking back. "I'll take the girl with me too. I suppose I did promise."

"No," spat Turlach. "She stays." And he rubbed the ruined side of his face ominously.

Aislinn glanced across at Emma, then shrugged. "Sorry, dear. If you see your friend Donovan again — which I rather doubt, if I'm being honest about your situation here — tell him I did try."

Emma snarled at Aislinn, but found herself staring at the woman's retreating back. Emma wanted to yell something suitably withering at the woman, but the words died in her throat as she felt Turlach's loathsome shadow fall across her. She swallowed, trying to stave off the mounting wave of terror which threatened to drown her.

"Not yet, Turlach. She is secondary. The stone, unlock the stone!"

Turlach paused and nodded reluctantly. He moved back away from Emma, returning to centre of the car park. Emma could see that he was now holding something in the pincers which had replaced his human hand. It was a small, thin rod, about six inches long, which terminated in a design very much like the bell-shaped rune embedded in the *fios* stone. Turlach pressed this end of the rod against the surface of the stone and, with a coruscating burst of electricity, the rod seemed to pass through the stone, although it did not protrude from the other side. Once about three inches of the rod had vanished, Turlach twisted it, a quarter-turn clockwise, and then stepped back hastily, wringing his alien hands in obvious anticipation.

The *fios* stone hung suspended in the rainy night air. It juddered and shivered for several seconds, as though it were about to explode. Sparks cascaded violently from its surface; a new volley of lightning sheeted through the sky above as if in harmony.

Then the *fios* stone seemed to unfold. Though it was already very thin, it opened first into an oblong form twice its original width. This folded over again, producing an even larger shape. Then, faster and faster, it spread out into a massive rectangle, fully twenty feet long on the greater of its sides. It remained hovering a yard or so off the ground, and Emma could see that its surface was now a roiling mass of colour, bleeding into every corner of the spectrum and beyond.

For a few seconds, nothing happened, and Emma watched as the colours surged and washed over each other. Then, in an instant, all of those dizzying hues imploded towards a small pinprick in the centre of what had once been the *fios* stone, glimmering against a field of nightmare black. And before Emma could draw another breath, the point of light erupted into the sky, quickly expanding into a column of wondrous fire which stirred the wind and rain into a frenzy, whipping at her face and stinging her eyes.

Turlach had retreated to within a few paces of her, and she could hear him chortling in his glee. "Yes!" he breathed, elated. "Yes! Behold… the fourth Waykey!"

Chapter Eighteen
In which all Ways lead to Twilight

Christopher was marvelling at the dizzying view afforded by his travels along the Ways. He no longer worried about the disorientation provoked by his initial journeys along the avenues of the city's collective memory. Instead, he felt a fascinated pleasure at seeing the years unravel before him, ebbing and flowing like the ocean tide.

He was walking now in the vicinity of Cavendish Square; Lochlann lead the way, his eyes fixed on some point to the south, while Chase silently brought up the rear, his countenance hooded with shadow. The landscape was flitting by at an astonishing rate, each step he took covering hundreds of paces in the real world. All the same, certain landmarks proved impossible for Christopher to ignore.

Just a little way off to his left, for instance, stood the Fort William property. Some moments, the eponymous fortifications were visible there, in various stages of construction or disrepair, and Christopher caught occasional glimpses of men dressed in ancient British — and, more rarely, French — military uniforms. Some moments, the fort seemed to be acting as a railroad station, with telltale plumes of smoke visible in the strange golden air of the Ways. And at other moments, no military battlements were present at all: instead, a large hotel was erected on the site, be it an older structure dating from the turn of the twentieth century or the newer building which had replaced it within Christopher's lifetime. He was entranced by the rolling chronicle of history, a fascination tempered only by the knowledge of Emma's captivity, and the mystery surrounding Aislinn's intentions with the *fios* stone.

Even these were nearly forgotten, though, as they advanced another pace and St John's Harbour came into view.

It wasn't the buildings on the shoreline which impressed Christopher, though they fluctuated faster than the ticking of a clock, and a strange orange-grey pall seemed to have settled over them. It wasn't the way Harbour Drive, which in modern times had been constructed to border the docks, was visible only as a pale outline barely distinguishable upon the harbour waters which lapped against the buildings lining the south side of Water Street. Nor was it the way the streets running perpendicularly to the harbour often appeared to be supplanted by long wooden wharfs, laden with barely-glimpsed goods.

No, what truly took Christopher's breath away was the harbour itself. It was at once empty and yet teeming with boats of all sizes, descriptions and antiquities. Here was a small, rickety fishing boat from the mid-1960s, laden with the day's catch. There was a trading vessel from the late nineteenth century, a rime of frost about its hardy wooden planks. Next to it, a World War II destroyer ploughed through the waters, an incongruous sight beside a towering twenty-first-century cruise ship which dwarfed the dockside with its sheer bulk. All of these and more did Christopher behold, like an encyclopaedia of maritime history brought to astonishing life before his eyes.

Chase jabbed him in the back with his walking stick to ensure Christopher didn't stop moving and drop out of the Ways. "It still impresses me, too," he admitted nonetheless. "There are few things in this world more powerful and more elegant than memory, Christopher, and the Ways are an embodiment of that. Count yourself blessed to have witnessed their wonders — and, moreover, to have appreciated it. I'm afraid that few amongst the Five Clans truly do, these days."

"I'll never forget this sight," Christopher uttered without an ounce of insincerity.

They walked on, and presently the golden glimmer of the Ways faded and the world regained the natural hues of night, blurred and distorted by the rainstorm which had only built in intensity since Christopher and Chase had first ascended the secret stair on the Memorial University campus. Thunder punctuated their arrival.

Christopher immediately looked about for Emma. "Where are we?" he demanded of Lochlann. A blustering gale howled around them, forcing him to raise his voice to be heard.

The trio stood on a narrow dirt path hugging the side of a cliff. Below, the hill fell precipitously away into the waters of the Narrows, the mouth of St John's Harbour. The lights of the city were barely visible through the rain behind them. Ahead were the endless tracks of the tempestuous sea. To their left, a dark jagged fissure rent the rock face of the slope; Christopher knew that he would not have been able to see to its bottom, even in the clear light of day. Strange, malevolent noises echoed up out of the evil-looking crack. Christopher was aware that it was simply the sound of the ocean roaring far below, but it seemed far more malignant than that — so much so that the eerie geological formation had long since entered popular folklore, with many folk in times past believing it to be an aperture into Hell itself.

"That's the Devil's Cleft," Christopher realised, answering his own question. "We're on the trail that runs around the back of Signal Hill. But where's Emma?"

Lochlann sneered at him contemptuously. "It occurred to me that it might not be the best idea to just appear right next to fair Emma, lest her captors be present also. So I've brought you to a point close by, where you might employ stealth to rescue her. She's up there," he said, gesturing towards the summit, where Cabot Tower was barely visible above the rise. "I trust my forethought does not invalidate the fulfillment of my favour to you?"

Christopher bristled at Lochlann's mock diplomacy, but controlled his temper and murmured, "No, of course not. Thank you."

Lochlann bowed exaggeratedly, and ran his hand through his rain-soaked hair. "Then my service to you is done?"

"You could stay, you know. Help us. Chase seems to think that this is a matter which involves all of your kind, not just me and him and Emma. Why not do your part?"

Lochlann stepped towards Christopher and grabbed him by his torn shirt. "Listen, Prescott, and listen well. I am not your friend. I am not your ally. I am most certainly not some kind of noble hero. I am a man of my word, mind you, and I have lived up to my responsibility — though in truth, the compact which binds me gives me little leeway to do otherwise. But know this: your bout of luck at the Parliament has cost me dearly. And the next time we meet, it will not go pleasantly for you. Are we understood?"

Christopher slapped the man's hands away from him, and glared into his one good eye. "Go away, Lochlann," he said without a trace of intimidation. "If you're not going to help us, you're a hindrance we'd do just as well to be without." And with that, the blond man was gone, the rain driving into the space he had occupied an instant before.

Christopher turned to Chase. "Shame," he sighed resignedly, "we probably could have used his help. What a jackass." He peered up through the rain at the apex of Signal Hill where, presumably, Emma was being held. "Not a stupid jackass, though."

"Indeed not," Chase concurred. "He was wise to divert our course like this. Stealth and subtlety can be great levellers when strength and power are not on your side, Mr Prescott — and we have no idea what forces Aislinn, or those with whom she's thrown in, have at their disposal."

Another series of lightning flashes darted across the sky, and the wind tore savagely at their clothes. "We'd better get a move on," Christopher suggested with a nod. "It's not a short walk from here to the top, and stealth or not, I don't want to leave Emma in Aislinn's clutches any longer than necessary."

They set off down the trail, jogging along the precarious path as best they were able in the stormy weather. There were stretches where not even a guardrail stood between them and a long drop to the jagged rocks far below, and Christopher forced himself to be patient and tread carefully, lest his foot slip on the muddy terrain — he would be of no use to Emma a broken corpse washed away in the surf. To make matters worse, there were places where tiny streams, which normally crossed the trail at a width of mere inches, had swelled to several times that size. Christopher and Chase, who was making considerable use of his walking stick, were forced to pick their way carefully through the rushing water. Within moments, both were thoroughly soaked to the skin, though Chase, despite the bulky suit he wore, seemed oblivious to the discomfort or to the weight of the water which had seeped into his clothing.

Finally, they reached a long wooden staircase which led steeply up the cliff face. It was a treacherous and draining climb — Christopher had hiked this along trail more than once with Cecily during their summers together and found this section, in this direction, to be particularly arduous. But both attacked it without delay, determination driving them onward and upward.

They were three-quarters of the way to the top when Christopher noticed something crawling along the steps ahead of them, and up the surrounding hillside for as far as he could see on either side. He stopped and motioned to Chase. "What the hell is that?" he asked, as quietly as the whipping wind and lashing rain would permit.

Chase strained to see past Christopher. "Bugs," he responded with a mix of horror and awe. And then a thought seemed to strike him. "Oh no… the Sixth Clan!"

But before Christopher could ask him to elaborate, the darkness of the night was pierced by a radiance more brilliant than any cascade of lightning. It erupted upward from the top of Signal Hill, and reached towards the grey clouds gathered above. Christopher started to think about how he had never seen such a swell of colours before... when he realised that, in fact, he had. The predominant hues were different — greens and yellows instead of oranges and reds — but the display was eerily reminiscent of the phenomenon that had engulfed him when Rose had transferred the *eochair* of the People of the Cat to him.

"A Waykey!" he exclaimed, his jaw dropping. "That's what must have been stored in the *fios* stone — the Waykey belonging to the People of the Serpent."

Chase's eyes narrowed. "Yes, that could be the knowledge Aislinn was planning to steal from her Clan." He pounded his walking stick against the wooden stairs in disgust. "I'm such a fool! The symbol on the *fios* stone, the same one which we found on Eachna's corpse... I thought it was left by the people who attacked her, but I was wrong. It appeared because of what was stolen from within her — it can only be the ancient mark of the *eochair*, the sigil of those powers who bequeathed them to the Five Clans! If only I had realised earlier... And to think, it was resting in your pocket all this time!"

"And yours too, for a while," Christopher reminded him.

"Yes, and mine too. The Sixth Clan... we can't let them obtain it. It's too potent, too dangerous! Hurry, Mr Prescott!"

The urgency in Chase's voice unmistakeable, Christopher spun about and ran up several more steps before halting abruptly. Chase nearly vaulted into his back. "What are you waiting for?" the British man demanded.

"You're forgetting the bugs," Christopher muttered over his shoulder. "And I don't think they want us to go any further."

In front of him, the creeping army of insects seemed to have taken notice of them and had stopped its ascent of Signal Hill to bar their path. Literally millions of the creatures were swarming the cliff; it looked as though the very rock itself was alive.

Then, much to Christopher's horror, a voice arose from the mass of bugs. How the rending, chittering noise formed into intelligible words he scarcely wanted to contemplate, but he could hardly ignore them.

"Ah, Donovan Chase. You are known to us. We are unsurprised by your appearance at this place, at this time. But you are too late to stop us, Chase."

"And who are you, exactly?" Chase demanded belligerently.

"We are the People of the Insect. We shall soon be masters of the Ways. We shall hold the very soul of the city in our thrall."

"Impossible! Even possessing two *eochair* isn't sufficient to seize that level of control. The other Clans will oppose you, defeat you."

And then there came a noise which made Christopher shiver to his very bones: the insects, as one, seemed to be laughing. "That can't be good," he murmured, though Chase appeared not to hear.

"Come to us, Chase. Be witness to our final ascension. We would be... honoured."

"You want me where you can see me, more like," Chase growled.

"But we can see you now, Chase. And there is no escape from us. Finish your climb. Your friend... Emma... is waiting for you."

"Emma!" Christopher gasped, picturing her drowning in a flood of insects.

"We were on our way anyhow," Chase griped, and prodded Christopher forward, towards the source of the incredible pillar of light which was now pulsating vigorously. The carpet of bugs parted slightly to allow them to proceed.

"What was that... that voice?" Christopher asked as they completed their now-fruitless journey.

"Eachna's Sixth Clan. The People of the Insect. A gestalt entity with delusions of grandeur... and, unfortunately, it would appear that they may have acquired the means to transform those delusions into reality."

"Using the Waykeys to dominate the city's own memories?"

"Yes." Chase's eyes narrowed. "And precisely how do you know so much about the *eochair*, Mr Prescott?"

Christopher felt a little guilty now that he had not divulged to Chase the unwanted gift he had received from the People of the Cat, but he still felt it would be safest if only he, Rose and her companions knew of it. Then he glanced ahead and saw that they were ascending the final flight of stairs to the top. "It doesn't matter," he called back at last. "So the Sixth Clan, the People of the Insect... what exactly can they do if they seize the Ways?"

"It would be monstrous, Christopher... the Ways are a link between every member of the Five Clans, between every living being in St John's, be they from your world or mine." Christopher wasn't so sure that the distinction was accurate anymore, but knew it was not the appropriate time to correct Chase. "They could use the Ways to absorb everyone into their gestalt — their hive mind."

Christopher tried to conceive of it — himself, Chase, Emma, his parents, Cecily, his friends, almost everyone he knew, subsumed against their will into a mental communion, a single being spread throughout thousands of bodies, acting with the instincts and desires of an insect. It seemed too hideous to be even remotely possible, yet it appeared that it was on the brink of coming horribly true.

"And don't think it would stop there," Chase continued. "The Ways, as Clansfolk here call it, are not isolated. Beneath the whole world — whole worlds — the mystery of our culture endures in the shadows and the cracks and the margins, and indelibly intertwined with that mystery is the memory of towns and cities, countries and continents, empires and realms. The People of the Insect could use the Ways as a bridgehead to the conquest and consumption of everything there is."

"But why start here?" Christopher cried. "Why St John's? This city isn't big, it isn't rich, it isn't really important in the grand global scheme of things. Why not do this in New York, or Toronto, or... or London, Moscow, Rome, anywhere other than here? Is it just a matter of seizing an opportunity?"

Chase considered the question for a moment as the summit of Signal Hill loomed directly ahead of them. "Perhaps, Mr Prescott, perhaps. But don't forget that St John's is the single oldest city in all of North America, and that makes it extremely special. This place is a nexus between the Old World and the New, in a way that nowhere else in the world can claim. I suspect that made it singularly attractive for our enemy."

"How do we stop it?" Christopher asked, nearly pleading for an answer.

But Chase just shook his head. There, amidst the rain and the wind and the darkness, he looked suddenly very old and very tired. "I don't know," he whispered, so faintly that the words were nearly lost on the breeze.

Christopher clambered up the last few steps and emerged onto the car park atop Signal Hill. He was breathing heavily, his clothes sticking to him with rainwater and humidity and sweat. As Chase followed close behind him, Christopher started to survey the scene.

Immediately, he was forced to shut his eyes tightly, as the column of radiance spiking up from the centre of the lot curved downward to form a spectacular arch. Its far end met the quivering black sea of bugs and erupted outward, consuming the insects. The brilliance surged towards them, blazing mercilessly into the teeming mass. Then, abruptly, the light was gone, leaving just sparks of green and yellow dancing in the air amidst the torrents of rain.

"It is done," uttered a strange, warbling voice. Christopher opened his eyes and realised that the speaker was not a person at all, but rather a hideous man-sized mutant insect, like something out of a Fifties horror comic book. The grotesque creature stood in the middle of the parking lot, not far from the source of the incredible illumination. "The *fios* stone is exhausted. The *eochair* is ours!"

"What in god's name is that?" Christopher demanded of Chase, slack-jawed. Aislinn's reptilian croney, Iollan, had been a gruesome enough sight, but at least some traces of humanity had still been evident in his form. This... this was nothing short of a monster come to life.

"He's called Turlach," came a tremulous voice to their left. As one, Christopher and Chase turned to see Emma standing there. She seemed to be handcuffed to the wall which ran around the perimeter of the car park. It was difficult to tell for certain, though, because nearly every inch of the girl's body was covered in writhing, undulating insects. She kicked and wriggled in a desperate effort to keep them from crawling too far up the uncharacteristically old-fashioned dress she wore. Only her eyes and mouth remained clear, and even then she was forced to squirm and shake her head constantly to keep the bugs from getting at them as well.

Despite her situation, Christopher was overwhelmed with elation at their reunion. "Emma!" he cried joyfully.

"Miss Rawlin," Chase acknowledged more reservedly. His gaze was fixed on the insect-man.

"Hello, boys," Emma replied through chattering teeth. "Hope you'll pardon my manners if I don't shake hands." Despite the horror of the situation, Christopher found himself grinning at her unquenchable pluck.

"Turlach, eh?" Chase said loudly. He began to cross the car park towards the insect-man, halting only when a wall of bugs moved together across his path. Chase set the butt of his walking stick down firmly on the pavement, crushing a beetle underneath. "I seem to recall a man named Turlach... he lived in Gloucester some considerable time back. He was a mindrapist," he spat, "of the worst order. He liked to befriend single mothers and convince them to let him babysit their children. He'd use the hours alone with the youngsters to get inside their heads, to the point that he could control them as easily as marionettes." Chase's expression had become as cold as ice in the intense heat of the night. "Then he'd have them perform… foulnesses for his pleasure and amusement." Christopher felt sick; Emma seemed no less disturbed.

"It's been a long time, Chase," Turlach chirruped with glee. "Those were good days, weren't they?"

"I thought I'd killed you," Chase told him in a voice which sounded quiet, yet carried clearly over the tumult of the storm. "I thought you'd died when I pushed you out of that tower."

Turlach beat his papery wings proudly, and for the first time Christopher noticed that of his three sets of limbs, the lowest pair — the legs — seemed utterly immobile. Indeed, the insect-man was placing no weight on them, instead appearing content to hover just above the ground. "Not quite," Turlach was saying. "Oh, my legs were shattered into uselessness and I spent a very long time convalescing. But after many seasons I became well enough to flee England and migrate here, to Newfoundland. And now, the People of the Insect have given me splendid new life!"

"You still can't use your legs, though, I see."

"That's her fault!" Turlach roared, gesturing in Emma's direction. "She forced the change prematurely."

"Good girl," Chase grinned, nodding towards Emma complimentarily.

"She will regret it," seethed Turlach.

"How interesting," Chase said loudly, changing the subject. "It seems the Sixth Clan has still permitted you some degree of independence, Turlach. Why is that, I wonder? Is it because deep down they know that their gestalt philosophy really isn't the best working model? Or is it simply because you don't actually meet the standards for admission into their collective? You always were of a lower rank than even the common cockroach."

The insect-man seemed on the verge of a heated retort when a ripple ran through the mass of bugs, on the ground and in the air, and that unnatural voice once again assailed Christopher's ears.

"Enough of this! Turlach, ignore his prattling. He seeks only to confuse you and delay our plans. We have now harnessed the eochair *of both the People of the Caribou and the People of the Serpent. It is time for us to consume the two remaining Waykeys in our possession."*

Turlach nodded with a small degree of reluctance, and tore something away from his carapaced neck. Christopher thought he could see the glimmer of two gemstones, but before he was able to get a better look, the insect-man had tossed them into his mandibled mouth and swallowed them both whole.

"No!" howled Chase in futile protest.

But the air around Turlach was already filling with two brilliant, competing glows: one dappled with blue and silver, the other awash with green and orange. After a few seconds, these swirled around Turlach, faster and faster, as if the coloured patterns were racing each other. Then, just as it seemed the energies could orbit him no more rapidly, Turlach exhaled noisily and they exploded outward, pelting down onto the bugs which surrounded him and finally fading from sight. Turlach tilted his head in satisfaction.

"Excellent. We can feel the eochair *of the People of the Great Auk and the People of the Codfish surging through us now as well. Only one Waykey remains beyond our grasp."*

"The one belonging to the People of the Cat?" queried Chase.

"Yes," said Turlach, rising a few feet in the air to loom above the little man.

"You'll never get your pincers on it," Chase declared dismissively. "You'll not catch them unawares like you did the People of the Caribou, nor find somebody in power corrupt enough to betray her own Clan, as with the People of the Serpent."

"We'll find a way," gloated Turlach. "It's inevitable now."

"No. Donovan Chase is correct."

"He is?" spat Turlach, floating back down to the ground.

"I am?" echoed Chase, caught a little off guard himself. "Erm, I mean, yes, of course I am!"

"*Which is why Chase and his friend will obtain the Waykey of the People of the Cat on our behalf.*"

"I'll do no such thing!" yelled Chase indignantly, his strangulated tone evoking his outrage. Behind him, Christopher merely watched the proceedings quietly. "Why don't you get Aislinn to do your bidding? She's come through for you so far. Where is she, anyway? I assumed she'd be here standing alongside you."

"*Aislinn of the People of the Serpent has fulfilled her role in our plan, and received the trifling reward she coveted so greedily. We will renew our acquaintance with her in the fullness of time. Now, will you obey our command?*"

"Never!"

"*Then your female friend shall die.*"

And Emma cried out, in pain and in terror, as more insects advanced towards her amidst the pounding rain. Her agony was echoed as a rolling burst of thunder exploded in the heavens.

"No, stop! Wait!" screamed Christopher, charging forward to stand beside Chase. The bugs retreated from Emma, just a little.

"*And what do you have to offer us, human? Will you do as we ask?*"

"I'll do you one better," Christopher said bitterly, the words almost torn from his throat.

"No, Christopher, don't offer them anything," warned Chase. "If the Sixth Clan gets their way, eventually we'll all be absorbed into their group mind. If Emma dies tonight, it will be a kindness compared to that living death!"

"I know," moaned Christopher. "Rationally, I know you're right. But much though I try to pretend otherwise, when it comes right down to it my actions are ruled by my heart, not by my head. That's the way I am, and there's nothing I can do about it. So I'm not going struggle against it any longer."

Chase seized his arms beseechingly. "Remember what happened with Aislinn, Christopher. Don't betray us just because you think you've fallen in love with some girl!"

Christopher shrugged him away. "I don't love Emma, Chase. I hardly know her, how could I love her? But she's done something for me that means as much to me as love."

"What's that?"

Christopher glanced over at Emma, still cocooned within a black shell of insects. Then he turned back to Chase. "She's reminded me that there is magic in the world, after all. There are marvellous things out there, Chase, if only you're willing to go look for them. I'd lost that for a long time — thanks to a relationship that settled into tedium, a livelihood that became routine, and most of all a life which drove the sense of wonder from me time and time again. I realise that now, because of Emma. And you have no idea how very much I value that.

"So I know now that I'd die for Emma, Chase. I know that with more clarity than I know anything else."

The bugs littering the ground chittered impatiently.

"*What is it you wish to say, human?*"

"The People of the Cat don't have their Waykey anymore. It was given away."

"*Then who wields it? Where does it reside?*"

Christopher remained silent for several moments, his head bowed, breathing in the sultry air. Then he looked back up at Turlach and at the legion of insects surrounding him.

"I've got it. It's inside me."

Chapter Nineteen
In which Prophecy is fulfilled

Chase's eyes boggled and seemed almost on the verge of popping out of his skull. "What are you saying?" he yelped. "Why didn't you tell me?"

Christopher regarded him with a cool, stoic expression. "I'm telling you now," he declared loudly. But under his breath, in a voice as low as he dared let it drop in the wind and the weather, he murmured, "Just trust me for once."

Chase narrowed his eyes suspiciously, but finally nodded his head.

"How is this possible?" demanded Turlach, his wings flittering agitatedly. "How can this boy already possess the final *eochair*?"

But an almost euphoric twittering arose from the insectoid throng.

"*It does not matter. It is all happening as was foreseen!*"

"What do you mean?" Chase bellowed, looking around himself in furious disgust.

But Christopher had already realised what the Sixth Clan was implying. "The People of the Cat... one of their number could... predict the future. Smell the winds of change, I think was the way they described it. There's one among you who has a similar talent, isn't there?"

"*Yes. It is hardly a feat of scent, but the principle is the same. We were certain that the girl would be the catalyst in our plan. That is why we had Turlach summon her through artifice. We knew that it would be because of her that we would obtain the final ele-*

ment we needed. And while we had not anticipated the circuitous route by which this was accomplished, in the end, all has come to pass as it was preordained."

"I don't believe it," muttered Chase. "Precognition is one of the rarest of abilities. In the whole world, there is only a precious handful with sufficient ability to see meaningfully past teatime tomorrow. And you're telling me that there have been at least two, right here in St John's, who can make predictions deep into the mists of time? Preposterous!"

"*Ah, Chase, always you and your kind reckon without the insect world. We are uncounted multitudes! What is more unbelievable is that we have discovered only one foreteller amongst our number. Soon, though, the handful of which you speak will be part of us as well, and then our vision of the glorious future awaiting us will be unsurpassed.*"

"If one of your bugs can see what's going to happen, why all the posturing?" wondered Christopher. "Surely that means you know how this is all going to play out."

"Not remotely, Mr Prescott," Chase replied. "Foretelling is a desperately elusive and cryptic ability, even amongst its mightiest practitioners. If the Sixth Clan's understanding of the future was so complete, then why didn't they know right away that you wield the final Waykey? Why didn't they predict that you would collect Aislinn's *fios* stone, thereby delaying their plans by at least a day?"

"*It no longer matters. Now the chain of events is inevitable. You will give us the* eochair, *human, and you will do so immediately.*"

Christopher grinned apologetically. "There's just one problem," he said, cringing theatrically.

"*No! No problems! What is the delay?*"

Christopher ran a hand through his dripping wet hair. "I don't actually know how to hand it over to you. It got put inside me — I didn't really have any say in the matter, let alone understand how it all worked."

"*Then we shall cleave it from your soul!*"

"Like you did with Eachna of the People of the Caribou," Christopher nodded. "Yeah, I was actually just thinking back to what she told us after you'd killed her."

The insects had begun to mass in a peculiar formation when abruptly they paused, as if taken aback by Christopher's words.

"You speak nonsense. Even the Unnoticed cannot communicate with the dead."

Chase chuckled darkly. "How ironic... even the bugs have forgotten the Forgotten Cemetery."

But Christopher was ploughing forward heedlessly, fully aware that he might only have seconds left to play his trump card.

"She told us you stole the Waykey she kept within herself before she was dead. And I've been asking myself — apart from sheer cruelty, why wouldn't you just wait until she was passed on before you sucked it out of her?"

"Because then it would be too late," said Chase, realisation dawning on him.

"Exactly," agreed Christopher. "Because the Waykey is bound up into the soul of the person it's hidden within. And if I'm remembering my admittedly rather neglected Catholic upbringing correctly, the soul isn't supposed to stick around once you've shuffled off this mortal coil."

"So if Eachna had died first, the *eochair* would have become... inaccessible."

Christopher nodded approvingly, like he would to a student who had just successfully struggled through a particularly difficult calculus problem. "Got it in one, Donovan." He winked. "It's been fun."

And in the same moment, he snapped his fingers. Instantly, Faolan's dagger was in his hand. Without even stopping to think, he slid it smoothly from its sheath and flipped the hilt so that the blade was pointed at himself. Then, with a cry of triumph, of terror, and of regret, Christopher slammed the knife towards his breast. Emma screamed in horror and Chase simply looked on, his face a mask of unvoiced despondence. Christopher waited for a brief flowering of pain as the dagger pierced his heart, preceding the interminable darkness that would quickly follow.

But it never came. For as swift as Christopher may have been in executing his self-sacrificial scheme, the People of the Insect were swifter still.

A bolt of sizzling black energy flashed out towards him from the insects massing into eldritch positions along the ground. Christopher was thrown back ten feet through the air, and landed with a painful thud on the asphalt not far from Emma's feet. Faolan's blade went clattering out of his hand, to be nearly lost beneath the forest of bugs.

"*We will not be so easily deprived of our prize, human! We are not mindless imbeciles!*"

Christopher lay there on the ground, twitching feebly as black sparks continued to torture the length of his body. Pain coursed through each nerve fibre, his vision swam drunkenly in and out of focus, and he was using every ounce of energy he still possessed just to struggle to remain conscious.

But Christopher Prescott was a man accused more than once of being stubborn and mule-headed. And there was no way he was going to submit to a bunch of bugs without fighting to the last. Concentrating on the agony wracking his frame, he channelled it into an anguished howl: "Chase!"

* * *

And, across the car park, the little man nodded in understanding, knew what Christopher was asking him to do even if the younger man could have no idea how Chase was going to accomplish it. He regarded his beloved walking stick one final time, his eyes tracing the intricate patterns engraved thereupon, and remembered the fate which had befallen its twin, long ago. "Goodbye, old girl," he murmured ruefully. Then he seized it in both hands and brought it sharply down upon his knee.

* * *

The stick cracked clean through. The severed lengths of wood erupted into two enormous clouds of roiling energy, blue like the cloudless heavens on a clear summer's day and golden-red like a sunset Christopher had once seen as a child, the swollen copper orb sinking low in the pink sky beyond the placid waters of Conception Bay.

Chase pointed to the storm-tossed clouds above and whispered, "*Marcach. Capall. Marcshlua.*"

At his command, the energy he had unleashed spiralled upward into the heavens. There it exploded with a frenzy to put even the greatest of the night's lightning strikes to shame.

And, for a moment, all was silent.

Then, above the noise of the rain and the wind, Christopher could hear another sound — low, rhythmic and percussive like the backbeat at the dance bar where all of this had started. As he watched, shapes emerged from behind the cover of the great grey clouds. They were enormous spectral riders, warriors in ancient armour astride massive steeds which snorted and frothed. From what Christopher could see of them, the phantoms' faces were fixed with a grim intensity, and there was no mistaking their target: the writhing mass of bugs atop Signal Hill. He could hear Turlach chittering in fright and alarm, and the entire body of insects seemed panicked in the face of the oncoming assault.

But Christopher was still virtually paralysed, his limbs spasming periodically but otherwise of no practical use. The never-ending pain continued to cripple his brain, making it hard to think of a new plan now that the Sixth Clan had foiled his original idea. And he knew that the supernatural army Chase had summoned would still only delay the insects: before long, they would renew their efforts to seize the cats' Waykey from him.

Behind him, the sound of clinking metal suddenly reached Christopher's ears. There was a rush of movement, the swish of a cream-coloured dress.

And then Christopher was a child again, dreaming. He wasn't certain, but he thought he was a little older than he had been when he'd had the dream about swordfighting in Bowring Park — closer to the age when such fantasies were beginning to seem foolish, when belief in wizards and goblins and Santa Claus was cause for scorn, not admiration.

All the same, he was dreaming that he was a knight on a quest, astride a snorting orange sphinx. It was a long quest which had taken him through many strange lands, from pleasant green fields to dark, sinister caverns, from vast halls of learning to the peak of a mighty mountain range. But as he finally dismounted his steed, he realised that though his goal (whatever that might be) was in sight, he had no idea what he was meant to do now to achieve it. And he stood there, perplexed, as the seconds drained away.

Then, just as it seemed all hope was lost, a woman stepped out of the shadows. In the way of dreams, she was at once old and gnarled, yet young and beautiful, but regardless, she was very, very wise. She pulled her shawl (or was it an extravagant fur stole?) tightly about herself, looked down at him — for he was, after all, still just a boy — and, smiling beatifically, said, "Remember the steps of your journey, Christopher. Remember what has gone before. Nothing in life happens without reason — not while you still believe in its essential magic."

And in a rainy car park atop Signal Hill, Christopher remembered again the words of the three unsettling schoolgirls: *One has betrayed them, one will betray them, and one of them will slay another.* Chase had stolen the *fios* stone from him. Christopher had handed it recklessly over to Aislinn. And Emma...

Oh no.

In that moment, Christopher Prescott's heart broke in twain. Because now he knew what had to be done.

*   *   *

Emma had watched the confrontation between Christopher, Chase and the People of the Insect with a mixture of dread and frustration. She was incensed that she could not stand there alongside her companions, that she was barely able to speak for fear that a red ant or centipede might take the opportunity to climb into her open mouth.

But Emma Rawlin was far from helpless. Ever since Iollan had chained her up, Emma had been using her particular talents to work away at the handcuff locks while the attention of others — first Aislinn and her reptilian flunky, then Turlach and his insectoid masters — was directed elsewhere. It had been a difficult process: her bonds had come into being through enchanted means, and so were less receptive to her efforts than normal cuffs would have been. But as the minutes ticked by, Emma felt herself becoming more and more familiar with their construction, could tell that she was getting ever closer to the point where she could convince the locks to relax and the restraints to open at her command.

And then, at the very moment that Christopher was hurled violently in her direction by the dark energies conjured by the People of the Insect, Emma felt the metal confining her right hand start to give way. As she watched her friend writhing in torment amidst the legions of bugs, she bent her mind implacably towards the task of unlocking the handcuffs, straining with all her might — and finally, as Chase's ghostly warriors materialised in the skies above St John's, she was free.

Angrily clawing away the insects which were clambering all over her, Emma raced to Christopher's prone form. She knelt beside him, brushing rainwater feverishly out of his face. To her astonishment, Christopher seemed to be trying to laugh.

"What's so funny?" she found herself asking, arching an eyebrow.

Christopher gestured towards the riders on the storm. "Aislinn said Chase was all tall tales and parlour tricks," he murmured, in a voice so pained and so quiet that Emma had to strain to catch his words. "And she was right! I think… I think those are just illusions. But lord, have they got the bugs running sc—" His sentence was cut off as he was gripped by a violent fit of coughing.

"Shhh," Emma said soothingly, coaxing the hair back from his face. "Try to take it easy."

"Nice dress," he quipped, grinning weakly.

"Thanks. I don't think it's quite me, though." She looked around desperately, trying to come up with some plan to save Christopher and stop the People of the Insect, but found no inspiration in the endless sea of bugs all around. More of them had moved into arcane formations, and black bursts of energy were spitting out towards the spectral warriors. Some of the riders dissolved away into nothingness as they bore the brunt of the insects' attack, but more boiled out of the clouds, and the lead horses were closing the gap with the bugs.

"Damn it, Christopher," Emma cursed, "we have to do something!"

Tentatively, Christopher reached his hand up to clasp hers. "I know what to do," he whispered, his lips barely working properly, his voice strained to the point of hoarseness.

"I hope it doesn't involve you trying to murder yourself again," she said seriously.

"No," he smiled wistfully. "Not in this condition." His smile vanished. "Emma, this time you have to kill me."

Emma dropped his hand as though it was burning hot. "Excuse me?"

Christopher's eyes bore into hers with a vitality belying the tortured state of his body. "It's the only way. I don't know what will happen to the Waykey, but the bugs won't get it. That's all that matters."

Emma shook her head insistently. "Not a chance. I can't do it, Christopher. There's got to be another way."

"Listen to me," Christopher pleaded, as fervently as he could likely manage in his state. "The cats… they did something to me when they gave me the Waykey. If the People of the Insect take it from me… I'll die anyway, and you know that's not going to matter to them. And if they get control of the Ways… I don't even want to think about it. Far better that my time should end… to prevent that from happening. Please."

"You can't ask me to do this!"

Christopher struggled to rise. "Please!" he cried, tears brimming in his eyes.

Thunder rolled sonorously, and lightning danced amidst the phantasms in the sky, now just moments away from touching down — at which point, she knew, their insubstantial nature would become plain even to the frantic bugs.

Emma's thoughts flashed back to her time with Lochlann, to the days she endured as Emmeline, a weak, fragile, submissive antithesis of her true self. She remembered how Lochlann had inveigled himself into her conscience — subtly at first, and then taking greater and greater control until he had twisted her into something she wasn't, something she had never wanted to be. And she remembered how he had maintained that control, through meaningless giftgiving, emotional manipulation, hollow flattery, tantalising glimpses of the mysteries of the Five Clans, and eventually much much worse. Her very being had been consumed by Lochlann: Emmeline had been little more than a puppet dancing on the end of his strings, or a pet dog, lapping at her master's heels, desperate to do whatever she could to earn his affection and approval…

And now the People of the Insect wanted to do the same thing, not just to her but to everyone she knew, and many more besides. And this time, there would be no escaping their insidious thrall.

Emma began sobbing uncontrollably as she realised that Christopher was absolutely right. She had no other choice.

"Please don't cry," Christopher said distantly, more than a little hypocritically. "Your face is far too lovely for tears."

Emma smiled despite herself, dabbing hastily at her eyes. "Christopher… I know you told Chase you didn't love me…"

"It's nothing personal," he sighed, resting his head back onto the sodden ground and closing his eyes. "I don't believe in love at first sight."

"Neither do I. Love comes in time, not in a flash of divine inspiration."

Christopher tried to nod his agreement, but his body was wracked by another prolonged spasm.

"But do you think that maybe, eventually, we might have…"

Visibly forcing his contortions to abate, Christopher reached a trembling hand up and caressed Emma's tear-stained cheek. He seemed about to speak, when suddenly his eyes went wide. "Hurry," he gasped. "Look!"

Chase's ghost cavalry was upon the bugs; only the bursts of crackling dark energy, now coming faster and faster as the People of the Insect redoubled their efforts, were keeping the wraiths at bay. But the Sixth Clan seemed to be growing tired. The expenditure of arcane energies was taking its toll, and it appeared that, imminently, either one of the warriors would have to physically assault the insectoid army, or else their reticence to do so would reveal the charade anyway.

Emma kissed the palm of Christopher's hand tenderly, and then eased it back down onto his chest.

"Faolan's knife…" he whispered urgently. "You have to find the knife."

Emma nodded, breathed deeply, and then propelled herself away from him, her head weaving back and forth as she scanned the pavement for any sign of the weapon. Lightning seared the sky, and in the momentary burst of illumination, she saw it: a glint of metal amidst a nest of writhing bugs. Heedless of the insects, Emma dashed over and grabbed the blade, then returned to Christopher's side as rapidly as she could. The dagger felt heavier than lead in her hands, and the hilt was slick with rainwater and perspiration, but she held on tightly as she knelt back beside her friend.

Again their eyes met, and Emma could barely quell a flood of tears. Gripping the knife in both hands, she held the point over Christopher's heart.

"Use all your strength," he moaned. "Make sure you break through the ribcage." He grinned bittersweetly. "No need to make this hurt any more than it has to."

Emma nodded and returned his smile for one final time. Christopher shut his eyes wearily. She raised the blade, ready to strike…

Something black and sharp clamped itself around Emma's neck. Kicking and gasping for breath, she was dragged roughly to her feet.

Christopher's eyes sprang open, and they widened instantly in fright. "Turlach!" he spat.

"Did you forget about me, Emma?" the insect-man chittered, his noisome mandibles nuzzling her ear. "You have spurned me, burned me, and disfigured me. But now there is no one to save you."

His claws tightened sickeningly around her supple neck. Emma's eyes bulged alarmingly, and all the colour drained from her face. Christopher struggled to rise, to lash out, to do something to save her, but his muscles were oblivious to his needs.

"Not quite no one, Turlach," came a richly-accented voice. There was a terrible tearing sound, and the insect-man squealed hideously, dropping Emma to the ground and crumpling onto the pavement next to her.

Christopher looked past Turlach and saw Chase standing there, his face ablaze with wrath. In his hands he held the remains of Turlach's loathsome wings, ripped from the monster's back and dripping with a grey-green ichor which bubbled and boiled as it hit the pavement. He regarded the abomination pitilessly as Turlach screamed an unending, unearthly scream.

"It's time I make amends for a past mistake," the little man muttered balefully. Chase reached down and grabbed Turlach by the stumps which were all that remained of his wings. And despite his diminutive stature, he hauled the insect-man across the car park to the edge of the barrier wall looking out onto the Atlantic Ocean.

"Despite the horror movie cliché," Chase spat, "I don't think you'll be coming back from the dead a second time." And he heaved Turlach over the side. Emma could hear the creature's body impacting heavily against the side of the cliff for several seconds, before the terrible noises were finally swallowed up in the storm.

Chase turned back to Emma, breathing heavily. "Finish this, Miss Rawlin! Quickly now!"

And indeed, the first of his phantasmal warriors were breaking against the tide of bugs. An uneasy ripple seemed to pass through the insectoid multitudes, as it dawned on them that something was very much amiss.

"*What... what is this?*"

Emma gathered her wits and reasserted her grip on the heavy, razor-edged knife.

"I'd give anything to get to know you better," she confessed shakily, looking down at Christopher's exhausted, ashen face.

His eyelids slid closed. For a moment, Emma thought that he hadn't heard her. But then his lips moved, almost imperceptibly, and he whispered, "Maybe in another time... another life..."

A final, furious explosion of lightning lit up the sky overhead and the blade gleamed in the brightness as Emma drew it up into the air over Christopher's heart.

"*Trickery! We must secure the* eochair!"

Emma couldn't bear to look at what she was doing; instead, she turned her eyes heavenward and let the rain wash over her face, mingling with the tears that now flowed freely.

"*No!*"

The dagger slammed down into Christopher's chest.
"*NO!!!*"
He died instantly.

Chapter Twenty
In which things Change

Chase tackled Emma to the ground as a charge of black energy swept through the space where she had been kneeling a moment before. But the dark shaft seemed less potent, more sluggish than the one which had felled Christopher, and Emma thought vaguely that the distraction of the skyborne warriors, now fading from sight like will o' the wisps, must have drained the People of the Insect even more significantly than she could have hoped.

Chase clambered off her back, and helped Emma to rise unsteadily to her feet. "I can't believe I just did that," she said in a very small voice, finding it difficult to look Chase in the eye. She realised that the dagger was still clasped tightly in her hand, Christopher's blood running in red rivulets off its edge. She wanted to drop it, forget she had ever held it, but she couldn't force herself to let go.

"You did what you had to do. As did Christopher," Chase told her. She supposed he was trying to make her feel better, but his voice lacked its customary conviction. "Never forget, the alternative would have been much worse."

"*WHAT HAVE YOU DONE?*"

The voice of the People of the Insect assaulted their ears again, but it sounded strident now, dissonant and even more distorted than usual — as if the concordance of so many bugs was faltering in its unity.

Hesitantly, Emma looked back across at Christopher's body. She gasped. Chase turned to follow her gaze.

It began with a point of light, glimmering amidst the blood which pumped from the wound at Christopher's breast. Then there was a second pinprick, and a third, and then a dozen or more, shimmering scarlet. And suddenly, radiance was pouring out of Christopher in waves, bathing the summit of Signal Hill with dazzling hues of red and of orange.

"The *eochair* of the People of the Cat," noted Chase. "Beyond anybody's control now."

But as the bewitching lights danced in the stormy night sky, the thousands upon thousands of insects covering the ground and obscuring the air began to emit a mournful, frustrated noise, all together. This was swiftly followed by a tremendous howl of wind, and abruptly there was an eruption of colour and energy, soaring upward from the hilltop. Greens and blues cavorted wildly around yellows and oranges. Streaks of glittering white traced pristine trails through fields of red.

"What's happening?" Emma asked in wonderment. Despite everything that had transpired on this night, despite all the horror and pain and tragedy, she found herself smiling in childlike amazement at the entrancing spectacle.

"The People of the Insect… they've lost their grip on the other *eochair*. Look, see — they no longer move and act as one." It was true: the bugs were now milling about aimlessly, confused and frightened. Many were spilling over the edges of the wall rimming the summit, trying to get away from the scene of their utter defeat. "Their spirit, their gestalt, has been broken. They no longer have the strength to bridle so much power."

As Emma watched, the gambolling hues began spinning faster and faster in the air, and a sound like the most glorious, angelic music never composed rose above the wind and the rain.

And then, with a deafening roar, the energies burst into a billion tiny specks of unutterable beauty, which began raining down upon the slumbering city. It was, Emma thought, like that first pristine snowfall in winter, but dappled with every colour of the spectrum.

Finally, the shower of radiance faded into the night.

"They're gone," Emma said, and breathed a melancholy sigh. "What does it mean?"

But Chase was silent. He was staring at Christopher, whose body now lay in an empty car park, devoid of even a single lurking insect. Only the puddles of rainwater still encircled him.

"What is it?" Emma asked, crooking an eyebrow.

Suddenly, Chase was running across the pavement, diving down next to Christopher. Emma raced over to join him, and found him with the flat of his hand hovering inches above Christopher's still lips.

"What the hell are you doing?" she asked. This close to her friend's corpse, she felt the euphoria of the light show wither inside her, to be replaced with a deep, bottomless grief she feared would never be dispelled.

"He's alive," whispered Chase, his voice rich with astonishment.

"That's not possible!" cried Emma. She pointed to the gaping wound through Christopher's heart. She wanted to grab Chase and beat her fists against him for playing this morbid trick on her.

"Feel for yourself!" the little man snapped irritably. He grabbed Emma's arm and dragged her down to her knees, placing her palm where his had just been.

And she could feel it. It was incredibly faint, to the point of non-existence, but it was undeniably there. One breath. Then, after a very long time, another. And another.

"It isn't possible," she gasped.

"Haven't you learned for yourself the lesson you drummed into Christopher?" asked Chase. "In our world, nothing is impossible." He looked up at the heavens, where the rain had ceased, the winds had calmed, the thunder was silenced, the lightning was stilled, and the clouds were parting to unveil the first grey glint of dawn. "The unimaginable power of the Waykey, which should have taken his life had he tried to give it up… instead, it has sustained him beyond death."

Emma just stared at Chase, and then back down to Christopher's near-motionless body. "But the wound…"

"Could still kill him," the British man concurred. "Even the *eochair* cannot keep him alive for long. We need to get him to help."

"But where?"

"I know a place." Very gingerly, Chase slid his arms under Christopher's back and legs, and hoisted him up. "Come on. There isn't a moment to lose!"

*   *   *

Esther was uneasily grooming her tail when suddenly Rose, who had been napping fitfully for the entire day and night, sprang rigidly upright in that preternatural manner that cats have. In happier times, Esther would have been searching about, assuming that the fattest, juiciest mouse in St John's had just trotted heedlessly into the penthouse. Instead, she merely nudged Rose with her head.

"How long have I… we… been asleep?" Rose demanded, her eyes wild, her pupils thin slits.

"Hours. You've missed at least seven meals."

"Are you okay now, First Minister?" Shadow asked, bounding across the room from where he had stationed himself beside the door.

Rose shook her head, her flattened ears returning to their more serene, upright stance. "Yes." Her whiskers bristled. "Do you smell it?"

Esther looked to Shadow, worried that their leader's mind had snapped under the previous day's exertions. But the black male was staring at Rose in something approaching understanding. "Smell what?" he asked encouragingly, an undertone of urgency apparent in his words.

"It has happened."

"What has?" demanded Esther impatiently.

"What was going to happen... has come to pass. There is a new scent upon the wind. We are no seer like our beloved half-brother, but we know that our world has changed."

"But for good or for ill?" Shadow rumbled ominously.

Rose met his stare for several seconds, unwilling or unable to answer the question.

Then the fragile silence of the room was shattered as a frantic white shape burst through the hatch in the door.

"Lady Rose!" Spot cried, her voice aflutter with panic.

"What is it, Spot?" the First Minister asked, maintaining her composure with some effort.

"We have unexpected guests. I think you'd better come see for yourself."

"Bring them here!" spat Esther. "You know full well that the First Minister receives visitors; she does not loiter after them."

But Shadow had been regarding Spot appraisingly, and nodded his head. "I think we need to make an exception in this case, my lady." Though his tone remained mild, there was no mistaking the earnestness he conveyed.

Rose was quick to react. "It shall be so," she concurred. "Follow," she beckoned to the assembled felines and, with Spot leading the way, and Shadow and Esther flanking the First Minister, they rushed from the room.

*   *   *

Christopher was lying upon the same bed the cats had allocated to him less than twenty-four hours earlier. Emma stood over him, sobs of frustration buffeting her form. She had torn a strip off her wet, dirty, ruined dress and was pressing it against the grievous wound to Christopher's heart, trying uselessly to staunch the bleeding. She glared at the fat white cat sleeping at the bottom of the comforter, who resolutely refused to wake up, much less find a new resting place and allow Christopher the entire length and breadth of the bed. If Chase hadn't warned her against offending their hosts, she would have pitched him out into the corridor ages ago.

Chase stood silently, like a statue, looking out of the nearest window. The first dim shafts of morning were breaking through the vanishing clouds, casting a gold-grey light upon the quenched grass and dripping trees.

"Dammit," Emma wailed, "it might already be too late. Where are they?"

No sooner had the words been uttered than the cat-flap flew open, admitting first one and then three more felines. The cat at the head of the party was the little white female who had greeted them, wide-eyed and borderline hysterical, in the main hall. This one, who introduced herself as Spot (and oh, how it still unnerved Emma to hear anything other than meows, hisses and growls coming out of a cat's mouth, even after all these years) seemed to know Christopher, and had led them quickly to this room before taking off to find her superiors. Of the rest of the coterie, one was a brash-looking ginger, while the other two, a female and a male, had black fur.

There was no mistaking which one was the First Minister, though: she held herself with a majestic bearing beyond what even the most self-assured of cats could usually muster, but it was tempered by a wisdom and a kindness that was rare even in humans. She glanced around the room, absorbing the tableau before her, then hopped quickly up onto the water bed next to Christopher and glared at Emma imperiously. "I am Rose, First Minister of the People of the Cat. Tell me what has happened to Christopher Prescott."

Emma was caught off-guard by the directness of the demand, was forced to relive the events of the last hours in an almost unbearable flash of memory. "I killed him," she replied in a dull, disbelieving tone. "He asked me to, and I killed him. And now we need you to save him."

"What lunacy is this?" the ginger cat growled.

"It's true, Esther." Chase had spun about suddenly, though Emma noticed that none of the cats so much as bent their ears or arched their backs. Instead, something approaching awe came over Esther and the black male. Spot was looking back and forth at them in bewilderment.

"Grimfarer," gasped Esther. "Shadow, it's Grimfarer!"

The other black cat, Shadow, shook his head in wonderment. "The Nine-Lived Man."

"I thought he was just a myth," Spot mumbled perplexedly.

"Hello, Donovan Chase," Rose meowed. "It has been many seasons."

Chase moved over next to Emma. "Too many, First Minister."

Emma looked back and forth between Chase and Rose. "You two know each other, then?"

"Oh yes," breathed Chase.

"Of old," agreed Rose. "We fear it is no coincidence that you come here now, at this crossroads in the time of men and cats."

"The Ways are safe, Rose," Chase murmured. "Thanks to Emma Rawlin here, and to Christopher Prescott. But the cost has been most high."

Rose looked forlornly upon Christopher's pale visage. "But what can we do? He is dead."

"Not quite," Chase said fervently. "He was, but the power of your *eochair* has brought him back from the brink. Yet the wound in Christopher's chest is still fatal. It must be healed, and swiftly, or he will perish anew."

Reluctantly, Emma lifted the makeshift cloth away from Christopher's body, and she felt her stomach churn as Rose looked upon the injury, then turned sadly away. "It is too severe, Nine-Lived Man," she said in a voice laden with regret. "We cannot do anything for him."

"Frankenstein can," the little man avowed.

"No, Grimfarer. It is beyond even his abilities. Christopher Prescott will die. It is as inevitable as the setting of the sun at dusk."

Emma wanted to cry out, to say something, to shake the black cat, or even just scream in anguish and loss. But before she could do anything, Donovan Chase erupted in fury.

"Nothing is inevitable!" he raged. "Nothing is impossible! You say the wound is beyond Frankenstein's abilities, but why can't he at least try? That is the root of the true problems with the Five Clans, Rose. We are so steeped in tradition, in the old ways, that no one will try anything new! We are stagnant, we are entrenched, and if we do not mend our ways then we will very shortly become obsolete and extinct. And it will not take the efforts of an insect hive-mind to propel us to our doom — through our inaction, we will accomplish it all by ourselves."

Chase fell to his knees beside the bed, and appealed beseechingly to the resolute Rose. "We must respect our traditions and the lessons of the past. Of course we must — only a fool ignores his history. But we have to look also to the future, or we will have none. Change, progress, development… these are not obscenities to be suppressed, but the watchwords for our survival. Let Frankenstein try, and try his best, First Minister. The worst he can do is fail."

Before Rose could respond, the overweight cat napping at the end of the bed suddenly rose to his feet, stretching languorously. Then his eyes — one blue, one green — met Chase's, and an understanding seemed to pass between them.

"Thank you," Chase murmured softly.

"Is that Frankenstein?" Emma asked uncertainly.

"He's supposed to be deaf," muttered Spot, looking rather hopelessly lost. "How did he even know we were talking about him?"

But the young cat's question went unanswered, as Frankenstein set to work.

Rose alighted on the carpeted floor next to Emma, leaving Frankenstein to his improbable efforts. "Christopher is a friend of yours, Emma Rawlin?" she inquired.

Emma inclined her head vigorously. "Absolutely. I mean... I only met him yesterday, but it feels like we've known each other for a lifetime or more. We've been through so much together: the Sixth Clan, the Forgotten Cemetery, the duel in Bowring Park —"

"Ah," the First Minister interrupted, "so it was your honour he so recklessly but valiantly defended at the Wandering Parliament. It was there that he discovered his true name, you know, though he has yet to recognise it."

Emma regarded the black cat quizzically. "What do you mean?"

"If Christopher Prescott were a cat — and there is, we think, more than a touch of the feline about him — he would be called by that which he declared himself to be in your service."

Emma inhaled audibly. "Champion," she realised.

Rose nodded once and swished her tail. "A most appropriate name indeed, we feel."

Then, without another word to Emma, she turned to face Donovan Chase, who was still kneeling at the bedside, watching Frankenstein sniff intently at Christopher's wound with his dirty pink nose. "What has become of the *eochair*?" she asked him. Emma listened keenly for his reply, as she was desperate to know the answer to that question herself.

But Chase merely shrugged. "They're gone. The Five Clans no longer hold any control over the Ways. The power of the *eochair* has been scattered all across the city, and perhaps beyond."

"To what end?" Emma asked.

Chase rose to his feet and smiled an enigmatic smile. "To tell you the truth, I have no idea. I suppose only time will tell."

*   *   *

... Along the shores of Long Pond, at the northern boundary of the Memorial University campus, an early-morning jogger finds his regular run interrupted by the sight of something gnarled and gangly flitting through the dense woods at the water's edge. He knows it is not a trick of the light and the shadow, not a figment of his imagination, not a half-remembered dream floating briefly back out of his subconscious. He has unmistakeably just seen a tree come to life...

* * *

... At a building lot for a new subdivision on the outskirts of the city, construction workers arriving to their jobs this morning are baffled by a most unlikely sight. Footprints, which might seem human were they not a yard long and half as wide, have been pounded into the soft, muddy earth. And ten feet above the ground, carved into the clapboard of a half-finished house nearby in big, shaky letters, is the improbable legend "Gok waz heer"...

* * *

... In the attic of an old house not far from the cats' dwelling, an old man cleaning out his attic happens upon a battered trunk he does not remember storing there. Curious, he manages to heave open the lid, though the rusty hinges groan in protest. Within is a large opaque flask, sienna brown, stoppered by a simple wedge of cork. He reaches for the vessel and tugs out the cork. As strange purple smoke issuing from the bottle envelops him, he is astonished to find that the arthritis which has plagued him these many long years is rapidly seeping away...

* * *

… A custodian, making her regular rounds of one of the city's oldest school buildings, is bemused to find that, during the night, someone has arranged a collection of antique porcelain dolls against a shadowed wall of the furnace room. Having crossed the dimly-lit room to do some maintenance, her bemusement turns to trepidation when, upon turning back towards the dolls, she realises that their shiny little heads have swivelled to follow her…

* * *

… And in a home in the east end of St John's, Naomi Holloway smiles a tired but grateful smile as baby Alec finally stops crying, and falls gently and deeply asleep. He is dreaming of guardian lions, and swordfights on a field of grass…

* * *

The first thought which passed through Christopher's mind as he drifted reticently towards consciousness was that the storm was over. He could not recall exactly what he had been dreaming, but thought it was joyful and filled with magic, bearing the promise of many more such dreams to come.

He opened his eyes, not sure what he should expect to see, and immediately his gaze found an open window. The sky was a blaze of light blue, touched by only sketches of thin, fluffy clouds, and the sun peeked cheerily around the edge of the curtains. The humidity which had hung oppressively in the air for so many days had dissipated, and now Christopher felt cradled in a pleasant, comforting warmth. Then his eyes drifted downward, and sitting upon the strangely wide sill he saw Faolan's knife, tucked back into its enchanted sheath. The sight of the weapon brought the memory of what he had thought would be his final moments crashing back to the forefront of his thoughts.

"Hey you," came a voice. Christopher swivelled his head to see Emma curled up on a chair placed next to the water bed. She was still clad in the remnants of the strange, old-fashioned dress she had worn atop Signal Hill.

"Hi," he replied. To his surprise, his voice was strong and clear. "I'm guessing that I'm not dead, then."

Emma smiled tenderly. "Not quite, even if you did give it a fair shot. Fortunately, Frankenstein was able to repair your wound, though it took a lot out of the poor little guy. He's got quite a feast of tunafish and milk waiting for him when he wakes up. Rose said it was a feat of healing unparalleled in recorded history."

"Wow," said Christopher, and he meant it. "So I'm back with the cats... I thought I recognised the décor. How long have I been out, exactly?"

"About thirty-six hours. It's Monday lunchtime."

"That would explain the pangs of hunger," Christopher acknowledged. Then he looked again at Emma's garb. "Wait... have you been here the entire time?"

"No, I just really like this dress. I think the mud and the bloodstains accentuate it nicely." She grinned disarmingly. "I called your parents, by the way."

Christopher sank back in his bed. "Mom must have been freaking out."

"Pretty much."

"What did you tell them?"

"That you'd been on an all-weekend bender, and ended up flying to Vancouver. They're expecting you home tonight."

Christopher groaned. "They'll never look at me the same way again."

"Actually, though he didn't say anything, I think your dad was kind of impressed."

Christopher rolled his eyes at the thought. "He would be. Hey, where's Chase?"

Emma shrugged. "He left already. His job here was done, et cetera, et cetera. He did leave a message for you, though." And she adopted an entirely ridiculous British accent: "You owe him a new walking stick."

Christopher laughed with abandon. His merriment abated only when a twinge of pain shot up from his breast, and he pressed his hand over his heart. Just a tiny scar remained there, a miniature version of that strange but now familiar bell-shaped symbol. Yet he knew that the wound would never be completely forgotten.

He looked back to Emma, and his face darkened. "I'm sorry... about what I had to make you do."

She glanced away from him for a moment, but then wrenched her gaze back to him. Christopher could see that her eyes were brimming with tears. "Do you remember when we were in that weird school corridor, and those three girls were saying something about how dark my life has been?" He nodded. "Well, they were right. I've done terrible things, Christopher, and had terrible things done to me."

"Lochlann?"

She shrugged sullenly. "And before. What I did to you... I've done worse, and for reasons that were far less noble. But never again. All of that is behind me now. For good." And she summoned a brave grin, which Christopher eagerly returned.

They sat there in silence for a while, basking in each other's company. Then Emma asked, "So what now, Christopher? Back to your regular life, to forget about everything that's happened this weekend?"

Christopher shook his head determinedly. "Not a chance. Emma, I never want to lose what I've discovered over the past few days."

She smiled, her expression flush with melancholy. "The Five Clans, you mean? With our secrets and our tricks and our... our magic?"

But Christopher stared deep into her blue eyes, and said, "No, Emma. I don't mean the magic. At least, not that kind of magic."

She looked back at him, and now each of them had tears touching the corners of their eyes. Without another word, Emma rose from her chair and crawled onto the bed next to Christopher. He put his arm around her shoulders and pulled her to him tightly, nestling her head beneath his chin.

"Champion," she murmured tenderly, caressing the stubble peppering his cheek.

"I'm sorry?" he asked warmly.

Emma sighed, and they both closed their eyes, content in each other's embrace. "I'll explain one day," she promised him in a gentle whisper.

And as they lay there together, Christopher Prescott realised that maybe Mondays weren't so bad after all.

Epilogue
In which a Loose End is tied up

Aislinn huddled into her furs. She cursed: no matter how deeply she buried herself in the heavy coat, her skin still felt as if it were being scoured by the frigid Russian air. She gratefully clutched a squat, chipped glass filled with another round of vodka. It was some of the worst liquor she had ever tasted, but it was the best defense against the polar climate.

She looked wearily over at Iollan, also clad in thick hides. The reptile-man was slumped over in his chair, snoring belligerently. Aislinn swore every time his forked tongue flitted out into the frosty air. She knew that they were already provoking curious glances from the thick-limbed, aggressively-bearded patrons of the seedy pub, and that was the last thing she wanted. It was bad enough that she'd already been solicited four times in this backward little hamlet lost amidst the snowy wastes; she didn't need anyone getting suspicious as to her identity.

Muttering angrily under her breath, Aislinn sank into her chair. She knocked back the contents of the fractured vessel and felt a brief, transient warmth spread through her innards. All too quickly, though, the heady glow faded away until it seemed as if it had never existed in the first place. She slammed the glass down onto the sticky, pitted surface of the table in frustration, and hollered for another.

As she waited for the peg-legged barkeep to serve her, Aislinn closed her eyes and let her hand drift to the coat pocket where she had secreted the treasures which had been her recompense from the People of the Insect, in return for her treacherous services. Even if things had not gone entirely to plan there — leaving behind witnesses to her involvement certainly hadn't been part of her original concept — at least she'd gotten paid. And when the heat died down, she would go back to St John's and —

Aislinn's green eyes opened wide. Her pocket was empty, the soothing bulk gone from its familiar resting place. Frantic, she began looking around the filthy tavern floor, desperate to find her riches.

And then her gaze fell on a pair of expensive-looking shoes, perched behind her chair. She swivelled around slowly, the intense cold pervading the air quickly giving way to a new kind of chill, one borne of mounting dread.

The figure wearing the shoes was grasping her precious treasure in one hand. He was clad in an all-too-familiar — and extraordinarily unseasonable — black-and-white pinstripe suit. And although his customary walking stick was conspicuous by its absence, this offered the red-haired woman precious little comfort.

"Hello, Aislinn," growled Donovan Chase.

About the Author

If the stories are to be believed, Shannon Patrick Sullivan was born in St John's, Newfoundland, in 1976. Public records suggest that *The Dying Days* is his first novel, though rumours persist that earlier works have been suppressed by the dark powers they offended. Popular legend has it that he was the contestant representing the Atlantic provinces on *Who Wants To Be A Millionaire: Canadian Edition...* but eyewitness accounts place him amongst the foothills of eastern Europe on those nights, baying in a forgotten tongue at the gibbous moon. It's whispered in shadowed corners that he is currently working towards his doctorate in math at Memorial University of Newfoundland, but no doubt he is being confused with the main character of this novel — for surely no author would base a protagonist so blatantly upon himself. He speaks with cats often, but they rarely respond.

Afterword
In which the Author rambles on

The first draft of *The Dying Days* was written between June 29th and August 3rd, 2004 on a keyboard whose spacebar worked only about two-thirds of the time (on a good night). It's the fulfillment of a lifelong dream of mine to write a novel, something I've been attempting in fits and starts since roughly the age of seven. It also occurred in the wake of the complete collapse of what had been, to that point, my most significant romantic relationship; to describe the experience as cathartic would be a bit of an understatement. Somehow, those five weeks of personal therapy have resulted in the text which, for better or for worse (but hopefully for better) you now hold in your hands. Inevitably, there are some folks I need to acknowledge for making all of this possible.

First and foremost, there are Shauna and Nicole, the two wonderful ladies to whom this novel is dedicated. Their support and advice have meant more to me than mere words on a page could ever adequately express. Nicole, especially, kept my enthusiasm kindled by agreeing to the thankless task of reading these chapters as I initially wrote them, and I can honestly say that without her, you would not be holding this work today. She is, without a doubt, a very wonderful muse and an incomparable friend.

Then there are the folks who came along after the first draft of the novel was completed, but who still had a huge influence on the final product you now hold in your hands. These include my editor, Lance Parkin, whose many suggestions include my editor, Lance Parkin, whose many suggestions were absolutely invaluable (and who let me borrow his title); cover designer extraordinaire, Maurice Fitzgerald; photographer equally extraordinaire, David Morgan; and everyone at Killick Press.

And I certainly can't forget Danny Dyer, Tara Stuckless, Charlie O'Keefe, Malcolm Rowe, Dan Reardon, and Jonathan Blum (the indispensable readthrough team), Joe Keeping and James Bow (whose story *In Tua Nua* is something of a thematic older sibling to *The Dying Days*), and the ranks of the Aspiring Lords of Chaos and the Special.K.Club (you know who you are)… and also Rebecca White, who I hope realises how special she'll always be to me, in spite of everything. Inevitably, I must lastly thank my parents, for providing me with a roof under which to unleash my imagination (and for not actually realising I was spending more than a month writing a novel, and therefore being incapable of bugging me about it while I was doing so).

A key thematic inspiration of this work is the Loreena McKennitt song *The Old Ways*, from her seminal album *The Visit* (it's also what Feaver hums in Chapter 14). Consider it highly recommended.

Readers outside the St John's area may be interested to know that while a few of the locations depicted in *The Dying Days* are my own invention, many are real places. Some, such as Signal Hill and Bowring Park, are easy to find and well worth visiting. Others, like the house belonging to the People of the Cat, may sadly prove rather more elusive, unless you're very very lucky…

Thanks for reading. I hope you enjoyed! Comments are always welcome at *shannon@shannonsullivan.com*.

Shannon Patrick Sullivan
February 6th, 2006